First published in the UK in 2023 by Stephen Pannett.
This edition published in the UK in 2023 by Stephen Pannett.

Copyright © Steve Pannett, 2023

The moral right of Steve Pannett to be identified as the author of this work has been asserted in accordance with the Copyright, Designs and Patents Act of 1988.

All rights reserved. No part of this publication may be reproduced, stored in a retrieval system, or transmitted in any form or by an means, electronic, mechanical, photocopying, recording, or otherwise, without the prior permission of both the copyright owner and the above publisher of this book.

This is a work of fiction. All characters, organisations, and events portrayed in this novel are either products of the author's imagination or are used fictitiously.

Paperback ISBN: 978-1-7392792-0-2
eBook ISBN:     978-1-7392792-1-9

If you no longer wish to keep this book, please donate it to a family member, friend, or your local charity bookshop. If you need to dispose of it please recycle it in an appropriate manner.

## *About the author*

Steve Pannett lives in Sheffield, UK, with his wife, Fraz, and their twin boys, Ethan and Lachlan.

Steve has an obsession for storytelling and fully believes in the power of a good book.

learn more at
**stevepannett.com**

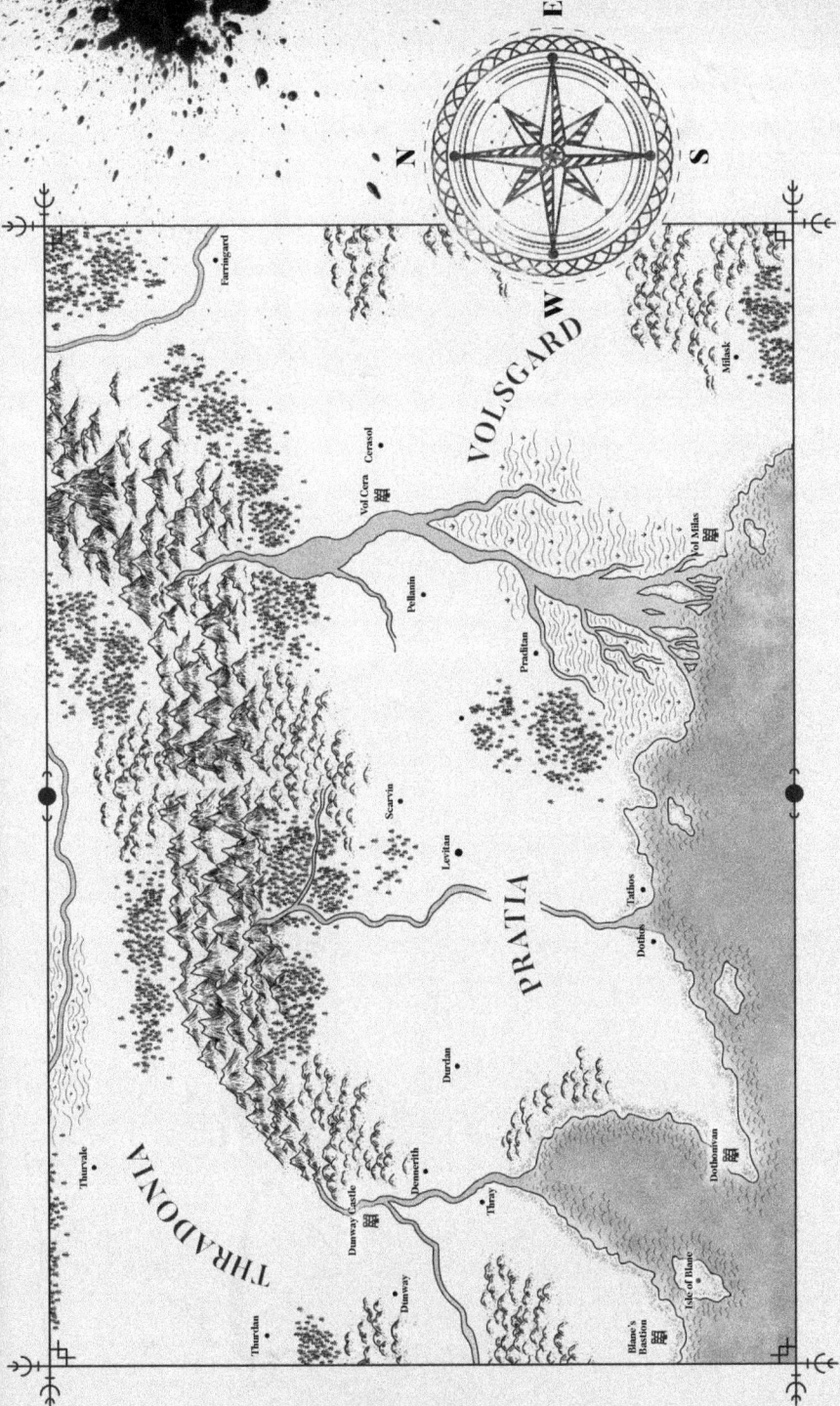

*For Fraz*
*For telling me to 'finish the damn story'*

# PROLOGUE

*Truth & lies*

## Truth is a weapon

THE HEAT PRICKLED at the back of Sweet's neck, beading among the coarse hairs between his shoulders and causing his skin to itch. He grimaced for the thousandth time and shifted uncomfortably in the saddle, one hand holding loosely to the reins as his horse walked slowly along the path leading out of the forest.

The heat was a bastard. It was supposed to be autumn, but it seemed to Sweet like summer had decided on one last hurrah. It was just his rotten luck that it had decided today would be the ideal date for that big send-off. The sun was hanging lower in the sky now so it was a little cooler than it had been in the closeness of the forest, but now the bastard was shining directly into Sweet's eyes as his horse plodded slowly along the dirt track. Heading west, back to Woodbyrne.

'Someone shoulda stayed with him,' a piping voice cut through Sweet's growing disdain for the cloying heat. He squinted sideways to see the small figure of Daraday half-turned in his saddle, facing back the way they had come. The youngster turned to look at Sweet, his big eyes wide and fearful. 'Y'know, in case...wolves or summat.'

Sweet snorted. There hadn't been wolves in these parts for decades. Might be a bear or two deeper in the forest or up in the hills, but there wouldn't be any wolves nearby for miles. Daraday took the snort badly, creases of hurt showing on his unblemished, beardless face. He was little more than a boy, was Daraday, but then—Sweet supposed—that was why he was struggling so much with what was really quite a simple truth.

No one else in their ragged little band seemed to share in Daraday's struggle. Truth be told, no one else in their ragged little band seemed to care a shit at all. Behind them Jenrick, Stover and the Wyn rode their horses with much the same looks on their faces as Sweet reckoned was upon his own. Something between boredom and being pissed off at the boredom. Up ahead of them Bryntas and Vi walked their horses just a few paces behind their captive, who trudged along at the head of their little column. Even the scraggly-haired, scrawny little shit himself—hands tied and scuffing his way along the dirt path—didn't seem fussed.

But, Sweet supposed, he was the cause of Daraday's discomfort in the first place. Kinda made sense that the man wouldn't give half a damn. The prisoner shuffled along with his head down, his hands tied tightly behind his back with a short length of rope leading up to Vi's gloved hand. She was gripping that coil of rope much more tightly than she was the reins to her horse. With good reason, too.

Sweet regarded the front pair of his little troop, passing over the hulking figure of Bryntas and being careful not to let his eyes linger for too long on the sleek, womanly silhouette of Vi in the saddle. There was a damn good reason she was called Violent Fey and she had been in Sweet's crew long enough for him to know that she had a sixth sense for being watched. Sweet remembered one silly bastard in a taproom back in Levitan; he had ogled her far too openly and for far too long. Vi had left him with his face in the sawdust and the stale beer and the puke, clutching at his manhood from where she had delivered several sickening blows with her booted foot. Sweet also knew that her boots were capped with cold, hard metal—for just such a purpose.

Sweet snorted again, this time at the memory of that unfortunate reveller. He hadn't blamed the man for looking. Vi was a good-looking woman, if you saw beyond the flint in her eyes and the scowl on her face; but the man had gone about his looking with all the subtlety of a punch to the face. Sweet tried to recall why Vi hadn't killed him, but couldn't remember. She had killed for less before. On the road ahead of him Vi turned her head slightly, as though listening for something. Sweet made sure to swing his gaze away from her, only to find himself staring directly into the big, wet eyes of the youngest member of the crew once more.

'Maybe I should go back?' Daraday cocked his head like a puppy waiting for instructions on where to piss. 'Make sure he's ok until you can send help.'

Behind them, Stover offered his own snort—this one much closer to a bray of harsh laughter. Daraday flicked his worried gaze back towards him, then returned it to Sweet.

Bitter Sweet, famed bounty hunter of the westerlands and scourge of any man, woman or child on the run, rubbed at the prickling sweat on the back of his head and sighed, eventually pulling his hand round the front of his neck to scratch at the silver-flecked stubble under his chin. He was dog-tired and sighed loudly.

'Ain't nobody going back,' he told the boy, keeping his tone even and his voice low. He pulled his gaze away from the youngster and squinted back into the sun again.

To the right of them, a field of tall grass bent over as a strong breeze blew through. The plants rippled like liquid and Sweet closed his eyes, waiting for the cool wind to touch his sweat-soaked skin. The only sounds were a bird chirping somewhere in the trees to their left, the slow clopping of their horses' hooves on the hard-packed dirt and the quiet shuffle of their prisoner as he reluctantly led the way back to Woodbyrne. Sweet almost found himself enjoying the moment.

'But will he be alright?' Daraday's reedy voice ruined it at the last.

Sweet opened his eyes and swung back to face the boy again. He fired him a look that he hoped would silence him, but must've ballsed it up something special, as it only seemed to spur the young lad on.

'How long will he have to wait, I mean?' Daraday tilted his head again. If he tilted it much further Sweet was sure he'd topple right out of his saddle. 'Until someone goes back to help him?'

Stover snort-laughed again. This time Sweet turned in the saddle and fired him the same look he'd just levelled at Daraday. He was relieved to see Stover transfer his gaze away in something of a hurry. The ugly bastard hawked and spat into the treeline, but avoided Sweet's fiery look like it was the most important task in the world. At least there's nothing wrong with my glares, Sweet thought with a smirk, it's just that the boy is too naive to read 'em properly. He returned his attention to Daraday, who was still staring at him with those big, wide eyes.

Sweet sighed again and pondered his next words.

Lies were useful. If anyone knew that in the whole of the westerlands then it was Bitter Sweet. The man who had the hunting of men—and women, when the coin called for it—down to a damn fine art. And if it was an art—and he the master of the craft—then lies were just one of the many brushes in his kit.

Hunting people wasn't like hunting animals. Animals were all instinct, no matter how much poets and bards wanted to imbue certain species with cunning or guile; at the end of the day, their behaviour was rational. It was understandable. It was predictable. Men, on the other hand—especially hunted men—were devious, desperate and downright *difficult* to deal with. They could run and hide and cover their tracks, but they could also lay down a network of false trails, misdirection and outright lies that would lead even the best bounty hunters hundreds of miles in the wrong direction. Not just the men you were hunting, either. There were always accomplices, friends or family desperate to help, or witnesses that needed a taste of metal—coin or steel—to loosen their lips, especially if the quarry had already offered something similar first. There were folks who wanted to seem brave who lied about tracking the fugitive themselves, folks who wanted to seem tough who lied about tussling with them. Folks who lied to preserve reputations or to invent whole new ones. And there were even folks who lied simply because they had a shitty relationship with the truth in general; some people just couldn't help themselves. Lies were damn tricky, but they were that way because they were so damn *useful.*

Lies were tools, and Sweet was a master craftsman. But the truth? That was something else entirely. Truth could strike to the heart of something with all the speed and ferocity of a viper guarding its nest. Truth could banish the fog of lies and show the way forward in just a single sentence. Truth could be more than a useful tool.

Truth could be a weapon.

'Ain't nobody going back for Aribor,' Sweet whistled the words between his teeth, squinting at Daraday and waiting for the inevitable reaction.

He didn't have to wait long. The young lad went from confusion to hurt to fear in a matter of heartbeats. He finally settled on a mix of the three that left him looking even younger and even paler than ever. A question began to form on his lips but Sweet preempted it, cutting in with a tone that ended most conversations this side of the Great Sea.

'Ain't nobody going back for Aribor because Aribor ain't there,' he told the youngster, speaking flatly. Sweet added a shrug for good measure, then lowered his voice a little. 'Just a corpse, boy.'

Stover made another noise behind them that Sweet took to be a grunt of satisfaction. This time Sweet ignored it, keeping his steely gaze levelled on Daraday. He waited for understanding to ripple over the boy's features before turning away from him, still being careful to ensure he wasn't left staring at Vi's arse up ahead.

Just ahead of them all, his hands still tied behind his back, the gang's lone prisoner had turned his head and was watching the exchange with the tiniest curl to the corner of his mouth. Sweet reckoned the man was enjoying what he'd heard. In years past that might've made Sweet angry. Go far enough back and he might've called a halt to their little caravan and given the murdering bastard something to smile about. Now though, he just ignored it, feeling little at all except contempt for the damned, late summer heat. He found himself picturing again their encounter with the man now tied at the head of their small column.

They had dismounted at the edge of the treeline, a troop of bounty hunters close to their quarry, leaving Jenrick and Bryntas to watch the horses. They had found the remains of a thrown-together campsite not more than a few hundred paces into the woods. It was so poorly concealed that they hardly needed the near-mystical tracking abilities of the Wyn. The tribesman could've led them to the camp blindfolded. They had searched the fugitive's camp, finding little of interest amongst the meagre belongings of a murderer on the run. Sweet had just been about to order the Wyn to start tracking away from the site when there had been a great whooping shout from above.

The mad bastard had been hiding up a tree, screened by the thick foliage and a lacework of branches. He had leapt down straight onto Aribor, knocking the youngster to the ground and falling atop of him. There had been a scuffle and the mad fucker must've pulled Ari's dagger from his belt because there had been a flash of steel and a gout of red. Ari had grunted, the man they were tracking had given a triumphant shout before the rest of the band had been on him.

Vi was in there first—when was she not, when it came to violence? She had delivered a thumping kick to the side of the man's torso, her steel-capped boot knocking the wind from him and sending him sprawling sideways off of Ari. The dagger was left standing in the youngster's gut, and Ari himself was left staring down at it, his eyes wide with disbelief.

Stover had been in next, smashing blows onto the fugitive's head and body. The man had cried out and moaned with each fresh smack. He had somehow scrambled up to a kneeling position and that was when Vi had stepped in again. Crunching another vicious kick under his chin and snapping his head back. The man had dropped to his back like a drawbridge, knocked unconscious. The Wyn had tutted at that—Sweet remembered—as though the man's feeble attempts to take on six armed hunters had disappointed him somehow. Sweet hadn't shared the Wyn's assessment. Feeble or not, the mad bastard had managed to stick one of them, hadn't he?

The entire exchange had been brief, but all the while Daraday had stood in the campsite, shaking and uncertain. Sweet didn't blame him. Violence did that to a boy, but thankfully—or not, he supposed, depending on your viewpoint towards it—you get used to it quickly. You get used to it so much that you start expecting it, sometimes even instigating it. Either that, or you end up like poor Ari.

By the time the prisoner had been trussed and tied, Sweet had been kneeling at Aribor's side, scrunching his face up at the dagger sticking from the lad's gut in the same way he might've examined a trinket at a market stall. Casual and with little actual interest in it. It wasn't that he hadn't cared. Not completely, anyway. It was just that he'd already seen enough to tell him the simple truth.

The others had gathered about and known what Sweet already knew. Even Ari himself seemed to have a measure of understanding beneath all that fear in his eyes. Of course, the knowledge did nothing to help his fear. It was a simple truth, though. The wound was a bad one.

'Get the prisoner back to the horses,' Sweet had grunted.

Stover and Vi had obeyed almost instantly, lifting the limp prisoner between them and dragging him out of the campsite, probably happy that they wouldn't have to look Ari in the eye one last time. The Wyn had swept after them, his eyes glinting from beneath his hood. Only Daraday had hesitated.

'But what about Ari?' the boy had quivered.

Sweet had looked up at him, contorting his face into something grim but reassuring.

'I'll take care of him,' Sweet had told the boy.

Daraday had hesitated a moment longer, but then seemed suddenly worried by the prospect of being left by the others and shuffled off into the trees after them.

And that had been that. Truth and lie somehow mashed into the same single answer. Artfully combined to make something that was somewhere in between.

*I'll take care of him.*

Another breeze swept across the land and this time Sweet felt a chill. Ahead of him, the murderer was still watching him with that odd little smile adorning his features. Vi snapped the rope in her hands and shunted him forwards, causing the man to stumble. When he regained his balance he was looking ahead, down the track again.

Daraday had fallen blessedly silent beside him, but where before that quiet had been serene and peaceful, now it felt laden, weighted heavy with judgement. The silence was bittersweet, Sweet thought drily.

He had always hated his nickname, but when folk started sending the name ahead of the man there was little you could do about it. Even less you could do by worrying about it, too. So if you started out your life as a bounty hunter giving a shit about justice and the like—if you spent time trying to find honour in your dirty line of work, then folk were likely to call you "Sweet"—mostly with an ironic grin. If you grew weary with age and learned that there was only dirt in dirty work, then someone adding

"Bitter" to your name wouldn't be far behind. He'd no doubt some bard somewhere was still nursing a stiff cock from pairing the two together. If he ever found the fucker then Sweet'd be sure to set Violent Fey on him. He'd pay her enough coin to make sure the punishment she'd meted out on the taproom voyeur would look like childsplay.

The quiet continued, even the chirping birds had fallen silent. Sweet reckoned silence would be the order of the day, now. The slow ride back to Woodbyrne would be conducted without further conversation. Most of the band would be thinking about their payment for the bounty that shuffled ahead of them, but Sweet knew that Daraday would be thinking only of one thing.

It didn't bother him though, because at least all that thinking would now be done in silence, instead of wide-eyed questions aimed in his direction.

The lies had been useful, for all of them. Tools that had worked, for a time.

But the truth had been a weapon. And it had gotten the job done.

## Same old shit

WOODBYRNE DRIFTED INTO view just as the last of the golden sunshine was sinking into a deep red over the horizon. Torches started to spring to life along the main street and firelight flickered in the shanty dwellings throughout the settlement. The prisoner, exhausted from his long walk—or perhaps just not too keen to see the little village again— stopped at the rise just above it. Vi didn't falter and nudged her horse into the man, flopping him forwards and getting him shuffling again. The horse itself snorted, apparently unhappy in its new role as a battering ram.

Sweet caught sight of a steady stream of people heading into the town from the north. They were loggers, having worked every inch of daylight available to them, returning to Woodbyrne to no doubt spend their pay in the settlement's taproom. Sweet frowned in the saddle as he realised his own little crew would likely want to do the same. Loggers were hardy folk, and Woodbyrne was a remote place. It was unlikely that the locals would enjoy entertaining outsiders. Plus, his crew were hardly the most hospitable of guests. Add plentiful amounts of cheap ale into the mix and you were asking for trouble. Probably violent trouble.

Sweet sighed, resigning himself to the distinct possibility. After all, what was he supposed to do? Forbid his gang from drinking and gambling? He might as well just ride out in the night and save them all the job of abandoning him. At least that way he wouldn't get his head kicked in for suggesting such a thing as sobriety.

Besides, now that Sweet considered it, he wanted a damn drink, too.

They started on their way down the slope towards Woodbyrne, the prisoner leading the way. As they neared the settlement's periphery, several of the loggers cast their scowls at the group. Sweet couldn't figure out if they were glaring at the prisoner, or the man's captors. At this point, he didn't much care.

The prisoner himself seemed to be revelling in the hatred and scorn thrown his way. He had murdered a woman in this town just a few weeks before, earning him the bounty that Sweet and his crew were now ready to claim. It was no wonder that the locals would be hostile towards him. Some of them hissed curses, others spat. Sweet didn't bat an eyelid, he had seen it all before. In some of the bigger towns rotten fruit or vegetables were hurled at the prisoner. Sweet hated that, because the aim of most townsfolk was as shitty as their food and it was more than likely that some of the rotted filth would end up splattered all over him and his crew, too.

Sweet had seen all the reactions of the prisoners themselves as well. Most would be downtrodden, weary from their time spent fleeing and wearier still that they had been caught and would now face whatever punishment awaited them. Some would plead, begging for mercy all the damn way. Sweet hated that sort, and more often than not would resort to delivering a swift blow to their head, just for a bit of peace.

Some would try to bargain, offering Sweet and his crew double the worth of their bounty, sometimes even more than that. Of course, the chances of these lowlife scum having access to that kind of coin was slim to nil, so again Sweet would nod at Bryntas and the big man would cuff some silence into them.

Others shrieked threats. Swearing revenge on the pox-ridden, pig-shagging, low-bastard bounty hunters that brought them in. Usually those threats got smaller and quieter as they neared the gaol to which they were to be delivered. Sometimes those sorts even switched into the begging kind as the sight of their retribution became clearer. Sweet had a special distaste for them. They spat and cursed and howled their threats until the hangman's noose came into sight, then they pissed themselves and melted like snow in the summer. Puffed up cowards, for the most part.

The last group was the worst, though. A special kind of bounty that, for whatever godforsaken reason they sold themselves on, seemed to actually *enjoy* being caught. They revelled in riling up the crowds and set broad grins at those they had wronged. Some of them even went to the noose still smiling. They were rare, but Sweet had seen a handful of them in his long years working bounties across most of the known world. Mad fuckers, they were.

Sweet hated them the most.

This prisoner was one of them, and in a town like Woodbyrne that could lead to violence of a deadly sort long before he even saw the swing of the gallows. A prisoner baiting an angry mob made a fine target for himself.

And for those charged with bringing him in.

The cursing and the spitting is fine, Sweet thought, so long as none of those tree-hackers take a pop at him. The bounty was a whole two crowns higher for the man being delivered alive. The last thing Sweet wanted was to lose two crowns within sight of the damn gaoler's office, just because some burly logger decided to take a bit of justice into his own hands and bury an axe in the little man's skull.

As if reading his thoughts, Vi angled her horse a little wide of the prisoner. She whispered something to Bryntas and the big man did the same on the other side, creating a bit more of a buffer between the prisoner and the townsfolk. Sweet smiled a little. She might've been a bit unhinged, but there was a damn good reason Vi was his second-in-command. She was savvy as a Velan merchant and sharper than Damsen steel.

The sunset cast the town of Woodbyrne in a pale orange glow, picking out the shadows in deep purple hues that turned innocuous villagers into potential threats. Most kept well out of their way—the sight of seven armed bounty hunters usually did that—but occasionally one or two would watch them go by with more than a little interest. Sweet squinted in the semi-darkness to see if he could pick out any faces he recognised, but mostly he saw the usual weathered expressions of folk living this far out from so-called civilised society. After the fifth face they all blurred into one and Sweet stopped bothering to look.

They rode past the tavern on their way to the gaol. A tall, wide building set atop a weathered wooden stoop, with outset bay windows that faced into the street. Already it sounded busy, the raucous noises of revelry spilling out through the open windows. Shadows swayed in the lamplight as tablemaids carried trays of food and drink to the patrons inside. Sweet didn't turn his head, but he knew that Stover would be craning in the saddle to catch a glimpse inside. He'd be looking for a card game in play. Stover liked nothing better than to brag at his prowess when it came to playing the tables. Sweet would be damned if he knew why. He could count on one hand the number of times Stover had woken up with more money than he'd had before the games started. Still didn't seem to stop him though, almost like he was addicted to losing.

Sweet's primary theory was a simple one. Losing at cards gave Stover an excuse to accuse someone of cheating. That was the sort of accusation that, more often than not, led to a fight. Stover might not have actually liked losing, but he sure as shit liked fighting. Not only that, but in the aftermath of a post-game fight, Stover was known to scoop up all of his coin again anyway—sometimes he'd even scoop up the money from his fellow players, too. Sweet reckoned that was Stover's idea of a perfect night. He'd game, he'd fight and he'd come out of the whole affair with heavier pockets to boot. Hardly honest work, but then, they weren't exactly honest folk.

Sweet heard the creak of saddle leather even as they rounded the corner, followed by a disappointed curse from Stover. No card game then. Sweet doubted it meant much, the evening was still new and a town like this would no doubt have a regular table. It would only be a matter of time before some upstart decided to kick up a game. Sweet wouldn't be surprised if Stover himself was the one to suggest it.

The gaoler's office was an unassuming building. Little more than an oversized hut set at the end of a row of equally dilapidated buildings. There was a battered old stoop out the front and the paunchy little constable was sitting with his feet up on the railing ahead of him. He straightened as the group approached, his expression twisting into a sickly-looking smile.

'Well well well,' the constable grinned his shit-eating grin and hitched his trews up, but not before they all got a good view of his pale, round little belly spilling over the top of them. 'So you found the bastard, then?'

'Found him,' Sweet grunted, pulling his horse to a stop beside Violent Fey. He dismounted, silently cursing at the ache in his hip as he did so. 'Caught him. Brought him in.' Sweet shrugged. 'Usually what we do.'

'Aye, so I hear,' the constable nodded, still grinning his yellow-toothed grin. 'You can take him straight in, keys to the cell are in the door.'

Sweet looked to the gaol, then back to the constable. Bryntas dismounted to stand next to the prisoner. The difference in the two men couldn't have been greater. The captive was scrawny, lean to the point of emaciation, with wild hair and even wilder eyes. Bryntas, by comparison, was an absolute giant. Muscles bulged across his chest and arms. His neatly trimmed beard and close-cropped hair framing a square jaw that sat beneath a small nose and careful, hard eyes.

'Usually we get paid before we hand over our bounties,' Sweet scratched idly at his chin. Bryntas bristled beside him and the pot-bellied constable's grin faltered a touch.

'Aye, of course,' the man nodded, taking the less-than-subtle hint. Sweet had dispensed with subtlety a long time ago. The gaoler turned on the spot and waddled inside, emerging a moment later with a small leather purse in one hand. He held it out to Sweet.

Vi flipped one long leg over her horse and dropped to the dirt in near silence. She strutted over to the constable and snatched the purse from his outstretched hand. As she walked back to her horse Sweet caught the constable following her gait with his eyes and he forced a cough, dragging the man's attention back to something that wasn't likely to earn him a sharp kick between the legs.

Well, Sweet thought, unless he's short-changed us, that is.

'It all there?' Sweet called over his shoulder.

There was a soft jangling of coins, closely followed by Vi's response.

'Aye, it's all here,' she reported.

Sweet slowly nodded his satisfaction, then motioned to Bryntas. The giant gave the prisoner a shove in the back so hard it was a wonder he didn't stove the man's spine in. The prisoner jolted forwards and nearly stumbled up onto the stoop. Bryntas moved surprisingly quickly for a man of his size and followed it up with another curt push between the man's shoulder blades. The pair disappeared inside while Sweet and the rest of his crew waited out in the street. Stover leaned over the saddle and spat.

After a time, Bryntas reemerged, ducking his head under the doorway and holding a heavy iron key in one hand. It looked like a child's toy in Bryntas' grip. The giant towered over the constable and dropped the key into his palm.

'Pleasure doing business with you,' Sweet said. He sighed as his crew remounted, then did the same.

'And you,' the constable nodded, his grin had disappeared completely now. His eyes brightened as he suddenly remembered something. 'Will you be staying for the hanging? Once I let the town council know he's caught, that bastard'll swing tomorrow before noon.'

'Doubt it,' Sweet grunted, ignoring the glint he caught in Stover's eye. The man loved a good execution almost as much as he loved gambling and fighting.

'You sure?' the constable tried again, 'see the fruits of your labour, an' all that?'

'Got all the fruits we need right here,' Vi answered for him, jangling the little purse with her best don't-fuck-with-me expression in place. It must've done the trick, because the constable swallowed and nodded his understanding.

Sweet didn't bother with a farewell. What was the point? It wouldn't be long before they rode into another shitpot town with another shitpot sheriff who needed them to risk their lives doing what he was supposed to do. After you'd seen one you'd seen them all, and all you'd do is see another one somewhere along the way. Saying farewell to them was as pointless as saying farewell to your own turds.

Sweet turned his horse and led the group back towards the tavern.

*

The taproom stank of stale ale and even staler sweat. There was a heady smog of woodsmoke, pipesmoke and body odour that was only occasionally cut through by the sharp tang of the cheap lemon perfume preferred by Woodbyrne's whores.

In short, the place smelled like every other taproom Sweet had had the mild displeasure of frequenting. He took another pull from his drink, more to bury his nose in the singular smell of the shitty ale instead of having it assaulted by the myriad of other shitty smells around him.

Despite its taste, somewhere between gritty and burned, the ale was strong and Sweet could already feel his senses numbing, softening around the edges a little. He had been out on the road for most of that day, hunting the murderer now safely in the care of the town's fat little constable, and during that time he had hardly eaten. The same was true for his crew, who seemed less aware of their own sensibilities being stretched by Woodbyrne's selection of beverages.

Jenrick and Bryntas were propped up at the bar, the archer talking animatedly with his hands while the bearded giant listened in near silence. Sweet knew Bryntas wouldn't give two shits what the other man was saying, but he would be comfortable pretending to listen if it meant he didn't have to talk himself. A man of few words, was Bryntas.

Beside Sweet, on their pokey little table near to the taproom's entrance, the young figure of Daraday sat nursing his drink—his only drink so far—looking both puzzled and glum in equal measure. The lad was still dwelling on Ari, Sweet reckoned, it would take him a while to realise that just a few more swigs would stop such thoughts from bothering him—at least until the morning, anyway. Beside the youngster sat the Wyn, and the table in front of him was noticeably empty.

Wyns didn't drink. Or, they didn't as far as Sweet knew anyway. After all, when it came to their sort he only knew this one, and *he* didn't drink, so it stood to reason that the whole lot of them avoided it. Normally not partaking in the liquid merriment would be a cause for raised eyebrows, even some snipes or jabs from someone eager to poke some fun. But not with the Wyn.

Wyns were hard bastards. And everyone knew it. They lived far in the north, beyond the bits of the wilderness that even wild folk went. Most were heavily tattooed, and the man two seats over from Sweet was no exception. The dark markings visible up his neck and onto his shaven head even from beneath his shadowy hood, swirling and jagging in a patchwork of intricate patterns. No one mentioned the empty table in front of him and most folk in the tavern gave his seat a wide berth as they passed. As well they might, Sweet thought, if they knew what was good for them.

The Wyn shifted in his seat, pulled out a small slip of paper and started crumbling some brown taffa into the folded centre. In seconds he had rolled himself a neat little papersmoke and perched it on his lower lip. At least the mad bastards have some vices, Sweet considered.

Beside the Wyn, directly opposite where Sweet was sat, Violent Fey slid the lit candle in the middle of the table over, the flame dancing as it went. The Wyn scooped it up with a silent nod and held the flickering orange tip to the end of his papersmoke. Moments later the sharp tang of the blue-grey taffa smoke was added to the taproom's general stench. Sweet sighed and took another deep swig of his drink.

'There'll be trouble tonight,' Vi observed, as though casually remarking upon the weather. 'Might even get deadly.'

Sweet followed her gaze. She had spoken without taking her eyes from something across the room. Through the crowd of drinkers, swerving barmaids and plying doxies he saw a group of men hunched over a semi-circular table against the far wall. Three of the four men looked at ease, happy even. They drank and chatted and puffed on pipes and papersmokes of their own. Only freeing up either hand to take their turn and play their cards.

The fourth man didn't look happy. He looked decidedly unhappy. In fact he looked surly and agitated as it came to his turn, casting suspicious glances—and the occasional glare—at his fellow players.

'Fuck,' Sweet whispered, with a sigh and an air of inevitability.

The fourth man was Stover.

'Mmm now there's a man who knows what he wants,' a nearby whore sidled over to Sweet's chair. Her painted face cracked at the corners of her eyes as she fluttered her eyelashes at him, blocking his view of the card game across the room.

'Piss off,' Sweet told her, craning to keep the table in sight.

The whore didn't look immediately discouraged. Quite the opposite in fact, as though Sweet was playing hard to get. She leaned in closer, providing Sweet with a better view of her tits and a wicked blast of that acrid lemon perfume.

'I can show you a proper night,' she promised, pushing her chest out as if to emphasise her guarantee.

Out of nowhere Violent Fey produced a long-handled dagger. She slammed the pommel down against the tabletop and caused the drinks atop it to leap into the air with a dull clang. Daraday, who had been staring listlessly into his drink, started with a yelp. The whore jumped too, and Vi cocked her head to one side.

'He said piss off,' she said, her expression darker than the tattoos on the Wyn's unmoving face.

The whore considered a retort, but her eyes flicked down the naked steel of the dagger—gleaming in the candlelight—and she hesitated. The woman hurriedly moved away from their table, turning back at what she clearly felt was a safe enough distance to fire a dirty sneer at Violent Fey.

Good job other shit's brewing, Sweet thought with a degree of bitterness, because ten paces wasn't nearly enough of a distance to be safe from Violent Fey when she had a dagger in her hand. At least she's got something to keep her distracted, he reasoned. Across the room, the card hand ended and the trio of men—locals by the looks of them—seemed jubilant with the results. Stover was bristling hotter than ever, somehow both sinking into his chair and rising from it at the same time.

'Time to stop it 'fore it gets out of hand,' Sweet nodded, draining the rest of his ale and slamming the tankard back onto the table with a tired thud. Daraday, who barely seemed to know where he was, jumped again. Maybe those two sips were enough to put him in his cups, after all. Maybe he'd skipped the fun part of being drunk and fallen headfirst into becoming a maudlin soup.

Chairs scraped as Sweet, Vi and the Wyn all rose together, leaving the scruffy-haired youngster sitting at the table, alone with his thoughts. Violent Fey had disappeared the dagger somewhere and finished her own drink as she walked. She plonked the empty tankard down on the table of some other patrons as she strode by. The men swaddled there looked ready to object to the sudden intrusion, but caught sight of the three strangers and thought better of it.

They were halfway across the taproom when a loud voice crowed out from a shadowy alcove somewhere to their left.

'Well well, if it ain't Bitter Sweet and his merry little crew!'

Sweet skidded to a stop, recognising the owner of that mocking cheer.

'Fuck' he whispered again. He stopped and turned to face the speaker, fixing his best eat-shit-and-die grin across his face before he did so.

'It is you!' Malvadas beamed, his gold teeth twinkling in the candlelight from his own table.

'Evenin' Mal,' Sweet nodded, taking a step towards the table. Behind him, Vi and the Wyn hesitated, unsure which potential shitfest to attend to. Should they go make sure Stover didn't get himself killed, or back up Sweet and make sure he didn't get himself killed? Sweet looked over his shoulder and made their decision for them.

'Go on over, I'll catch up,' he told them, forcing a smile. He turned back to face Malvadas, his smile fading. 'Won't be long.'

'Won't be long,' Malvadas mimicked, feigning hurt and drawing a grim smile from the grubby band of cutthroat bastards sitting around his table. Sweet recognised a few of them, but not all. The ones he did know were pricks—nasty folk who would've slit their own mothers' throats for a bent copper coin—so it was safe to assume the others were no better. More likely worse. 'But we've got *so* much to catch-up on, Sweet.'

'Way I see it,' Sweet hitched his belt, purposely letting his sword swing into view a little. 'Now that we've both said 'lo we're probably about as caught up as needs be.'

'Sweet,' Malvadas tutted, shifting a strand of his greasy black hair away from his hawkish face. The man's own false grin faded away as his tutting concluded, and when he spoke next his voice was hard and cold. 'You wouldn't want to be rude now, would you?'

His crew seemed to bristle at that, as though an accusation of ill manners was an invitation to get ready to start raining down on someone with fists and steel. Malvadas himself finished the question with his teeth ground together, his sharp little eyes flashing with the prospect of violence.

Sweet didn't falter. He had seen this kind of performance a thousand times before and—if anything—it bored him more than it scared him. Might be that was bravery, or just experience—either way, it probably wasn't smart. Sweet found that he didn't care.

'The fuck do you want, Mal?' he asked, sighing and casting a glance across to the cardgame. Vi and the Wyn had arrived on the scene, but didn't seem to have gotten themselves involved just yet. They were hovering around the periphery for the time being, watching closely. For the best, Sweet thought, Vi knows when to pick her moment.

When he turned back to face Malvadas and his band of surly arseholes, the whole lot of them looked about ready to boil over. Sweet caught a short flash of steel as one of the ones he didn't recognise pulled something free under the table. At the last, Malvadas softened and broke back into his sly smile, exposing the golden teeth that nestled alongside his yellowing ones. His crew seemed to take that as a signal to stand down and they relaxed a little.

'Heard you had some trouble collecting my bounty today,' Malavadas grinned at Sweet, nodding back to where Daraday was still sitting, now running his finger miserably around the rim of his drink. Malvadas' grin morphed into a mocking pout. 'Lost a man, did we?'

'Aye,' Sweet nodded, 'aye I lost a man collecting *my* bounty, but I daresay the pay will ease his passing. For the rest of us, at least.'

Malvadas said nothing to that, so Sweet took the opportunity to press back on the shit-eating bastard.

'Looks like you've lost your fair share too,' he said, motioning to the gaggle of frothing filth sitting around Malvadas' table. 'Can't say I recognise too many of your boys these days. Misplace some o' them, did we?'

Malvadas' golden grin hardened again. The men around him bristled again, though Sweet was quietly delighted to see that not all of it was aimed in his direction this time. One or two swapped a glance and a few concerned eyebrows were raised. Discontent in the ranks, it seemed.

'Had our fair share o' troubles,' Malvadas acknowledged through gritted teeth. 'A couple o' contracts up in the High Places. Hard going, they were, but times are tough.'

'That they are,' Sweet nodded, more sincerely than he would've liked. He suddenly brightened. 'But I think you're a little late to this one, Mal. As I said, the bounty's all accounted for. Hope you and your boys didn't go too far out of your way, coming all the way out here.'

The men seated around the table shifted angrily for a second time. One of them muttered a curse under his breath. Malvadas himself didn't seem too put out by the jibe and took a sip from his drink before placing it down on the table.

'Win some, lose some,' he shrugged. 'There'll be plenty o' work once this war starts proper. Won't be long before the Vols are jabbin' at Pratia with more'n just hard words.' Malvadas smiled slyly. 'War brings out the worst in folk.'

'I reckon so,' Sweet agreed, 'and the worst in folk means there'll be plenty of work to go around.'

'Plenty for *us*,' Malvadas replied, nodding towards his crew and meeting Sweet's eye.

Sweet smiled and stepped closer. He leaned down, fired his best grin at the seated men and scooped up the drink in front of Malvadas at the same time. He tipped the drink back and swallowed it in one pull. Sweet straightened and wiped foam from his stubbled chin. The men around Malvadas looked ready to pounce, but Malvadas himself simply sat in watchful silence.

Sweet flicked a coin up, it flashed through the air and landed on the table with a dull rattle before spinning to a halt.

'Have one on me,' he grinned. 'After all, *we* can afford it.'

Sweet turned and started stalking away from the table. Ignoring the glares from the men around it. He burped and called over his shoulder.

'Good seeing you, Mal.'

Sweet was just admiring his own quick wit when there was a shout from across the room, followed by a great crash as a table was upended. Coins and cards flew high into the air as a man was pole-axed by a thrown fist.

'Fuck,' Sweet whispered again.

It seemed that Vi had picked her moment.

*

Sweet arrived just in time to deliver a hard punch to the lower back of a logger facing the other way. It was hardly a fair blow, hitting someone from behind like that—but then in Sweet's experience fights were rarely fair. Not if you wanted to win them, anyway.

The man grunted and turned to face his attacker, leaving his face exposed enough for Violent Fey to crunch her own fist into it. The logger was thrown backwards into a table of seated drinkers nearby.

'Come on then you loose-toothed sheep-fuckers!' Stover screeched, grabbing a fistful of a man's shirt, pulling him in and butting him hard on the nose. The man went down, sending a tray full of drinks and taffa ash into the air as he dropped.

A big logger lurched up behind Stover, but the Wyn ghosted in beside him and delivered a sickening blow to the man's throat with the side of his hand. The logger staggered backwards, whooping for breath and scrabbling at his neck. Sweet had time to pray that it wasn't a mortal blow—the last thing they needed was for one of the locals to get killed—before an angry logger with a pock-marked face took a swing at him. Sweet ducked back and Violent Fey moved in, kicking the man in the side of his knee with a sickening crack. He screamed and fell, clutching at his leg.

Someone barrelled into Sweet's side, knocking him into Vi and sending them both crashing against a table. Sweet heard Vi growl, low and urgent, before she shoved him off and reached for the dagger at her belt. Sweet grabbed at her wrist and she snapped her head up, eyes swimming with the violence that leant her her name. He felt his balls tighten as that gaze turned on him and it took all his resolve to hold to it with a grim warning of his own.

'No steel,' he hissed at her.

Sweet turned back to face the carnage and raised his hands, letting go of Violent Fey's wrist and praying that she didn't whip out that dagger and sink it between his shoulder blades.

'Ho!' he bellowed, raising both arms. 'Enough!'

The desperate fighting slowed, then eased to a halt. Chairs had been upended and a table had been smashed in two. Broken tankards and playing cards were scattered all about. The sawdust on the floor was soaked in ale and spattered with blood, though a quick scan of the combatants told Sweet that most of it had come from punches or kicks. As far as he could tell no one had been stabbed or cut.

That's a start, Sweet thought.

Stover, blood streaking from his nose in a pair of black rivers, was being held by the enormous figure of Bryntas, who had left his spot at the bar to join the fray. The Wyn was stood close by, calm but coiled, his cold eyes scanning the room for threats. Four men were on the floor around him, including the man still clutching at his throat. That particular unfortunate was sitting with his back against a wooden strut and Sweet was grimly pleased to see that his breath seemed to be returning to him, albeit in ragged, choking gasps. He glared balefully at the Wyn between his snatched breaths.

The man Violent Fey had kicked was nursing his leg, but Sweet reckoned it wasn't broken. Dislocated the knee, maybe, but no broken bones. Several other loggers stood just a few short strides away, fists clenched and eyes narrowed at Sweet and his crew.

'Enough,' Sweet repeated, quieter this time but no less fierce for it. He fixed his hardest-bastard stare at each of the men in turn. Their eyes returned the challenge in kind so Sweet turned his hip to show the sword sheathed at his side and smiled grimly. 'Wouldn't want this to turn nasty now, would we lads?'

The men glanced down at the blade and hesitated. One of the men on the floor clambered to his feet to stand in the middle of the group. His nose looked worse than Stover's and his eyes were wild.

'This fucker attacked us!' the man jabbed an angry finger at Stover, who flexed against Bryntas' grip, grinning bloody teeth like the murdering lunatic they'd locked up just hours before.

'Truth is,' Sweet sighed, 'I don't rightly give a shit. I said *enough*.'

'I'll teach him some respect,' the logger spat blood to the sawdust.

'I'll run you through, you cheating piece of shit!' Stover hissed.

'You come at us again,' Sweet barked, cutting short a retort from the logger, 'and we draw blades.' He cast his eyes around the busy tavern and raised his voice. 'Fair warning, and everyone here heard it. Respect ain't much use to you if you've a gut full of steel now, is it?'

The logger tensed, as though he was about to leap at Stover, but at the last he relented. He frowned across the broken tables from under thunderous brows, but said nothing.

'Good,' Sweet whispered, trying desperately to steady his own heart as it beat like a drunken drummer. 'Now, we've all said our piece. We've all thrown a few punches and ain't nobody dead,' he lowered his arms, slowly. 'Now I'd call that a result. Let's keep it that way. We'll be leaving.'

Sweet fired Stover a warning with his eyes, sure that the other man would offer some sort of protest—something about not being done drinking or playing cards—but the mad bastard only grinned his bloody grin all the wider. Sweet sighed again. The prick was actually enjoying himself.

Sweet motioned to Bryntas and the big man started hauling Stover away towards the doors. Violent Fey pierced the loggers with a wicked glare of her own before turning and slinking after them. Sweet stood for a moment longer, making sure none of the locals had a last surge of ale-induced bravery, then he turned away from the whole mess and started shuffling towards the exit with the Wyn at his shoulder. Jenrick and Daraday joined him, casting wary glances at the rest of the patrons as they passed. The eyes of the entire taproom were fixed on them, watching them balefully as they picked their way towards the exit. There was near silence inside the taproom except for the sound of their shuffling footsteps and the odd scrape of a chair as a drinker cleared the way for them.

They had nearly made it to the door when Sweet heard a single chuckle echo from way behind them. The sound was dry and mirthless. He didn't need to look over his shoulder to know it was Malvadas, still sat in his dark little booth with his gaggle of low bastards huddled around him.

Sweet considered cursing under his breath again, but decided even that was pointless now. He gave the door a rough shove and stepped out into the night.

# Hanging around

THE MORNING SUN shone brightly, painting Woodbyrne in an altogether too-crisp shade of yellow. Sweet covered his eyes as he stumbled out of the rooms—a collection of dilapidated shacks near the far end of town that they had paid far too much in silver for—and into the morning warmth. Somewhere in the distance a dull banging echoed through the air, the noise drumming into Sweet's sleep-addled brain.

'You're up late,' Violent Fey remarked. Sweet squinted from beneath the canopy of his fingers and tried to pinpoint her. Eventually his eyes landed on where she was sitting. She was perched on an upturned bucket in the shade of her own little shack. Her sword was in her lap and she ran a whetstone along its edge. The noise scraped at Sweet's ears and he winced. She fired him a dangerous smile. 'Too many ales, was it?'

'Not enough, by all accounts,' Sweet replied, stretching his back and not enjoying the now familiar pops in his hip and shoulder. With every passing season he seemed to add a new one to the growing collection—and he didn't much care for any of them. He straightened up and looked over to the cabin at the end of their sorry little row. The one occupied by Stover. 'Couldn't he have gotten into a fight *after* we'd drunk our fill?'

Vi shrugged, running the whetstone along the blade again.

Sweet's eyes had adjusted enough now and he looked skywards. Vi had been right, he was up later than he would've liked. A smart man would've bet that the sun was closer to noon than it was to dawn already.

'No one else awake yet?' he asked, scratching at his chin.

'The Wyn disappeared early,' Vi responded, examining her work. She frowned down at the weapon and set to dragging the whetstone along its edge again. 'And the kid headed into town to get some supplies.'

Sweet raised an eyebrow at that. He mused on the fact that Daraday might not be rejoining their crew. The boy was obviously dismayed by what had happened the day before, so maybe he had decided this life wasn't for him after all. Maybe he'd decided to slip away whilst they all slept, never to be seen again. Sweet didn't blame him. It was a pretty shitty life, all things considered. Bringing folk to justice sounded all high and mighty, fluffed up with notions of honour and righteousness and the like. But once you started in the work, it became pretty clear that dealing with the filth of humanity all day, every day—well, it meant that you got plenty dirty yourself in the process.

'When did he go?' Sweet asked.

Vi shrugged again.

'Not long 'fore you dragged yourself out of bed.'

'Bryntas and Jenrick?' he asked.

'Ain't seen 'em yet,' another shrug. 'Though from Bryn's snoring I can make a pretty educated guess at what he's doing.'

Sweet smiled at that, but he didn't let it linger. Vi liked her jokes to be received with a grunt and a raised eyebrow at most. Anything more than that got her plenty suspicious, and when Vi got suspicious she tended to reach for her knives.

Despite the late hour of the morning, it was altogether too early for that shit.

'Argh my fuckin' head!'

The door to the end shack clattered open and Stover staggered into the daylight, his trews only half done up, revealing the top of a pasty leg that looked nearly white in the morning sunshine. He took a stuttering step forwards, fumbled some more with his clothes and then looked about him with a pained squint. 'Why'so fuckin' bright?' he mumbled, almost to himself.

'Cos it's late!' Sweet barked. Stover jumped and Sweet allowed himself another smile. This one he did let linger. 'We shoulda been gone with the sunrise.'

Vi grunted her agreement and the whetstone shrieked along the blade again. Stover winced at the sound and Sweet was sure she had angled it to purposely make the worst noise possible. He smiled again.

'Need some food,' Stover muttered, hawking and spitting a glob of brown to the hard-packed dirt. 'Breakfast.'

'The kid's gone to fetch some supplies,' Sweet told him. 'Let's get a fire going and we can see if he brings back anything worth eating.'

*

Daraday did indeed return from the market of Woodbyrne, to Sweet's mild surprise. He still looked upset, but too scared to simply abandon the group he had found himself in, like a lost puppy among feral dogs. Except most lost puppies didn't come back with a bundle of food, complete with sides of bacon fresh from the butcher's block. The group fried the bacon and wolfed it down alongside some eggs and a knob of hardbread each.

By the time they'd packed away their gear the town of Woodbyrne seemed to have livened up. People wandered by their ramshackle accommodation in pairs or small groups, talking excitedly amongst themselves. Most of the townsfolk gave Sweet and his crew a wary look as they passed their little camp. Sweet reckoned he recognised one or two faces from the taproom the night before.

'Where's everyone going?' Stover asked, picking at a bit of gristle lodged between his back teeth.

'The hanging,' Daraday replied, not looking up. He sat staring into the dwindling fire, watching the grey embers as they pulsed red in the morning breeze. Stover paused in his battle with the gristle to raise an eyebrow at him.

'Hanging?' he asked, speaking between his own fingers.

'Aye,' Sweet sighed, tonguing at a bit of bacon stuck between his own teeth. 'You not remember the murderer we brought in last night?'

Realisation dawned on the other man's face and he brightened.

'We should watch him swing,' said Stover, almost gleefully growling the words. To Sweet he sounded the way some men did when a woman's shape caught their eye.

'It's a long ride back to Levitan,' Sweet remarked, trying to sound innocuous.

'Won't matter if we leave it another hour then,' Stover grinned—his first smile all morning—as though that had somehow settled the matter in his favour. Sweet grimaced but didn't offer a reply. Stover had been in his crew long enough for Sweet to realise that arguing with him would be like arguing with the tides of the sea. Sometimes it was better to just let the water come in and then dry off later.

They finished packing away their gear. Stover seemed to have shaken off the ales from the night before and worked as brightly as any member of the crew. Or at least, he had some renewed energy about him anyway. With their gear stowed on their horses, the group started walking them towards the centre of the town.

\*

The source of the banging noises that had accompanied their breakfast became clearer as they neared the middle of Woodbyrne. Four main roads intersected at the centre of the town, a holy building nestled between two of them and what looked to be some sort of town hall stood across the way.

Between them, where the crossroads sat, a hangman's scaffold had been thrown together. Several men were hammering the last of the nails into place, pushing and pulling at the beams to test the strength of their handiwork.

'Hope they know what they're doing,' Stover remarked, grinning at Sweet. He seemed to have perked up remarkably ever since news of the hanging had reached his ears. 'Remember that mess in Gambury?'

Sweet did remember. The sleepy little village had put their own gallows together, same as the folks of Woodbyrne were doing now. Only, the people of Gambury obviously hadn't been well practised in that particular craft. By the time the criminal—one of the pleading kind that grated at Sweet's ears—had been bundled under the gib, the wooden beams were already creaking ominously. The village elder had kicked the stool away from under the man's feet and the whole platform had collapsed as his weight tightened the noose. Three people had been injured, including the village elder, who broke a leg as he fell under the crumbling scaffold. The criminal himself had been found under a stack of splintered timbers, a potato sack still over his head and the noose still round his neck, gibbering and mumbling questions about whether or not he was dead. Sweet and Bryntas had hauled him out of the mess themselves. After the wreckage had been cleared away, the villagers had reconvened and quietly hanged the man in a nearby forest instead.

Sweet sighed at the memory, and at the gleeful glint in Stover's eye.

Sweet hated hangings.

One of the carpenters gave the gib a final slap with a heavy open palm. Satisfied it would hold true, he followed his colleagues down off the platform, grim-faced in the bright autumn sunshine. A crowd had gathered in front of the gallows and Sweet and his crew stopped their horses at the back of it. The smile on Stover's face faltered a little— Sweet knew the bastard wanted to be down the front—but he kept his silence and made no efforts to move through the crowd.

The doors to the town hall opened and the murmuring from the crowd swelled. Sweet squinted into the sunlight and saw a small group of hunched figures emerging from the gloom. At the head of the group was a tall man wearing a tattered old robe of office. From the way he held his head—forehead up high and chin pointed outwards—Sweet knew immediately that he took his oath far too seriously. He was closely followed by a pair of men. Local militia, judging by their grim faces and poorly maintained swords at their hips. To one side shuffled the paunchy constable of Woodbyrne, a taffa papersmoke hanging from the corner of his mouth. At the back of the group came the prisoner, flanked by two more armed militiamen. His hands were bound behind his back and he wore the same filthy rags that he'd been dressed in when Sweet and his crew had captured him the day before. For a man being led to the gallows, he looked surprisingly serene—almost content. Definitely a madman, then.

The group, led by the painfully slow pace of the tall headman, stepped out into the noon sunlight and made their way to the newly-erected gallows. The noise from the crowd went up another notch, but they weren't shouting or hollering. Not yet anyway, that would come later. Sweet knew that was how most of these things went, after a time.

The group climbed the short series of steps leading up onto the platform and turned to face the crowd. The headman with the weathered robes stood, solemn as a priest on a holy day, waiting for silence. After a few moments it became apparent the best he would get was a dull quiet and he cleared his throat to speak.

'This man has been found guilty of murder,' he intoned, pointing a withered finger at the prisoner. The crowd immediately began to grumble more loudly and the headman had to raise his voice to be heard. 'By the law of the exalted kingdom of Pratia, The punishment for such a crime is death. Are there any here who would speak in his defence?'

The cursing started then. Folks in the crowd began shouting insults, one at a time at first, but soon it became a cacophony of angry voices. Sweet sighed as he caught sight of Stover's smile widening. Loved a bit of chaos, did Stover.

The headman, apparently satisfied no one would speak in favour of the prisoner, turned back to face the town hall and gave a slow nod. Another man emerged from the darkness within. He wore black boots, black trews and an ill-fitting black shirt. Over his head was a sack, cinched about his neck with a length of twine. Two badly-cut eyeholes, one slightly higher than the other, just about allowed him to see.

The gathered crowd's baying turned to cheers as they saw the hangman appear. The black-garbed man ignored the crowd and strode purposefully towards the gallows. Sweet was glad of that. Sometimes a hangman would play to the crowd, waving his arms and riling them up. Sweet hated pricks like that. A death sentence didn't need more spectacle, and it definitely didn't need that kind of jumped-up pageantry.

The hangman stumbled on the first step and Sweet wondered if the reason he wasn't playing to the mob was because he couldn't see them through the damn sack on his head. He sighed again.

The hangman approached the prisoner and motioned for him to climb onto the stool set in the centre of the platform. The man looked momentarily puzzled, but climbed up readily enough. Sweet thought he almost looked happy. The hangman settled the noose over the man's head. He wasn't gentle, but he wasn't overly rough either and Sweet found himself respecting the executioner more and more. Here was a man who didn't enjoy dark work. He just did what needed doing.

With his preparations complete, the hangman gave the tall headman a sharp nod to indicate he was ready. The robed official cleared his throat again.

'Do you have anything to say?' he asked, addressing the prisoner, 'before you are to hang?'

The crowd quieted, waiting to see what the murderer would say. Even Sweet found himself straining to listen. The man had barely said a word the entire time he had spent as their prisoner and he was strangely curious to hear what his voice would be like.

'Darkness comes,' the man said, his voice weirdly songlike. He was looking beyond the crowd, beyond the buildings even, as though staring into a great distance. 'Darkness comes on swift wings.'

There was a pregnant silence from the gathered crowd. All the cheering and the baying faded down to a confused murmur. Sweet heard Stover mutter beside him—

'What the fuck did he say?'

—then the mob began to hurl insults once more. As though they had been cheated by this last refrain of the condemned. They had expected him to beg for mercy. Or to shriek defiance. They had wanted it, just so they could bare their teeth and cry their disdain. They had needed it. Instead they got the lightly-spoken utterances of a madman, moon-touched and seemingly unaware of the noose around his neck or the gravity of his predicament. Even Stover looked disappointed now. At least that gave Sweet a small sense of satisfaction.

The headman had raised a wispy grey eyebrow in response to the prisoner's remarks, as though waiting for more. When he found nothing forthcoming, and perhaps in response to the growing anger from the crowd, he nodded to the hangman once more.

The black-garbed executioner gave the stool a rough kick and the prisoner dropped. The noose snapped tight and the crowd suddenly switched back to wild cheering. The prisoner danced on the end of the rope, for the drop had only been an inch or two—not nearly long enough to break his neck. His legs kicked and bucked and his eyes bulged as he struggled for breath. Sweet watched with a mix of mild disgust and disinterest. The crowd continued to cheer.

After a time the man's kicking fell still. His eyes rolled into the back of his head, and the crowd cheered all the louder as he swung gently from side to side on the end of the coarse rope.

Sweet turned to face his crew. Bryntas and Jenrick mirrored his own feelings of apathy. Violent Fey had narrowed her eyes to angry little slits. Daraday looked both solemn and nauseous in equal measure and Stover looked hungry for more.

'That's that, then,' Sweet told them with a weary sigh. 'Let's find the Wyn and get going. No point hanging around in this shithole town any longer.'

# PART ONE

*The hunters*

# Different wolves

L EVITAN MIGHT HAVE new rulers, but it still stank the same.
Sweet resisted the urge to curl his nose as the first wave of the stench hit his nostrils. His horse whickered softly, as though it was offended by the smell, too. Sweet wondered why he was surprised. The city of Levitan wouldn't have won any beauty contests even before it was sacked by an invading army. So there was little wonder as to why it was such a tableau of repugnancy now. He looked around at the trash-strewn streets and tried to remember if it had actually been any different when the Pratians had still been in charge. Probably not, he reckoned.

Stover hawked deeply from the saddle beside him, then pressed a finger to one side of his nose and blew a gob of snot out of the other. He sniffed and wiped his face on his travel-stained sleeve.

'Still a shithole, then?' he chuckled, his grizzled features wrinkling together to form a grin.

'Aye,' Sweet agreed, guiding his mount around the remnants of a wagon left in the middle of the road. Only one wheel of the vehicle remained, and even then it was charred to a cinder. There was a dark stain to the ground around it. Soot or blood, Sweet didn't know. Probably both, he reckoned again.

'The Vols didn't fuck around did they?' Stover smirked, as they skirted their horses past the wreck.

Sweet grunted his response this time. The fires had all been put out now, but occasionally their little group rode past the blackened shell of a building or two. Down one particular street the squat little dwellings on one side of the road had all been torched to ash. Several men, women and children were still hanging around the ruins looking lost, as though the destruction had happened mere moments ago. In reality, it had been nearly two weeks since the armies of Volsgard had descended upon the capital city, effectively winning their war against Pratia. At this point more damage was probably being done by looters, chancers and opportunist criminals, instead of by Vol soldiers. Though the lines between those groups were blurry at best, depending on who you asked.

Sweet spotted a child—couldn't have yet been ten winters old—with dirty hair so roughly clipped that he couldn't tell if they were a boy or a girl. The child, dressed in threadbare rags that might've been sackcloth in a past life, was picking through the soot-covered ruins of a miserable little building with grubby little hands at the end of gaunt little arms. The child looked up as they passed by and Sweet felt a twinge of something as he looked into those forlorn eyes.

Sorrow? Guilt, maybe?

He stifled it, almost angry with himself. Wasn't his fault, after all. The war between the Pratians and the Vols had nothing to do with him. He hadn't even been in the kingdom for most of the war. He'd stayed well clear of the whole affair, as any sane person should. If anyone should shoulder the guilt for this mess it was the Pratian king.

Hard to shoulder guilt when you were dead, of course.

The ruler of Pratia had been a proud bastard. All accounts of the man had him pegged as arrogant, loud, brash and stupid. Where others had recognised the strength of Volsgard, he had openly mocked and provoked them. Under the guise of patriotism he had whipped up his nation into defying the most powerful empire in the world. When the invasion had finally come, and war had arrived in Pratia, at first the people had celebrated. They had been drunk with a nationalistic fervour, certain that they would repel the enemy and defend themselves against the aggressor. At first they even had some cause to celebrate—the Pratian defenders held their own, even claiming a handful of victories along the way.

But as the weeks bled into months, and more and more battles had ended in defeat or—at best—a bloody stalemate, the good mood in the kingdom had begun to wane. The promises of rising up to slay the onrushing beast that was the Vol empire were slowly forgotten, replaced with a knowledge that chilled them all. An inexorable truth that eroded their confidence like endless waves eating at the base of a cliff.

They were losing.

And then, as the losses mounted and it became clear that there were no able-bodied men left to be conscripted into the fight, the end had come in a rush. In just a single month the Pratian army had all but collapsed and the Vols had pushed forwards like an unstoppable flood.

With the Pratian army scattered to the winds in a pitched battle just a week's march away from the city itself, the Vols had entered Levitan largely unopposed. The king had sealed himself and his family inside the Royal Palace, along with the remnants of whatever madly loyal soldiers he could find. The defenders had been quickly overwhelmed and the Vols—not known for their mercy at the best of times—had shown none of it to the leadership of the fallen kingdom.

The citizens of Levitan themselves had been left to fend for themselves during the invasion. Sweet had seen cities in the aftermath of a sack before—and once you'd seen one you'd seen them all. With no one enforcing the laws and desperation everywhere, folks quickly turned on each other. Looting, robbery and murder were all fairly common even before a single enemy soldier arrived on the scene. Men and women with long-standing grievances saw good opportunities to take action on them, and others who just saw something they wanted simply took it.

When the soldiers did show up, what happened next largely depended on the quality of the general in charge of things. If they were half-decent—or at least in some way competent—then their soldiers wouldn't kill everyone who crossed their paths and raze the entire place to the ground. If they weren't competent...well there were plenty of ghostly ruins to the south that had once been thriving cities. Happily—or unhappily, depending on how you saw it—for the people of Levitan, the sack of their city had been conducted by a competent general.

Say what you want about the Vols—and most people here would've been happy to do exactly that just a few months ago—they were damned good at war. Ruthless, efficient fighters who prided themselves on their military might and strict discipline. Whichever of their storied generals charged with the taking of Levitan had done so with the least amount of mess possible. They had assumed control of the city quickly and efficiently and with none of the rampant slaughter heard of in other campaigns.

Sweet doubted such a thought would offer much comfort to the child sifting through the blackened rubbish. He found it didn't offer him much comfort either, so instead opted to turn his head back to the middle of the road and keep his horse moving. Better to just put some things from your mind, after all.

'Think the Vols did all this?' Daraday asked, motioning to the derelict buildings.

The youngster had grown over the past three years. Since he had joined Sweet's crew he had shot up in height by another half a foot or so. His shoulders had broadened and—though he wasn't nearly as bulky as Bryntas—his muscles were lean and taut. Most of all, though, he had toughened up plenty in his mind. Gone was the boyish, wistful sheen in his eyes. Replaced now with a hardened, flint-like gleam. Sweet could still remember the childlike fear and naivety of the younger Daraday. He could still remember the defining moment that naivety had started to fade, too. What was the town called, Woodbyrne? That had surely been a moment of reckoning for the boy. The day they had tracked the madman in the woods. The day Aribor got stuck. Three years of living and working among Sweet and the rest of the crew had surely changed the lad. Sweet swallowed as he found himself wondering if that was such a good thing.

But it was better to put some things from your mind, after all.

Most things, if he was being honest.

'I reckon they did this to themselves,' Sweet answered, not deigning to look upon the broken ruins again. 'Folk get panicky when there's an army at the gates.'

''specially a Vol army,' chimed in Violent Fey.

'Aye,' Sweet sighed, ''specially then.'

They walked their horses for another half a mile, navigating broken streets and broken people. Sweet made plenty sure that his blades were on full show, lest any of the more desperate folk take a fancy to the mounted group riding slowly through their ruined city.

Levitan's industrial district looked mostly untouched by the fall of the city. But Sweet supposed that made sense—what use was there in acquiring a new city if you destroyed the main reason for its continued existence? The forges and tanneries even looked to have reopened, plumes of smoke billowing from their smokestacks and chimneys. Perhaps they'd never closed—only now there were pockets of Vol soldiers standing in the doorways, their dark armour matched perfectly by the dark looks on their faces. They eyed Sweet and his crew with great suspicion as they slowly rode by, as though they expected a scrap. Wanted one even, judging by the ferocity of the scowls. Sweet ignored the looks. After all, it wasn't his first time in a sacked city.

The presence of Vol soldiers soon became even more clear as they rounded a street corner and came upon a hastily-erected barrier blocking the road ahead. Upturned tables, chairs and other furniture had been thrown together to create a makeshift barricade. Vol soldiers—looked to be a whole troop of them milling about—were standing in a line in front of it. A small group of them were bunched in the centre of the barrier, where enough space had been left to allow passage for two horses to ride through side-by-side. The men bristled as Sweet and his crew approached, their horses' hooves clopping loudly on the cobblestones.

Two of the soldiers stiffened, spears in hand, and several others reached for the hilts of their swords.

'You there!' one of the soldiers called out. Sweet noted the insignia on his uniform and guessed him to be a First Sergeant, probably the man in charge of the barricade. 'State your names and your business.'

Sweet pulled his horse to a stop and cleared his throat. Riding through the smoking ruins of the city's poorer districts had given him a bastard of a dry mouth, but he didn't dare reach for his waterskin just yet. These boys look jumpy enough as it is, he thought. Wouldn't want to give them reason to fly off the handle completely.

'Most call me Bitter Sweet,' he told the Vol officer, ignoring the wary gazes of the soldiers around him. After a moment of silence, Sweet shrugged and motioned to the others. 'This is my crew. We're bounty hunters, we're here to—ah—see if there's any work needs doing.'

The officer smirked at that.

'You're aware this city is now a part of the Empire of Volsgard?' he asked, drawing ire from some of his compatriots.

'Aye, I'm aware,' Sweet nodded, accepting the mocking tone with the utmost nonchalance. He shrugged. 'S'why we figure there'll be work available. New management usually has some loose ends that need tying up good and tight.'

The officer's smirk faded a little. He thought about that for a moment, then slowly nodded.

'There're still some who refuse to accept their place,' he said at last, the corner of his mouth curling up as though one such a person was kneeling before him right this second. 'As well as plenty o' folk who need bringing into line. In Volsgard the law is iron.'

'So we've heard,' Violent Fey muttered over Sweet's shoulder, thankfully quiet enough for the soldiers not to hear it.

'Plenty that needs doing then?' Sweet asked brightly.

'Plenty,' the officer agreed, smirking again now. 'General Gamvan has control of the city, but he's busy up at the palace. Make for the Hall of Justice, state your business to the officer on duty and he'll see you get eyes on any contracts we have open.'

With that, the soldier waved them through. Sweet tipped him a nod and a smile as he walked his horse towards the opening in the barricade, his crew following close behind.

Violent Fey nudged her mount closer to Sweet's as they left the barricade behind them.

'Arrogant bunch, aren't they?' she raised an eyebrow. 'I thought the

Vols were supposed to be ruthless bastards? All business? Not much for the swagger?'

Sweet shrugged.

'Winning wars'll do that to men,' he replied with a weary sigh. 'They're no different to any other conquering army.'

An elderly man was standing in a doorway to their left, his clothes clean but his hair unkempt. He watched Sweet and his crew with hard-eyed suspicion, but he looked frightened as they neared. He disappeared into the building and pushed the door shut with a slam. Over Sweet's shoulder, Stover chuckled.

'Besides,' Sweet added, irritated by the laugh, 'to all the folk here not much'll change. Not really, anyway. Just a different flag flying above the palace and a new set of nobles to bow to.' Sweet sighed, frowning at nothing. When he spoke again it was barely a whisper, spoken almost to himself. 'Same sheep, different wolves.'

Sweet angled his horse off at the next turning and led his crew towards the centre of the district. Towards the former Pratian—now Volsgard—Hall of Justice.

*

The Hall of Justice was an imposing structure. Sweet supposed that was by design. If you wanted people to obey the law then what better way than to make the seat of those laws look formidable beyond reckoning?

Tall walls of smooth stone rose high above every other building in the district. On the higher floors, lines of thin, lead-lined windows ran in perfect symmetry. Despite not being wide enough to accommodate even the most emaciated of figures, the thick iron bars that covered them sent a clear message. Even so, Sweet knew that most criminals in the former kingdom of Pratia feared the lower floors more. Those windowless rooms, some deep below the streets themselves, were where interrogations took place. Under Pratian rule they had been places that struck terror into the hearts of even the hardest bastards in the criminal underworld. Under Vol rule, Sweet shivered thinking about what horrors might await any man or woman consigned to imprisonment down there.

What made Sweet even more uncomfortable was the knowledge that every cell down there would likely be occupied already. There would be Pratian captives who knew the whereabouts of whatever remaining military units were still active. There would be loyalists to the old kingdom who would know the names of others organising any resistance to Vol rule and where they would meet to discuss their plans. And then there would be people simply caught up in the wrong place at the wrong time. Unfortunates who were taken prisoner by the Vols under the misgiving—or the pretence—that they would have information that might prove valuable.

And, under the questioning of the Vols, all of them would sing.

Sweet shivered again as they neared the entrance. Two huge stone pillars, as devoid of decoration as the walls they flanked, stood strong beside giant doors of dark wood, studded with crossbars of blackened iron. A troop of Vol guards, even more stern-faced and wary-eyed than the ones guarding the barricade, stood to attention at the feet of the pillars.

Sweet drew rein a good distance away from them, his crew did the same. The lead Vol soldier stepped forwards, looking up at them with a practised eye. He scanned the group, lingering on the Wyn and arching his brow.

'Bounty hunters?' he grunted the question once his assessment complete.

'Aye,' Sweet nodded, 'we hear there's work available.'

The Vol nodded.

'I can't let you all in,' he told Sweet, 'three of you can go, the rest wait here.'

'Fine by me,' Sweet agreed, he turned to face the group and nodded at Vi.

'I'm coming,' Stover announced, snorting loudly. He was already dismounting before Sweet could object.

The Vol looked on, impassive as to which of them would enter.

'Leave your weapons here,' he told them. 'Speak to Lieutenant Renauld, he's at the desk inside.'

Sweet climbed down from his horse and handed his weapons over to the Vol guards. He watched Vi do the same and was irked by Stover's smirk as he passed across his hatchets, his short-sword and a wide array of daggers and knives. Thankfully, the Vols clearly saw him as no threat, ignoring the expression as though he wasn't there. Their lack of reaction seemed to irritate Stover and his face darkened, like a child who hadn't got his way. Sweet enjoyed that, at least.

Vi fired Sweet a questioning look, as though bringing Stover might be amongst the shittier options available. Sweet already knew that, but Stover was a stubborn bastard and sometimes it was easier to give him an inch than let him steal a mile.

Once disarmed, the three of them climbed the short flight of steps leading up to the enormous doors. Two Vol guards pushed them open and waved them inside.

The entranceway was a cavernous expanse that stretched up two storeys high. A horseshoe-shaped balcony overlooked the vast floorspace below. Just like the exterior of the building, there were no adornments and little by way of decoration. It was gloomy inside, the only light provided by the slitted windows high above the doorway. Dust motes danced in the air as the doors were pulled shut behind them.

At the far end of the room, flanked by another pair of Vol soldiers and sitting behind a small desk that looked to have been liberated from somewhere else in the building, was a Vol officer. He was studying a parchment on the desk intently, another stack of papers piled beside his arm. He ignored the trio of newcomers as they entered the Hall of Justice.

Sweet swapped a glance with Vi, then started approaching the desk. The echoes from their boots sounded in the high alcoves above them. Sweet saw more Vol soldiers lingering in the shadows there. He stopped a few feet short of the officer behind the desk and waited for him to greet them. When he didn't, Sweet gave a short cough. Still the Vol studied his parchment. Before Sweet could stop him, Stover leaned forwards.

'We're here for work,' Stover sneered, casting daring glances at the two soldiers who had bristled at his sudden movement.

'This is not the Hall of Employment,' the officer replied, his voice soft and unassuming. He still hadn't looked up from his papers and Sweet felt a queasy feeling in his gut. Not normally something he was like to ignore. Stover obviously hadn't cottoned on and leaned forwards again, jabbing a finger through the air.

'Well we're—'

'It is customary in Volsgard,' the officer interrupted, slowly drawing his attention away from the contents of his desk, 'for subordinates to wait for instruction.'

The Vol officer sat straight in his chair to regard the trio. His pale hair was neatly trimmed, his face clean-shaven. His nose was small, his lips thin. His bright blue eyes were deep set and swam with a sharp intelligence. His entire demeanour was one of quiet confidence. Normally Sweet could respect a man like this easily enough, but when those blue eyes locked onto him he felt a cold icicle seep through his belly and tug at his balls. Every fibre of Sweet's being screamed the same thing at him.

This man was dangerous.

'My name is Lieutenant Renauld,' the officer announced, folding his hands together in front of his neatly-pressed uniform. He made his introduction affably enough, but Sweet detected no warmth in its depths. Beside him, Stover had gone from pissed-off to confused in a matter of heartbeats. Luckily, that confusion came with a side-serving of shutting-the-fuck-up.

'Sweet,' Sweet nodded, dragging Renauld's uncomfortable attention back to him. 'These are two of my crew, Vi and Stover.'

'Vi being shorthand for *Violent Fey,* no?' Renauld asked, with a smile that never touched his eyes. He almost sounded amused.

'That's right,' Vi replied coldly, interpreting the inquiry as mockery. 'There a problem with that?'

Sweet winced as she barbed the question, but the Vol officer barely flinched. He sat with his cold, dead smile fixed in place, as though he had gone momentarily deaf.

'Not at all,' he said at last, causing Sweet to release a breath he didn't even know he'd been holding. 'Just that your reputations precede you.'

'We're here to help,' said Sweet, trying desperately to wrest back some control of the situation. He didn't like this slick bastard and he didn't like that both Vi and Stover were already riled up. 'No doubt you've got some folk who need bringing to heel,' he flapped his arms out to his sides, gesturing stupidly towards his comrades, 'we can help with that.'

Renauld continued smiling his queer little smile. Sweet wished he'd stop. Iciness he could deal with. Burning anger he could deal with. Creepy little shits like this rubbed him up the wrong way entirely. They were the sort of men who started life pulling the wings off of insects because it amused them, before quickly escalating to drowning puppies and—eventually—skinning men alive for pleasure. Sweet swallowed as he suddenly remembered where he was standing.

A place like this was made for a man like that.

'You gave your name as Sweet,' Renauld remarked, carefully placing his elbows on the surface of the desk. 'I thought your full moniker was *Bitter Sweet.*'

'It is,' Sweet agreed, eager to get away from the desk and—more importantly—its occupant, as quickly as possible. He swallowed the feeling down and shrugged. 'Bit of a mouthful, though.'

'So called because you entered your...business with high hopes for a noble profession,' Renauld continued, his eyes twinkling dangerously. 'But found the reality to be...less palatable. You started out sweet, then got bitter along the way—that's the story, is it not?'

'Something like that,' Sweet grumbled, his empty sword belt suddenly feeling decidedly light.

'You've worked Pratia for the best part of two decades?' asked Renauld, either oblivious or uncaring towards Sweet's discomfort—he guessed it was the latter.

'S'right,' Sweet answered.

'There's not a man or woman alive who could hide from your crew in this kingdom,' Renauld continued.

'Part of the empire, now,' Sweet corrected, somewhat mockingly. He saw one of the soldiers beside the desk suppress a half-smile. Sweet regretted making the quip almost immediately, expecting the officer's face to darken at the remark. Perhaps there would be anger now. Heated words, maybe even yelling. In Sweet's experience powerful men didn't like having their mistakes pointed out to them, especially if it was done in jest. Instead, Renauld's strange little smile returned in full force—and somehow that was even worse.

'Yes, quite,' was all he said.

'But aye,' Sweet mumbled, eager to steer things away from his misstep, 'we're good at what we do.'

'The best,' Stover added, looking down his nose at the seated Vol as though he was the one in command of the situation. Sweet had a moment to wonder if Stover might just be the stupidest man in the city before Renauld was talking again.

'Take the stairs to your left,' he told them sharply, snapping his head down to study his papers once more. 'Second corridor on the right at the top, end of the hall. Knock and wait.'

It took Sweet a moment to realise they had been summarily dismissed. He muttered something that might have been quiet thanks, though whether it was to Renauld or to some higher power that had somehow engineered their escape from the charged encounter with the Vol officer, he couldn't say. He turned on slightly shaky legs and made for the stairs, Vi and Stover following close behind.

'Arrogant prick, int he?' Stover asked, loudly enough to make Sweet wince again.

'Dangerous, that one,' Vi commented. She spoke more quietly than Stover, but saying anything aloud in a room as large an echochamber as this one was not something Sweet would recommend. He left it a moment to see if there would be a response from below. When there was none he breathed again.

'Ain't that the truth,' he said, addressing both of them.

# The golden rule

∘⊢⇥ ✗ ⊦ • ⇥●⟨⇥ • ⊦ ✗ ⟨⊢ ⊦∘

T HE CORRIDOR WAS just as sparse and uninviting as the entrance hall had been. The ceiling was uncomfortably low and the walls were more endless stretches of bare stone. Vol soldiers were stationed at each of the plain, functional-looking doors set along its length. They were disciplined men, standing to rigid attention even before Sweet, Stover and Vi stepped past them. Their uniforms were pristine and their weapons looked well cared for.

No wonder the Pratians lost the war, Sweet thought, remembering some of his encounters with soldiers of the defeated kingdom. A patch of dirt on a uniform here, a patch of grime on a blade there, stubble along jawlines and dark rings under bleary eyes that had seen too little combat and too much of gambling dens and seedy taverns. They'd not been exceptionally lazy or careless in their work, certainly not compared to the circles that Sweet usually moved in anyway. But by the impeccable standards set by the armies of Volsgard, it was no surprise they had been beaten into bloody submission.

Annihilated was probably a more apt description, from what Sweet had heard. The war had raged on for the best part of three years, triggered by a Vol incursion as their emperor set his sights on yet another expansion. There had been bloody skirmishes at first, ambushes and the like, but it had quickly escalated—as these things usually did. Before long the Pratian king had started recruiting more men to bolster his forces, Sweet and his crew had even been approached by the recruiting officers themselves. A veteran Pratian who had first talked of glorious purpose and—when that hadn't whetted their appetites—began reeling off what different ranks could each hope to earn during the campaign. It had been a fruitless exercise on his part though. Sweet was savvy enough to know the best place to be during a war was anywhere but in it.

After a year the two sides were in deadlock, but then the Vols had taken a key river crossing in the east of the country and had started to exert their superior military advantage. They had chipped away at the Pratian forces—and their resolve—for months after that, culminating in the sacking of two cities that—by all accounts—had been much less lucky than Levitan. In the final year of the war, the Pratians had gotten desperate, coercing old men and boys into the starving maw of their war machine, handing weapons to farmers and shepherds before pitting them against the most hardened fighting force in the known world. What followed then had been slaughter after slaughter, until at last the two sides had met in a pitched battle, not more than twenty miles away from Levitan itself.

The Battle of Scarvin, where the Pratian king had gathered all of his remaining forces—battle-scarred veterans and wide-eyed new recruits alike—and faced them up against four battalions of Vol soldiers. The Pratians had outnumbered the Vols by more than two-to-one; but they were inexperienced, weary and—quite rightly, in Sweet's opinion—terrified of the army they found themselves facing.

The battle had been short but bloody. When the fighting was done, over eight thousand Pratian men and boys lay dead in the fields of Scarvin, with two thousand more taken prisoner by the victorious Vols. The Pratian king himself had fled the field as the battle had turned into a rout, abandoning his soldiers and fleeing to Levitan where he had barricaded himself inside his palace—for all the good it did him.

Sweet walked by another Vol guard and found himself wondering if the man had been there. Had he seen the horrors of Scarvin and rejoiced? Had he fought and killed so that his emperor could claim another part of the map for himself? Sweet shook the thought from his head, finding it both grim and insane in equal measure. He sighed. Such was the way of the world.

At the end of the corridor, yet another pair of Vol guards flanked a doorway. This time, the door had been given more attention than its counterparts further down the hall. The wood panelling had been expertly carved into patterns inspired by Pratian iconography. The door handle was polished brass and inlaid with decorative swirls, reflecting distorted mirror images of the Vol guards that stood either side of it. Sweet cleared his throat.

'Lieutenant Renauld sent us,' he told the men, 'told us to...err...knock and wait.'

The guards didn't say a word, but one of them snapped out of his rigid posture and curled a hand towards the panelled door. He gave three sharp, solid raps with his knuckles and then returned to his original position, every movement quick and efficient. They even knocked on doors like it was a damn military manoeuvre.

The Pratians never stood a chance, Sweet thought.

After a long quiet, broken only by Stover snorting—as loudly and as disgustingly as he could manage—a soft voice called out a single word from the other side.

'Enter.'

Sweet cleared his throat again and opened the door.

\*

The room they entered was just about as far as could be from the cold, imposing hallways and atriums that made up the rest of the Hall of Justice. It was a vast and welcoming space, with massive windows facing out onto the canal outside that let in an inordinate amount of stark white daylight. Wooden floorboards, set into zig-zagging patterns and polished to a high sheen ran the length and breadth of the room, broken up only by a rug so intricately woven that Sweet had to squint to see the detailing. To their left and right, huge bookshelves, each twice as high as a man, rose up towards a cavernous ceiling embellished with rich panelling of its own. An enormous chandelier—unlit for now—hung from the centre of the ceiling, carefully-worked glass and crystal shimmering in the dull light of the overcast sky outside. Behind the bookshelves were the walls themselves, dark wooden boards flowed up from the floor to waist-height, where they were met with painted paper stuck fast to the wall itself. It was something of a trend amongst the high and mighty of Pratian society—or so Sweet had heard anyway, his line of work usually saw him spending more time with the low bastards of the kingdom than it did the high and mighty ones. The dark green patterns of the papered walls were interrupted only by detailed oil paintings hung in gilt-edged frames and depicting all manner of serious looking aristocracy. A broad, ornate fireplace was set into one wall, an inviting pile of burning logs crackling happily in its firebox. Through a gap in the bookshelves to his left, Sweet saw a carved bust—presumably of the now-dead Pratian king—staring vacuously into space. To the right, in the shadows behind the shelves, an enormous suit of armour was half-hidden in the gloom. Sweet had been in the Hall of Justice many times before, when Levitan was the Pratian capital and they had accepted bounties from the Pratian magistrates, but he had never been in this office, nor any quite as lavish.

In the middle of the room, just in front of the lead-lined windows and directly beneath the expensive-looking chandelier, was a desk the size of a galley. Carved from the same wood as the wall-panels—so dark it looked almost blackened—it rose up high and wide. The Pratian Royal Seal had been carved into the front, an unsubtle reminder to any visitors of the office of the sheer depth of shit they were in, should they find themselves standing before it. Though Sweet reckoned the effect was somewhat lessened now, with a Vol inquisitor sat behind the desk. Or maybe that was worse, he considered.

Atop the desk were various writing implements and stacks of parchment, blank loose sheafs and piles of texts with tiny lettering covering them from top to bottom. Leather wrappings bound with cord held yet more papers and rows of ink pots, their lids screwed tight, ran along every remaining inch of space available.

Behind the desk sat an unremarkable man in a Vol uniform. Presumably the owner of the soft voice that had granted them entry. He looked to be about the same age as Sweet, though Sweet knew his own grizzled face added an extra decade to the nearly-five already under his belt. From the looks of it, this man's life had been considerably different to Sweet's own. His face was weathered but not beaten, his skin was much lighter from a lifetime spent indoors—no doubt behind a desk similar to the one he occupied now—and his clothing was neat and well presented. He had short-cropped, mousy-coloured hair that was more grey than brown and thinning on the top. He was clean-shaven, with a slim jawline and high cheekbones. He wasn't overly threatening to look at, but his eyes sparkled with the confidence of a man used to being in charge. He sat at the desk like a man who belonged, despite the obvious disparities between his garments and the seal emblazoned on the front of the desk he now occupied. His hands were set before him, fingers entwined and he watched Sweet, Vi and Stover step forwards with an expression somewhere between bemusement and apathy.

'Lieutenant Renauld sent us,' Sweet started, 'he said—'

'You are Bitter Sweet,' the man interrupted, carefully pronouncing each word in turn. A slight smile twitched across his face. 'And your companions, the notable Violent Fey and...Stover, was it?'

'S'right,' Stover almost growled, visibly irked that he had been considered something of an afterthought. Sweet hoped he could hold his tongue. A Vol didn't get to sit behind this particular desk without having some significant clout available to him. Pissing him off because he didn't consider you noteworthy would be a monument to stupidity itself—and Stover was something of a champion craftsman when it came to erecting those.

'My name is Lennick Sylvanus, High Magicker of Volsgard and councillor to his supreme eminence, the Emperor Thranovin.'

Sweet swallowed and did his best to keep the surprise off his face. It was unusual for Vol magickers to leave Volsgard itself, let alone be stationed in the seat of law-making for a conquered nation. And this man had called himself *High Magicker,* too. Sweet didn't know a lot about the structure of Vol politics, or where magickers sat within it—they tended to stay put inside the inner reaches of the sprawling empire—but he knew that anyone with the emperor's ear was worth reckoning well. Dealing with such a man would require a deft touch. The utmost caution was required.

'We're here for work,' Stover grunted, folding his arms across his chest as though challenging the man. Sweet closed his eyes and sighed, wondering how many sentences it would take for Stover to get them all locked up in the dungeons below the building. Or maybe they'd be cut down on the spot for their insolence.

'And work you shall have,' Sylvanus' smile only grew wider. He unlinked his fingers and threw his arms wide to emphasise his point. The size of the desk warped Sweet's judgement a little, but he guessed that the magicker wasn't a big man, perhaps even on the slight side of things—though he supposed magickers didn't rely on their muscles so much as they did—well, their magick.

'You have contracts open?' Sweet asked, speaking quickly to cut off a reply—no doubt something confrontational and arsehole-ish—from Stover. He skipped the introductions. After all, it seemed as though this man already knew all about them. The very thought made Sweet a little nervous. The magicker seemed to know all of them well enough, but so far the only things Sweet knew about the man sitting across from them was his name and title—the very things that he had just told them.

'Just one, actually,' the little magicker continued smiling, letting his arms fall and reaching for a small stack of parchment wrapped in hide and stamped with the mark of Volsgard. He paused and looked up at Sweet. Something in the man's twinkling gaze pulled at Sweet's guts, similar to the feelings evoked by Lieutenant Renauld downstairs, only this one was somehow worse. Maybe it was all Vols, Sweet thought. They're all dangerous bastards. Ambition will do that to men. 'I hear you and your companions are the best in Pratia?' Sylvanus continued, raising an eyebrow.

Sweet kept his expression blank. Was he taunting them? Patronising them? Or was he being sincere? And if he was being genuine, why? Here sat a magicker, in a city full of friends with sharp blades and with a supposed direct link to the most powerful ruler in the world. Here sat a man with the strength and authority of an empire at his back, and he was toying with them the way a cat did with its unfortunate prey. More often than not—Sweet knew—that prey was tortured before being devoured. Sweet decided that—faced with such a question—the best way of avoiding a similar fate would be to offer humble neutrality.

'Best in the world,' Stover put in before Sweet could respond, cocking his head and looking down his nose at the magicker as though he had offered a personal slight against them. As though even suggesting that there could be others who plied their trade better than they did was something worth dying for.

'Stover,' Sweet warned aloud.

You dumb fuck, his eyes said, silently.

The little magicker leaned back in his stolen chair and chuckled. The sound held real mirth, but something in it ground at Sweet's ears like fingernails down a chalkboard. There was joy, but it was a malicious kind of joy. The kind that took pleasure in the suffering of others. Hell, Sweet had heard it often enough from Stover himself.

The other bounty hunter was scowling at Sweet now, as though being quietly admonished was the worst possible outcome for him. Sweet—recognising the potential depths of shit they were in—knew better.

'How delightful,' Sylvanus finished his bout of laughter, tailing off with a forced sigh. 'The best in the world indeed, well—as luck would have it—that is *exactly* what we need.'

'Who's the mark?' Sweet asked, ignoring Stover and doing his best to ignore whatever game this Vol prick was trying to instigate, too. His initial fear was starting to give way to frustration now. If this man was a cat toying with its prey, Sweet had no intention of playing the game. He hated the greasy feel of politics at the best of times and this man was dripping with it.

'Straight to business,' the magicker remarked. He wagged an appreciative finger through the air at Sweet, though it felt more like something a parent might do when disciplining a wayward child back to good behaviour. 'I like that,' he said, 'no wasting time.'

Except for all this bullshit, Sweet thought, wondering exactly how many Vol soldiers were stationed in the Hall of Justice. A hundred? Two? Three? Enough to butcher him and his crew a thousand times over, no doubt. None in here though, if we needed to, maybe we could overpower this bastard before he called for help. Not bloody likely though, you don't get to be High Magicker—whatever the hell that was—without knowing a trick or two. He could probably turn us all to ash before we could get halfway around that bloody great desk. Sweet's mind recoiled at the thought, but he remained silent and stony-faced.

'Very well,' Sylvanus leaned back in his chair once more, folding his hands into his lap and regarding the trio with a supreme sense of self-satisfaction. 'As you know, our esteemed emperor's forces have conquered this...tired little nation. When General Gamvan and his troops took this city, the kingdom of Pratia ceased to exist.'

Tell that to the people picking through the ruins, Sweet thought.

'The king himself died in the melee,' Sylvanus reported, his sympathy ringing so false he might as well have laughed the words instead of speaking them. 'He and his men fought to the last. A noble, valiant effort—albeit one offered in vain.'

Sweet had to resist snorting at that. He doubted very much that the last stand had been either noble or valiant. Sweet reckoned there was more chance of the sun never rising again. By all accounts, the king of Pratia had cowered as the Vols invaded his palace, and had been killed quickly to avoid any loose ends for what came after. After all, without a king, Pratia was just another scrap of land for the emperor to add to his collection. Why take a king prisoner when you can just kill him and his family, erasing his kingdom in the process? It was neat, Sweet had to admit, if not a bit ruthless for his taste.

'The queen sadly took her own life,' Sylvanus continued, his feigned sympathy grating at Sweet's ears. 'She consumed poison as our soldiers entered the palace.'

Sweet had no doubt that the poison had actually been forced down her throat, probably by those very same soldiers the magicker was talking about. Damn it he hoped the man would stop talking soon and get to the bloody point.

'The Crown Prince, though,' Sylvanus locked eyes with Sweet, who suddenly saw a hardness that hadn't been there before. Something every bit as cold and ruthless as he would've expected from a Vol sorcerer. 'Is nowhere to be found. He is missing'

Sweet tried to exhale slowly, the sound coming as a hoarse whistle through his pursed lips. Now *that* was a rumour he hadn't heard before. The king's son had been a member—albeit an honorary one—of the king's personal bodyguard. It was therefore widely assumed that he had died in the fighting alongside his comrades, protecting his father as the

Vols closed their grip on the palace itself. As far as Sweet knew, no one considered him to still be alive. Alive and unaccounted for, to boot.

'Missing?' Sweet queried, clearing his throat.

'Just so,' Sylvanus replied coolly. 'It appears that, in the chaos of the city falling, the Crown Prince Orsen slipped our net and escaped. His current whereabouts are unknown.'

Sylvanus paused for a moment, letting Sweet and his crew absorb the information.

'And this is where you come in,' the magicker wagged his finger again, returning his attention to the small stack of parchments.

'You want us to find him,' Stover grinned, showing yellow teeth.

'Very astute,' Sylvanus remarked without looking up, his bored tone causing Stover's grin to falter a little. 'We need men—and women—' he glanced up to tip a nod at Vi, ' who know this land, who know its... people. You say you are the best in the world,' he settled back in his chair, 'now you can prove it.'

Sweet exhaled again. He found that his heart was racing and his belly was churning with a heady mix of fear and sudden excitement. Mostly though, there was a bitter taste about the whole business that he couldn't shake. He trusted this Vol magicker about as much as he trusted Stover's skill with cards. The man spoke sweetly enough but there was something in his voice that Sweet didn't like. Moreover, there was a lack of something in his eye that Sweet really didn't like.

The man lacked any sense of humanity.

Sweet didn't expect to see the warm, innocent eyes of a child—or even the open, friendly eyes of an adult who had somehow avoided being ground down by the world around them. But usually there was *something.* If not happiness or contentment, it was bitterness, anger or naked hostility. Too much pride or too little. Ambitions, frustrations, strengths and weaknesses. All of these flickered and shimmered in the eyes of a man. But with Lennick Sylvanus, High Magicker of the Volsgard empire, Sweet didn't detect a single flicker of humanity.

Just a void.

Sweet didn't have many rules—in his line of work it was difficult to keep to any, let alone a full set of them—but he did have one. It was a simple rule, but it was Sweet's golden rule and he had lived his professional life by it ever since it had been passed down to him by the crew he had joined as an over enthusiastic teenager all those decades ago.

Never work for a complete cunt.

Of course—as had been explained to the young Sweet—the definition came more from an instinctive feeling than from any specific set of criteria. But it was his job to hone that instinct whenever possible. To train his gut to identify a wrong 'un well before he got in too deep with them.

When it came to bounty hunting, you could expect to take contracts from the corrupt, from the dirty and even from the downright unhinged. Your marks were usually not far from any of those things, either. Everyone involved in the whole sorry business was a liar and a cheat. They were sly and they were dangerous. Scum through and through. The lowest of the low. But Sweet's singular rule towards rejecting contracts was ironclad, and so far it had kept him and his crew—mostly—alive and in business.

'You have no idea where the Crown Prince is?' he asked, stalling for time as he considered how best to let the magicker down.

'We believe he fled the city,' Sylvanus replied smartly, his eyes narrowing as though he saw through the tactic.

Sweet raised an eyebrow.

'Information given to us by captured Pratian soldiers,' Sylvanus explained with a mild shrug.

Sweet shuddered inwardly and tried not to think about exactly how freely that information would've been given. His imagination betrayed him as it conjured images of glowing hot irons and fingernails being slowly peeled away.

'It's believed he and a small retinue of guards disguised themselves as commoners and fled the city through the west gate,' Sylvanus continued. 'After that,' he held out his hands and smiled again, 'well, that's where your renowned skills are required.'

'Anyone else know about this?' Sweet asked, avoiding the compliment as though it were poison.

'If you're asking if this contract is exclusive, then sadly no,' Sylvanus smiled again. 'Grand though your reputation may be, I am far too cautious to put all of my eggs into your basket. No—whilst we are not advertising it to every man in earshot—the contract for the capture of the Crown Prince has been opened to parties other than yourselves.'

Sweet grunted at that, wondering if it could be useful in rejecting the offer. If the magicker had others looking for the prince then maybe he'd be less offended when Sweet declined the option of his crew joining the hunt.

'I even have my own men in pursuit,' Sylvanus had continued talking, he relaxed back into his chair.

A heavy footstep sounded from behind one of the bookshelves and

Sweet, Vi and Stover all turned to face the noise. For a moment Sweet had to fight down a flutter of panic as he saw that the suit of armour had moved. Then he realised that he had been mistaken before and the armour was actually worn by a man, half hidden in the shadows behind the shelves. Sweet's panic soon turned to dread as the man took several more juddering footsteps into the grim daylight seeping through the vast windows.

He was enormous. Bigger than Bryntas—which took some doing—and armoured in the heavy metal plate from head to toe. A full-faced helmet covered his head, but Sweet could hear the man's heavy breathing rattling behind the plates, echoing out like the wind around some deep, dark cave mouth. Draped over one shoulder was a heavy cape the colour of the night sky. Sweet saw the blades of not one but two axes flaring out either side of the titan's broad back, their short handles poking up either side of his battle helm. Sweet didn't scare easily—not really—but the man taking slow, steady steps out of the shadows looked every bit a demon from legend.

The others clearly felt the same. Sweet felt Vi tighten beside him, every muscle seeming to tense at the same time. He could practically hear her thoughts, wondering madly if her daggers—sharpened to vicious hell and back—would be any good against such a brute, even if they hadn't been surrendered at the entrance. On his other shoulder, Stover seemed to shrivel at the sight of the armoured warrior. He shrank into himself and swallowed loudly.

The man tramped over to the side of Sylvanus' desk and stood, staring at the trio of bounty hunters through the slit in his full-faced helmet. Sweet couldn't see his eyes amongst the shadows there, but he didn't much like the feel of the man's gaze. He had expected to be sized up like a bear eyeing its next meal, but instead he felt a cold disdain. As though the man knew he could crush them all like insects, but that the idea bored him.

'Thond here is my personal bodyguard,' Sylvanus announced, still speaking as though a bonafide weapon of war hadn't just entered the conversation. 'I believe you have a Wyn of your own, on your crew?'

'H-he's a Wyn?' Stover managed, his eyes darting up and down the man's enormous figure, lingering worriedly on the visible blades of his axes.

'That he is,' Sylvanus nodded, still smiling. 'He and his men are also expert trackers, as I'm sure you're well aware from your own... companion. Though they don't know this land, or its people, quite as well as you do. I have opened the contract to them, as well as a few other parties. The full bounty goes to the crew that brings the Crown Prince back to me, alive.'

If Sweet had needed one more reason to reject the offer of the contract then this was it. Competition was expected in any hunt. After all, it was rare for a contract to be given to a single party on an exclusive basis. There were enough crews and individuals knocking about to pick up the same jobs on more than one occasion. Mostly they kept out of each other's way, but—of course—some competitors were more dangerous than others. Some crews would seek to hobble their opponents, as well as track their quarry. Fights were common, injuries too. Murder between bounty hunters wasn't as rare as Sweet would've liked, either. And one look at the enormous, silent, armoured, axe-wielding Wyn told Sweet that this man wouldn't think twice about crushing his skull and stepping over him before his body hit the floor. Not a good quality in someone competing for the same prize.

Sweet shifted on his feet and hooked his thumbs deeper into his belt. He took a deep breath and wondered how often this magicker heard the word "no". It would take some careful tact to ensure the three of them left the Hall of Justice alive—and not in chains.

'How much?' Stover snorted, his greedy eyes shining bright.

Fuckssake, Sweet thought.

Sooner rather than later he was going to have to stop considering his next move and just make it before this idiot landed them all in a Vol dungeon—or worse. Sweet's mind began picturing just what 'worse' might look like when the magicker answered, his voice steady.

'Five hundred thousand gold pieces.'

There was a silence then. Long and hollow.

Sweet scrunched his face up as though he hadn't heard properly. Probably he hadn't. Beside him, he heard Vi gasp. It was a noise he'd never heard from her in nearly ten years of her running in the crew. Come to think of it, it was the first time he'd ever heard her caught off guard at all. On the other side, Stover was gaping at the little magicker. His slack jaw, covered in three-day stubble and what looked suspiciously like a little bit of that morning's breakfast, hung open. His eyes had widened to the size of dinner plates.

'Five hundred thousand?' Sweet asked, tipping his ear at Sylvanus and squinting through one eye, as though lessening his visibility might somehow improve his hearing. Beside the desk, Thond stood, statue-like.

'That's correct,' the magicker replied, his dead-eyed smile unmoving.

'Split evenly seven ways—if that's how you do things of course—that would equate to just shy of seventy-two thousand pieces each. A rich reward, wouldn't you agree?'

'Rich?' Stover slammed his jaw shut with an excited swallow, thoughts of the armoured Wyn stood just feet away from him forgotten completely, 'you could buy a fuckin' palace for five hunnerd thousand gold pieces!'

'Quite so,' Sylvanus agreed, with evident distaste for Stover.

Sweet's thoughts were racing. Stover's valuation of the average palace felt a bit off to him, but five hundred thousand gold pieces was an extraordinary sum nonetheless. It was a sum that Sweet couldn't properly comprehend. Godly, almost. With that kind of money—even split seven ways—Sweet could hang up his boots and live out his days in a semblance of peace. It would certainly be enough for a modest house and supplies for a lifetime or more, even a servant or two. Someone to clean his clothes, prepare his meals and call him "sir".

Sweet's excitement abated a little as he considered it further. Did he really want to be called "sir"? For most of his forty-something years he'd found the noise cringe-inducing at best and downright obscene at worst. Besides, most of the folk Sweet met who insisted on being called "sir" were complete arseholes. Did he want servants at all? Being waited-on all day every day sounded good in principle, but what the hell would he do with his days then? Did he even want peace? Even a semblance of it? Would that just leave him with nothing to fill his time except an endless silence into which his own thoughts would spill? Thoughts about his life. All the things he'd done, all the things he'd allowed to get done without a word of challenge. All the shit he'd seen. All the shit he'd been an active participant in. All his regrets.

Something deep inside Sweet shuddered at that.

Then there were other—more pragmatic—questions. This creepy bastard knew that Sweet ran with six others in his crew. He knew that they ran with a Wyn. Hell he even knew their names. The little magicker appeared to know more about them than they did. Sure, Sweet and his crew had a deserved reputation as successful bounty hunters, but that news wasn't likely to have reached the magickers of Volsgard. So why so much bloody interest? Usually a contractor wouldn't care who you were or how you brought a bounty in, so long as the bounty came in. So why did this sinister little bastard know so much about them, even before they'd committed to taking the job? It wasn't a comforting thread to pull at. Not only that, but with the terrifying Thond—and who knew who else—also on the hunt, they would spend more time looking over their shoulders than they would looking for the missing prince.

Then there was the money. The more Sweet turned over the unimaginable sum of five hundred thousand gold pieces the more, well, unimaginable it became. He had no doubt the emperor of Volsgard could come up with such a figure, but why stick it on the head of a friendless prince fleeing a destroyed country? Was he really that valuable to them? Was it really the reward? Or was it bait intended to hook them onto the chase without thinking things through?

Finally, Sweet thought, there is this bastard himself.

This bastard and my golden rule.

Even Sweet's initial fear of the giant Wyn was abating now. He was just another big hard bastard in a world full of them. Sweet's shock at the mention of the bounty purse was also fading into memory, too. His numbed senses tingled back into life. Including the distrustful ache in the bottom of his belly. The more he looked at Sylvanus' joyless smile and those glassy little eyes, the more he realised he would gladly *pay* five hundred thousand gold pieces just to leave the city with the clothes on his back and breath in his lungs. Leave and be well shot of the Vols forever. Pratia was gone, and so should they be. Coming here had been a mistake.

Sweet made his decision and swallowed.

'We'll do it!' Stover clapped one of his hands into the other, a shit-eating grin plastered across his face, so wide that it was a wonder the top half of his head didn't fall off and expose the empty cavern where a brain should be.

Sweet had to double-take. It was his turn to gape, astonishment quickly followed by a surge of anger. That was even more closely followed by a dousing splash of reticence as he remembered where he was.

'What he means is we'll think on it,' Sweet said, trying to glare at Stover and smile at Sylvanus at the same time. And failing at both. 'Lots to consider, you see.'

'Five hunnerd thousand in gold!' Stover barked out a laugh, gesturing to Sylvanus as though the gold was already laid out on the desk in front of him. 'What more is there to talk about?'

'I understood you were the best,' Sylvanus cleared his throat.

'Best in the world!' Stover parroted back, gleefully puffing his chest out with pride and apparently unable to even temper his fanatical grin.

'Quite,' Sylvanus acknowledged. 'The emperor therefore felt it was important to offer a reward worthy of such talents.'

'Damn straight!' Stover practically cheered.

'We need to think on it,' Sweet insisted, much to Stover's obvious chagrin.

'Ain't nothin' to think on!' the other man argued, 'the man wants to pay five hunnerd thousand for the best, so let's show him the best!'

'Stover,' Sweet held out a hand, trying to calm him. He looked to Vi for support and was more than a little upset to see that she was cautiously avoiding his gaze. She had folded her arms across her chest and was looking to the floor instead. 'Vi?' Sweet asked.

'It *is* a lot of money,' Vi sighed, looking up and meeting Sweet's eye. Her gaze swam with the usual steely defiance, but now also something akin to regret. Contrition maybe. As though she didn't *want* to challenge his authority, but that maybe he was about to make a bad fucking call by rejecting this man's offer. 'It's the biggest contract we've ever had. Maybe even the biggest we'll ever have.'

Sweet felt his heart sink a little. She was right, of course – the contracts they'd worked before had never even broached a few hundred gold pieces. Five hundred thousand was simply unheard of. This would change all of their lives. Well, except maybe Stover's—the dumb prick would no doubt lose it all at a card table on the first night.

Sweet glanced over to the idiot now. He was staring back at Sweet with an expression that read somewhere between anger and confusion, as though the most obvious response in the world was to accept the contract and Stover couldn't understand why Sweet couldn't see that. Maybe it was the most obvious response. Maybe Sweet was overthinking it. Overcomplicating it all with years of built-up bitterness and distrust.

Sweet looked back to Vi. She was still watching him with those piercing eyes, challenging him but somehow apologising to him at the same time. He glanced up at Thond, but the Wyn was still unmoving, radiating silent menace. Then he looked across the vast expanse of desk to where Lennick Sylvanus was sitting, patiently waiting for a response with his fingers entwined once more like a spider waiting for a string on its web to thrum.

The magicker looked smug. What man behind a desk like that wasn't smug? Moreso, there was a hint of something in his eyes now. It took Sweet a while to realise that it was the glint of the victory. It seemed the magicker's game had played out exactly as he had planned. Every piece had moved as expected and he had settled in to bask in the final move that would seal his triumphant glory.

Sweet took a deep breath.

'We'll do it,' he sighed.

# A great start

⇥ → • ⊢ • ⇒●⇐ • ⊢• ← ⇤

T HE KNIFE SPUN and twinkled in the cold light of the morning, flashing dangerously as the occasional sunbeam managed to sneak through the iron grey clouds overhead. Sweet stood, momentarily mesmerised by the twirling blade, before shaking his head and pushing himself away from the rickety post he had been leaning against. He unfolded his arms and pulled up a stool beside Daraday. The youngster ignored his presence, his concentration—firmly fixed on the spinning knife dancing across his fingers—written across the frown on his face, the tip of his tongue just poking out from the corner of his mouth. He'd gotten good at ignoring people over the last few years. The lad's demeanour had changed from wistful puppy to ill-tempered hound over that time. Life as part of a bounty hunting crew did that to a boy, Sweet reckoned, unsure if it was something he should take the credit—or the blame—for.

'You're gettin' good at that,' Sweet remarked, unhappy with the silence. Truth be told, he had been unhappy with most things since he had been press-ganged into accepting the Vol magicker's contract the day before. Daraday only grunted in response, not taking his eyes off the little dagger as he twirled it between his fingers.

'He had a good teacher,' Violent Fey observed. She strode out into the dingy little courtyard, a steaming cup of tisane clutched between her hands. She wore a tunic of dark green, cinched at her waist with a simple leather belt and a set of dark leggings. Her own daggers, honed to razor-sharpness, were hanging at her belt. She had tied her long, dark hair back with a strip of fabric and tilted her head towards the sky. It was another grim day in Levitan—though Sweet supposed they were all grim days for the city's inhabitants now—the ground was wet with rain from the night before and the sky overhead was threatening more, and soon.

Daraday had stopped dancing the dagger along his fingers and looked up at Vi.

'Reckon we'll have time to throw at some targets before we leave?'

the youngster asked. Even his voice had deepened in the three years he had been on the crew, though Sweet could hardly take the credit for that.

'You're asking the wrong person,' Vi shrugged, motioning to where Sweet was perched on the stool beside Daraday. She was trying to make amends for questioning his authority in Sylvanus' office—and without much subtlety either—but Sweet was grateful for it all the same. No use crying over what's done now, he reckoned. They had taken the contract, now all that was left was to see it through. Besides, he reasoned, if the job got too hot they could always back off from it to avoid getting burned in any serious way. It wasn't as though bounty hunters were bound by some noble code to see a job through to its end. That shit belonged in bad poetry and the songs of washed-up bards.

'We'll leave as soon as everybody's up,' he told Daraday, trying to read the younger man's face. He thought again about how much the boy had changed since joining their party. In his dour mood, Sweet found himself really wondering if all the change had been good. The boy had joined the crew as a bumbling innocent, sure of his notions of right and wrong and doing what was honourable. Or what the poets and bards had taught him was honourable, anyway.

Now he was a man, hardened to the worst of humanity, distrustful towards the rest of it. Apathetic towards the violence and suffering that inevitably came along with both. Sure, it was useful for the job, but what had he lost along the way? What had he missed out on? What had it cost the young man?

What has it cost me?

The thought leapt unbidden into Sweet's mind and he frowned deeply as he turned it over, his mood darkening further still. Thankfully, a loud bang interrupted his moment of grim self-reflection. Stover had thrown open the door to his lodgings and emerged into the grey morning, an ear-to-ear grin plastered across his face. That same grin had been ensconced there since the moment they had left the Hall of Justice with some papers detailing the Crown Prince's last known movements and a list of his notable associates. Also included was a writ, signed by Lennick Sylvanus, High Magicker of Volsgard himself, granting them safe conduct throughout the newest piece of the ever-growing, ever-sprawling Vol empire.

Sweet loathed that grin.

'Are we going?' Stover asked brightly. It was rare for him to even be awake this early, let alone so full of vim and vigour. Clearly the thought of hunting a fortune larger than all of their previous jobs combined was enough to change a lifetime of habitual misery.

'Bryn isn't up yet,' Sweet told him, and none too warmly either. He was still pissed at the way Stover had barged his way through the previous day's meeting with the Vols. It was a damn miracle they were even still alive. 'There's a pot of tisane over there, get yourself a cup and we can talk about where—.'

'Bryn!' Stover bellowed, cutting across Sweet and ignoring the suggestion of a hot drink entirely. 'Bryn!' he marched over to the door of Bryntas' room and began pounding on it with the bottom of one fist. 'Get up you big lardy bastard! We've got work to do!'

Sweet snorted at the idea of Stover eager to do work. The sound drew a wry smile from Vi but did nothing to improve his mood.

'Bryn!'

The door was wrenched open and a bleary-eyed Bryntas stepped out from the shadows. He was bare-chested, somehow looking even bigger as a result, and his face was thunderous, but Stover only grinned wider for seeing it.

'That's the spirit!' he clapped the big man on one heavily muscled arm, 'now come on, let's be away!'

'The Wyn ain't back yet,' Daraday reported, spinning the dagger in his hand once more and not looking away from the blade. 'He left wi' the dawn.'

Stover spun away from Bryntas, looking distraught.

'Well where the fuck did he go?' Stover demanded, his voice rising in pitch.

Daraday shrugged, not even flinching at the aggressive nature of the question.

'It's the Wyn, innit,' he replied, as though that was answer enough. Sweet reckoned it probably was. 'Does what he wants.'

Colour rushed into Stover's pock-marked cheeks and Sweet tensed a little, half-expecting the older man to rush the boy. Though he would've been a fool to do so, to be honest. Daraday really had gotten good with Vi's knives. After all, he did have a damn good teacher.

'Not when there's a bloody fortune on the line he don't!' Stover threw his arms up like an angry child. 'We need to get after—'

'Calm down, Stover,' Sweet raised a palm for peace, 'Jenrick ain't up yet either, we can't just go traipsing off into the wilderness two men down. Hardly a great start to the job now, is it?'

Stover looked around urgently, seeking out the door to Jenrick's room next.

Before he could find it, a dark-clad figure swept around one of the buildings and into the mud-spattered courtyard. It was the Wyn, and even from under his hood Sweet could tell something was awry. The man's tattooed face rarely gave much away, but when you spent the best part of five years with a man you got to read him pretty damn well. There was an unease around the corners of his features that made the hairs stand tall on Sweet's neck, like he had something to tell them all and they weren't gonna like it. The tribesman was hardly one to deliver any kind of news, which usually meant that the only kind he did deliver was the bad kind.

'What's wrong?' Sweet raised an eyebrow.

The Wyn motioned with his head, back the way he'd come.

'Come see,' he grunted.

*

The clouds made good on their threat and the rain had begun to fall by the time they arrived at the scene. Small and drizzling at first, but now coming down in slow, fat drops. Heavy enough to drive most folks inside, leaving the streets largely empty. Despite his cloak and his hood, Sweet was soaked through by the time the Wyn led them to the canalside a short walk away from their lodgings.

The body was ghostly pale and already beginning to bloat a little. The man's pallid skin looked puckered around his closed eyes, lank hair stuck to his face like the long legs of a dead spider. The Vol soldiers fishing him out with their long-staffed pikes grimaced as the body turned a little in their grip, sending a splash of water back down into the canal below.

From the far bank, Sweet and his crew watched in grim silence as the body was lifted clear of the stonework and rolled up and onto the quay. A small crowd—those who either didn't care or didn't have the means to escape the rain—had gathered to watch the proceedings. Sweet supposed it was the closest they got to entertainment in a city just recently under siege. He looked along the line of people gathered at the quayside. Then he swept his gaze across the faces of his crew. All of them were frowning, but Sweet could feel from his own aching brows that he was frowning the hardest.

Jenrick's dead hand flapped out and slapped against the cobbles of the quayside like a white fish. The man's eyes were closed but his tongue lolled out of his mouth and Sweet grimaced a little.

'Silly bastard must've fallen in,' Violent Fey looked disgusted, though Sweet couldn't tell if it was the corpse of their former colleague or at the thought of such an arrantly stupid and pointless way to die. He reckoned the latter.

'I left him after a few drinks,' Bryntas motioned further along the canalside. He had pulled a shirt on now but it was soaked through and the man's massive shoulders were slumped. Sweet followed the gesture and saw several alehouses and taprooms lining the cobbled road, not more than ten paces from the water's edge. 'He was talking my ear off all night,' Bryntas added somberly, 'said he'd stay for one more.'

'More'n one, I reckon,' Sweet sighed, watching as the Vol soldiers started bundling Jenrick's body onto the back of a small hand wagon. He peered over the edge of the canalside. It was a solid seven foot drop into the murky waters below, and who knew what hidden dangers lurked beneath the surface. Jutting stones maybe, grasping weeds perhaps, or a tricky combination of both. Streaks of slimy green algae clung to the stonework that lined the canal walls. They looked slippery. Too slippery to climb out from, especially if you were too drunk to fall in in the first place.

'You talk to anyone else?' Vi cocked an eyebrow at Bryntas. The big man shook his head. He looked a little saddened, but nothing a day's ride wouldn't shake out of him. Jenrick was hardly a popular member of their crew. Not disliked, but not what anyone would've considered a friend. Sweet wondered idly if any of the crew considered each other as friends. He doubted it.

Sweet caught sight of Daraday watching as Jenrick's corpse was manhandled into the wagon. The lad was squinting with hard eyes and a face of stone. Impassive and uncaring. Sweet found himself thinking about the last time they had lost a member of their crew, three years before, just outside of Woodbyrne. Daraday hadn't looked on like that back then.

Then Sweet saw Stover, standing at Daraday's shoulder. If anything the man's shit-eating grin had somehow grown wider, his eyes wet with excitement under scraggly hair wet with rain.

'Th'fuck're you smiling at?' Sweet asked, his anger momentarily taking control. Stover snapped his eyes from Jenrick's drowned corpse and looked over to Sweet. He looked almost confused by the question.

'Well,' he shrugged, 'one less share, I suppose.'

It took a moment for Sweet to process the response. When he finally did he thought he would feel more anger, but instead he felt a cold dose of apathy. Jenrick had been with them for about four winters, but in truth he didn't add much to their crew other than another pair of eyes for watch duty. He had been pretty good with a bow, but that was about it. Like the rest of the crew, Sweet hadn't considered the man a friend, just another useful body in the team. Now he was a useless corpse on a hand wagon, dripping brown canal water to the cobbles below. The more Sweet thought about it, the deeper his frown became. He was uneasy at feeling so little at Jenrick's death. He felt uneasier still that a part of him—small though it might've been—found himself actually agreeing with Stover.

A great fucking start, Sweet thought, turning away from the canal.

*

The western gate of Levitan was a throng of human chaos. Gaunt-looking refugees returning to the city—or perhaps just fleeing the countryside—jostled with gaunt-looking city-dwellers desperate to get out, or fight for the ruins of their lives. Wagons, laden with goods or possessions—depending on the driver—tried to squeeze through spaces that were far too tight for them. Ponies and oxen pulled at their traces, growing ever more anxious by the rising pandemonium all around them.

The air was thick with smells. The scent of sweating men and women permeated every breath, as well as the stink of cargo animals and a few mangy dogs sniffing around for scraps of whatever they might find suitably unguarded. Sharp smoke was drifting in from somewhere and the rain—now eased to a light drizzle—did little to cleanse the nostrils.

There were Vol soldiers everywhere. Some stood grim-faced in lines, spears and pikes held across their bodies to create a barrier of armour and blades that herded folk one way or another. Others watched in little groups, barely able to keep the disgust from their expressions. As though the chaos of the scene was abhorrent to them. Which, Sweet reckoned, it probably was.

Even more soldiers tried desperately to restore a semblance of order. A Vol lieutenant was bellowing out instructions to several wagoneers who had clogged up the main road, his efforts hampered by the fact that one of them clearly didn't speak the same tongue as the others. The foreign driver gesticulated wildly, his mad eyes bulging as he screamed back something even Sweet—who knew enough of most languages to get by—didn't understand.

The gate itself was an enormous structure of stone set into the wall that wrapped the vast majority of the city. A wrought iron portcullis, the tips edged with flaking orange rust, had been drawn up high under the archway and the gates themselves were stood open, fastened in place by thick chains. From one side of the gate to the other was maybe twenty feet, the thickest part of Levitan's protective perimeter. The city walls—crafted from the same heavy, grey stone blocks—ran off to the north and south away from it. More Vol soldiers patrolled the battlements above, keeping an eye out for trouble in the crowds below. Sweet guessed the same chaos inside was mirrored outside of the city too, with people queuing to get back into Levitan now that the war was over. He grunted as somebody shoved at his shoulder and instinctively checked for his purse. The milling crowd and noisy clamour was a pickpocket's dream and he had no intention of falling prey to them. Satisfied his money was still hanging from his belt where it was supposed to be, Sweet looked for an opening in the maelstrom.

The crowd parted a little and Sweet saw a row of Vol soldiers blocking passage through the gate. He motioned to the others and then strode off towards them, barging at anyone unfortunate enough to move into his path. A stream of curses followed him as he led his crew towards the Vols. His horse whickered at all the commotion and Sweet whispered a soothing word to it as he led it by the bridle.

The soldiers tensed as Sweet approached, though he had no doubt that was the effect of some of the others in his crew, rather than his own appearance. Bryntas and the Wyn tended to draw wary behaviour wherever they went, and even Violent Fey had a good way of projecting her aura that made sure no one fucked with her. The array of weaponry they sported probably didn't help their cause. The lead soldier swallowed and called out as they neared the line.

'Halt! State your—'

'Aye, aye names and business,' Sweet interrupted, eager to be away from the closeness of the people all around them, as though the desperation and desolation might somehow be contagious. He shook water from his hair as he stepped under the shadow of the gate. 'My name's Bitter Sweet, these are my associates,' he motioned to the others as he reached into his coat.

The Vols around him tensed even more.

'Easy lads,' Sweet told them, slowing his movements and producing the signed writ Lennick Sylvanus had given him. He offered it to the soldier who had spoken. 'We're bounty hunters, on a job for your High Magicker. We need to get out of the city, sharpish.'

The Vol hesitated, but only for a moment. He took the writ and scanned it quickly, at last looking up to inspect the motley crew standing dripping in front of him.

'Says here there're seven of you,' the Vol said, somewhat suspicious.

'We lost a man,' Sweet sighed and gave a half-apologetic shrug. 'Drowned in the canal last night. Too many ales.'

The Vol nodded slowly, looking at each of them in turn. At last it seemed as though he accepted the explanation. Why shouldn't he? Sweet thought. If we were a man extra I could understand his concern, especially with a fugitive prince on the run. But a man light? That was arithmetic even Stover could probably fathom—if he had an abacus and a few days to work on it. The soldier passed the writ back to Sweet.

'Let them through!' he bellowed, and the Vol soldiers stood aside.

Members of the gathered crowd behind started shouting their objections, demanding to know why Sweet and his crew got such special treatment. The Vol soldiers started bellowing back, even shoving a few folks with the hafts of their spears. Sweet sighed and trudged through the shadows under the gate, feeling a spark of danger as he passed under the heavy portcullis. His horse snorted again, as though echoing the feeling— or perhaps it just wanted to get the hell away from the festering mire that was the city of Levitan. Either way it seemed a pretty reasonable request.

An identical line of Vol soldiers parted at the far end of the gate and Sweet led his crew out into the rain once more. They walked their mounts through the crowd—thankfully thinner than the one inside the walls— and Sweet turned back to face them.

'Feels like this rain'll only get worse,' said Violent Fey. Her hair was still tied back but a few strands had pulled free and were plastered against her face. 'Maybe we should've stayed another day.'

'Fuck that!' Stover laughed, 'the sooner we get after this royal bastard the sooner we're all rich as shit!'

Vi's eyes narrowed, but she said nothing in return. Sweet supposed it wouldn't do any good to point out to Stover that—as a native Pratian himself—the "royal bastard" he was describing was actually his rightful king. After all, the man didn't have enough loyalty in him to fill a thimble. Unless loyalty to gold coins counted, of course.

'Don't matter,' Sweet cut in, 'we've left now anyway, so no use thinkin' about what we should've done.'

Stover seemed to take that as a vindication of his point and puffed himself up with a champion effort at a punch-me-now smile. Sweet was glad Vi was a few paces further away or she probably would've taken the bait and chinned the silly prick.

'Well then,' Stover grinned, 'shall we be—'

'Make way!' a great shout went up from a nearby Vol soldier. It was taken up by others and soon the air was alive with the shout. 'Make way!'

The spearmen manning the gate wrestled the crowds aside, butting and shunting them with the hafts to clear a passage under the gate. One woman fell with a yelp and a bloody nose. Another man was shoved up against the stone walls with a grunt. The noise of thundering hooves on rain-spattered mud filled the air, sounding like the roar of a great beast as they echoed from under the arched gateway. Sweet and his crew watched as a troop of Vol horsemen rumbled out of the city. The men slowed as they exited the gateway and Sweet felt a cold clench at his belly as he recognised the man at their head.

'Master Bitter Sweet,' Lieutenant Renauld nodded at him, pronouncing each syllable with distaste. Despite the weather, the man looked utterly unfettered. His dead eyes still stared blankly, as though they were staring through Sweet rather than at him. 'It seems that you liked the High Magicker's proposal.'

Sweet said nothing. The Vol horsemen around Renauld were watching them closely and he didn't much like the way they stared.

'Good luck in your quest,' Renauld continued, his voice dry. 'May the best team win.'

With that, the lieutenant turned his horse and nudged it into a trot, leading his men away from Levitan to the west. Sweet watched them go, a frown scrunched onto his face.

'Th'fuck did he mean by that?' Stover asked, leaning so close that Sweet could smell the man's foetid breath. Stale taffa smoke and whatever he had thrown down his neck for breakfast that morning. Raw onions, judging by the tang of it.

'It seems that the Vols aren't relying on just us to find the runaway prince,' Sweet sighed, shifting his head so he could breathe some fresher air.

'I thought he said he was sending that creepy Wyn bastard after him,' Stover whined. Sweet glanced over at their own Wyn to see if Stover's casual invective of his creed had troubled him, but the tattooed tribesman was as unreadable as ever. Sweet sighed again.

'I would guess that Sylvanus has set more'n a few folk after this prince,' Sweet frowned up at the darkening clouds. 'Us, that big armoured bastard Thond and his lot, now Lieutenant Renauld, too.'

'Probably others,' Bryntas put in, his voice echoing the unease that Sweet felt. A nervousness about the job that he'd managed to shake for just about all of the time it had taken them to pass under the gates of Levitan. A few fleeting moments of worry-free thoughts, now plagued by them again.

'Aye,' Sweet nodded, trying not to think about it. He shook his head and motioned to the few buildings built outside of the city walls. 'Let's get under some cover, this bastard rain is hanging about. We'll wait it out for a bit.'

'But they're getting ahead of us!' Stover protested, pointing after the Vol horsemen as they thundered off into the distance. 'They'll run this royal bastard down before us! We need to get out there and get after them!'

Sweet followed the man's grubby finger and snorted.

'Them?' he scoffed. 'They're going the wrong way.'

## Wild country

THE SKY WAS slate grey and the air was cold with the promise of a punishing winter ahead. A harsh wind blew across the rolling slopes, causing the drab grass to sway back and forth like ripples in cloth. It had rained the night before and the ground was damp, the air thick with the metallic scent of more stormy weather to come. Sweet took in a deep breath, savouring its cold touch in his lungs, and found himself strangely at peace.

They were not more than a few days' ride outside of Levitan, having decided to wait out the worst of the bad weather in an abandoned stable once they'd exited the city itself. If you'd put a knife to his throat Sweet would admit that he had taken that decision more to annoy Stover than from any great dislike of the rain. The other man had brooded and grumbled as they had waited, mumbling about how they were going to miss out on the bounty of a lifetime. He had been sullen and irritable but—blissfully—quiet enough to ignore whilst Sweet, Vi and the others had gone through their plan of action.

The Vol lieutenant, Renauld, seemed to think the prince had struck due west from the city. There was some logic to that. The western border was closest to Levitan, and it nestled neatly against the lands of the Thradonians—who might not have exactly been allies to Pratia, but they certainly had no love for the Vols and their ever-growing empire. They would have even less love now that the empire now bordered their own lands. It made sense then, that the prince would strike out west and seek sanctuary amongst the Thradonians. Besides, all the reports that Sylvanus had gathered for them suggested the prince had fled through the city's west gate. However, a city under siege was a chaotic place and Sweet reasoned that getting out of *any* gate would've been the prince's priority. Once he was outside the city walls, the prince, and whatever retinue travelled with him, would be free to pick a direction of travel.

Sweet reckoned the prince wasn't alone. It didn't add up that a member of the ruling royal family would've been able to slip through Vol fingers without help. Though there couldn't be more than a handful of men with him. Loyalists who had helped him evade capture. Honourable fools, Sweet reckoned. The kind who would lay down their lives for the young royal.

Once they'd escaped the city, they would've had more options available to them. To the west were more Pratian cities and settlements, but these had been under Vol control for some time now. Vol soldiers would be patrolling the main roads and probably some of the lesser ones, too. The landscape didn't help, either. The countryside was mostly rolling grassland, good for farming but not great for hiding in or fleeing through. In short, Sweet reckoned it was a damn good direction to go if you wanted to get caught, outnumbered and out in the open.

But Sweet hadn't spent decades hunting men and women without learning a thing or two about how they tried to avoid just such a situation. Sweet thought that this prince would be savvier than that. After all, he had managed to get through the Vols as they besieged the city—and that was no mean feat in itself. So once he was out of Levitan, he would've known that to head directly west would be fruitless. To the east was much the same problem, more farmlands and more Vol soldiers, followed by a river border with Volsgard itself. The south held even less by way of escape, with the Pratian coast curving round to eventually meet the border with Volsgard again. He could try for a ship of course, and escape by sea—but the ports were all overseen by the Vols now. There was a blockade stopping all but essential ships from coming in, and any vessels that tried to leave would be thoroughly checked. It would be beyond risky to travel all that way south just to get stopped at the docks of some shitty harbour town.

But north? North was more interesting.

To the northeast of Levitan was—after a time—yet more borderlands with the Vols, but due north there was a glimmer of hope. Deep in the wild country, far from where Pratian civilisation ended, there were mountains that marked a natural border for the former kingdom. But there was a mountain pass, vaguely well-known in its day. Once used by miners who toiled in the cold stone depths for silver. The pass and accompanying mining town had been abandoned when the silver ore dried up, but it was still there all the same. If Sweet wanted to get a fugitive out of a defeated kingdom occupied by ruthless enemies—that would be where he would strike for.

It was hundreds of miles away, much further than any other border, and across some of the most rugged terrain imaginable. Added to which, the pass could already be blocked by rockfalls or earthquakes, dooming the whole venture from the start. At the very least, the journey would need to be made before the winter snows set in. During the cold months the prince would have more luck braiding fog than he would traversing those mountains in deep snow. But despite all of that, Sweet knew it was the man's best chance.

Which is why it was also theirs.

So they had stayed longer in the city outskirts, hunched together over a map, and figured out the route they would take. All except Stover, who had sat sullen, sulking over a cold meal, smoking taffa and muttering to himself about falling behind the competition whilst they wasted time poring over scribbled lines and making their stupid plans.

Sweet had to admit that, despite his reticence over the contract itself, he had enjoyed mapping out their journey. Some of the old fire of the job had flickered back into life in him during that time poking at the ink drawing laid out in front of them. Second-guessing which way the fugitive prince might have gone and what decisions he might've made along the way. They put themselves in his boots and argued about what they would have done in his place. Where they might seek assistance, or particular places they would look to avoid. The whole thing had awakened a sliver of excitement deep within him. Truth be told, it was something he hadn't felt excited about in years.

The hunt was on.

Maybe that was why this dull, grey morning was lifting Sweet's spirits. Like a cool breeze over his sour mood he felt refreshed by the thought of tracking their quarry. Outwitting him at each turn as they closed in on him.

Doubts still tugged at him. After all, he hadn't lasted this long in the business without being a cautious man. But now they were tempered with the beginnings of excitement, too. The danger posed by their newfound employer—and dangerous he most definitely was—was strangely thrilling, where before it filled him with nothing but dread. The thought of an arduous trek through Pratian wildlands now felt like something of an adventure. Even the weight of their proposed bounty no longer felt so oppressive. The thought of all that gold didn't excite him in the same way it clearly did Stover, but Sweet supposed he wouldn't *have* to spend it, if he didn't want to. He could earn the bounty and then it could just be there, if he needed it. No need to buy a palace or hire servants or change anything, really. Maybe he didn't care about it at all. Maybe he just wanted to have been the one to win the prize.

The one to *earn* it.

It was a strange thought, but also somehow reassuring.

Sweet took in another deep breath and flicked his eyes skyward. The wind was blowing fast and the heavier clouds would roll in before long, shedding their rain just as sure as they would block out the sun. Sweet had to suppress an odd little smile. He felt a touch giddy.

Gonna be a beautiful day, he thought.

'Gonna be a shit day,' Violent Fey appeared at his shoulder, startling him. Nearly ten years now she had been a part of his crew and she could still sneak up on him like it was his first day on the bloody job. She was looking at him with one eyebrow raised, clearly not understanding the boyish gleam that he could feel in his eye.

'Gonna be rain alright,' Sweet agreed, ignoring that curious look and urging his horse forwards. The beast obeyed and started carrying him down the gently sloping road. His crew followed behind.

They had passed very few people on the road, but those they did come across had the same haunted looks as they had seen on the faces of the people inside Levitan. There were plenty of farms dotted along the way but most were abandoned, their owners no doubt having fled the Vols as they had approached the city. One had even been burned down. The farmhouse was a blackened skeleton standing atop a low rise, a broken beam poking out of the wreckage like a rib of charcoal. The sight of it made Sweet wonder why a man would want to burn a farm. With your enemies defeated, what possible gain could there be from it? His improving mood dampened a little as he realised he already knew the answer.

For some men, the burning was enough.

For the next hour they walked their horses along the dirt path leading north. A wagon passed them, heading south. The vehicle was pulled by a donkey that looked like it would drop dead any minute. The driver was an elderly man, his tanned face etched with deep wrinkles and his clothing tattered and worn. He eyed them with a combination of fear and suspicion as their paths neared.

'Seen a prince travelling this way, old grey?' Stover called out from behind Sweet, following it up with a harsh chuckle that quickly turned into a roasting cough. He cut it short by spitting to the side of the road and taking another drag on the papersmoke between his fingers.

The old man said nothing, but his eyes widened a little. Sweet ignored both Stover and the wagoneer, and the vehicle rumbled by without further interaction, save for another whooping chuckle from Stover, who was clearly enjoying himself.

Now there was a man who'd burn a farm, Sweet thought to himself, his mind wandering as his horse led them up the road. Stover had joined the crew because Sweet knew he would be useful. Each member of his little bounty hunting gang brought a particular skill, or set of skills, to the party. Stover's had been the threat of violence. Sometimes a job needed someone with a particular look in their eye to prove that the crew meant business. Stover could call upon that particular look at will. Hell, there wasn't a day when he *didn't* have that look. He was—put simply—a man who was too stupid to understand and too violent to care.

Sweet had Vi for when calculated aggression was needed, and he had Bryntas for when brute force was required, but Stover had provided the final piece of that particular puzzle. He was unpredictable and wild and it showed, plain as the sun in the sky. Unfortunately for the rest of the crew those particular traits also made him somewhat volatile. Not to mention an insufferable arsehole. Still, Sweet had reasoned when he had hired him, he'd prove useful.

And the simple truth was that he had. Over the four years that he had been running with them, Stover had—paradoxically—deescalated situations simply by demonstrating he had no limit. He forced folks who pretended to be crazy to back down when confronted by someone truly unhinged. He also worked hard—provided that work involved roughing someone up for a bit of information, or threatening someone's family to find out which way a bounty had gone. They weren't pleasant jobs, but he did them. The truth was—Sweet knew—Stover loved those kinds of jobs. To Stover, they were his way of burning farms.

Sweet's mood darkened a little as he remembered his crew had left Levitan a man short. Jenrick's own skillset had mostly involved the bow and arrows that were now stowed across Daraday's saddlebags. The man had been a damn fine shot. Not enough to win competitions or the like, but good enough to keep them fed in the wilder parts of the world and competent enough to hold a drawn bow on a cornered bounty until they finally surrendered. Jenrick had talked too much for Sweet's liking, rambling on about some mundane shit or another, but he had been another useful member of their crew. He would be missed, Sweet knew, but only until they could find another archer worth a damn.

His odd mood darkened a little more when that thought crossed his mind. Did he really care so little about Jenrick? The man had been with them for years. Not as long as Vi or Bryntas maybe, but definitely a few more months than Stover had been, and Stover was a prick. Was simply not being a prick enough for Jenrick to be mourned somehow? Had Sweet even liked the man?

*Did he like any of them?*

The question leapt unbidden into his head and startled him a little, dampening his spirits even further. Of course I like them, he reasoned, they're my crew. Maybe I don't like Stover—because he's an arsehole—and maybe I didn't like Jenrick—because he never shut up. But Bryn was a reliable pair of hands and the Wyn was so good at tracking that Sweet was sure the tribesman used magick. Then there was Violent Fey, his second-in-command and the person he trusted most—maybe the only person he trusted, now that he thought of it. And finally there was Daraday. Sure the boy had been all green and innocent when he and Ari had first joined the crew, but in the three years since Woodbyrne the lad had hardened up into a bounty hunter worth his weight in gold. He worked hard, did the tough parts without complaint and earned his place in the crew. He had gone from a lost lamb to a seasoned wolf, much like Sweet himself had done, all those years ago.

And that's a good thing?

Damn this self-reflection! Sweet shook his head, as though trying to dislodge a bee inside his brain. His good mood was truly on the wane now and he cursed under his breath just as the first drops of rain began to fall. Lightning flashed off to the east and Sweet's horse whickered, he patted its neck just as the low rumble of thunder followed a long moment later.

The group rode carefully up a steep hill and rounded a small stand of trees, their leaves mostly shed as autumn threatened to turn into winter, making a carpet of rust and brown. As the road arced around the last of the mangy vegetation Sweet's horse whickered again, though this time he didn't pat its neck. He was too busy surveying the scene ahead of him.

The road fell away for a few feet in a steep bank of long grass, strands of it desperately reaching to make it to the top of the rise. Then the ground levelled out and rolled into another one of the low, flat fields that dominated the Pratian countryside around the capital city.

Only this one was filled with corpses.

The first lay less than a stone's throw away from the road itself. Facedown in thr mud and still wearing what had once been a bright Pratian uniform, no doubt worn with pride. A stump of wood poked out from between the man's shoulders. Sweet guessed it was the broken haft of a spear that had plunged through his back. The second and third corpses lay across one another. Sweet reckoned a poet might've seen them entwined like lovers in eternity. Sweet reckoned they were two dead men lying across one another where they fell.

After that there was little point in counting them. The bodies lay, broken and deranged and rotting, across the entire length and breadth of the field. Crows still fluttered from corpse to corpse to pull at a stray sinew or strip of grey flesh, but most had already been picked clean in the weeks that the bodies had lay here. Flies still buzzed in the air and as the wind changed Sweet was greeted with the sickly smell of death after rain. He grimaced just as Vi walked her horse alongside his.

'Scarvin,' she said.

'Scarvin,' he agreed, his good mood completely gone now as he gazed out over the sea of corpses. There must've been thousands of them. Hell, there *were* thousands of them.

'The Vols just left 'em all here,' Vi said, wrinkling her lip in disgust.

'Not their own,' Sweet observed, noting that he hadn't spotted a Vol uniform amongst the grisly tableau just yet. 'Only the Pratians.'

'Why?' Vi breathed.

'They were in a hurry,' Sweet shrugged, 'once they won this battle they wanted to take Levitan before the king could muster any sort of defence of the city. A long siege would've been costly to 'em.'

'But after that?' Vi asked, turning her head as the wind blew across the fields again. The rain was falling steadily now. 'Why not come back and bury them? Or burn them, at least?'

Sweet shrugged again.

'Why would they care?' he asked, uneasy with the question even as he voiced it.

Lightning flashed again and both Sweet and Vi's horses startled a little. The thunder that followed was closer behind the flash now and Sweet knew that a storm was blowing in. He turned to face the rest of the crew, who were all staring out over the field of the dead. Bryntas looked sombre, as did the Wyn. Daraday looked unmoved and Stover looked somewhere between awed and a little bored.

'There's woodland not much farther north,' Sweet told them, 'let's get there before this storm breaks proper.'

He turned back to the battlefield of Scarvin. More thunder rumbled and a lone crow took flight from the head of an unfortunate Pratian soldier, cawing loudly as it went. Another flash of lightning illuminated the morning scene, painting the corpses in a ghastly white light that made them seem somehow alive again. The light was gone so quickly that

Sweet could've sworn one or two of them had moved, inching closer and reaching towards him up on the road.

He shivered and turned his horse, urging it onwards even though it needed little encouragement.

'Let's get out of here,' he muttered, just as thunder growled again.

*

The forest that Sweet knew of was really just a bigger stand of trees than the one that marked the other edge of the Scarvin battlefield. The road north bisected the woodland, leaving the group flanked by the tall trees on each side. Not all the leaves had fallen yet and so the morning darkened even more as they entered the little wood. At least the trees screened the worst of the rain, Sweet supposed.

The horses were already nervous from the stench of death and the coming storm, so the closeness of the trees made them even more skittish still. Sweet patted the neck of his mare again, whispering soothing words and trying to calm her. Some woodland creature scurried away in the undergrowth to his left and the horse snorted its discomfort. Sweet sighed, long and loud.

You and me both, he thought.

'Now where in the fuck is *he* going?' Stover's voice rang out from behind Sweet. He turned in the saddle to see that the Wyn had dismounted and was deftly picking his way through the foliage to the side of the road. Sweet pulled his own horse to a stop and watched the hooded tribesman step carefully around a patch of brambles. Sweet sighed again and dismounted, cursing the dull ache in his hip as he swung his leg over the saddle.

'Why're we stopping?' Stover demanded.

'Because he's seen something,' Sweet muttered, more to himself than in response to the other man's question. Sweet looked up at Bryntas. 'You and Dara stay with the horses,' he told the big man. 'Vi, you're with me.'

Violent Fey gracefully swung herself to the ground, the daggers lining her belt glimmering in the grim morning light. She tossed the reins of her horse to Daraday and then strode over to where Sweet was already following the Wyn's trail deeper into the woodland.

Not more than forty paces into the trees, the Wyn had stopped by the foot of a large oak. He was looking down at something on the ground just in front of it. Sweet joined him and followed his gaze.

A neat stack of flat stones had been carefully arranged in the dirt.

There was a stream not far away and Sweet reckoned the stones had been pulled from there, then arranged—almost reverently—into this quaint little tower. Sweet found himself wondering how in the hell the Wyn had spotted it all the way from the road, especially in poor light, but decided it was best not to question the tribesman's abilities. Wyns had a way about them, everyone knew that. Instead, Sweet frowned down at the sad little pile of rocks.

'A cairn,' he murmured.

'For the dead,' said the Wyn, his soft voice barely audible over the rain that pattered across the forest. The tribesman shifted his head just enough for Sweet to interpret it as a nod back towards Scarvin.

'What is it?' Vi asked, arriving at the scene with her hands on her hips.

'A cairn for the dead of Scarvin,' Sweet explained. 'Someone built a waystone for the souls of the fallen.'

'Out here?' Vi scrunched her face up in confusion.

'Prince,' the Wyn whispered. He nodded again, this time towards the stand of stones. Sweet followed the motion and dropped to his haunches in front of the cairn to inspect it more closely. Something glimmered between two of the stones and Sweet reached for it, being careful not to disturb the rocks themselves. He pulled his hand back and straightened. Vi leaned close to see what he had found.

It was a ring. Expertly crafted from well-worked silver and with a deep green gemstone set into its face. There was a symbol engraved into the metal beside the gem. Sweet's eyes weren't what they were and he couldn't quite make it out, but he didn't reckon he needed to see it fully to know what it was.

'The Pratian seal,' Vi whispered. She looked down at the cairn. 'The prince did this?'

'Aye,' Sweet nodded thoughtfully, 'reckon so.'

The runaway prince had come across the field of the dead, just as they had done. Only where they had passed by as quickly as they could, he had stopped to pay his respects, even building this cairn both as a memorial to the fallen and as a beacon for their souls, so that they might not haunt this place and find peace instead—or so the stories went.

Sweet was surprised to find himself touched by the gesture. Even fleeing from a ruthless enemy this prince had tried to honour those who had fought and died for their country. He looked down at the little stack of rocks. It wasn't much, sure, but it was something. It was certainly more than the boy's father would've done, by all accounts.

'What the fuck are you all staring at?' Stover crashed through the undergrowth, wet leaves stuck to his trews. He sneered down at the little column of stone. 'What the fuck is that?'

'It's a cairn,' Sweet sighed, turning away from the structure and showing Stover the ring he had found. 'Reckon the prince built it to honour the Pratian dead,' he motioned back towards Scarvin.

Stover absorbed this information and his face slowly brightened, his eyes growing suddenly excited and hungry.

'He came this way,' the man breathed.

'Aye,' Sweet nodded, 'reckon so.'

'Then what're we waiting for!' Stover nearly shouted, he spun on his heel and started marching back towards the road. He waved an arm and called back without turning. 'Let's get after him!'

Violent Fey and the Wyn trudged away from the oak tree, following Stover back to the road. Sweet sighed again and looked down at the signet ring, then back at the cairn. It was so small—no higher than his knee—and looked pitiable in the relative vastness of its surroundings.

So small, Sweet thought, looking back towards where they had left the battlefield of Scarvin. So small to commemorate such a catastrophe. He closed his fist round the ring and pocketed it with another sigh.

So small, he thought.

But it was something.

*

They made their camp a little way up the road. A row of boulders lined the eastern side so they led their mounts through the trees and into the relative shelter of the rocks. The Wyn got a fire going and Sweet pulled a sheet of tanned doeskin from his pack. He set it over Violent Fey's shoulders and the pair of them crouched down to study the map, sheltered from the rain.

'He came this way then,' Sweet muttered, pointing a grimy finger at the part of the map that marked out Scarvin. Before it had been known as the battlefield where the Pratian military was utterly annihilated by the Vols, Scarvin had signified a burgeoning settlement just to the northeast of the battle site itself.

'You reckon he went through the town?'

'They would've needed supplies,' Sweet nodded, tapping at the marker on the map. 'Food, provisions, winter gear. Could be they even got themselves some horses. Weapons, too, if they'd had to leave theirs in

Levitan in order to slip by the Vols.'

'You don't think he would've been recognised?' Vi raised an eyebrow.

'Maybe he didn't go into the settlement himself,' Sweet scratched at his chin. 'Might be he has some men with him, could've sent one or two of them to fetch the supplies they'd need. Besides, even if they were spotted—these folk are Pratians, they've got no love for the Vols.'

'Might have love for gold, though,' Vi offered.

Sweet shook his head.

'If they'd turned on the prince he'd be captured by now, probably before we even heard about this job.'

Vi accepted that with a silent nod of her head.

'How far ahead of us do you think he is?'

'Could be quite aways,' Sweet shrugged, scratching at his neck now. 'They had a decent head start on us, but we don't know how long it took him to get out of the city. We might've only missed him by a few days, and I doubt he made it out with a horse. They'll have come this way on foot, we'll have made up some good ground on them by now.'

'So what next?' Vi asked, her eyes shining bright in the shadow of the doeskin rain cover. Sweet shifted his position, the dull ache in his hip joined by a sharper one in his knee. That secondary pain was a more recent addition to the growing repertoire that seemed to wrack his body with every passing season, and it wasn't one Sweet welcomed.

'We'll get somethin' to eat,' he told her, frowning down at the map, 'rest up a little, then head into Scarvin to pick up their trail from there.'

Vi said nothing for a moment, then bit her lip and looked up at Sweet.

'You alright?' she asked, barely a whisper, 'you don't seem…happy with this job.'

Sweet thought about the question for a moment, then gave a dry chuckle and answered.

'I'm alright,' he said, and meant it.

'This is a once-in-a-lifetime opportunity,' said Vi, still searching his expression for any hint of a lie.

'Aye, I know,' Sweet nodded, his smile failing a touch.

'We could sit pretty on that bounty. Wouldn't ever have to take another job.'

'Aye I know that, too,' Sweet nodded again.

'That what's bothering you?' Vi asked, her voice still low but her tone sharper than the knives strapped all around her. Sweet thought about the question. It was as though she'd heard his thoughts from earlier that day. Had he even been satisfied with his own conclusions then? Had he even reached any?

Sweet held her gaze and eventually shrugged.

'It is what it is,' he offered.

Vi studied him for a moment, then sighed.

'We get the job of a lifetime and that's the best you can do?'

Sweet shrugged again, another wry smile breaking out across his face.

'Gotta do the job first,' he replied, 'and then get paid for it, to boot.'

'You don't trust the magicker?' Vi raised an eyebrow.

Sweet forced a dry laugh.

'You know me,' he grinned. 'I don't trust anyone.'

# The price of things

SCARVIN WAS A grim little town filled to the brim with grim little people. Before the war with Volsgard the settlement had been part of a key trade road that struck east-to-west across the kingdom. It was positioned neatly between several major Pratian cities—including Levitan—which made it a perfect mid-point for trade deals to take place, particularly those that needed conducting outside of the watchful eyes of tax collectors and lawmakers. Like any place that showed the vaguest promise of opportunity, Scarvin had attracted a rich variety of opportunists to go with it. All of them shifty, hustling and untrustworthy in equal measure. It was well known that most of the town were crooks, of one ilk or another.

Hard-eyes and suspicious stares followed Sweet and his crew as they walked their horses down the main street—a wide scratch of dirt with dwellings and businesses lining either side. At the centre of Scarvin was the town square, a wide, open patch of land which had been so well trodden over the years that not a blade of grass grew in the dirt there. This was where the town had its marketplace—though no stalls were laid out today—and met for important gatherings. In the centre of the square was a wooden structure with a strong base of mortared stones.

The town gallows.

Unlike the wilder parts of the world, Scarvin was closer to civilised society—which meant it was closer to the scum of humanity who preyed on those they deemed weaker than themselves. This close to the city of Levitan, crime was as common as rainclouds in the autumn. Pickpockets and thieves, brawlers and thugs, even rapists and murderers—Scarvin was nothing if not diverse. The gallows were therefore not temporary, like in smaller towns and villages where their use was considered a special circumstance. No, these gallows were a mainstay of Scarvin's town square—and a well used mainstay at that, too.

Sweet and his crew had been through the town before—the last time not more than two years ago—and little had changed, except there were a few more dank buildings and the sullen townsfolk looked even more downtrodden than usual. Even so, considering the destruction that had rained down on the rest of Pratia—and considering the corpse-covered battlefield less than a few miles to the southwest—the people of Scarvin had been lucky in avoiding the worst of things.

From the naked glares they cast at the bounty hunters, the townsfolk didn't seem to share Sweet's thoughts on the matter. He supposed they were wary of anyone as heavily armed as he and his crew were. With the Pratians gone and the Vols frying bigger fish, it was more than likely that bandits and roving gangs had increased in both numbers and boldness. If the crime rate in Scarvin had been high before the war, it would be somewhere in the clouds by now.

At least they've got the gallows already, Sweet thought.

It was another drab day, but as they neared the town square the clouds thinned long enough for a few shafts of sunlight to stab their way through. The effect was less than impressive. There were murky puddles on the ground and they glistened like oil as the sunlight hit them. The only structure worth highlighting—the stone-based gallows themselves—cast an ominous black shadow to the west. The townspeople shuffled to and fro, laden with buckets or baskets or bundles of cloth-wrapped goods. Off to the eastern side of the square, Sweet spotted what he was looking for.

The North Road Tavern was a wide, squat building that must've been conceived by a blind architect and built by a drunk construction crew. A long and warped, stooping porch ran the width of the building, with a rickety railing and hitching posts for those passing through. For those staying a little longer, a hastily-built stables had been erected around the back and along one side of the building. It always looked to Sweet like the stable was an afterthought, but according to the tavern's owner—a hatchet-faced man by the name of Arc—it had been designed from conception with overnight travellers in mind.

Inside the North Road was a low-ceilinged taproom with just a few too many tables. Arc always claimed he'd tried to make the place feel cosy, but Sweet knew all he really cared about was fitting the most people under his roof as possible. Like most, Arc's true thoughts and actions were governed by the glint of coin. The man also lacked a single honest bone in his body, so Sweet's general rule was to assume he was lying.

Leading off the taproom was a wonky hallway, one wall slightly higher than the other. And leading off this hallway were rooms that Arc claimed were for the overnight travellers, but Sweet knew were more often than not occupied by Scarvin's whores, earning their pay. A cut of which—naturally—would go straight into Arc's grubby little palm. He was—in all but name—Scarvin's chief pimp.

'We stayin' the night?' Stover asked, a hint of hopefulness in his voice. It was the first time since they had left Levitan that the other man had even hinted at slowing their pursuit of the runaway prince.

'It's not even noon,' Vi snorted. 'We'll be gone before lunch.'

Stover looked a little disappointed, though Sweet could read the man well and knew that he had immediately started calculating how much time that would leave him with. Less than a half hour, which probably gave him more than long enough for what he had in mind.

Sweet led his horse to the front of the North Road Tavern and dismounted, he hitched the reins to one of the splintered posts and glanced up. A toothless old man was sitting under the stooping porch not far away. He was perched on a weathered-looking chair with a wilting papersmoke stuck between his lips. Sweet reached into his pocket and pulled out a silver coin, he flipped it over to the man who caught it with practised ease.

'Watch the horses,' Sweet told the man, who only grinned in return, revealing a single brown tooth. Sweet grimaced a little and led his crew up the stoop and into The North Road Tavern.

*

It wasn't busy inside the long hall. Only two of the battered circular tables were occupied. A pair of old timers who looked as though they never left, nursing drinks that no doubt never ended. They looked half-asleep, or most of the way towards slipping into a more permanent state of sleep. The only other movement inside the taproom came from a portly woman in a filthy apron. She was scrubbing down one of the tables closest to the door. The lack of custom inside the taproom was hardly surprising, given the freshness of the morning.

Could do with some of that freshness in here, Sweet thought, as he ambled into the gloomy interior. Clouds of dust motes drifted around them and the air had a stale smell about it. The woman in the apron stopped her scrubbing and looked up as they entered, blowing an errant curl of hair away from her face with a snuff of her lips.

'Take a seat,' she told them, her voice gruff and heavily accented. 'Kitchen ain't open yet but y'can drink. Might be some cold food left in the back if yer after some breakfast.'

'Not here for food, hot or cold,' Sweet told her, scanning the bar at the far end of the room. He saw nothing but the rows of bottles stacked onto shelves. They were set underneath a row of enormous barrels mounted above. A kingdom-ending war might've just concluded, but Scarvin was never likely to dry up, no matter the circumstance.

'Drink then?' the woman nodded, returning to her cleaning—though judging by the state of the rag she was using, Sweet wondered if she was actually making things worse.

'Not here for a drink either,' he told her.

'Speak for yourself,' Stover muttered.

'Well what are'y here for then?' the woman asked, straightening from her task again and blowing the stray curl of hair away for the second time in as many moments.

'Information,' Sweet said, with a stare that he hoped was hard but somehow always felt a bit flat when faced with complete and total ambivalence. The same ambivalence she was offering right now. The woman seemed to consider his answer for a moment. She glanced at Sweet's crew, her eyes stopping on their assortment of weapons and their grimset faces. Sweet thought he saw a moment's hesitation before she shrugged and went back to her cleaning.

'Take a seat,' she told them again. 'Arc's in the back, I'll fetch him once I'm done 'ere.'

Sweet nodded, thinking he probably wouldn't do much better than that, then motioned for his crew to take a big table nearby. He had no idea if the woman had already cleaned it, but the wooden surface was still damp so he supposed she'd given it a go at least. They filed past him and pulled out the chairs with sharp wooden screeches, making one of the dozing old-timers startle over his drink. Not dead yet, then, Sweet supposed. The aproned woman finished wiping the tables nearby then angled towards the bar.

'I'll fetch him for you now,' she told them as she squeezed by.

'And those drinks, too,' Stover flashed her a grin. The woman looked unimpressed and said nothing more as she walked away.

Several minutes passed and the only sounds inside the long taproom were the thrumming of Stover's fingers as he drummed them against the tabletop and the occasional wheezing cough from one of the old timers. Eventually the portly woman reemerged from a door behind the bar, followed closely by the enormous figure of Arc Malmont.

Arc was a barrel of a man. Broad-shouldered and heavily-muscled, but with short arms and legs and a layer of fat that seemed to round off most of his features. He was dressed in greasy brown trews, matching braces and a stained shirt that had probably been white at some point back when the world was young, but had now settled into something more akin to a yellowy grey colour. The sleeves were rolled up, revealing hairy forearms and faded tattoos. Arc's face was red, his eyes set back behind a bulbous nose. He sported a long, drooping moustache, similar to the style in which Stover wore his, though Arc's was marginally more kempt. He smiled as he saw who his guests were, though Sweet recognised a well-exercised greeting when he was fed one. It was all part of the dance.

'Sweet, you old dog!' Arc threw his arms open wide, grinning broadly.

'Arc,' Sweet nodded, not getting up. The tavernkeeper let his arms drop, but kept his smile bright.

'And you've brought your crew,' he beamed, before turning to the aproned woman. 'Fetch us some drinks, Tula. Ales apiece.'

'Not for me,' Sweet waved a hand, 'bit too early in the day.'

'Never stopped you before!' Arc barked out a laugh, then he frowned at the woman. 'Oh well, ales for the rest of us then.'

'This one don't drink!' Stover motioned to where the Wyn was sat, silent and unmoving. Stover was smart enough not to clap his hands on the tribesman's cloaked shoulders—and instead they just hovered close enough to make Sweet wince a little. Stover only grinned wider, 'so I'll have his one, too!'

The bounty hunter laughed, loudly and stupidly. No one else joined him. But Arc forced another smile.

'What brings you to this neck of the woods?' The big pimp asked, ignoring Stover's shit joke and returning his attention—and his false charm—to Sweet.

'Sit down and let's talk,' Sweet motioned to the empty chair at the table.

Arc took it, easing his enormous frame into the chair, which gave a creak of protest as he dropped his prodigious bulk into place.

'Which way did you come through?' the tavernkeeper asked.

'South,' Sweet replied. 'Levitan.'

Arc's eyes sparkled at the mention of the city.

'Any news?' he asked, almost hungrily. 'Heard the Vols took the city pretty quick, always best that it happens like that eh?'

'Aye,' Sweet snorted, 'quick, but no less painful for it.'

'You must've passed the battlefield then?' Arc raised an eyebrow and lowered his voice, as though speaking of the dead might somehow disturb them. Sweet didn't reckon that was likely.

'Aye,' Sweet sighed, 'we saw it.'

'No one left to clear the bodies,' said Arc, shaking his head but not with any sincerity. 'Terrible thing.'

'Crows don't seem to mind,' Sweet sighed. He glanced up and met Arc's eye. 'And I'd bet my last bent copper there was some loot to be had.'

'Most likely there was,' Arc replied, the glint in his eye telling Sweet what he already knew. That glint told Sweet that Arc himself had sent a gang of urchins to root through the bodies of the fallen—probably whilst they were still warm—to search for anything of value. The country might've changed hands, Sweet thought grimly, but this big bastard is still the same as ever. As crooked as they came and without a scrap of morality to him. Sweet sighed inwardly.

The aproned woman, Tula, weaved her way back through the jumble of furniture with a carefully balanced tray of clay jugs. She set one down in front of each of the table's occupants, skipping out Sweet and the Wyn. Stover didn't seem too aggrieved that he was only given one cup, despite his earlier jibe—for which Sweet found himself grateful.

'Didn't see many Vols in town,' Sweet observed, changing the subject. 'They not been very "hands-on" in Scarvin?'

'You know how it is,' Arc shrugged, offering another smile. This one was a little sharper and a little more dangerous than before. 'We govern ourselves, for the most part.'

Sweet knew exactly how it was. The strongest governed Scarvin, usually to the detriment of the weakest. Not much different to the rest of the world, he mused again, but just a bit less subtle about it.

'When was the last time you had any around?'

'Oh there's some,' Arc nodded, 'they left a little detachment behind after the battle was over. But they mostly keep to themselves up at the far end of town.'

'No hunting parties then?' Sweet asked, holding to Arc's gaze again. The big tavernkeeper held firm, but a sly smile began to spread out from under the wings of his drooping moustache.

'Hunting for what?' he asked, his tone a picture of false innocence.

'The fucking prince!' Stover sprayed ale as he spoke, slamming his other hand onto the table for emphasis and causing the same old-timer to jump for a second time. Sweet wondered if a third surprise might kill the man outright.

'Stover,' Sweet growled. He caught the other man's eye and silently told him to shut up.

'The prince,' Arc's smile grew wider and he took a deep swig from his own drink, wiping his face with the back of one meaty hand. He let out a soft belch and raised one eyebrow. 'Crown Prince Orsen?'

'The very same,' Sweet nodded slowly.

'He wasn't killed in Levitan?' Arc raised the eyebrow higher, 'I heard the royal line ended in the siege.' He put on a mocking voice of proclamation, 'Pratia is hereby assimilated into the grand vastness of the Vol Empire. The kingdom is no more, an' all that.'

Sweet sighed and closed his eyes. When he opened them, the tavernkeeper was still staring at him with that badly painted expression of faux probity. Like a shit actor in an even shittier play.

All part of the fucking dance.

'Let's stop this, shall we?' Sweet asked, growing weary of the same old nonsense. 'You know I can never be bothered with this dumb-fuckery.'

Arc's smile grew wider still.

'There's the Bitter Sweet I know,' he said, chuckling softly. Then his face hardened. 'But very well, you want to be all business then let's be all business.'

Sweet nodded, already wondering if he would come to regret such a direct approach.

'The prince came through here,' Sweet said. He wasn't asking. Didn't need to. Arc didn't respond. He didn't have to. 'Or at least someone he's travelling with did.'

'Could be they did,' Arc half-agreed, somewhat more slyly than Sweet was comfortable with.

'I thought we were done with the games?' Sweet asked, narrowing his eyes. Arc gave him a look of mock hurt, then chuckled again and nodded.

'We are,' he said, then cleared his throat. 'I have the information you want.'

'Then give it to us,' Stover growled, the thin foam from the ale still clinging to his moustache.

'I will,' Arc replied, half-sneering at the other man. He returned his gaze to Sweet, eyes glinting hungrily. 'For a price.'

'Name it,' Sweet said, fixing him with a cold stare, 'and no fucking about trying to haggle, I'm not in the mood.'

'Very well,' Arc agreed, straightening in his chair, which screamed in protest again. 'But I don't want your coin.'

'What kind of shitty price is that?' Stover smirked.

'Shut up, Stover,' Sweet snapped. He frowned across the dirty table at the big pimp and tipped his head questioningly. 'What *do* you want, Arc?'

'I want your help,' Arc replied, his voice steady, but cold. 'Your gold is no good to me without it.'

'No one said anything about gold,' Sweet corrected him, 'and if you want our help then that *is* the price. Gold won't come into it.'

Arc remained silent, so Sweet took a deep breath.

'What do you need help with?' he asked.

'There's a new game in town,' said Arc, his lip curling in barely-disguised anger as he spoke. 'Bunch of thugs have moved into a property at the end of the west road. Unscrupulous bastards that don't know the way of things. They're stealing away my business.'

'You want us to shut down another tavern?' Stover scoffed. Arc fired him a glare and Sweet rolled his eyes.

'He's talking about a brothel, idiot,' Sweet sighed. He looked back to Arc. 'Where're they getting their girls from?'

'Most of 'em used to be mine,' said Arc, his voice heavy with regret, though Sweet doubted it was out of concern for the womens' welfare. More likely he was mourning the loss of the coin they brought to him each night. 'Only got a handful left now, and I don't reckon they'll stay too much longer.'

'I thought you had an agreement with them?' Sweet asked, knowing full well what the agreements between pimps and whores usually resembled. *Give me your coin and I'll stop your customers from beating you, or worse,* was the usual outward agreement. *Give me your coin and you get to keep your teeth,* was usually the underlying gist of it.

'I did,' Arc nodded, still looking somehow wistful, 'but these new bastards threatened 'em. Even killed one, to prove they were serious.'

'They killed one?' Sweet raised an eyebrow.

'Making a point,' Arc shrugged, as though he was a rancher discussing a lost cow. Sweet reckoned that was probably how Arc saw it.

'And no one did anything?' Sweet asked.

Arc snorted at that.

'What's anyone gonna do?' he gave a bitter laugh.

Sweet thought about it for a moment.

'Right,' he muttered, more to himself than to Arc. 'You govern yourselves.'

Arc nodded. Sweet sighed again.

'So,' he said, 'this new gang rolled into town, threatened your girls and forced them into working for them instead of you, that about the rub of it?'

Arc nodded again.

'You need a crew to keep yourself safe,' Stover sneered. His voice hardened. 'And to keep your girls in line.'

'I had one,' Arc replied, 'but most of the daft bastards got swept up in the recruitment drive for the war. I'd bet any money most of 'em are lying dead on that field you passed on your way in! More useless now than they ever were.'

Yeah, no doubt the children you sent to pick through the bodies found their purses for you though, Sweet thought grimly.

'So you want us to step in?' he said aloud. 'Shut these newcomers down and get your girls back to come back here? That's your price?'

'That's my price,' Arc agreed.

Sweet pondered it for a moment. He felt Vi stiffen in her seat beside him and knew her thoughts without even looking at her face. The same feeling was written plainly across the faces of Bryntas and Daraday, too. Sweet sighed and clasped his hands together.

'It's a shit deal,' he told Arc. The tavernkeeper's eyebrows shot up in surprise. It was just about the only genuine gesture he had shown since emerging from the door behind the bar.

'But—'

'One,' Sweet cut him short with a wave of one hand. He held up a single finger to enunciate his point, 'we're bounty hunters, not muscle for hire.'

'But—'

'Two,' Sweet held up two fingers, 'we don't give a rat's arse who pimps out the women in this shitpot little town.'

Arc remained silent this time and Sweet flicked up a third finger.

'And three,' he said, pushing himself to his feet at the same time. 'You already told us the prince came through here, so I'm not sure we need much else.'

Sweet turned to leave, hearing the chairs scrape behind him as his crew all made to follow. Stover was a little slow on the uptake but eventually joined in, throwing the last of his ale back down his neck first. Sweet had made it only two steps towards the door when Arc's laughter started up.

Sweet slowly turned to face the fat tavernkeeper. He frowned down at him in his chair.

'Something funny?' he asked, narrowing his eyes at the big man, 'because the way I see it, you haven't got long before you go out of business, and I don't reckon you'll earn nearly as much as the girls will in plying the same trade. That is, if these newcomers don't decide to just take you out of the game permanently first. If they've killed a whore then why would they blink at killing a pimp?'

'Former pimp,' Vi corrected, her voice hard as a coffin nail. 'Can't be a pimp without whores.'

Sweet had to resist a smile. She always knew what to add to drive his point home all the more fiercely.

'I'm laughing,' Arc grinned up at him, ignoring the jibe, 'because some things never change.'

Sweet only stared back at the man, waiting for more of an explanation.

'The rain is still wet, the sun still bright,' Arc's smile turned more lupine again, 'and Bitter Sweet is still a shit liar.'

Sweet said nothing.

'You need my information,' Arc continued, all confidence again now. 'You *think* you know the prince came through this way. But you have no idea how many he travelled with, or who they might be. You have no idea how well armed they are. How well equipped they are. You have no idea if they're on foot, or what mounts they might have. You have no idea how long ago they passed through, or which way they went.'

Sweet swallowed.

'And you know all that, do you?' he snorted, but the noise sounded false even to his own ears. Arc's grin grew even wider and even more satisfied.

'I do,' he smiled up at Sweet, 'for a price.'

# Painted faces

‘WHY WE DOIN’ this?’ Stover asked for what felt like the thousandth bloody time. The grizzled bounty hunter took another deep puff from his papersmoke and blew it out through flared nostrils.

‘Because if we did it any other way we might not get reliable information,’ Sweet told him—also for the thousandth bloody time. ‘If we rough Arc up he’ll spin us a lie or two just to get us out of his face. And if we go down that road then he wouldn’t ever tell us another truth again, and you never know when we might need him. But mainly,’ Sweet breathed, ‘because I say so.’ He increased his pace as he spoke, partly to reinforce his point and partly because he wanted nothing more than to get this over with.

Vi was the first to match his new walking speed—they’d left their mounts at The North Road in the esteemed care of the toothless old feller on the stoop, who had been slumped, dozing in his seat as they left. Vi glanced over at Sweet.

‘He’s got a point,’ she said, leaning in and speaking quietly enough for Stover not to hear it. ‘Why *are* we doing this?’

Sweet frowned at her as they trudged down the street leading west through Scarvin. She still looked as hard as coffin nails, but there was something else bubbling just beneath the surface. It wasn’t something Sweet was used to seeing on Vi’s face. It looked a lot like doubt.

‘Because of all the reasons I just said,’ Sweet told her, perhaps a little too bluntly. He saw the briefest flash of anger in her eyes and wondered if it was about to be followed by the flash of a blade. He breathed a sigh of relief as the moment passed. The relief was closely followed by a wave of guilt for snapping at her in the first place. He shifted his shoulders and grunted. ‘Besides, if these new folks put Arc out of business for good then he’ll never be able to sell anyone up the river to us again. The man’s an arsehole, but even arseholes are useful.’

Vi said nothing in response, and Sweet found some of that doubt in himself. He frowned again as he turned it over in his mind. Why *were* they doing this? They were clearly on the prince's trail, and with the Wyn in their crew there was little doubt they would pick up warmer leads as they headed further north. Was Arc's information really worth it? They would find out what kind of entourage the prince had managed to escape with when they caught up to them. Horses, weapons, supplies – they were all things they would discover if they just followed the prince. Was it out of some weird sense of loyalty to a reliable—if not prickly—source? Was Sweet doing this because he actually liked Arc?

Those questions, at least, were easy to answer. Sweet had no loyalty to a man who would just as quickly sell information about bounty hunters to their target as he would information about the target to their hunters. As for liking him? That was the easiest answer of them all. Arc was a prick from every angle. No one fucking liked him.

So why then, was Sweet going out of his way to help him? Why was he running this errand for the man? Wasn't it just an unnecessary danger on what already felt like a dangerous enough hunt? Did he really want more in the mix? It occurred to Sweet that that might well be his answer and he frowned all the harder for it.

The whorehouse came into view, close to the edge of town, just like Arc said. It was a two-storeyed building with another ramshackle stoop poking out of the front of it. There was no sign, but the women standing outside of the building passed for one all the same. There were two of them, leaning on the stoop railing and passing a papersmoke between them. Even from a distance Sweet could tell they were working girls. Gaudy clothing with more skin on show than the season called for, trussed up hair and painted faces. They straightened a little as Sweet and his crew approached, casting nervous glances to all the weapons on show but doing their best to look past them.

'You here for a good time?' the first one tried what she thought was a seductive expression. To Sweet it looked like she'd clamped down hard on a lemon wedge.

'Here to see Bennett, as it happens,' Sweet answered, giving the name Arc had supplied and not returning the false smile. 'He about?'

'He's inside,' the second woman answered, blowing a stream of blue-tinted smoke between her stained lips. The first whore gave her a stern look and the woman screwed her own up in reply as if to say "what?"

Sweet ignored them both and climbed the step up onto the stoop. He reached for the door handle and the first whore stepped up beside him.

'We're closed,' she told him, trying to sound tough but falling well short of the mark, 'business hours ain't started yet.'

'Not for us you're not,' Sweet told her, turning the handle.

He didn't wait for a response. Sweet opened the door and strode inside.

The building was smaller than the North Road Tavern, but no less densely packed with tables and a mismatch of chairs and benches. A bar had been thrown together at one side of the room, with two big cabinets standing behind it, displaying all manner of liquor bottles in various states of depletion. There was a closed door behind them, presumably leading into storage or management quarters for the taproom. A set of stairs led up to the second floor, where a gallery overlooked the tables and chairs below. A series of closed doors led off this gallery, which was no doubt where the women with painted faces plied their trade. In fact, Sweet could hear the forced cries of one of them—muffled by the distance and the doors in between them—as she gave a performance that would've embarrassed the very worst of the street theatre hacks.

The air inside was stale and gloomy and reeked of debauchery. Sweet took a deep breath of it and grimaced a little. A group of four men were sitting huddled around a small table near to the bottom of the stairs. They had been playing cards but looked up as Sweet entered, their expressions hard. Those expressions changed to confusion, and then surprise, as the other members of Sweet's crew filed in behind him. Sweet noted that all four of the players were armed.

'Afternoon lads,' Sweet said, amiably enough. 'Looking for Bennett. He here?'

The men all pushed away from their table a little, their card game forgotten. They glanced between the swords, hatchets and daggers hanging from the newcomers that had entered their domain.

'No need to get up,' Sweet assured them, holding out his palms, 'we just wanna speak to Bennett.'

'He's upstairs,' one of the men responded gruffly, nodding in the direction of the whore's wailing moans. A scar ran down the side of his nose and into his top lip. 'Who're you?'

'Just passing through,' Sweet told the man. 'You think you can call him down here or should we just go up and fetch him?'

The room filled with the sounds of scraping chair legs as the men rose in unison. The man with the scarred lip was easily as tall as Bryntas, though not as broad. The men flexed their hands as they reached for their weapons.

'Now lads,' Sweet held his palms up again, gesturing for peace but knowing he wouldn't get it. 'We really do just wanna speak to Bennett. Ain't no need for anything more'n that.'

'He's busy,' the man with the scar sneered, 'best you leave now.'

Sweet sighed, though he knew there had never been any hope for anything less than violence. That was the way of things.

'Six on four, lads,' Sweet tried again. He cocked his head to one side. 'I wouldn't back those odds.'

'No?' Scarlip raised an eyebrow. Then he raised his voice. 'Darvas!'

There was a rustling sound from behind the door next to the drinks cabinets. It swung open and a round-shouldered man barged into the taproom, he was followed by four others. Two of the men had crude-looking cudgels hanging from their waists, long-bladed knives were sheathed at the hips of the others. The round-shouldered man had a hatchet tucked into his belt, he surveyed the scene with narrowed, pig-like eyes and then nodded his understanding of the situation.

'Nine on six,' Scarlip's sneer grew larger. 'Reckon them odds are better.'

'Aye,' Sweet nodded, turning wistfully to his crew. 'Try not to kill them,' he said.

Scarlip's sneer turned into a snarl and he lunged forwards, pulling a knife from his belt as he came. At the same time the round-shouldered man—Darvas—charged his men forwards from the door beside the bar.

Sweet's crew were ready. They had been since they had left the North Road Tavern, knowing full well what their task entailed. Probably before that, if Sweet was being honest.

His crew were always ready for violence.

Scarlip had steered for Sweet, but Bryntas cut across his path, batting the man's knife-hand away with one huge arm like a bear swatting a fish from a river. His other arm arced round at the same time, slamming into Scarlip's face and sending him flying onto a nearby table.

A second man from the card game swung a club at Bryntas' exposed back, but the Wyn stepped in and raised a knee into his stomach. Air rushed out from the man's lungs and he was folded in half. The Wyn spun on his planted foot—his dark robes swaying with the movement—then brought his raised leg spinning round. His booted heel caught the downed man square in the face with a sickening crunch. The man was spun from his feet and crashed to the floor.

From the other side of the room, Darvas was nearly on Sweet, who kicked a nearby chair into his path. The round-shouldered thug stumbled, losing the swing of his raised hatchet. Sweet stepped in and grabbed that hand to stop him from swinging it again, he landed three punches to Darvas's side before receiving one to his ribs in return. Sweet grunted, but gritted his teeth and forced himself to hold onto the man's hatchet. The two grappled before Sweet used his weight to toss the smaller man over the nearest table. One of the other men came at Sweet with a dagger levelled at his chest, but Violent Fey slapped his outstretched arm downwards and crunched the pommel of one of her own knives into his surprised face. The man grunted and fell to the floor, but not before his own blade cut into his leg. The pain from his newly-broken nose must've been outmatched by the gash in his leg because he shrieked and clasped at the flesh above his knee.

Vi turned and delivered a full-bodied punch to the face of the nearest thug. The man staggered backwards but lashed out himself, catching her high on the cheek and spinning her back into the others.

Then all was chaos.

Tables and chairs clattered about as men were thrown into them, or they were picked up and thrown into other men. Blades were slashed and smashed aside. Cudgels were swung in anger, drawing gasps when they hit bodies and dull thuds when they were turned away. Stover had drawn his sword, but was too close to his opponents to use it in earnest. He grappled with a thin man with a pockmarked face before kicking out, catching him in the knee. The thug cried out and his leg buckled, Stover pushed him over then lunged with his sword. It lanced through the unprotected chest of another man, who stared down at the blade in his chest with a look of wide-eyed surprise.

Daraday had launched himself into the fray, guarding Violent Fey as she recovered from the blow to her face. He spun lithely, darting away from a swinging club and stabbing out with a dagger, catching the wielder in the wrist and causing him to drop the weapon. There was a primal snarl stretched across the boy's face as he fought. Sweet grappled with a knifeman, the man's face so close to his own he could smell the stink on his breath. From somewhere came a shattering crash as glass was broken.

A door burst open on the gallery above and a half-dressed man appeared at the railing, closely followed by a naked whore, her painted face smeared and her eyes wide with fear.

'What the fuck?' the man bellowed, his open shirt billowing around him as he laid eyes on the carnage below. Sweet just had the time to see him disappear back into the room and reemerge with a short sword in his hand before another fist came swinging at his face. Sweet ducked it and tackled the fist's owner, spearing his shoulder into the man's midriff and sending him flying.

Pain seared across the top of Sweet's arm as a dagger sliced across it, cutting through his shirt and the flesh beneath it. Sweet half-turned to face his attacker but Bryntas got there first. His huge hand clamped around the knifeman's throat and lifted him high into the air. The man's eyes went wide as he was carried up and up before being sent spinning onto a nearby chair in a melee of splintered wood.

Sweet saw Stover slash at another thug, who cowered away from the singing blade. A second man stepped forwards to stab Stover but Daraday lunged at him and the two wrestled for control of the knife. The sound of thudding footsteps on the stairs drew Sweet's attention away from the fight.

The half-dressed swordsman—whom Sweet assumed was Bennett—came clattering down the stairs, his shirt still wide open and his trews only half-tied. The Wyn, still with no weapon drawn, knocked down another of the thugs and rushed up the stairs to meet the bedraggled pimp.

Bennet swung his sword, but it was a wild attempt and the Wyn easily ducked out of its path, swaying like a branch in the wind. The tribesman delivered a series of crunching blows to Bennet's exposed chest, using the side of his palms and his extended fingers to do the damage. The man lost the grip of his sword and was shoved back against the balustrade. He looked dazed. Even more so when the Wyn hit him square in the face, this time with a clenched fist.

The cacophony of noise that had filled the taproom had quieted now, and Sweet turned to see that the fight was all but over. Bits of broken furniture lay everywhere. At some point one of the drinks cabinets had been toppled, which accounted for the smashing glass Sweet had heard. An unconscious man—one of Darvas' lot—lay facedown next to it.

Sweet's crew were all still standing, breathing heavily and sporting the odd cut or bruise but no injuries of note. Vi's nose was red with blood and already swelling from where she'd been punched. Daraday had a long cut across one cheek that was bleeding worse than it looked. All in all, Sweet reckoned the slash across his own shoulder was the worst of it.

Bennett's men had not fared so well. Three were down in a trail leading up to where the Wyn now propped Bennett himself up against the stairs. Sweet hadn't even seen the tribesman take down two of them, but the way they were lying suggested they wouldn't be getting back up for a little while longer. Across to Sweet's right the carnage was worse still. Scarlip hadn't ever risen from where Bryntas had swatted him, and the man who'd been lifted by his neck was groaning softly and holding one hand to his spine where it had connected with the chair. Stover, his sword still streaked with blood, was kneeling beside another unconscious man, busy relieving him of his purse. The hatchet-wielding Darvas was the only man left standing, and he was carrying a deep cut all down one arm courtesy of Stover's sword. The arm hung uselessly by his side, dripping blood to the boards below as he flicked his eyes from Stover to Daraday to Violent Fey to the corpses on the floor.

There were two men dead, or at least from what Sweet could tell. The one Stover had lanced through the chest was laid flat out on his back, arms and legs akimbo in a growing pool of blood. One hand was twitching a little but he was otherwise still. The second was the knifeman that Daraday had been wrestling with. The handle of said knife could be seen jutting from the man's breast, right where his heart was. A dark stain had already spread wide around the weapon. All the other downed men appeared to still be breathing.

Darvas licked his lips and looked back from the corpses to Sweet. His face curled up in a snarl, but Sweet saw the fear in the man's eyes. Like a cornered animal, Sweet thought.

'Best you be getting gone,' Sweet told him, breathing heavily himself.

The man looked a little puzzled at first, but soon realised he was being granted a reprieve. He took two shuffling steps backwards before turning and hurrying through the door beside the bar, leaving it swinging on its hinges behind him.

Sweet frowned down at the two dead bodies, then turned his attention to Bennett. He motioned for the Wyn to bring the man over and the tattooed tribesman dragged the groggy pimp across the room, unceremoniously dumping him into one of the few remaining intact chairs.

'You Bennett?' Sweet asked, leaning down to catch the man's eye.

'Fuck you,' Bennett responded, one eye already swelling shut from where the Wyn had hit him.

Sweet immediately punched him full in the face, snapping his head back sharply. Sometimes words fall short, he reasoned.

'You Bennett?' he asked again, as the man's head lolled forwards once more. His nose had exploded under Sweet's fist and blood was running freely across his lips. Just like the painted faces of the whores, Sweet thought. As he had the thought, he glanced up to see the railing of the gallery above was lined with nearly a dozen women now. Most were looking down with weary, almost expectant expressions. One or two looked shocked, but not overly so—Sweet doubted this was their first exposure to sudden violence. The main doors to the taproom creaked open and the two women who had been sharing their papersmoke outside stepped indoors. The first woman surveyed the scene with a grim sense of acceptance, the second looked altogether more stunned.

'Ugh,' the seated figure of Bennet burbled.

Sweet frowned at the women gathered on the balcony above and then punched the man in the face again. Hard. Time to prove a point, he thought.

'Simple question,' he told the seated man, roughly grabbing his shoulders to stop him from spilling out of the chair. 'Are. You. Bennett?'

The man spat to one side, sending blood, phlegm and what looked like a piece of tooth to the boards below. He nodded glumly.

'Aye,' he breathed.

'See,' Sweet smiled, patting the man's cheek, 'that wasn't so hard. Next question is an easy one, too.' Sweet motioned to the men in various states of consciousness around the taproom. 'When your boys wake up,' he frowned at the two corpses, then added 'the ones that can, anyway. You'll all be leaving town, right?'

The man looked up at Sweet, a spark of fire in his eyes. It died as he saw Sweet's grim smile, and he looked down again, nodding for a second time.

'Aye,' he whispered.

'Excellent,' Sweet clapped the man on the shoulder, as though they'd come to an agreeable business deal. He supposed in a way, they had. He straightened and addressed the women up in the gallery above him.

'Ladies,' he called out, 'if you're still of a mind for good business, I suggest the North Road Tavern. Arc Malmont has some vacancies, as I hear it.'

Several of the women nodded knowingly, most just watched in stony silence. They knew how this worked. They'd played this game before. Sweet sighed and leaned down to look into the battered face of Bennett once more.

'You'll be leaving town, right?' he growled at the man.

Bennett nodded glumly.

Sweet exhaled loudly, reasonably happy with the outcome of their little excursion to the shittier end of the shitty little town. None of his crew were dead, none of them were carrying wounds on the bad side of serious and it seemed that they had accomplished their task. Arc would be back in business by nightfall and would furnish them with the information they needed to make good on their pursuit of the runaway prince—and the enormous bounty placed upon his capture. All in all, things had turned out as well as could be expected.

Yet somehow Sweet felt flat. Empty and dulled. As though all the doubts and questions he'd had before still itched at him, even though the answers were now meaningless in light of the carnage inside the taproom. Why had he taken on this job? Was he looking for trouble? Looking for violence? Was he just frustrated? Was it as simple and stupid as that? Sweet frowned, angry at his inability to unpick his own feelings.

Then he punched the man again.

## Ends of the bargain

‘ I KNEW THERE was some of the old Bitter Sweet still in there,’ Arc
beamed a smile across the bar, jabbing a meaty finger towards
Sweet's chest. Sweet was glad the bar was too wide for Arc to reach him,
if that finger so much as brushed the front of his shirt he might've leapt
over it and throttled the man.

Arc rambled on about the good old days—whatever they were—and
Sweet tuned him out. He looked down at his own hands, turning one over
and seeing the dried blood that had crusted in the valleys of his knuckles.
He rubbed at it with his other hand, pulling some bits off in rusty little
flakes. Some of it wouldn't shift at all, ingrained into the contours of his
skin.

'...and look at us now, eh!' Arc finished, his grin wider than ever
and his arms held out wider still. Sweet, as though waking from a daze,
followed the big man's gesture and glanced around the taproom.

The North Road Tavern was heaving with people. A stark contrast to
just a few hours before when Sweet, his crew and the unmoving pair of
old-timers had been the only souls in the place. The old timers were still
there, Sweet could see them amongst the bustling crowd—it looked as
though they were still nursing the same drinks from that morning—but
now they were surrounded by a heaving, laughing, jostling mass of men
and women, all in varying stages of drunkenness.

Sweet was propped up on his elbows at the North Road's generous
length of bar. Arc's staff—including the portly woman who had been
cleaning the tables earlier that day—busied themselves around the big
tavernkeeper, taking drink orders, pouring them out and palming the
coins that were tossed lazily in their direction, or left spinning on the bar
itself. The man stood beside Sweet was having an animated conversation
with his friend and backed into Sweet, their shoulders knocking together.
The man turned with a drunken apology already forming on his lips. The
look on Sweet's face must've stopped him from issuing it as he quickly

turned back to his companion, took another deep swig from his ale cup and resumed talking loudly. Something about a fish he'd nearly landed that afternoon.

Sweet sighed and returned his attention to Arc.

'We held up our end of the bargain,' he told the man, rubbing at his knuckles again, as though realising for the first time that they were aching. Even stinging a bit, he must've cut them on one of Bennett's teeth. 'So tell me what you know about Crown Prince Orsen. When did he come through?'

'Straight to business, eh Sweet?' Arc gave a knowing wink..

'Arc,' Sweet fired him the same warning glare he'd given the drunken fisherman beside him. The tavernkeeper relented with an exaggerated sigh.

'Just over two weeks ago,' he said.

'Just over?' Sweet raised an eyebrow.

'Can't be more'n a day or two over that.'

Sweet masked his surprise. The news meant that the prince was closer than expected. Maybe he had encountered problems between Levitan and Scarvin, or maybe it had taken longer for him to escape the city than Sweet first supposed. Either way, the news should've excited him. A bounty worth more money than most men would ever see was well within their reach. But Sweet only felt a strange numbness at the thought.

'Who was he with?' Sweet asked, trying to shake the feeling.

'*He* wasn't here at all,' Arc replied, reaching under the bar and pulling out a bottle of rust-coloured liquor and two small glasses. 'Sent two of his men into town instead.'

'Two of his men?'

'Guardsmen, is my guess,' Arc continued, pouring himself a glass.

'Not for me,' Sweet held out a hand as Arc started for the second glass. Arc glanced up at him for a moment, as though his former assessment of a return to the glory days had gone awry. Then he shrugged.

'Suit yourself,' Arc said, 'and aye, two fancy bastards—trussed up like paupers as best they could, but not fooling anyone—they had swords, too. Good steel. Reckon one might even have been Damsen.'

'Well-spoken Pratians, badly disguised as peasants and carrying Damsen steel,' Sweet mused, 'sounds about right.'

'Exactly,' Arc nodded, tossing the contents of his glass down his neck in one go. He grimaced a little, wiped at his chin and then set about pouring himself a second. 'They wanted supplies, winter clothing and horses, too.'

'They came in on foot?' Sweet raised an eyebrow. That would also account for the prince's slow progress. It made sense, he supposed. Escaping Levitan unnoticed on horseback would've been nigh on impossible.

'Aye, I reckon so,' Arc nodded. 'Left on foot, too.'

'No one gave them the horses?'

'Pfft,' Arc leaned back, looking offended at the very suggestion. 'Ain't nobody in Scarvin just *giving* horses away. And they didn't have the coin to pay for them.'

Sweet absorbed this news with grim deference. The fugitive might've been the Crown Prince of these lands, but the folk of this town didn't much care a shit about who lorded over them. At the end of the day, a prince's gratitude wouldn't put food on the table or keep a roof over their heads.

'You said they wanted supplies,' Sweet looked up at Arc again. 'Supplies for how many?'

'Hard to say,' Arc downed his second drink and rubbed at his face, as though feeling the warm tingling through his hand. 'If they're heading where I think they're heading then enough for ten, maybe twelve men.'

Sweet cursed inwardly at that. A dozen men was more than he had expected. Such a group wouldn't have fled Levitan together, it would've been too obvious. Maybe they'd escaped in twos and threes with an arranged rendezvous point so they could regroup once outside the city walls. That's what Sweet would've done. Smart boy, this prince, he thought.

'Did they get the supplies they need?' Sweet asked.

'Oh aye,' Arc nodded, pouring himself a third glass of the dark liquor. 'They had enough coin for that, at least. Food and winter clothing.'

'But no horses.'

'Well,' Arc grinned, 'they got a pair of pack ponies, to help carry their provisions.'

'I thought your stables were looking a little empty,' Sweet muttered. Arc only grinned wider. 'Anything else you know?'

Arc's grin tempered a little and he leaned across the bar, lowering his voice just enough to still be heard over the raucous din inside the taproom.

'I know you ain't the only crew looking for him,' the tavernkeeper met Sweet's eyes, then darted away to one side. Sweet nodded then slowly followed the gesture across the room, passing over a myriad of drunken patrons, to a table set against one wall. He swore aloud this time, under his breath but full of feeling. Sweet turned back to face Arc and the man gave a knowing nod. Sweet returned it, then scooped up the glass of liquor the tavernkeeper had poured for himself, he tipped his head back and swallowed hard. The drink went down his neck like liquid fire.

Sweet turned away from the bar and began easing his way through the crowd to the table at the far wall. The group seated there stiffened as he approached. The man seated at their head opened his arms wide as though offering a warm greeting of old friends. Gold glittered from his wolf's smile.

'Bitter Sweet,' Malvadas grinned. 'Well met, old boy.'

*

Sweet stared down at the other bounty hunter with a withering look. Lamplight danced in the gold dotted throughout the misshapen rows that made up his teeth—he'd acquired more since the last time Sweet had seen him, though Sweet could never understand why a man would want to put gold in his mouth. Seemed damn inconvenient. Not to mention it was something of an invitation for anyone on the wrong side of desperate to knock them out and take them. Not that anyone needed another reason to knock Malvadas' teeth out, mind you.

'What, no smiles for your old pal?' Malvadas' eyes flashed just as much as his teeth did.

'Alright, Mal,' Sweet flicked the other man a nod. 'It's been, what? Three years?'

'Something like that,' Malvadas agreed. 'Woodbury? Or something like that?'

'Woodbyrne,' Sweet grunted.

'That's the one!' Malvadas poked a bony finger up at Sweet. 'You always did have a good memory, Sweet.'

'Can't say I remember many of your crew,' Sweet replied, folding his arms and casting his eyes over the men seated at Malvadas' table. Mean bastards, every one of them, but not a single face that Sweet recognised, even in passing.

'Aye well, a lot can happen in three years,' Malvadas scratched at his ear, his feigned regret sounding as hollow as it surely was. 'I suppose your own band of merry companions has changed a mite, eh?'

'Nope,' Sweet answered, before thinking for a moment and adding, 'cept for Jenrick.'

'Ah yes,' Malvadas clasped his hands together, making a little tent out of his fingers. 'I heard about that. Drowned, was it? Back in Levitan.'

Sweet said nothing. He held Malvadas' gaze, trying to figure out if the man was playing a game. Most probably he was, but Sweet couldn't work out what it might be just yet.

'Aye that's right,' Sweet said at last. He cocked his head to one side. 'You keepin' close tabs on us, Mal? Didn't realise you missed me so much.'

'Well, you know how it is,' Malvadas pulled his eyes away and smiled into his drink as he took a swig. 'Damn but that's good. Won't you join us for a drink?'

'I'm not staying,' Sweet replied, seeing more than one of Malvadas' men shift as they brought weapons closer to hand. The faces might've changed, but some things never did.

'Ah yes,' Malvadas repeated, still smirking. 'Got a prince to hunt, am I right?'

So there it is, Sweet thought. This gold-toothed prick is toying with me because he knows our business here. That must mean...

'That Vol magicker make you an offer, did he?' Sweet raised an eyebrow, keeping the anger from his face. The fear too, for that matter. Competition of any sort was never welcome. Competition in the form of this dangerous bastard was about as unwelcome as it got.

'That he did,' Malvadas leaned back in his chair, one finger sliding around the rim of his ale cup. Toying with it, just like he was toying with Sweet. 'Not somethin' any sane man would turn down lightly.'

'Not sure any of this is sane,' it was Sweet's turn to smirk. 'Chasing a runaway prince for a Vol magicker don't seem like easy work.'

'No,' Malvadas agreed, 'but then easy work don't pay so nicely as the tricky stuff, does it, Sweet?'

'Reckon you've got a lead on him then?' Sweet asked, ignoring the question.

'That we do,' Malvadas picked up his cup once more, 'all thanks to our esteemed tavernkeeper,' he tipped it in the direction of Arc. Sweet followed the gesture and saw the big man busy himself at the bar, looking distinctly abashed. So he should, the duplicitous bastard.

'Lined his pockets, have we Mal?' Sweet asked, nodding his understanding.

'Actually no,' Malvadas took another swig of ale, tasting it between his teeth afterwards. 'He's really very chatty, once you threaten his fingers, his eyes and whatever passes for his manhood.'

Sweet felt a tightening in his own stomach. A bit lower down, if he was being honest. Malvadas had threatened Arc, then. The same threats hadn't carried much weight when they'd been made by Sweet and his own crew, but Malvadas was a different breed of madness. Even the way he'd so casually mentioned his dark methods had been laced with danger. Malvadas had made the comment so blithely, but it had been underpinned by a venom in his voice that Sweet knew all too well. It might've been three years since their paths had last crossed, but Malvadas was still a mad bastard all the same. One who wouldn't bat an eyelid about torturing someone for information.

'Heading north, then?' Sweet tried, concealing his fear as well as he could manage.

'Now Sweet,' Malvadas flashed his gleaming smile once more, 'what kind of businessman would I be if I gave away trade secrets to the competition?'

Sweet shrugged.

'Could always take him in together,' he ventured, but truly wanting nothing more than to be a hundred miles away from this gold-toothed lunatic. Malvadas laughed, but the sound was devoid of humour. Like an echo in a mausoleum.

'Now Sweet,' he chided, 'I don't think we're much in need of your help, but thank you for the offer all the same.'

'Suit yourself,' Sweet shrugged again. He turned to stalk away from the table, having had his fill of talking for one day. Had his fill of just about everything, to be perfectly honest. 'Be seeing you, Mal.'

'Aye,' Malvadas voice followed him away from the table, even through the raucous noise of the taproom. It made Sweet's spine tingle. 'Be seeing you, Bitter Sweet.'

# *Friendly competition*

O VER THE NEXT few days Sweet led his crew northeast. They followed the road out of Scarvin for a few miles before veering off to follow a beaten track that ran alongside the course of a fast-flowing river. The track was only wide enough for them to ride in single file and it was pitted and rough in places, making progress slower than it would've been had they stuck to the trade road due north. But Sweet didn't want to take that route. He had told his crew that the prince was more likely to keep off the main roads in order to hide from Vol patrols, but truthfully he didn't want to share the route with Malvadas' crew. The man was a snake, and in Sweet's experience it was better to go around a snake than to test if it had fangs. And since no one had offered much of a challenge to his suggestion they took the road heading northeast.

Sweet led the way, his horse picking its way over scattered rocks and dusty divots, with the sound of rushing water echoing back off the small lee of rock beside the path. He wondered if it wasn't such a bad call after all. Northeast actually angled them towards the borderlands with Volsgard, but if a fugitive wanted to make good on their escape then sometimes taking the less considered routes worked in their favour. Besides, the prince had already done it once, having left Levitan and travelled for Scarvin instead of fleeing for the eastern border with Thradonia. It stood to good reason that he might make the same choice again, just to be sure he was throwing pursuers off the scent. Unfortunately for him, those same choices had kept Sweet—and now Malvadas—well on the prince's trail. At least the Vols themselves were still chasing shadows somewhere to the west of Levitan.

Sweet's thoughts turned to Malvadas. Considering him a snake probably didn't go far enough. The man was a viper. He had been a rival for as long as Sweet could remember, competing with the gang that Sweet had first joined when he started out in the game. Malvadas couldn't have been more than ten years older than Sweet himself, but his own crew had been ruthless even back then. The gold-toothed bounty hunter had drawn to him a band of like-minded folk—all hard bastards with a dark streak inside, little more than criminals themselves. They had very quickly established themselves as an outfit that were not to be fucked with under any circumstances.

Competition between bounty hunters wasn't a new thing, but most operated on a fairly simple code of "leave alone what you want to leave you alone". Funnily enough it was a pretty similar approach to dealing with snakes again. However, Malvadas' crew had challenged that code, stealing bounties captured by rival crews and leaving their competitors bruised or worse. Several times over the years Sweet had heard of other crews going missing in the wild, or being cut down—supposedly by bandits or outlaws—as they sought their quarry. Every single time, Malvadas and his crew had been the ones to finally bring the bounty in. Sweet wasn't the only one to assume that Malvadas and his crew had been involved in the deaths, but there was never much evidence and the contract was still fulfilled. Most clients couldn't give a shit if one team of hunters got themselves killed in the process, so long as they got their mark.

Malvadas' callousness wasn't just reserved for his competitors, either. Each time Sweet ran into the gold-toothed hunter—which, thankfully, was rare—he had a new band of vagabonds riding with him. They were always hard-eyed, grim-faced and clearly dangerous, but they never seemed to last long under his leadership. Again, rumours abound that Malvadas took mad risks with the lives of his crew, putting them in danger in pursuit of their contracts. It was obvious to anybody—save maybe the crew themselves—that Malvadas saw them as extremely expendable. Probably he even saw them as a needless expense. One more mouth to feed, one more purse to pay from the bounty.

Sweet frowned as he remembered Stover's own delight at Jenrick's death in Levitan. Maybe it wasn't an attitude that was specific to Malvadas, after all.

Not only that, but Sweet had heard that Malvadas was as ruthless with his own crew as he was with those of his rivals. One story told of a planned mutiny within Malvadas' outfit. Two men—apparently sick of the wily hunter's leadership—had reportedly plotted to remove Malvadas as the head of the operation and install themselves in his place. Malvadas had gotten wind of the scheme and slit the throat of one man. The other he had beaten to a bloody pulp, then he'd dragged him to a bridge. With the rest of the crew watching, Malvadas had looped a noose over the man's neck and taken a sickle to his belly. He'd dragged the blade across the man's stomach and kicked him from the bridge. The rope had snapped taut and the man's guts had been thrown from his body. It had—according to one man who'd left Mal's crew not long afterwards—been a lesson about loyalty.

Sweet shivered and pulled his coat tighter about himself. It fit his frame a little too snugly and he found himself cursing inwardly. Let myself get a bit soft these past few months, he thought. Too much comfort and not enough sharpness. And with Malvadas' crew nearby the one thing Sweet wanted to be was sharp.

Still, he considered, a few weeks' hard toil out here in the wilderness would soon fix that.

The ground rose a little, the river beside them ran faster and even dropped down a small step of rock in a little waterfall. The loud splashing made Sweet's horse nervous and he patted its neck and stroked at its mane. Not for the first time, he found himself wondering just what in the hell they were doing out here. Hunting a prince, of all people.

Sweet didn't much care for politics. In his long years leading a crew he had hunted Pratians, Thradonians and even Vols—though the latter were thankfully few and far between. The Empire tended to deal with internal issues itself. The nature of a man's birthplace was immaterial to Sweet, as was the flag he swore allegiance to or even the deeds he'd done to earn a bounty on his head. To Sweet, it was just business.

And business was good, as it usually was following a long and bloody war. There were plenty of contracts available. Thieves and looters, rapists and murderers—all with a price on their heads. There would be plenty of gold available for Sweet and his crew to see them through the winter, at least.

But this contract would see us through every winter, for the rest of our lives.

Sweet frowned again as he considered the thought. One contract that would set them up for the rest of their days. One big score that would carry them into a life of luxury. It sounded too good to be true and—in Sweet's experience—such things usually bloody were. Suppose then, that the rest of their days didn't extend beyond the completion of the contract itself. Sweet trusted their new employer about as much as he trusted Malvadas and—even if they somehow retrieved the prince and fetched him back to Levitan in one piece—he was conscious that both Lennick Sylvanus and Malvadas obviously shared a common trait.

They were both vipers.

So, supposing they *did* manage to capture the prince out here in the wild. Supposing they did manage to drag him all the way back to his former capital city, evading Malvadas and who knew what else on the journey back. Supposing they delivered him to Sylvanus. What then? The magicker would thank them all for their service and give them each a heaving cart of gold to take away as promised?

Sweet's face contorted as he even considered such a fantasy.

No, Sweet thought, a man like Sylvanus didn't get to his position of power by doing right by people. No one rose that high in the world by keeping their word. And rich men didn't get rich by paying folk, either. Sweet reckoned that—even if they were to be successful in this most lucrative of contracts—their payment might well last them for the rest of their lives, but those lives would probably be measured in hours instead of years.

And that—Sweet thought with a heavy sigh—would be an awful lot of gold in the hands of dead people. Sweet reckoned dead folk would have a hard time spending it. They usually did.

'You look troubled,' Violent Fey nudged her horse alongside Sweet's own and he looked up to see that the track had widened without him realising it. He transferred his gaze across to Vi and nodded slowly.

'Aye,' he replied simply.

'Malvadas?' Vi enquired. The flint in her eyes grew harder at the mention of the man's name. As far as Sweet knew, Vi had no specific reason to dislike the man. But—Sweet supposed—you didn't exactly need anything specific to dislike a man like that.

'Aye,' Sweet nodded again, scratching at his neck. 'Doesn't bode well that he's here. He tracked the prince north, too. Others might've done the same.'

'We'll know soon enough,' said Vi, scanning the far side of the river.

She was right. The Wyn had rode on up ahead. The landscape rose steadily and there was a sloping ridge not more than a few miles to the west of them. He had made for the high ground that morning to scout the land ahead—and the land behind, too. The tattooed tribesman was an uncanny tracker and by the time they regrouped with him Sweet reckoned they would have a good idea if anyone else was following in their footsteps. Anyone besides Malvadas and his band of cutthroat degenerates, that was.

'Still having doubts about this job?' Vi asked, lowering her voice so that it wouldn't carry back to the others. The question caught Sweet off guard and he took a moment to think about it. He considered a cheap laugh or an outright lie, but then his eye caught Vi's own and his expression softened.

'Aye,' he admitted, letting loose another deep sigh. 'You really think Sylvanus has the money to pay us?'

'Are you asking if he has it, or if he'll give it up once the bill is due?' Vi raised one eyebrow.

Sweet smiled at that. He might've dulled over the past few months, but Vi was sharp as ever. When had she ever not been?

'He has it,' Vi answered for him, looking back to the beaten track ahead. She sounded certain, but Sweet reckoned she was convincing herself as much as she was trying to convince him. Her eyes hardened and she added, 'and when the time comes, we'll make sure he pays.'

Sweet kept quiet. When Vi's thoughts turned to violence or threats it was often best to say nothing. You didn't want that kind of light shining on you if you could avoid it.

In principle, he knew she was right. They'd dealt with folks like Sylvanus before. Folks who wanted their help but then found that they didn't want to pay for it. Folks who'd even tried to cheat them out of their payment after the job was good and done. Sweet had seen it all. Weighted bags to make a purse feel bigger than it was. False coins, the counterfeit quality of which varied from close to looking genuine right the way through to being a scratched up disc of scrap metal. Some had even turned on Sweet and his crew and instigated violence in an attempt to get out of paying them.

All of them had regretted it.

But something about Sylvanus oozed a different kind of danger. The man was a magicker and—in Sweet's admittedly limited experience with them—magickers were about as trustworthy as a starving fox in a henhouse. Every word the man had offered them back in Levitan had seeped and dripped with a poison disguised as sweetness.

And yet, Sweet sighed aloud as he became lost in his troubled thoughts, here we are.

*

By the time they regrouped with the Wyn the sky had darkened considerably. Heavy, brooding clouds the colour of wet stone had rolled in from the north. It hadn't started raining yet, but it wouldn't be far off. It looks like winter is shaping up to be a real bastard, Sweet thought as he frowned up at the sky.

His frown deepened as he saw the Wyn's face. It was mostly hidden in the shadows of his hood, not helped by the ailing light of the day. Even with no hood and good visibility, the Wyn's expression would've looked unreadable to most men. To Sweet though, the message was plain.

Bad news.

'Let's hear it,' Sweet told the tribesman as he approached, handing the reins of his horse to Daraday. He, Bryntas and Violent Fey began setting up their camp for the night, nestled in the relative shelter of a cluster of boulders. Stover had wandered away to stand at the lip of the ridge, overlooking the landscape far below. A quick glance over told Sweet that he was pissing over the edge. Standing damn close to the edge, too. He was either very brave or a complete idiot, and Sweet would've bet his life on being able to answer which one.

'Fourteen men,' the Wyn replied, his accented voice so soft that Sweet had to strain to hear it. As well as the darkening clouds above, the wind was picking up again and it rattled around his ears like flapping canvas.

'Fourteen?' Sweet's frown deepened further still. The Wyn only nodded solemnly. That was more than he'd seen sitting with Malvadas at his table in the North Road Tavern. He'd probably had others dotted around the taproom. Others had probably been in the backrooms with Arc's whores, too.

'All armed?' Sweet asked, knowing the answer.

'Swords, axes,' the Wyn nodded, 'four bows.'

'Damn it,' Sweet whispered under his breath. His own crew only had the one bow—recovered from Jenrick's possessions—and none of them were half as good a shot as he had been. The bow and a quiver of arrows now resided amongst Daraday's other belongings, strapped to the packs of his mount. 'What about scouts?'

The Wyn shook his head.

At least that was some small comfort. Malvadas was confident enough—or arrogant enough—to not bother setting scouts further up his trail. The gold-toothed bounty hunter was obviously banking on simply riding the prince down. Without horses, the young royal and his retinue wouldn't be able to outpace mounted hunters. It would only be a matter of finding their trail and then eating away at the miles between them.

'Six others behind,' the Wyn spoke again and it took Sweet a moment to realise what he'd said.

'Six more hunters?' he queried, 'Malvadas is riding with twenty men!?'

The Wyn shook his head, his face still solemn.

'Not bounty hunters,' the tribesman said. For the first time since Sweet had known him, his expression flickered a little. It took him a moment to register what it was. The tattooed man looked troubled, even a little fearful. It did nothing for Sweet's own confidence.

'Who, then?' he asked, already feeling a knot in his belly.

The Wyn met Sweet's eye and slowly raised a hand to tap at his own chest.

'My people,' he said.

'Wyns?' Sweet was confused as well as worried now and he scratched at the side of his head. Then he remembered. 'Was one of them a big bastard? Two great big bloody axes?'

The Wyn nodded, that troubled look still swimming in his gaze.

'Fuck,' Sweet muttered.

There could be no mistaking it. The second hunting party that the Wyn had seen had been sent by Sylvanus directly. At their head was the enormous bodyguard they'd encountered in the Hall of Justice, Thond. Sweet's mind raced as he sought to factor this new complication into their plans. He came up short and turned away from the Wyn in frustration. He wandered over to the lip of the ridge, feeling the wind clawing at his clothes as though eagerly pulling him towards the edge. At this exact moment Sweet wondered if it would be such a bad thing—it would certainly be much simpler. A moment of weightlessness, followed by a short plummet and a quick end, dashed upon the rocks below. Even as he neared the ridge he knew even that wouldn't be that simple. More likely the fall wouldn't kill him outright. He would break some bones, then lie in agony until he died from dehydration.

'Fuck,' Sweet said again, louder this time. His thoughts dark and swirling, a reflection of the sky above him.

'What's wrong?' Vi called out. She must've seen his exchange with the Wyn and wandered over to see what the score was.

'Trouble,' Sweet told her, his mood grim. Vi came closer and raised an inquisitive eyebrow. 'Mal has thirteen others with him,' Sweet told her, 'four archers in the group.'

Vi said nothing, but Sweet saw a shrug forming in her eyes. Fourteen men competing with them for a bounty was nothing new, even if they were led by a deranged and ruthless sonofabitch.

'Plus,' Sweet sighed, 'that big bastard, Thond, is not far behind them.'

'Thond? The Wyn with Sylvanus?'

'Aye,' Sweet nodded. 'Reckon he's tracking the same way we all are.'

'Or he's tracking Mal?' Vi offered.

Sweet considered this and found a small ray of sunshine shining through the clouds in his mind. If Sylvanus had set his hound to follow Malvadas' crew, then there might be slim hope still. If Sweet and his crew could find and capture the prince first, they might be able to loop back behind the other hunters before they knew what was happening. Malvadas might well lead Thond's group on a merry chase to nothing.

'Or he's tracking us,' Vi continued, spearing the good thought as quickly as it formed in Sweet's mind. She shrugged. 'Either way, we'll deal with it.'

'Deal with what?' Stover asked, sidling over whilst still lacing the front of his trews back up.

'We have company,' Sweet sighed. He explained the nature of the other groups in pursuit of the prince again. Stover swore.

'Then what're we waiting for!?' he threw his arms wide. 'Let's get after him before they get there first!'

Sweet swapped a glance with Vi, then sighed again.

'We'll talk more once we've got a fire going,' he said, turning away from Stover before he could offer further protest. Sweet stalked back to where Bryntas and Daraday were setting up the camp, his mood darker than ever.

*

With a campfire crackling and their bellies full of bacon and bread they'd bought in Scarvin, Sweet's crew relaxed in the relative warmth of its orange glow. The rain had held off—much to their surprise—and the dark clouds had made way for a field of thinner ones that now drifted overhead, edged with the silver glow of moonlight. Daraday and Bryntas lazed off to one side of the campfire, their backs against the shared face of a tall boulder. Vi was beside them, stabbing a dagger at the ground between her legs. Stover was next to her, and beside Sweet, picking at some bacon fat caught between his teeth. The Wyn was sat cross-legged on the rocks above, facing outwards and keeping watch for movement in the night.

'So then,' Sweet rubbed his hands together, feeling infinitely better for a warm meal and a warm fire. 'Some news on our contract.'

Vi stopped spinning her dagger. Stover stopped picking at his teeth. Bryntas and Daraday looked up.

'As you all know, we've got some...friendly competition,' Sweet forced a grim smile, 'only they ain't too friendly.'

The group shifted a little at that, swapping knowing glances.

'Malvadas is a hard bastard,' said Bryntas, drawing nods from the others.

'It ain't just Mal we've to worry about,' Sweet replied, leaning forwards and hunching his shoulders a little. 'It seems like Sylvanus' has set his right-hand man on the trail, too.'

'That big Wyn you all met in Levitan? Thond?' Daraday asked, raising an eyebrow.

'That's the one,' Sweet nodded.

'He weren't that big,' Stover grinned, back to picking at his teeth. He gestured across the fire. 'Bryn could take him.'

'I know a dangerous man when I see one,' said Sweet, a flicker of irritation prickling his voice. 'And this fella is up there with the worst of 'em. Not to mention he's travelling with five others. The prince himself is said to be travelling with around ten of his own. Add that to the thirteen men Malvadas is riding with and it puts us at a disadvantage if it comes down to a scrap.'

'One helluva disadvantage,' Bryntas muttered, idly throwing a pebble into the fire.

'So we don't fight 'em!' Stover tried his grin again, 'not part of the job anyhow, is it? We just grab this royal shitbag 'fore they get a chance to do it first.'

'Aye that's one way o' doing it,' Sweet nodded, then he shrugged. 'Come to think of it, it's the *only* way o' doing it.'

'So what's there to talk about?' Stover huffed. 'We should be hunting him down right now!'

'That's the *only* way o' doing it,' Sweet repeated, before taking a deep breath. He wasn't sure exactly what kind of reaction his next words would get, and that troubled him. He sighed loudly. 'The other thing we need to talk about is…not doing it at all.'

There was a moment of quiet, through which only the crackling fire and the rise of the wind outside of the rocks could be heard. Sweet looked at each of his crew in turn as he saw his words sink in. Bryntas only nodded. Vi remained unmoved. Daraday looked a little surprised, but masked it well. It took Stover a moment longer than the others, but then his face darkened.

'Ain't nothing to talk about then,' he nearly growled.

'This job is a hot ticket,' Sweet continued, ignoring Stover's scowl. 'And it's only gettin' hotter with three groups all closin' in on the party,' he sighed, 'there's an awful lot of steel about, and folks itching to use it.'

'So fucking what!?' Stover erupted. 'Ain't nothin' we haven't dealt with 'fore!'

'It's exactly that,' Sweet shot back, just about keeping his anger in check and his voice quiet and even. He looked across at the faces of the others and was somewhat relieved to see that they appeared to agree with him.

'That's a lot of armed men, Stover,' Bryntas put in, concentrating on turning over another pebble that he had picked up in his massive hands.

'We're all armed!' Stover protested, 'and deadly to boot. Ain't reckoned you were such a bunch o' cowards.'

The group bristled at that and Sweet held out his hands for calm.

'Ain't nothin' cowardly about bowing out of a fight you can't win,' he reasoned.

'We don't gotta fight!' Stover insisted. 'Like I said, we get to the prince first, grab him and ride like hell back to that magick bastard to get our gold!'

Sweet considered raising the point that he didn't trust Sylvanus—or that the money on offer would even be paid—but he decided against it. To do so would've brought into question why they had bothered travelling north at all and the others were already studying him carefully. Last thing he needed was for the crew to fall apart at the same time as the job did.

'Besides,' Stover continued, eagerly grasping at the opportunity to fill the silence, 'we already agreed to the contract. Ain't no *bowing out* o' anything now.'

'That's not how it works,' Vi snorted her derison. Stover bared his teeth at her in response.

'That's never how it's worked,' Bryntas agreed, tossing another pebble into the fire. Stover switched his attention to the big man, his mouth falling open in shock.

'I can't believe you lot!' he cried. 'All that gold and you want to turn back just because other folk are chasing it, too!'

Sweet considered pointing out that they had only agreed to the contract in the first place because Stover himself had launched them bare-arsed into the deal, but decided it would only add fuel to the fire and tensions amongst the group were taut as it was. Truth could be a weapon, and sometimes it was better not to draw it in anger.

'Five hundred thousand in gold!' Stover carried on speaking his piece, the exasperation written all over his face. 'We could do anything wi' that kind o' coin!'

The group bristled again, but this time Sweet reckoned it wasn't anger. It was a discomfort of another kind, like maybe they didn't much like the thought of missing out on all that gold.

*If it even exists,* he thought sourly.

'It is a big promise,' Sweet said, picking his words carefully. 'And if Sylvanus holds up his end o' things then aye, we could do anything with that kind of coin. But, this job is getting more complicated and more dangerous with every hour that passes.'

Stover opened his mouth to speak again so Sweet cut across him first.

'Which is why I wanted us to talk it through,' he looked at each of them in turn. 'So that everyone gets to say their piece. Stover, we all know where you stand.'

'Damn right,' Stover huffed, folding his arms across his chest and glaring at the others.

'Vi?' Sweet asked.

Violent Fey sighed, still turning her dagger over in thought.

'I say we keep going,' she said at last. Stover brightened at that and Sweet ignored him. Vi met his eye. 'At least until it gets *too* dangerous. For now though, we've still got a chance of taking the bounty quietly, without a straight fight.'

'What about the prince's men?' Bryntas questioned.

'We kill 'em,' Stover answered, smirking now.

'We deal with them when the time comes,' Vi replied, her face darkening. 'But if we turn back now then the whole thing'll have been a waste, and we already risked our necks for that fat bastard back in Scarvin.'

There was a small murmuring of agreement at that and Sweet couldn't argue with it. Running Arc's competition out of town hadn't exactly been a noble deed, but it had been a risk all the same. Bennett and his thugs had hardly been a sophisticated bunch of fighters, but in a scrap with blades drawn anything could've happened to any one of them.

'Very well,' Sweet nodded. 'Bryn?'

Bryntas looked troubled. Deep frown lines wrinkled the skin of his forehead as he continued to play with a new pebble in his hand.

'I don't like it,' he admitted. 'Malvadas is ruthless as they come, and from what you told me this Thond feller ain't someone who'd show much mercy in a fight.' He sighed. 'But it is a lot of gold, and I've a mind to buy myself a farm.'

'A farm?' Stover snorted, seemingly unaware that Bryntas had cast his thoughts in favour of the cause he was advocating. 'Didn't reckon you for a farmer, Bryn?'

'No,' Bryntas nodded, looking a little embarrassed. He looked up at Sweet. 'But a man can't do this forever. Sooner or later this life comes to an end,' he grinned sheepishly. 'Might as well do that with a mountain o' gold to fall back on at the end of it.'

Sweet nodded. He could understand that. Hell, Bryntas was a few years younger than he was. Maybe he should've been thinking the same thing himself. No sooner than he'd considered it, Sweet dismissed the thought. The idea of himself turning over crops or raising livestock was so ridiculous he nearly laughed aloud. Looking at Bryntas though, he could see it. The big man was a hard bastard and didn't shirk away from violence, but he wasn't built for this life. There was something in him—a gentleness at his core—that was too soft for it. Sweet didn't reckon it was a weakness, as such. But in this game any bit of softness could be exploited, and that could mean destitution—or worse. The more Sweet thought about it, the more that Bryntas the farmer made more sense than Bryntas the bounty hunter.

'Dara?' Sweet turned his focus to the youngster.

Daraday leaned forward. Dark shadows—cast by the flickering orange fire—danced across his face.

'Let's take him,' he said, his voice firm. Stover brightened further still.

Sweet was a little surprised by that. He'd expected the boy to weigh up both sides of the argument more, but instead he'd committed to continuing the hunt with almost no hesitation. He'd become a real hard case alright. There was even something in his eyes that looked a little haunted. It made Sweet uncomfortable. Was the lad trying to prove to Sweet he could handle this job? Was he only agreeing with Stover to prove to them all that he had the stomach for it? In Sweet's view that was a shit reason to put your life—and the lives of your crew—on the line.

'You sure, lad?' Sweet asked, concerned.

'He said so, didn't he?' Stover smirked. Sweet ignored him and watched Daraday closely. The youngster nodded, the steel in his eyes unflinching.

'Aye,' he said. 'Let's finish it.'

Sweet nodded and leaned back a little. He cocked his head up towards the rocks above.

'Wyn?' he called out, 'you been hearing all this talk?'

There was a moment of silence, followed by the Wyn's surprisingly soft voice drifting down to them all.

'You go, I follow,' he said.

Stover looked as happy as a pig in shit. He unfolded his arms and beamed at the others as though they were his family again, rather than folks he had—just moments ago—accused of abject cowardice. Sweet nodded, mostly to himself.

'So it is,' he muttered. 'Get some sleep, we'll set off before dawn.'

*

The following day saw a rare spell of autumnal sunshine break through the banks of rolling grey cloud overhead. The landscape was bathed in a gentle yellow glow and scattered golden spears lanced through the thin cloud to highlight parts of the rugged terrain ahead.

They had abandoned the river now, and rejoined what was left of the northern trade route. There had been little sign on their track that the prince's group had travelled alongside the waterline and Sweet reckoned he had called it wrong after all. Most likely the prince had stuck to the well-trodden road and gained something of an advantage over them. It also meant that Malvadas and his crew would likely be ahead now, too. Somewhere between Sweet's own group and the prince. It also put Thond and his smaller—but no less ominous—band somewhere behind them. It didn't feel so much as being between a rock and hard place as it did being inside a cave when the walls start to crumble. Sweet frowned as the uncomfortable thought trespassed in his head.

He had told the Wyn to keep something of a rearguard. The tattooed tracker had agreed without a word and was now ranging somewhere to the south of them. Sweet didn't want Sylvanus' personal bodyguard to happen upon them unawares. The big, armoured Wyn worried Sweet just as much as Malvadas did. If Sweet was being honest, the man had worried him when they'd first met back in Sylvanus' stolen office. If he was being *totally* honest then the big man had scared the shit out of him. He didn't want the axe-wielding bastard stumbling into their camp one evening, so the Wyn had been told to watch their backs as they continued their hunt northwards.

That just left the very present danger of Malvadas and his sour-faced bunch of cutthroats, somewhere on the road up ahead. Bryntas had ridden ahead of the group, with orders to find Mal's crew and keep them in sight, but nothing more. The idea was pretty simple, if Bryn kept eyes on Malvadas then there was little chance the gold-toothed snake could lie in wait, ready to ambush Sweet and his crew as they rode by. It might've been paranoia—after all, Mal had the numbers and so probably didn't need to worry about them—but Sweet knew the other bounty hunter well, and he reckoned Malvadas would want to eliminate any competition *before* he reached the prince.

That left just four of them travelling together, riding two abreast on the weathered old road. Gorse had started to appear in scraggly patches and rock formations sprouting from grassland soon gave way to grassy knolls sprouting from rock. Sweet knew that the road continued for many miles yet, but it wasn't often travelled. It would be rough going at best. When it did eventually end, they would have to strike northwest for the mountains—and that would be real wilderness. So for now, Sweet decided to make the most of the rare showing of sunshine and the relative flatness of the road beneath his horse's hooves. He closed his eyes and tipped his face up towards the sky, feeling the warmth of the sun gently settle on his cheeks.

An hour or so passed and Daraday lifted Jenrick's old bow from Sweet's saddlebags. He volunteered to go hunting for some game—whilst there would still be some—and Sweet had to admit it was a good idea. When the grasslands disappeared entirely there would be little else to hunt but rabbits and badgers. They'd bought plenty of provisions in Scarvin but most of those would keep, so getting fresh meat whilst they could get it made good sense. Sweet felt more than a little pride as Daraday heeled his horse off the beaten track, angling slightly to the west. Maybe not everything the boy had learned was so bad, Sweet thought, watching him go.

Overhead, the clouds parted further and the sun warmed his face even more. In a thin stand of trees away to Sweet's right, two birds chirped loudly to one another. He sighed, as close to content as he had come since they'd ridden into Levitan. Maybe none of this is so bad, he thought. Maybe this is what I could do with my share of the bounty. Just take quiet rides out into the countryside, with the sun on my back and the birdsong in the breeze.

Sweet's good spirits continued unabated throughout the morning. Stover was unusually quiet and Violent Fey kept to herself, which left him with his enjoyment of the fresh air and his newfound contentment. His worries—heavy though they were—seemed far away right now and he was happy to be able to ignore them for the moment, at least.

After a few hours Daraday returned, cantering his horse up from the south. A young doe was tied across the back of his saddle.

'A good hunt?' Sweet asked, impressed.

'She's not that big,' the lad replied with a ghost of a smile on his face.

Sweet suddenly realised it was the closest thing to a smile he'd seen from the lad in months. 'But she'll keep us fed for a night or two.'

The four of them shared a meal of hardbread and crumbling cheese in silence and Sweet found himself beginning to wonder if he'd ever really wanted to bow out of the hunt at all. Sure, they didn't have the strength to match Mal's crew, but they were smarter than he was. They were more resourceful and more cunning. They had the guile to steal the prince from under Mal's nose and the experience to spirit their bounty back to Levitan without so much as needing to raise a voice against the other hunters, let alone raise a blade. Sweet found himself beginning to believe that collecting on this job might actually be possible.

As for Sylvanus. Well, Vi was right on that count, too. They'd dealt with his kind before and would probably deal with his kind after, too. If he tried to double-cross them then they'd be ready for it. They'd plan the exchange the way *they* wanted it to go, and if they suspected treachery then they'd plan for that, too. They'd do things like they always had done.

Slow, careful and right.

They finished their meal and mounted up again, riding slowly but evenly, eating the miles up at a steady pace. Sweet was turning over the practicals of that particular issue in his mind—figuring out how they might exchange a live prince for a mountain of gold without complications—when they crested a low rise and the road turned into a small patch of woodland. The sun was shining brightly now and there was something in the road up ahead.

'What the hell is that?' Stover whispered, shading his eyes from the sun with one hand. Beside him, Vi and Daraday squinted down the track. Sweet's eyes weren't as good as any of the others' so he didn't bother trying to spy what the shape was. Instead he just carried on walking his horse carefully down the road towards it, one hand moving towards the sword strapped at his waist and one eye on the trees surrounding the road. They were thin, scraggy things, and didn't provide a lot of room to hide, but the undergrowth was thick and Sweet knew from experience that men could conceal themselves just about anywhere if they tried hard enough.

By the time they were close enough to realise what the shape in the road was, Sweet heard Stover's whisper from just behind him.

'Fuck.'

It pretty much summed things up, as far as Sweet was concerned. It was just as eloquent as it needed to be and it was the tripwire that brought his surprisingly contented mood crashing down all around him. He should've been used to that cliff-drop by now, but somehow he was never truly ready for it. Suddenly the warmth from the sun felt stifling and the birdsong grated at his ears. Sweet's frown returned in full force as his horse neared the hulking shape that lay unmoving across the middle of their path.

It was Bryntas.

Sweet dismounted—still keeping an eye on the trees either side of the road but seeing nothing—and approached the big man. He lay on his side, stretching across the full expanse of the road, with his broad back facing towards them. Sweet barely registered the others dismounting as he crouched down beside the giant's still form. He carefully reached out and pulled at the big man's shoulder, rolling him over.

Half of Bryntas' face was caked in dirt from the road. His nose looked broken and there was bruising around one eye, which were both closed. It looked almost as though he were sleeping it off after an irksome fight.

Except that his throat had been cut.

Blood had caked the road below him, creating a red-brown sticky mess that also stained the big man's clothes. Sweet observed the body in a grim silence. Bryn's sword was still buckled at his side, but the blade looked clean. He hadn't even drawn it, by all accounts.

'What the hell?' Stover whispered again, approaching from Sweet's left shoulder.

'He dead?' Vi asked, from over his right shoulder.

Sweet nodded, either unable or unwilling to say anything. He wasn't sure which. He just stared down at Bryn's dead face, wondering why the hell the big man looked as content in death as Sweet had felt just moments before. The more he looked at that strangely serene expression on Bryntas' face the more Sweet felt angry. A hard anger, cold and calculated, rising from somewhere deep in his stomach.

'Malvadas,' Vi breathed, coating every syllable of the man's name with an icy edge.

'Aye, reckon so.' Sweet nodded again, tearing his eyes away from Bryntas' body and pushing himself to a standing position. His hip ached and his knee popped but he ignored them both. Didn't reckon Bryntas would be bothered by a crumbling hip bone, so it didn't seem right that he should either. He turned to face the others. 'This was a message,' he told them, his voice cold as he pointed down at the body—almost accusing Bryntas' corpse of being in on the threat. 'Mal wants us to turn back.'

'Fuck that,' Stover muttered, still staring down at Bryn's body. He sounded a little nervy, but resolved all the same. Beside him, Daraday looked down at the big man's motionless body with a cold and impassive expression on his face. But Sweet could see the anger in his eyes. Damn it, he could recognise the same anger he felt himself.

'They murdered him,' said Vi, something between sadness and fury in her voice.

'Aye,' Sweet nodded for a third time, trying hard to contain his own growing rage. 'He wants that gold.' Sweet ground his teeth together. 'But we're not gonna let him get it.'

'We can't take him on,' Vi replied, still blankly staring down at Bryntas' corpse.

'We won't have to,' Sweet told her, scanning his eyes across the group. 'We just need to get to the prince before he does.'

*

The four of them buried Bryntas just off the road aways and waited until the Wyn rejoined them. He arrived, trotting his horse to a halt, and surveyed their dirt-caked clothes in silence. His eyes tracked across to the riderless horse—Violent Fey had found it wandering half a mile up the road—and then to the mound of earth just behind them. The Wyn nodded his understanding.

'Malvadas,' Sweet told him, not sure the explanation was entirely necessary but somehow feeling the need to do it anyway. 'We reckon he left a few men behind, waiting for Bryn to fall into their trap.'

'He was a good brawler,' put in Vi, 'but he wasn't much of a woodsman. Poor bastard probably got jumped before he knew what was happening.'

The Wyn nodded again and Sweet sighed loudly. His initial anger had subsided now and he felt a queer sense of emptiness. He felt wronged, but knew that wasn't the case. This was just how things were in their line of work. It was the nature of things. But no matter what he told himself, the void in his chest wouldn't go away. The tightness it brought wouldn't dissipate. It wasn't despair, Sweet reckoned, but it was unpleasant all the same.

'What about our friends to the south?' Sweet asked the Wyn, eager to pull the subject away from their dead companion, lying in a shallow grave not more than a stone's throw away.

'Far behind,' the Wyn reported, waving an arm back down the road. 'Riding slow.'

'Slow, eh?' Sweet considered this for a moment, scratching idly at his chin. 'Might be they're waiting for somebody else to snatch the prince, then they'll swoop in and snatch him themselves when they're on the way back.'

'A good plan,' Vi raised an eyebrow, 'maybe we could take some pointers?'

'Maybe,' Sweet scratched again, 'but we…' he hesitated, then stiffened, 'we don't have the numbers to take him off a larger group. We need to get to the prince before Mal does.'

'And if we don't?'

'Then we'll take pointers,' Sweet agreed, almost growling, remembering Malvadas' twinkling sneer back in Scarvin. 'But one thing is for sure. One way or another, we're not letting that rat-bastard collect this bounty.'

## *Decisions*

THE SUN DISAPPEARED over the next few days, giving way to a dull white sky that always threatened rain but never quite managed it. The wind picked up, chilling both horses and riders as they continued tracking the road north. Even the land itself looked more grey. Bare rock grew more prominent and the patches of grass had turned from a leafy green to more rust-coloured stands of tough-looking plantlife. Grey-purple oceans of coarse heather covered much of the land ahead, which peaked and troughed like an undulating ocean. Larger hills and valleys started taking shape and the road grew less and less well-trodden.

Sweet posted no further scouts. The Wyn's talents were useful enough even when he was riding with them, and Sweet reckoned they'd be safer as a group of five anyway. Well, he reasoned, as safe as we can be, caught between a murderous group of merciless bounty hunters and the behemoth personal guard of an untrustworthy sorcerer. Sweet's dour mood had returned alongside the tempestuous weather, and with every mile he found himself living up to his name more and more. The whole enterprise felt somehow bitter, now.

Bryntas hadn't been a close friend. Sweet wasn't even sure he had any friends—let alone any close ones—but he had always been a reliable companion. Damn it, Sweet thought, that was unfair; he had been more than just reliable. The big man had been about as close to likeable as Sweet reckoned someone in this profession could manage.

And now he was dead. His throat slit by some cutthroat bastard who wouldn't have given the deed a second thought. His body was buried in a shallow grave at the side of a dilapidated trade road in the arse end of nowhere, but not before his pack and pockets had been emptied by those who had buried him. His funeral—such as it was—was attended by four people who'd spent the last few years riding with him, side by side, day by day, but had almost nothing to say as they piled the thin earth over his corpse. No kind words about how he had lived, and no lamenting of his legacy and adventures. The final mourner had arrived late to proceedings and added no more to the matter—though Sweet reasoned that might be a touch unfair given that the Wyn rarely said anything, so he could hardly be expected to deliver Bryntas a long-winded, heartfelt eulogy, could he?

But damn it, Sweet cursed inwardly again.

The big man deserved better.

'Ain't about what you deserve,' Sweet murmured to himself aloud, 'that's the truth of it.'

And truth was a weapon.

'You say summat?' Violent Fey edged her horse a touch closer to Sweet's own. He shook his head and said nothing. After a time she eased on the reins until he pulled away again. Sweet could feel her eyes fixed on his back. He could feel the concern in that icy stare.

She wasn't worried about him, Sweet knew, or even worried about herself. She was worried about everything else. Sweet had always kept things together, even on their toughest assignments. He had always had a plan and they had always pulled through. They did things slow and careful, and that approach paid dividends. They had been in some tight scrapes together sure, but everything had always seemed controlled, somehow. Sweet knew exactly why Vi was worried now.

Nothing about this felt controlled.

Jenrick was dead, drowned in a poxy canal. Bryntas had been murdered in cold blood. They were in the employ of a deadly Vol magicker who could be trusted about as far as he could be thrown. There were enemies all around them and their quarry was still out there, somewhere in the wilderness. The edges of things were starting to fray, and both Sweet and Vi knew that frayed edges could quickly lead to things unravelling altogether.

These worries plagued Sweet's mind as they topped the latest rise. Below them the road angled away to the west, cutting through a sea of purple heather and scattered rocks. It curved away from the long, winding crack of a ravine, the rocks still slick and dark with the morning's rain. Sweet couldn't see the bottom from where his mount was standing but he reckoned it would be a fair way down. The ravine ran a snakelike path to the north, like an angry scar in the fauna of the landscape ahead.

The Wyn heeled his horse beyond Sweet's own and cantered it down towards the curve in the road. He dismounted and casually tossed his reins into the gorse to his left. His horse snorted, but waited dutifully nonetheless.

'He's found summat,' said Stover, hungrily. Sweet nodded and they walked their horses down the slope to where the Wyn was now crouched over the road. As they neared, Sweet could see a multitude of muddy tracks in the bend of the path. Didn't need to have the Wyn's otherworldly talent for tracking to see them either. A blind man could've spotted them.

'Malvadas?' Sweet asked.

The Wyn continued to observe the tracks for a moment longer, then straightened and looked up.

'Yes,' he said, his plain-speaking voice mirrored by his expression. 'And a group on foot.'

'On foot?' Stover cocked his head, his face straining with thought. His eyes took on a dangerous glint once he landed on an idea. 'The prince?'

'Aye,' Sweet muttered, cursing under his breath. 'Looks like they'll catch up to him before we do.'

Stover looked disappointed, Vi looked downbeat and even Daraday took a break from his hardest-bastard-in-the-room routine to look a little disenchanted. Sweet sighed, long and loud, his mind ticking over their next options. Probably weren't any, as it happened. If Mal's group had caught up to the prince then the job was as good as over. The five of them couldn't take on Malvadas' group alone, and trying to steal the prince from his grasp was riddled with risks. Bryntas and Jenrick were dead for naught. Sweet took a deep inhale of cold, blustery air. That bitter feeling was getting worse with every second, and he wondered how long it would take for him to admit aloud that this whole sorry debacle was at an end.

'No,' the Wyn said, cutting his thoughts off sharply.

Stover, Vi and Daraday all looked up at the tattooed tribesman in unison.

'No?' Sweet questioned.

'Tricked,' the Wyn pointed to the mess of muddy tracks, as though the answer were written there as plain as day.

'Tricked?' Sweet queried, 'what do you mean?'

The Wyn returned his attention to the tracks and pointed at several of them—though it all looked like an indistinguishable muddy mess to Sweet—then he took some careful steps along the road as it swept west, pointing at more. He was mumbling something in a language Sweet didn't understand now. Finally, the Wyn pointed back along the road and towards the lip of the ravine.

'Tricked,' he repeated. 'Men on foot make tracks,' he gestured at the road, 'but not go that way.'

'They laid a false trail,' Violent Fey nodded her understanding. She looked around at the openness of the land around them. 'They must've realised they were being followed, so they left a false trail along the road.'

Stover hawked and spat, folding his arms across his chest.

'So where did they go?' he asked.

Sweet turned on his heel and looked to where the Wyn had pointed last. There was a ledge of rock leading up onto the roadside, but it was no wider than a man's feet if he stood with them pressed tight together. Below, the deep drop into the earth below yawned wide. Sweet sighed and gave a shrug.

'That way, I reckon,' he said.

\*

The rocks were slippery and the high walls of the ravine meant they were mostly picking their way through shadows. The ledge was narrower than Sweet had supposed and it seemed to slope away from the safety of the wall, as if trying to topple anyone stupid enough to risk walking along it. The deeper darkness on the other side was a constant reminder of the peril they were in. There was a faint glimmer of light far below, flickering reflections from running water that Sweet could just about hear if he strained his ears.

They'd doubled back to the south at first, finding a stand of rocks where they could tether their mounts out of sight of the road. The ravine would be no place for horses and Sweet didn't fancy leaving anyone behind to watch over them alone. They'd taken a small amount of provisions and only a few weapons. Sweet and Daraday had also shouldered their tents as a last thought—Sweet didn't want Thond and his crew happening upon the horses with all their gear. From there they'd walked back to the curve in the road and eased their way carefully into the chasm. With any luck, the horses would still be there when they reemerged from the darkness.

*If* we reemerge, he thought, swallowing hard as a loose stone slipped out from under one foot. It clicked and clattered as it flipped into the yawning blackness below. A moment of silence followed before a low splash echoed back up to them.

The Wyn had gone first, and was now a few feet ahead of where Sweet was clinging to the rockface. The tribesman had tied any loose clothing tightly around his lean form and seemed perfectly at ease with the deadly drop beside him. Wyns were just built different, Sweet reckoned. Behind Sweet came Vi and then Daraday. Stover was bringing up the rear, though Sweet could hear his muttered curses as he inched his way along the ledge.

'Quiet,' Sweet whispered, as loudly as he dared. Sweat was beading his brow and he wanted to wipe it away, but he didn't dare loosen his grip on the rockface and so let the droplets run their course.

They toiled for nearly an hour, though to Sweet it felt like a lifetime. Every step of the way he regretted bringing his sword, the hilt of which kept digging into his hip or stomach. Or—worse still—it butted against the rockface and threatened to push him over the ledge as he moved along it, like some possessed lever that just wanted to see what happened when a man fell several hundred feet onto the damp, sharp rocks in the darkness below. The gap overhead widened a touch and let in a little more of the bland daylight. Sweet saw that the Wyn had strapped his own blade to his back, trying it so that the pommel barely reached out over the top of one shoulder. Smart move, Sweet thought, wish I'd thought of that. Bit late now, though.

The ledge began to widen and Sweet felt eternal relief as his footing became more assured. The Wyn was waiting for him up ahead on a section of rock that looked just about big enough to hold them all. It wouldn't be a comfortable fit, but no one would be hanging out over the darkness, either. To Sweet, that seemed like a victory worth celebrating.

As Sweet approached, the Wyn raised a solitary finger and pressed it firmly against his lips, indicating silence. Sweet looked baffled for a moment, then realised he could hear something over the natural noises of the ravine. The sounds were muffled and confused by the echo within the chasm, but Sweet could definitely hear something. Were those voices? And what was that? Steel?

The others huddled close behind him and Sweet repeated the Wyn's gesture for quiet. Stover was the last to arrive and he grumbled as he nudged his way onto the relative safety of the rocky shelf.

'What's going on?' he whispered in the semi-darkness, louder than Sweet would've liked. Sweet curbed his anger and gestured for them all to listen. There was a moment of quiet—the only sound was the soft bubbling of running water far below them—and then the sound of voices drifted to them again, louder this time.

Suddenly there was a great shout and the unmistakable ring of steel. A man cried out and the ravine was suddenly awash with sounds, distorted as they echoed against one another. Men grunted and bellowed. There was a crashing noise and a scuffing sound as something scraped against rock. Someone screamed, the sound piercingly loud in the confines of the chasm, then it was cut short with a wet gurgle. There were thuds and grunts and clangs and cries, and weird echoes that sounded through the ravine like melancholy ghosts of the chaos.

Then the noise faded, and only those ghostly echoes were left murmuring within the depths of the darkness. The Wyn listened a moment longer, then met Sweet's eyes and gestured for them to continue. Sweet nodded and turned to the others, repeating the gesture again and leading them back out onto the rocky ledge.

Sweet was breathing heavily as he followed the Wyn along the ledge. His heart was racing and he slipped on another loose stone, muttering a curse aloud despite his own insistence on quiet.

Then he rounded a corner and the rocky ledge was suddenly a flat-topped open space. The rock wall above opened out and daylight spilled onto the stone. Puddles of water had coalesced and reflected the light further still, illuminating moss-covered walls and jagged brown faces of rock. Water ran in from above in a frothing stream that crossed the space in a jagged line before tumbling off the ledge into the darkness below.

There were bodies everywhere. Doubled over and bloodied. The man closest to where Sweet was standing had a sword right through his stomach, half of which poked out from his back, the blade tip slick with red. Two others lay nearby, their dead eyes staring up at the overcast sky above. More bodies were scattered further about the rocky shelf, one so close to the edge that it would only take a nudge to send it spinning into the darkness below. Sweet saw that about half of the men were garbed in simple cloaks of dark wool, but he could see more expensive clothing beneath. The clothes were travel-stained and worn thin, but expensive nonetheless. The other half were dressed more appropriately for the dark confines of a muddy ravine. They wore battered old travelling gear and were laden with knives and close hand weapons. Bounty hunters, from the looks of them. Some of Mal's men? Maybe the wily bastard hadn't fallen for the prince's false trail after all. Or not totally, at least, judging by the number of dead hunters lying on the rocky ground. Sweet counted five in total. It looked like Malvadas had split his force, sending half of his men into the ravine and taking the others along the road. Another reckless move, Sweet thought, staring at the bloodied bodies.

The prince's men—which Sweet felt he could safely assume were the more well-dressed corpses—looked to have fared little better. Sweet counted seven dead men in total, including one slumped up against the rock wall with his chin resting on his chest. Sweet started to piece together some of the noises they had just heard, too. No doubt one or more men from both sides had taken a tumble off the ledge. The others had fought, blade to blade. Stabbing and thrusting until their opponents were dead.

But not everyone in the little expanse of cold, slippery stone was dead.

Three men were still standing. A raven-haired youngster and an older man, who looked to be about Sweet's age, were backed against the rocky wall. The older man clutched one hand to his stomach and Sweet could see blood leaking between his fingers. A grim-faced bounty hunter stalked towards them—Sweet recognised the man from Arc's tavern back in Scarvin—a bloodied sword in his hand.

'Back my lord!' the older man urged the raven-haired youngster aside, still doubled over and clutching at the wound in his stomach. Sweet didn't need to be a surgeon to know it looked like a bad one.

My lord? Sweet turned over what the older man had said. The younger man must be The Crown Prince!

The grey-haired warrior suddenly charged at the hunter, who was taken by surprise. The two men grappled and in the melee the old man's sword slashed across the bounty hunter's arm, drawing a cry of pain. The hunter quickly regained his composure and landed a punch to the older man's midriff, folding him in two and causing him to cough blood, the wound in his stomach spurted more still. The grey-haired man sank to his knees and put out a hand to steady himself.

The bounty hunter backed away, giving himself enough space to examine the wound on his arm. Satisfied the cut wasn't too deep, he turned back to finish the job.

But the raven-haired youngster had stepped into his path. Unarmed, the prince faced the bounty hunter with an expression of grim resolve. His fingers opened and closed into fists. Behind him, the old man tried in vain to rise to his feet, but his strength was rapidly draining away and he instead settled for grasping towards the youngster.

'My lord,' the man breathed, blood staining his lips and chin. 'Get back…behind me.'

Sweet found himself strangely impressed. Even mortally wounded as he was, this greybeard warrior's only thought was to protect his charge. Not so long ago Sweet might've chalked that up as foolishness, but now he found himself wondering what could inspire such devotion in a man. Especially a dying man. And then there was the prince himself. Barely older than Daraday, the raven-haired youngster stood defiant against an enemy who stood nearly a head taller and was armed with a sword. The blade of which was already slick with the blood of the prince's companions. That took nerve, and no mistake.

The bounty hunter bellowed and charged at the prince.

The prince stepped in to meet him, catching the man by surprise and giving him no room to properly swing his sword. The prince grabbed at his wrist and threw his head forwards, butting the bounty hunter square in the face. The man grunted and fell back a step, blood streaming from his broken nose. Stunned as he was, he didn't have a chance to set his feet and the prince followed in and gave him a violent shove. The bounty hunter went spinning backwards, the sword falling from his grip to clatter onto the stone. His arms flailed as he tipped over the edge of the rocky ledge, he screamed as he fell into the darkness. The sound was cut short by a squelching thud.

The prince, breathing heavily, turned to kneel beside his older companion.

'Carthin,' the prince urged, placing a tender hand on the man's shoulder, 'Carthin,' he repeated. But the man was dead.

The prince looked around and suddenly laid eyes on Sweet and his crew for the first time. He scrambled around for the bounty hunter's fallen sword and pushed himself to his feet, adopting what looked like a fencing pose and levelling the point of the blade at Sweet's eyes.

'Come on then you miserable Vol bastards,' he spat at them, his dark eyes blazing. 'You'll not take me alive.'

'We ain't Vols, boy,' Sweet sighed, raising his palms. Beside him he felt Stover bristle. 'Lower your blade.'

'If you're not Vols then you're working for them,' the prince kept the sword raised, his eyes flashing with anger. 'It's all the same to me.'

'We ain't even with these bastards,' Sweet said softly, motioning to the corpses of the fallen bounty hunters. He felt a grim anger, dull but hot, wash over him as he thought of Bryntas. 'They murdered one of ours just yesterday.'

The prince wavered a little at that, but kept the blade levelled at Sweet all the same.

'Who are you, then?' he demanded, taking half a step forward.

'We're here to take you home,' Stover grinned, fanning out to Sweet's side and letting his hand fall slowly towards the hilt of his own weapon. The prince tracked the movement with the raised sword.

'Easy boy,' Sweet kept his palms raised, he turned his head. 'Stover, stay where you are.'

'Why?' Stover shrugged, 'we can take him.'

'You do that, you'll be doing it alone,' Sweet growled. 'Reckon you can do better'n that feller did?' he motioned to the part of the rocky ledge the last bounty hunter had fallen from. Stover's grin faltered and he scowled over at Sweet.

'Well what're we doing, then?' he barked.

'We're talking,' Sweet replied sharply, then he turned back to face the prince. Sweet softened his tone once more and held the young man's gaze. 'Just talking, is all.'

'Then talk,' the prince shook the swordpoint at Sweet. His eyes were blazing but his arm was steady. Sweet took a deep breath.

'We're bounty hunters,' he said, 'that much is true enough. But we ain't with these bastards,' he motioned with one hand towards the corpse of one of Malvadas' men. 'They're part of another crew.'

'It hardly seems to matter,' the prince snarled, 'if your objective is to take me captive then it doesn't matter who your damn friends are.'

'Can't argue with that, lad,' Sweet tried a faint smile. The prince stood, unwavering. 'But think about what you're saying. There're five of us and one of you, and you're tired, and we're not.'

'Then try and take me, you old bastard!' the prince hissed.

Sweet was impressed again, despite the insult hurled his way. He'd expected the prince to be a pampered nobleman, frightened and meek in the face of capture or death. Out of his element and hunted by his enemies. Instead he was defiant, bold and holding his fear in check. This boy had nerves of steel. Sweet felt oddly proud of the lad. It was a bizarre feeling.

'If it comes to it, we will,' said Sweet, still speaking softly. 'But if it's all the same then I'd rather we did this without another scrap.'

The prince only glared back in the semi-darkness of the ravine. He'd been holding the sword out for awhile now and Sweet reckoned his arm must be getting a little tired, even if he wasn't showing it. At last he saw a flicker of doubt cross the younger man's face and he slowly lowered the weapon. Sweet could feel the grin returning to Stover's face beside him and he felt a twinge of distaste.

'Who hired you?' the prince asked, his voice more even-tempered now.

'A man called Sylvanus,' Sweet answered. 'A Vol magicker.'

The prince scoffed.

'And you trust him to pay my bounty?'

Sweet shrugged.

'We figure that we'll cross that bridge when we come to it. Got bigger problems right now.'

'Oh?' the prince feigned concern.

'Aye,' Sweet nodded, ignoring the mocking tone. He gestured to the bodies again. 'This lot aren't *all* of that other crew. And I can't see their leader among the dead, so I reckon he was with the group that followed your false trail back on the road. That was a nice play, by the way.'

The prince's face softened a little and sadness filled his eyes as he glanced down at the body of the older man behind him, still in a kneeling position with his head resting on his chest.

'That was Carthin's idea,' the prince whispered. 'We knew we were being hunted, he thought we'd throw them off the scent.'

'Smart man,' Sweet nodded, 'and it worked, too. I reckon this is only half of the crew that were hunting you, the rest of them followed the false trail.'

'Not you, though,' the prince looked up again. Sweet saw defiance there, still burning strong, but beneath it all a growing acceptance that he was cornered. Defeated. Even so, Sweet reckoned the youngster still wouldn't go lightly. One wrong word and that sword point would come roaring back up. Sweet stayed silent, but offered a faint conciliatory smile by way of a response. The prince cocked his head suddenly.

'What's he paying you?' he asked.

This time it was Sweet's turn to be caught by surprise.

'What's it matter to you?' Stover snarled.

'Because I want to know what my life is worth to a Vol dog,' the prince shot back. Stover glared at him but offered no reply.

'Five hundred thousand in gold,' Sweet answered, impressed further still by the way the boy was handling himself. Truth be told, it helped that he was pissing off Stover. That never failed to endear.

'I'll double it,' the prince said, straightening his back and meeting Sweet's eyes. It was a firm gaze. A gaze that dared Sweet to call him a liar.

'Bullshit,' Stover coughed out a hacking laugh.

'I will,' the prince replied, not breaking eye contact with Sweet. 'One million in gold.'

'For what?' Stover scoffed. 'Letting you go?'

'For seeing me to safety,' the prince replied instantly, drawing another hacking chortle from the grimy hunter. Sweet only stared back at the boy, narrowing his eyes a little at this new game. 'One million in gold,' the prince continued, talking as though a plan was forming in his mind. Maybe it was. 'If you see me safely across the border to my allies in Thradonia.'

A charged quiet followed the prince's offer, punctuated only by the low burble of water below and—eventually—the scoffing, hacking laughter of Stover once more.

'What utter bullshit,' the bounty hunter crowed. 'This royal prick doesn't have a bent copper coin to his name and he wants to offer us a million in gold. Let's take him now, Sweet!'

'Stay where you are!' Sweet barked, holding out a hand before returning his thoughtful gaze to the prince. The young man had made an impression on him. The cunning he must've used to get out of Levitan. To make it this far at all. The way his men had laid down their lives for him. The way he had killed the final bounty hunter, stepping in to face him when every instinct must've been screaming at him to back away. The way he'd spoken to Sweet and his crew in the face of certain capture or death. The lad had stones. Not only that, but he was damn near right about the rest of it, too. Sweet trusted Sylvanus as far as he could throw the man. The gold he'd promised was a myth and Sweet knew it. There were warriors and fighters who wanted them dead, both ahead of them and behind them. Two of his crew had already been put in the ground and for what? If they turned back now they'd be two men short and they'd return home with empty pockets, if they returned home at all.

The whole thing was fucked. All of it.

In the semi-darkness of the dank ravine, Sweet felt a deep well of frustration rise within him. It must've been building, maybe even before the job had started—maybe even for years—because its release felt cathartic to the extreme. Like a great weight that had been pressing down on him suddenly lifted and he could move freely again. A tightness that had gripped his chest loosened and when he breathed it felt like fresh air, crisp and whole, for the first time in decades.

'You know,' he said, meeting the prince's eye. 'I reckon you've got yourself a deal.'

There were gasps from his crew.

'What the fuck?' Stover cried.

'Sweet—' Vi sounded concerned.

No words from Daraday or the Wyn.

Nothing much new there, Sweet thought, with a wry smile.

The prince himself looked shocked, but quickly recovered as he tried to figure out if he was being tricked. His gambit had clearly been to stall for time, so never in a thousand years had he expected for his offer to actually be taken up.

'We do?' he asked at last, his tone tentative at best.

'Aye,' Sweet nodded, more firmly this time. 'We do. We'll get you to the border and into Thradonia, for one million in gold.'

'Sweet, he don't *have* a million in gold!' Stover protested, his voice shrill with disbelief. 'He don't have—'

'Then he'll get it,' Sweet interrupted, he locked his eyes on the prince's own once more. 'Right?'

The prince took a moment and then straightened again, adopting that regal look the same way Sweet himself might have thrown a cloak around his shoulders.

'Right,' the prince agreed.

'Sweet?' Violent Fey's voice sang with worry, 'what're you doing? Are you sure about this?'

'Aye,' Sweet nodded, feeling more sure than he had done since the moment they'd ridden out of Levitan. 'Sylvanus was never gonna pay us, Vi. And we never would've made him pay, either. He's not like the others who've tried to con us out of a bounty before. He's a damn magicker! A magicker with the Vol army at his command. We've more chance of getting blood from a stone than getting payment from that slimy bastard!'

'Then why not just go back?' Vi demanded, her expression tightening. 'Turn around and walk away?'

'Vi we can't do that,' Sweet's shoulders sagged, 'Bryn would've—'

'We ain't turning back!' Stover protested, near shaking with rage now, 'and we ain't taking this prick anywhere but back to Levitan!' he motioned to the prince. 'And—'

'Stover shut the fuck up!' Vi stormed, her anger blazing. Stover cowered away from her, stunned by the suddenness of her redhot fury. 'It's your damn fault we're in this mess in the first place, so for once in your damn life just shut the fuck up!'

Stover recovered from the heat of her rage quickly and looked ready to fire an angry retort back when Daraday's voice suddenly cut through the echoes of Vi's outburst.

'Sweet's right,' he said, his voice firm and steady. The group turned to face him, confused and astonished. Daraday only shrugged under their stares. 'He's right,' he repeated. 'If the magicker wasn't gonna pay us, then this is the next best way of getting...somethin' out of all this.' He looked down at his feet, speaking his next words more softly. 'Bryn shouldn't die for nothing.'

Sweet felt a surge of emotion rise in his chest and for a moment wanted nothing more than to comfort the lad. But he resisted it, and instead tried to let his rationalities take control again. This whole enterprise was a mess, but the boy had spoken the truth. The only way they got out of this with something to show for it now was to take the prince up on his offer. Whether he was good for one million gold pieces was almost immaterial. Sweet reckoned they'd be rewarded to some degree, and even a modest purse would be better than whatever Sylvanus had planned for their triumphant return.

'What about you?' Sweet raised an eyebrow at the Wyn. The tribesman stared back at him, his expression blank as the sliver of sky overhead.

'You go, I follow,' he said, simply.

'Vi?' Sweet turned to face her. She still looked angry. There was confusion there, too. She was torn again. Torn between following Sweet's lead and what felt like the more sane idea of just abandoning the job altogether. But after a moment she relented, her shoulders sagged and she shrugged, sighing loudly.

'Fine,' she said. 'Out of one madness and into another.'

'Like old times,' Sweet agreed with a wry grin. He turned back to face the prince. 'Looks like the deal is on.'

'Like hell it is,' Stover interjected. 'Don't I get a vote in this?'

'As it happens, Stover,' Sweet smiled his best shit-eating grin at the other man, but his eyes stayed cold as ice, daring the other man to keep pushing his luck. 'No, you fucking don't. Vi's right, this mess is your doing as it is. At least this way you might see some gold in your pocket at the end of the ride, instead of some steel in your belly.'

Sweet's voice had hardened as he spoke, his eyes never leaving Stover's own. The other man fell into a sullen quiet, his pock-marked face a picture of surly petulance. Sweet ignored him and turned back to the prince.

'Now what?' the raven-haired youngster asked, the stolen sword still in hand and looking more than a little confused himself. As though he couldn't quite believe what had just happened. Sweet reckoned it would be awhile before he could wrap his own head around it, for that matter.

'Now,' Sweet sighed loudly, the noise ending as a low whistle. 'Now we're all being hunted.'

# PART TWO

*The hunted*

# *Hunted*

THE NEXT FEW days passed in near silence, with members of Sweet's crew speaking only to ask a question pertinent to their travels. Sweet didn't mind the quiet—he even found it something of a relief. It gave him space to think. He'd expected their journey to be fraught with the same kind of heated exchanges as they'd had inside the darkness of the gorge. Instead a brooding silence had settled amongst the group, with each of them clammed up inside their own heads, alone with their own thoughts.

A large part of that had to do with the fact that they had faced an immediate setback in their new quest. Sweet had sent the Wyn back along the ravine to see if it was safe to collect the horses. The tribesman had returned a few hours later, as the daylight was waning, only to report that their horses had been taken. It was safe to assume that the thieves had been led by Malvadas, no doubt having figured out that his own pursuit of the prince was a phantom chase. The Wyn had also reported seeing more, fresh tracks heading back up the road leading north. When the pieces of that particular puzzle were put together, it looked like Malvadas had doubled back, found—and stolen—the horses belonging to Sweet's crew, and then ridden at speed back up the road. Perhaps hoping to find the other end of the gorge and cut them off as they tried to emerge from the darkness of the ravine. After all, that's exactly what Sweet would've done.

As soon as this information was absorbed, the group set off again through the ravine, picking their way along the ledge in a bid to outrace Malvadas to the far end. They had managed it within just another half hour, emerging onto more rocky outcrops scattered with gorse and heather. The sun was setting and there was no sign of any hunters, so they had angled their route to the east before cutting north once more.

That had been three days ago, and the quiet that had descended over the group still remained. Though Sweet reckoned he didn't need to hear their words to know their thoughts. The Wyn remained as impassive as ever, smoothly moving from job to job without so much as a word or a flicker to his expression. Sweet reckoned he could've declared they were to ride against the entire Vol army and the tattooed tribesman would've simply nodded, sharpened his blade and fallen in line.

Stover still seethed, his anger as plain to read as an open wound gone bad. It had about the same stink to it, too. He spent half his time glaring balefully at the prince and the other half glaring balefully at Sweet. It didn't take a scholar to understand where his mind was. In truth, Sweet was beyond caring. The man was a prick, let him seethe and fester all he wants.

Violent Fey had looked troubled, but it hadn't lasted long and she had soon settled back into her usual calculated demeanour. Sweet reckoned she was still concerned by the sudden change to their plans, but that she was dealing with it in the only way she knew how. She was turning her focus onto how to make this new venture a success. If nothing else, she was reliable, was Vi. Sweet was damn grateful for that.

Daraday was almost unreadable, but Sweet had a keen sense for people and could tell that the boy was on the same page as Violent Fey. Now that the decision had been made, he was getting his head down and getting on with the task at hand. Sweet was damn grateful for that, too.

The prince himself was just as visible to Sweet's keen eye. He still walked tall, holding his head high, but Sweet could tell it was mostly an act. The young man was trying to project an air of regality. He was still trying to prove he was able to make good on his promise of riches in exchange for a safe escort into Thradonia. Truth be told, Sweet didn't much care whether he could or not. They'd made their call now, and there'd be no reneging on this one. Beneath that regal mask though, Sweet reckoned the lad was tired. There were deep, dark rings under his eyes and his face looked drawn and sallow. It was no wonder really—his family had been deposed and killed, his countrymen had been butchered damn near to a man, he'd fled a city under siege and he'd spent weeks in the wilderness trying to evade hunters of all codes and creeds. If anything it spoke volumes that the young man still had the strength of mind to even try to maintain the facade of control.

Sweet himself had adopted his usual frown as they picked their way over the bare rock—as though troubled by a tricky puzzle. If any of the group were to look at him, they'd see a man figuring out the details of an already carefully put-together plan of action.

If they looked a little harder they'd see that—underneath it all— Sweet's mind was roiling.

In the three days since they'd taken the prince on as an employer rather than a captive, Sweet had had plenty of time to cool off. All of his anger and his frustration had burned away almost as quickly as it had come, and it had left him with a sea of doubts churning away inside his head. They nibbled away at his sanity like a swarm of persistent midges. Chief amongst them was a simple, blunt question.

What the hell were they doing?

With the decision they'd made, Sweet and his crew had essentially pitted themselves against the might of the entire Vol empire. The prince was—to the Vols at least—a fugitive. An enemy of the state. Now Sweet and his crew were aiding that fugitive. He doubted if the Vols would make a distinction between them now. That thought was ugly enough on its own.

Sweet had never had time for politics. So why had he embroiled them in such a volatile situation? He'd never had time for cheap notions of honour or "doing the right thing" either. Those things were for poets and fools—as he had so often lamented himself. So why had he felt a sense of relief when he'd agreed to see the prince to safety? Was it even relief that'd he'd felt? Or was it something even more stupid? Some ridiculous sense of pride, maybe? Pride that was likely to get them all killed. What good was pride to a dead man?

Who cares? Sweet thought, stepping up over a trickling stream of water as it cascaded down the rocks they were clambering over. It's done. This is our job now. Time spent focussing on *why* it was their job would only serve to get them captured or killed. And Sweet didn't relish either outcome.

'I suppose at some point I should thank you,' the prince's voice cut through Sweet's thoughts. The younger man had moved alongside him, lithe and quiet, and was looking at him carefully with piercing grey eyes.

'For what?' Sweet grunted, climbing up another stone and following the Wyn as he picked a way through the rocks.

'For saving me,' the prince replied.

Sweet scoffed at that.

'Don't reckon you needed saving,' he muttered, 'killed that last hunter right enough.'

'And then I'd have been on my own,' said the prince. He swallowed. 'Carthin was the one in charge, I just followed his lead.'

Sweet saw the pain on the other man's face. Heard it in his voice, too. That the old soldier had been special to the prince was in no doubt. It made Sweet a little uncomfortable but he softened his frown all the same.

'Not heard of a prince taking orders 'fore,' he said, offering a conciliatory chuckle. 'Usually the one givin' 'em, I reckon.'

The prince gave a wry smile.

'If I had done that we never would've made it out of the city,' he said, then his face darkened. 'I wanted to face the bastards as they stormed through the gates.'

'Fair,' Sweet nodded thoughtfully, wondering if the boy's father had done the same, at the end. By all accounts the king had cowered until the last, cut down as he threw servants and chambermaids into the path of his attackers. It seemed that his son held more romantic notions of staging a last stand. 'But your man Carthin was right,' Sweet told him, 'his way you got to stay alive.'

'And fight for my kingdom's freedom another day,' the prince murmured, his voice hardening as he spoke. Sweet said nothing to that. Wasn't much to say. The Vols were in charge of Pratia now and there wasn't much anybody could do about it, least of all a fugitive prince out in the wilderness with only a ragged bunch of bounty hunters for company. All the same, the steel in the lad's voice was there. He was determined. He was resolute.

Even if he was naive.

'Your man—Carthin—was leading you to the mountains, eh?' Sweet asked, more to change the subject than anything else. 'The pass next to the old mine?'

'Yes,' the prince nodded. 'He said we could get into Thradonia through the pass, move west for a while and then turn south to make for the capital. I've friends in the Thradonian court. If they know I'm alive they'll help me.'

Sweet said nothing to that, either. He didn't know much about politics, or the nature of kings and queens, but he wondered if the Thradonian king would truly give two shits about reinstating a renegade prince to the throne of Pratia. Especially considering that his own kingdom now directly bordered the newly-conquered Vol territory. After all, the Vols were not renowned for being nice neighbours to have—just ask a Pratian. Sweet reckoned that—before long—the Thradonians would have bigger problems to concern themselves with than the fate of a powerless, refugee royal. But—he thought—best keep that notion to myself. Truth could be a weapon, after all.

'But,' the prince sighed, filling the silence. 'We need to get there first.' He looked back across at Sweet. 'Carthin said it would be tough going.'

'Aye,' Sweet nodded, grimacing as his hip sent a twinge of pain coursing up his side, 'can't argue wi' that,' he glanced up at the sky, which was thick with clouds once more. 'And we need to get there before the winter sets in, otherwise the pass'll be blocked.'

The prince nodded soberly. He looked even more weary now and the sea of doubts inside Sweet's head boiled all the harder for the sight. For the first time since they had met him, the prince looked suddenly forlorn.

'Maybe I should hand myself over,' he whispered, more musing to himself than speaking to Sweet. 'It all seems so bloody bleak, anyway.'

'Maybe we shoulda done that,' Stover put in, climbing beyond them and puffing taffa smoke over one shoulder. He turned his head and spat, the brownish-yellow glob landing just in front of where the prince was walking. 'Then we could be climbing a mountain o' gold instead o' these fucking rocks.'

The prince said nothing, but his face fell further still.

'What's done is done,' Sweet heard himself say, his voice surprisingly soft. 'Besides,' he offered another weak smile, 'you'll be giving us an even bigger mountain o' gold once all this is over.'

The prince brightened a little and gave another wry smile.

'Not sure he wants my gold,' he muttered, motioning up the slope towards Stover.

'Him?' Sweet chuckled. 'Ignore him,' he said, 'the man's a miserable bastard.'

A hint of smile cracked at the corner of the prince's mouth and Sweet saw past all the tiredness and exhaustion, all the grime and the dirt, all the pain and the stress. He saw the face of a young man who'd no doubt got himself into plenty of mischief as a boy, and then tested the patience of more'n a few folks as he'd grown older. A man with strong features and intelligent eyes. A handsome young sort—and royalty no less—who probably caused highborn maidens to go weak at the knees and other young noblemen to turn green with envy. A man who had escaped the hellfires of war but still taken the time to leave behind a token of remembrance for his fallen countrymen. The lad had heart, that much was for sure.

'So,' Sweet sighed, changing the subject. 'Should we address you as "your highness"? Or "your majesty?" I never was one for paying much attention to how royalty works.'

The prince's cracked smile grew a little wider.

'Call me Orsen,' he said.

*

147

As the group travelled further north, the heather slowly began to fade into the distance behind them. The slopes grew steeper, the plantlife more stunted and the rocks bigger and more precarious to climb. At one point they even had to scale a sheer face of some twelve feet in height—the only alternative was to swing wide of it, but Sweet reckoned the ridge spanned a mile or two both east and west and he was unwilling to lose the time trying to find a way around.

The weather continued to provide a grey and grizzly backdrop for their struggles. The clouds bunched in angry, slate-coloured masses before unleashing a torrent of driving rain each time they grew too fat and too encumbered. The wind whipped and howled as they climbed ever higher and the cold was biting harder than ever.

Hunting became nearly impossible, though Daraday managed to bring down a brace of hill rabbits with Jenrick's old bow. The animals were scrawny at best, but the stew they supplemented at that evening's camp went down a treat all the same. Sweet was glad they'd not left all of their supplies with the horses before entering the ravine or they'd have really been in trouble. They'd taken winter clothing from the dead men inside the gorge, as well as stocking up on whatever provisions they could scrounge from the corpses. By Sweet's reckoning they'd do alright if they made it to the mountain pass before the winter snows came. A nervous glance skywards told him that might be sooner than he'd like, but he kept that thought to himself. No doubt the others had considered it themselves, anyway.

The edge seemed to have completely fallen away from Vi and Daraday now. Both of the dagger-wielding hunters seemed to have accepted their new job and were fully engaged in seeing it through. Stover was still sulking like a pissed-off child and spent most of his evenings glaring across the campfire at the prince. They didn't see much of the Wyn—save for those evening camps—as Sweet had instructed him to watch their trail for signs of pursuit.

So far the hooded tribesman had reported little of note. If Thond and his men were tracking them then they were still far enough behind not to worry about just yet. Sweet didn't fancy the big bastard would chance the ravine, so it seemed likely that they would've had to take the longer route around. And it appeared that Malvadas and his crew hadn't pursued them on foot after all. That was good news, because it meant there would be no immediate threat from the gold-toothed bounty hunter either. But it was bad news, because the trade road—pitted and rough though it might be—still continued for a way north yet. Not to mention they had horses. That meant Mal could ride his men as far north as he wanted and then either circle back on foot to cut them off, or he could simply wait for them to come to him. Sweet knew what he would do if the roles were reversed. Setting a trap for your prey was much easier than tracking them through the wilderness. Either way it put them in deep shit. Sweet just didn't know how deep, right now.

*Prey.* The word sounded strange in Sweet's thoughts. That's what we are now, though. We're the prey. The hunted. It felt equal parts exhilarating and terrifying at the same time and again Sweet found himself wondering if he'd lost his senses. Strangely, the notion that he might've gone completely mad wasn't entirely unpleasant.

Sweet glanced over at where the prince was clambering up a steep pile of rocks, the man was saying something to Violent Fey. Sweet watched as Vi said something in return. She didn't smile—Vi never bloody smiled— but Sweet reckoned he saw a slight curl at the corner of her mouth. She liked the lad.

And why not? Sweet considered. He was a likeable sort, after all. Since travelling with their little crew he'd not shirked any of the camp duties, nor had he slowed them down in any way. He'd not been too brash, nor too quiet, both of which could put anyone off a man. He'd also not spoken any further of his proposed offer, or how he might come into possession of such a vast amount of money—considering that he was currently residing in the wild without a coin to his name. Sweet liked that. Most men in his situation would've felt the need to constantly reinforce the prize at the end of the road, fearful that their newfound companions might have a change of heart. The prince, though, seemed to understand that once Sweet's crew set their mind to something, they didn't need reminding *why* they were doing it, over and over.

Well, except maybe Stover, of course. He was the one member of the crew that didn't seem to like their latest addition. One night, as the campfire burned low and the group had been picking at the remnants of their meagre meal, Stover had asked the prince about the gold he'd promised them. Before Orsen could answer, Vi had cut him off—cold and sharp—quieting Stover just as she had done in the ravine. She'd only said three words—three and a bit, really—but they had been delivered so finitely and with a quiet ferocity that had stopped the conversation dead.

'He'll get it.'

The grim-faced bounty hunter had grunted, scrunched his face up and then shuffled off into the darkness muttering something about needing to piss.

Sweet watched Orsen clamber to the top of the rocky outcrop and turn on his heel, offering a hand out to Daraday. The young bounty hunter took it and the two men worked together to climb over the rim of the stone. Almost like he's part of the crew, Sweet thought.

From up ahead the Wyn came climbing down a tricky-looking section of boulders—he stepped lithely, barely even glancing at where he needed to place his feet and Sweet was reminded that this kind of terrain must've been second nature to him. Not much was known about Wyns, save that they were nomadic by nature and kept to the high and cold places of the world. It was no wonder then, that the Wyn in their crew seemed completely at ease in such a hostile environment.

'What is it?' Sweet asked gruffly, carefully picking his way around a scraggly bush that appeared to have thorns poking at every conceivable angle.

'High ground,' the Wyn gestured over the next rise. All Sweet could see right now was the grey blotches of sky above, but he knew that the tribesman meant there was high ground a little further on. He looked to the east.

'Reckon you'll be able to see the trade road?' he asked the Wyn.

The tattooed man only nodded, his eyes glinting from the shadows of his hooded cloak.

'Good,' Sweet nodded, 'how far?'

'Nightfall.'

'Good,' Sweet nodded again. 'Get up there and see what you can see. Find us somewhere to camp, too. We'll meet you in a few hours.'

The tribesman nodded and moved away, climbing back up the treacherous rocks as though he were striding across flat grassland. He passed the others and eventually clambered from view. Sweet huffed and continued struggling up the rise.

Time to see just how deep the shit is.

*

After they'd crested the rise, the ground dropped steeply into a narrow gully with a dark and muddy bottom, before rising again even more steeply on the far side. Already they could see the Wyn, close to the top of the far slope and picking his trail with expert precision. The rain had started again, but it was little more than a drizzle. Sweet was tired and sweating from their exertions and the cool touch of rainwater on his face wasn't entirely unwelcome.

'Fuckssake,' Stover breathed, standing with his hands on his hips. His latest papersmoke had been discarded now and he scrunched his nose as he stared up at the challenge ahead. 'How much further?'

'A way yet,' Sweet told him, trying to calm his own breathing. Unwilling to talk to the other man, he instead transferred his gaze to the west. The land was lower over there, with a dense patch of trees marking a forest far in the distance. Somewhere within that woodland—Sweet knew—was the road north. He switched his eyes back to the steep climb ahead of them. 'No use standing here moaning about it,' he muttered, picking his way down into the gully.

The going was tough, and the rain—falling a little heavier now and drawing curses from all of them—made it even tougher. The rocks became slippery, and where there wasn't rock there was dirt that quickly turned to mud – and that was even slippier still. Twice Sweet lost his footing, the first time crashing his knee against a jutting stone. A jarring pain cannoned up his leg and he gritted his teeth against it. The second time he felt himself falling backwards, his eyes went wide and his mouth opened ready to cry out, but a strong hand clamped around his wrist and pulled him back to the relative safety of the slope itself. He nodded his thanks to Vi, who nodded back, stern and grim-faced as ever. She slowly released her grip and they continued their climb.

Eventually they made it up the craggy hillside and the ground levelled off for a bit. They gathered their breath and trudged wearily towards the next rise. It looked a little less daunting than the one they'd just tackled, but by all accounts they were all too tired to complain anyway. Beyond that slope, Sweet could see a stand of enormous grey rocks, jutting high and wide like sentinels on the hillside.

The high ground that the Wyn had spoken of.

Somewhere in those rocks, the tribesman would have a campfire going for them all. Warm and welcoming and shielded from the biting wind and driving rain. Just the thought of it brought a shiver of pleasure to Sweet's cold, wet frame and spurred him on.

'Regretting your decision yet?' Violent Fey asked him as they clambered up a stretch of scree-covered slope. She had a glint in her eye that Sweet recognised as her version of mockery.

'Maybe,' he grinned through the rain, with more than a little truth to it. 'But damn if this doesn't feel like living.'

'The Sweet I know would've laughed at such a thing,' she told him drily.

'Reckon I'm mellowing in my old age,' he grinned again. 'Or maybe it's just all this fresh air.'

'Lost your senses, is what it is,' grumbled Stover, from just below them.

'You say summat, Stover?' Sweet called down the slope. Beside him, Vi shifted her feet a little. Not enough to have done it obviously, but enough to send a small scattering of stones and pebbles down towards the surly bounty hunter.

'You heard me, right enough,' Stover breathed, reaching where they were standing. He straightened and leaned in close, narrowing one eye at Sweet. 'Losing sight of what's real, I reckon.'

'Oh?' Vi raised an eyebrow, 'and what's *real,* Stover?'

'Ain't none of this, that's for damn sure,' Stover gestured to the hillside. His eyes landed on where Orsen was climbing the slope. 'We don't bed down with our bounties, we *hunt* 'em. We hunt 'em, bring 'em back—warm or otherwise—and we get *paid.*'

'We'll get paid,' Sweet told him, looking away as though he was surveying the landscape. He cleared his throat. 'Just a change of employer, is all.'

Stover grumbled again and pushed past them, still muttering about lost senses and what was real. Sweet swapped a glance with Violent Fey and she narrowed her eyes a touch. It didn't look like Stover would come round anytime soon, that look said.

Sweet found it hard to disagree.

*

They entered the rocks through a small archway. Two enormous boulders had fallen into one another, creating a gap between them through which they could all squeeze through right enough. Once through, they were faced with more huge boulders, but most of the stone lay flat and they could see a fairly straight path through. To the east, the rocks rose in a series of giant steps, eventually plateauing again around half a mile away. Sweet reckoned the Wyn would've had a damn good view of things from up there and was eager to catch up with the tribesman to learn about their would be captors. Though, at this point, Sweet reasoned that only Orsen would get to sample captivity at the hands of their pursuers. After all, the contract laid down by Lennick Sylvanus was only for the prince's capture. It didn't say anything about the fate of anyone assisting him. Sweet and his crew were just obstacles now. Bodies that needed climbing over in order to get to the prince.

Shaking such sombre thoughts from his head, Sweet led the group through the passage of boulders until they came out onto a wide, almost circular section surrounded by a sheer wall of rock on one side. Part of the cliff was eroded inwards and a dark cave lay beyond. The shadowy cave mouth cut deep into the rock and disappeared into blackness. Sweet paused and scrunched his nose up against the wind. The air smelled damp—though the rain had stopped now—but there was something else, too. Something that smelled a bit musty, somehow.

Sweet had stopped to sniff at the air so suddenly that Stover nearly clattered into the back of him. The man swore loudly as he sidestepped, nearly tripping over a jutting shelf of stone in the ground below their feet.

'Shut up,' Sweet told him, speaking quietly and straining his ears. He could've sworn he'd heard something.

'What is it?' Vi enquired, emerging from the passage they'd just traversed. Her hand moved unconsciously to the long-bladed dagger sheathed at her left hip. The favourite of all her many knives, judging by the number of times she went for it.

'Not sure,' Sweet whispered, sniffing again. Damp and musty for sure, but also something coppery on the breeze now. *Was that—*

A roar sounded from within the cave.

*—blood?*

Sweet tensed as a shadow detached itself from inside the cave, huge and lumbering and heaving itself out of the darkness in a rolling lope. Sweet felt a bolt of fear run the length of his spine as an enormous bear emerged from the cave. The creature's fur was so dark that its form seemed to grow from the shadows themselves. It unfurled its massive head, opened a huge set of jaws and roared again. Sharp yellow teeth flashed in the overcast light of the afternoon.

'Fuck,' Sweet whispered.

Daraday reacted first. The young hunter swung the bow from his shoulder and reached for an arrow to nock to its string. Sweet thought about yelling for him to stop, but the bear looked pissed enough already so staying calm wouldn't have done much good anyway. The creature roared again, its ears pressed flat against its skull. It took another huge step out of the cave mouth.

Sweet's heart was racing, but his muscles retained their memory and his hand reached for the sword buckled at his hip. It was Damsen steel, recovered from the body of the grey-haired soldier, Carthin, and a damn sight better than Sweet's previous blade. Even so, the weapon looked so small in comparison to the enormousness of the bear. Like trying to fight the thing with a letter opener. Sweet would've found it faintly comical, if there hadn't been a fucking great bear standing in front of him.

Daraday loosed an arrow and it cut into the bear's shoulder. The creature roared again and shook its head, rising up onto its hind legs. It was tall and powerful and Sweet saw that its maw was slick with blood. No wonder he's pissed, he thought, we disturbed his meal.

Daraday was reaching for a second arrow when the bear suddenly dropped to all fours and charged at them. Orsen gave a shout and the group scattered. Stover dove to his left, Vi and the prince scrambled away to their right. Sweet stood for a moment, sword in hand, before swallowing hard and bellowing as loud as he could. He waved his arms, high and wide, drawing frantic circles in the air with his flailing limbs. The bear paused in its charge, lowering its head and watching them more warily. Sweet remembered being told by a huntsman once that bears usually offered a challenge before attacking for real. He had no idea if it was true or not, but the huntsman had suggested you could scare a bear away if you acted big enough and tough enough. Sweet might not've felt big or tough right then, but he damn sure hoped the bear would buy it.

The creature slowed, grunted and circled a few steps, glaring at Sweet and flexing its jaws, baring those wicked-looking teeth and dripping saliva to the stone below in great glooping strings. It tensed again and Sweet knew its next charge wouldn't be turned away by waving arms and loud shouts.

Daraday fired a second arrow just as the beast lunged forwards once more. The missile flew somewhere into the bear's midriff, drawing another deep howl of pain—or maybe rage—but not slowing it at all. Sweet tried to sidestep and lance his sword at the bear but it was so damn fast, a great paw swept out and cannoned into Sweet's side. The force of the blow sent him flying and he became vaguely aware of a burning sensation across his arm. Then he crashed into the rocky ground and the air was knocked from his lungs. He rolled over with a groan.

Daraday had fired another arrow, this time into the bear's exposed flank, and was busy notching a fourth to the little hunting bow. Vi had abandoned the long-bladed dagger and opted instead for a series of throwing knives that she kept strapped across her chest. She pulled each of them free with well-practised ease—her face locked in a defiant snarl—and hurled them one after the other at the beast as she tried to keep a stand of rocks between them.

The bear roared, rising up on its hind legs again and turning to its right, where Stover was cowering against the rock wall, his sword all but forgotten as he stared up at the angry beast. The bear lunged for the man, but Sweet saw the slim figure of Orsen rush forward. His arms were raised and he bellowed as loud as he could, the sound echoing through the rocks. The prince was unarmed—Sweet had made that one stipulation of their newly-struck deal—but he charged in, hollering and flailing to distract the beast. Seemed like a pretty stupid stipulation right about now.

The bear looked momentarily confused, unsure of which man to attack, but it quickly settled on the prince and dropped on him like a shadow. Sweet clambered to his feet and looked around for his sword, he saw it a few feet away and scrambled for it at the same time as he stumbled towards the bear. He let loose a roar of his own and charged at the bear's side with the sword point levelled like a spear. The blade cut into the creature's side and pain jarred through Sweet's shoulders, it was like striking a great sack full of sand and rocks. At first the weapon bit into the bear's fur and flesh, but it soon became stuck and the force of the charge ran back along Sweet's own body.

Even so, the bear roared again, spinning with incredible speed and batting Sweet with the back of one huge paw this time. For the second time in as many moments, Sweet was hurled from his feet and came crashing down on the rocky ground with a jolting thud. From where he lay, he could see the prince also on the ground, almost directly beneath where the bear was standing.

Daraday had run out of arrows now and was also throwing knives at the bear. He and Vi might as well have been throwing stones, for all the good it was doing. It seemed to Sweet the hurled daggers were doing more to make the bear angry than they were to slow its attack.

Just as the thought came to him, one of Vi's throwing knives pierced the bear's left eye, sticking right to the hilt. The creature howled, this time the sound was borne more of pain than it was of anger. It wrenched its enormous head left and right, as though trying to dislodge the weapon. Then it rounded on Stover again, who was still standing with his back to the rockface, watching in open-mouthed terror as the carnage unfolded before him.

The bear lunged at Stover for a second time, but Sweet saw a dark blur suddenly drop down from the rocks above. The shape landed on the bear's shoulder with a dull thud, the force of the blow driving the creature to its stomach. The shape rolled clear and Sweet saw that it was the Wyn. The tribesman straightened and threw his cloak back from one hip. Sweet saw that the man had no sword, then realised that it was jutting from the bear's shoulder. He'd leapt from the rocks above and plunged it deep into the flesh beside the beast's neck.

The bear was wobbling a bit now, its lower jaw hanging slack. The Wyn pulled a long, curved dagger from his belt and ran at it. He stepped onto the bear's planted knee and leaped into the air, holding the dagger in both hands high over his head. Without so much as a sound the Wyn slammed the weapon into the flesh on the other side of the bear's head, then landed and rolled away again in one smooth motion.

The bear tried to roar again, but this time the sound was muted. To Sweet it sounded mournful and confused. The beast wobbled again, took a staggering step to one side and then fell forwards with an enormous whumping noise. Its huge chest rose and fell for a few moments more, before finally falling still.

The silence that followed was malleable. Sweet pushed himself gingerly to his feet. Every bone in his body was aching at once. He was faintly aware of a ringing in his ears, no doubt caused by cracking his head against the unyielding stone ground. He glanced down at the hot pain on his upper arm and saw that both his cloak and the shirt underneath it had been torn by the bear's claws. Three angry red gashes ran across his exposed bicep, the middle one was the deepest and Sweet reckoned it would need stitches, but he seemed otherwise unhurt.

'Sweet?' Vi asked, two throwing knives still in hand as she glared at the still body of the bear, as though she expected it to suddenly rise again. Hell, Sweet was watching the great shaggy body of the beast closely too, just in case. Vi raised an eyebrow at him. 'You alright?'

'Aye,' Sweet breathed, feeling anything but alright. 'I'm fine,' he said, then he glanced over at where Orsen lay. 'The prince!'

Prince Orsen was lying face down on the ground, but at the sound of Sweet's voice he groaned and rolled over. He had a matching set of gashes on his own shoulder, as well as some cuts and scrapes where he had been crushed against the rocky ground. He looked shaken, but relatively unharmed.

'You alright?' Sweet asked, leaning down and placing a hand on the prince's uninjured shoulder. Orsen nodded, his expression groggy, like a man who'd ordered another ale when he should've called it quits on the drink before.

Or like a man who just fought a bear, unarmed—Sweet considered.

'I'm alright,' Orsen answered. 'The bear?'

'Dead,' Sweet looked up, then gave a deep nod to where the Wyn was stood, his face as impassive as ever. 'Thanks to this man's impeccable timing.'

'No thanks,' said the Wyn, he motioned to the far side of the rocks, where a steep path led up the cliff face from which he'd leapt onto the bear in the first place. 'Come see.'

'Eh?' Sweet questioned, a dull throbbing beginning at one temple where it had struck the stone. He was breathing hard and his legs felt unsteady. He frowned at the Wyn. 'Come see what?'

The Wyn looked unsettled. Or—at least—as unsettled as Sweet reckoned he *could* look. The pain in his head seemed to swell further still as he caught sight of that expression.

'Trouble,' the tribesman answered.

*

Sweet had been exhausted before the climb up to the top of the rocks. He'd been exhausted before they'd been set upon by a bloody great bear. But the rush he'd felt when the creature attacked had quickly faded, and he was left feeling even more weary than ever now. By the time he reached where the Wyn was waiting for him, staring out to the west, he was about ready to keel over. His limbs felt shaky and his breath came in short, sharp bursts. He bent over to take a moment, leaning hard on his knees. The one he'd cracked against the rocks twinged with pain and he winced.

Sweet straightened and squinted towards where the Wyn was facing. He was momentarily staggered by the scene. From their position up on the high peak, they could see for miles. To the south, the ground slowly turned from grey to brown to purple as the swathes of heather they'd passed through took hold. Sweet could even see a dark smudge in the far distance that marked the ravine in which they'd caught up to the prince. To the west, the forest spread over the land like a dark green blanket, cut apart only by rising hillocks and rocky ground like the patch they were now standing on. To the north, the terrain was more bleak and foreboding, with sharp ridges rising and falling away like jagged ripples in the land. Beyond the ridges, on the far horizon, Sweet could just about see the outlines of the mountain range that marked the northern edge of the Pratian kingdom. Or—rather—the land that had formerly been the kingdom of Pratia and was now the westernmost part of the Vol Empire.

The mountains were shrouded in fog and flecked with white streaks the higher up Sweet looked. Their peaks were lost in the clouds themselves, but Sweet knew they would be snow-capped all year round.

The landscape, coupled with the biting wind that stung at Sweet's face, was charged with a raw and monstrous beauty. It made Sweet feel small and insignificant, just as his encounter with the powerful beast at the base of the cliff had done so—only there he had felt terror for his life. Up here the sheer majesty of the land made him feel dread for his very existence.

'What is it?' he asked the Wyn, eager to both drink in more of the view and to get away from it at the same time.

'There,' the Wyn pointed to the forest away to the west. Sweet tried to follow the gesture with his eyes but could see little save for a grey-green blur in the distance.

'What?' he asked, just as the throbbing at his temple pulsed a warning not to squint so hard.

'Riders,' the Wyn said, nonplussed.

'Malvadas?' Sweet asked, a little worried. The blur that the Wyn had pointed to was further north along the road than Sweet would've preferred. Truth be told he'd prefer if the gold-toothed bastard turned his men around and headed home. 'The other bounty hunters?'

The Wyn nodded, then shifted his arm to the south, back along the way they had come.

'There,' he intoned.

Sweet squinted again, ignoring the flare of pain it caused. Again he could see little, the distances were so great and the fog and rain were playing havoc with his vision.

'Bloody hell man, just tell me what you see,' he told the Wyn.

'Hunters,' the Wyn said, his voice as stark as the sky above. He solemnly tapped at his chest. 'Like me,' he intoned.

'Wyns?' Sweet questioned, 'you mean that big bastard, Thond?'

The Wyn nodded again.

'How far?' Sweet asked, feeling a lump in his throat at the thought of the axe-wielding giant walking in their footsteps.

'Getting closer,' the Wyn answered.

'Damn it man,' Sweet swore, 'how close?'

The Wyn didn't react at first. It felt like getting angry with a statue—and that thought only made Sweet angrier. Damn he was tired. Sweet wanted nothing more than to curl up under his blankets beside a warm campfire and sleep for several days. Instead he forced himself to take a deep breath and tried to find some calm. He steadied his gaze and raised it to meet the Wyn's own. Eventually the tribesman gave a short shrug.

'Three days,' he said, then added, 'getting closer.'

Sweet's mind reeled, and it was already reeling from the fight with the bear. The wound in his arm was stinging wildly now and his head was starting to pound like a drum.

'There,' the Wyn spoke again. He had transferred his pointing finger across the landscape a third time. This time he had angled his arm to the northwest, but he'd raised it higher, as though pointing beyond the road. Confused, Sweet tried to follow the gesture. The clouds were lighter in the far distance and it looked like the rain hadn't reached that part of the land yet. It might've been his eyes, or the pain in his head, but Sweet reckoned he could see a small cloud of brown in the far distance. Without the Wyn pointing at it, it would've been almost imperceptibly small. Damn near invisible, even.

'Is that dust?' Sweet grimaced as another wave of pain pulsed from his temple. 'Horsemen?'

'Yes,' the Wyn answered.

'More bounty hunters?'

'No,' the Wyn shook his head.

'Well,' Sweet gesticulated, 'what, then?'

'Soldiers.'

'Soldiers?' Sweet frowned. 'Vols?'

'Yes.'

Sweet considered this for a moment. It could've been a patrol, but why would they be patrolling the wilderness? What was there to protect this far north? And if they were on patrol, why were they riding so fast as to send a cloud of dust into the air? No, if there were Vol soldiers riding hard out this way then they would be out here for a reason. And Sweet knew of only one good reason. He also had a pretty good idea of exactly who might be leading that particular little excursion.

'It'll be Renauld,' he muttered, more to himself than to the Wyn, who absorbed the information without response anyway. 'That creepy bastard from Levitan. I'd hoped they'd take longer to figure out that they'd gone the wrong way. Looks like he got wise.'

Another thought occurred to him then. If the Vols were riding at speed for the north, there could only be one destination for them. His head pounded all the harder for the realisation. They were heading for the mountain pass itself.

They were going to cut them off.

'Come on,' Sweet gestured to the Wyn, his head aching as though he'd be kicked by a horse. 'It's bloody freezing up here, let's get back down to the others.'

By the time they reached the bottom of the rockface, the light was beginning to fade. The others had lit a fire and—by its light—Sweet could see the colossal corpse of the bear. It lay unmoved close to the mouth of the cave, though blood had pooled around its head from the mortal blows that the Wyn had struck.

Stover was squatting in front of the fire, feeding more sticks into the flickering blaze and doing his best not to look at anybody. Daraday was sat beside him, examining his recovered arrows with a frown on his face, one glance told Sweet he didn't reckon many of them would be much use again, if any at all. The other weapons—Daraday's and Vi's knives and the Wyn's sword—lay beside him, having first been carefully cleaned. Prince Orsen was next in the circle, leaning forwards with his shirt pulled up over one arm as Vi stitched the wound on his shoulder with a hooked needle of bone, the thread held between her gritted teeth as she worked. Sweet nodded to the group as he and the Wyn returned. Vi tied off a stitch and pulled the thread from her mouth.

'Good news?' she asked, seeing the look on Sweet's face.

'Not the best,' Sweet admitted, hunkering down beside her and the raven-haired Orsen. He told the group of what the Wyn had spotted and they absorbed the information with grim deference. The only way you could think about it, Sweet supposed. Wasn't much point panicking about things you couldn't control.

'We camping here, then?' he asked, changing the subject and motioning to the fire. Vi shrugged.

'As good a place as any,' she said, then added, 'we checked the cave, no more bears.'

'Good,' Sweet nodded, transferring his gaze to the motionless body. He felt a touch of sadness then, as he stared at the dead bear. 'He would've been alone, getting ready to hunker down for the winter.' Sweet sighed and turned to face the prince. 'Brave work today, lad,' he said.

Orsen only shrugged, wincing as the movement pulled at his new stitches. He didn't look embarrassed by the comment, but nor did he puff up with pride at it either. Sweet found himself warming to the boy more and more.

'Reckon you'll be needing this,' Sweet continued, unbuckling the sword at his hip and holding it out to the prince. The younger man only looked at him. 'Y'know,' Sweet shrugged, 'next time I don't fancy you charging in unarmed.'

The prince gave a tired smile, then took the weapon and laid it across his lap. Sweet swapped a glance with Vi and Daraday and was pleased to see that they agreed with his decision.

'Take this, too,' Violent Fey said, offering out one of her daggers by the hilt. Sweet raised an eyebrow at that. Those knives were like bloody children to Vi, so her offering one up was no token gesture. Judging by Orsen's reaction, he had come to the same conclusion and took the dagger gently—damn near reverently—and nodded his gratitude to Vi. The prince half-drew the blade from its scabbard and turned it over a few times, before snapping it shut and sliding the whole thing into his boot.

Removing the stipulation that the prince go unarmed seemed like a pretty solid call, by all accounts. Sweet caught Stover's eye but the other man looked away quickly. He might've disagreed with the idea, but he was smart enough to recognise that Orsen had saved his life when the bear charged at him.

That ought to shut him up at least for the night, Sweet thought.

Sweet settled down around the campfire and the group shared a meal in silence, too exhausted to talk. Soon after, Stover and Daraday had both laid down, wrapped in their blankets—the former was snoring within moments. Vi stitched Sweet's wound and then moved aside to sit and sharpen her daggers while the Wyn took the first watch of the night. That left Sweet sitting beside the prince. He saw that the younger man was looking down at the scabbarded sword still laid across his legs. He lightly traced one finger along the hardened leather of the sheath.

'It's a good blade,' Sweet observed. Then he gave a wry smile. 'Though I think it needs a better man'n me to wield it,' he added. 'Damn near snapped it in half trying to spear that bloody bear.'

'It wouldn't have snapped,' the prince said softly, still not looking up from the weapon. 'It's Damsen steel.'

'Everything snaps, lad,' Sweet replied, just as softly. 'If you apply enough pressure.'

'It was Carthin's sword,' the prince sighed, unable to keep the edge of sorrow from his voice. Sweet cursed inwardly as he remembered taking the weapon from the old man's body.

'You were close?' Sweet asked, eager to change the subject but almost immediately regretting his choice of tangents. He took a swig from his waterskin and wished like hell he had bought some dark spirits from Arc back in Scarvin.

'Aye,' Orsen said, sighing again. 'He was master-at-arms in the palace.' The prince drew a deep breath and frowned, as though that description wasn't enough. He sighed again, then added. 'He was...like a father to me.'

Sweet said nothing more and the prince didn't elaborate. Sweet reckoned the raven-haired youngster had a feel for conversations and had realised how uncomfortable he was. Or perhaps, he thought, the lad just doesn't want to talk to a near stranger about his dead friend.

Hell, his dead father-figure, as it turned out.

Sweet shuddered, although the warmth from the fire and the protection from the wind afforded them by their rocky surroundings meant he wasn't cold. He felt suddenly weary beyond all measure and reasoned that a dram of Arc's dark spirits might've knocked him out instantly. Maybe that wouldn't have been such a bad thing. He yawned and stretched, feeling the tightness of the stitches high on his arm.

'Do you think we'll make it to the mountain pass?' Orsen asked suddenly, cutting through Sweet's weariness. He blinked a few times and thought about the question, then shrugged.

'We will or we won't,' Sweet answered, suddenly not sure it truly mattered either way.

'And if we do, the Vols will be there?' The fire reflected in Orsen's piercing grey eyes and Sweet felt a wave of power emanate from the young royal.

'They will or they won't,' he answered again, with an apologetic smile.

'If they are,' the prince whispered, 'we'll go through them.'

Sweet said nothing to that at first. He pulled his blanket tightly around his body and laid down on his side, feeling a mutiny of aches and pains ripple through his tired muscles. He yawned again and exhaled deeply.

'We will or we won't.'

## Sacrifice

THE NEXT FEW days passed without incident. The group left the stand of rocks and headed out onto more open ground. The wind seemed to whip harder than ever, driving rain under the hoods of their cloaks and snapping them back in constant mockery of their attempts to stay warm and dry. The wound on Sweet's shoulder had turned from a sting to a dull ache and fast became an annoyance he could've done without, but his nightly inspection from Vi suggested that the cuts were clean and would likely not become infected. Prince Orsen's was the same, though the wound drew no complaints from the young royal.

What bothered Sweet more than the pain in his arm was how slow their progress was. The worsening conditions and the tougher terrain, coupled with their general state of exhaustion, meant that they crawled through the miles at a snail's pace. He found himself glancing over his shoulder time and time again, half-expecting to see the big warrior, Thond, and whatever men he had with him just a hundred paces away. But there was always nothing. Occasionally Sweet could see the figure of their own Wyn, scouring the land behind them for signs of hot pursuit. The hardy tribesman ranged both ahead and behind, seemingly unbothered by the challenging terrain or worsening weather. Sweet pictured again how calmly the Wyn had plummeted from the rocks above the bear. He must've dropped twenty feet or more onto the creature's shoulder. And even after he had delivered the blow, he had rolled away and risen to attack again. It highlighted to Sweet just how formidable a warrior the Wyn was—and he was on their side.

Sweet didn't want to think what Thond might be capable of.

They were still climbing upwards, and before long the view that he and the Wyn had shared above the bear's cave became visible to the entire group. Sweet saw Orsen, Vi and Daraday all giving it the same watchful study he had. Each of them regarded the scenery with the same amount of begrudging respect and admiration that he had felt. If you didn't respect this kind of place, he thought, it would swallow you whole and spit you out without a second thought. Better to be cowed by it than killed by it, he reckoned.

Only Stover didn't give the stunning vista a second glance. He trudged on, marching with his head down and a dark look spread across his face. He had clammed up since the bear attack—for which Sweet was grateful—but his brooding silence spoke for itself.

'At what point do we consider ourselves in the mountains?' the prince asked, breathing hard but with the hint of a smile around the corners of his mouth. Sweet couldn't help but return the gesture.

'Another few miles yet,' he replied, 'you think this bit's hard going, wait until we get into the high places.'

Orsen whistled loudly.

'And here was me, thinking these *were* the high places,' he chuckled, hitching his pack and traipsing ahead.

As the morning drifted into afternoon the clouds overhead began to dissipate. The heat from the sun—meagre though it was this high up— was a welcome addition, but it was so low in the sky that Sweet found himself blinded in one eye as they tramped north. He crested a rise and saw Daraday leaning against a large rock, filling his waterskin from a small stream that trickled down over its face.

'How much further?' the youngster asked, his voice gruff and blunt.

Sweet shrugged and scratched at his chin, feeling the itchy growth of a new beard there. He'd last shaved back in Scarvin and didn't reckon he'd get another chance at it until the winter was over. *If* he got another chance at it.

'Quite a way, yet,' he answered, voicing the answer he hadn't wanted to give the prince just moments before. He glanced over his shoulder for the thousandth time that day. 'And we've got company not far behind.'

Daraday nodded.

'Sylvanus' dog?'

'He's more'n a bloody dog,' Sweet replied, tipping the contents of his own waterskin down his throat and moving to refill it. 'He's a great big bloody wolf, and he's right on our trail.'

As if to hammer the point home, the lithe figure of the Wyn appeared at the nearest rise. He was moving quickly in their direction. Not panicked or even rushed, but certainly not out for a leisurely stroll in the country, either. Sweet straightened as he caught sight of him, the others had arrived at the crest now and stopped to catch their breath.

'Fill up your waterskins,' Sweet told them all, watching the Wyn as he danced his way up the slope. 'Let's see what he's got to say.'

'A day behind us,' Sweet said, rubbing his hands together as he squatted amongst the group. Grim eyes set in grim faces stared back at him. 'And getting closer by the hour.'

'What'll we do?' Vi asked. She asked the question bluntly, cold as the oncoming winter.

'Not much we can do,' Sweet acknowledged, pulling his hands apart and showing his palms. 'We clearly can't outrun them – eventually they'll catch up to us.'

'So we hide?' Stover suggested. The man had seemed much less sure of his prowess for confrontation since Bryntas had been murdered and they'd been set upon by a bear. He glanced at the others. 'Let them go past us?'

The looks on the faces of the rest of the group—uncomfortable at best—told Sweet they already knew what he was about to respond with.

'We can't hide,' he said, sighing loudly. 'This big bastard that leads them is a Wyn, might be the men he's travelling with are Wyns, too. They'd find us with their eyes closed.'

'So what then?' Stover asked.

Sweet took a deep breath.

'We'll have to fight them,' he said, almost wincing as the words left his mouth.

'Fight them?' Stover wrinkled his nose, 'us six, against...how many of them?'

'Six as well,' answered Sweet, 'including the big man.'

'Six on six,' Daraday nodded, taking a drink from his newly-filled waterskin. He gave a shrug. 'There're worse odds.'

'And we could choose the ground,' Orsen put in. All eyes turned on him and he reddened a little, but swallowed and pressed on all the same. 'Carthin used to say picking the field of battle is where half the fight is won.'

'Yeah?' Stover sneered. 'Well this ain't a battle, and killing those fuckers is the half we should worry about.'

'He's right,' Sweet said, speaking before Vi could offer Stover a reprimand. Sweet reckoned the other man had just about had his fill of the acid from her tongue and it wouldn't be long before violent words gave way to violence of a more physical nature. They always did.

'What?' Stover frowned at Sweet.

'Orsen is right,' Sweet repeated wearily, 'if we can pick some high ground, maybe somewhere narrow where they have to come at us in pairs, or—better yet—one at a time, we've got a chance.'

'But you said yourself, they're Wyns!' Stover protested, 'they'll smell a trap from a mile away!'

'Aye,' Sweet nodded, 'but I'm betting this Thond bastard is arrogant enough to assume he can spring it and still come out on top anyway. We'll just have to prove him otherwise, eh?'

'We won't all get out of that fight alive,' Stover warned, his brow furrowed deeply. 'We'd need a damn miracle to take them on and win.'

The Wyn suddenly straightened and Sweet looked across at him. There was alarm in the tribesman's eyes and he reached for the sword at his waist. For the first time since Sweet had known him, he was too slow. Out of nowhere, a sword blade sprang up against the Wyn's neck and the tribesman stopped cold before his fingers could touch the hilt of his own weapon. The wielder had appeared so suddenly that—to Sweet—they seemed to have materialised out of the very air itself. He was still registering the shock when he felt the cold, unmistakable press of a blade against his own neck. A quick glance across told him that Vi and the prince were in similar predicaments. Only Stover and Daraday were left without sword points touched against their throats.

Daraday sat as still as a statue. His eyes narrowed but he didn't make a move. He watched the scene unfold calmly and carefully and Sweet could see him calculating how far away his nearest dagger was from his fingertips. Too far, by the looks of it.

As soon as Stover registered the danger he scrambled backwards and lurched to his feet, clipping a rock on his way up and nearly stumbling over and into the stream.

'What the fuck!' he cried, scrabbling for his own sword.

'No!' a sharp voice barked from behind Sweet's shoulder. No doubt its owner was the same person who was holding a sword to his neck. Stover stopped, midway through pulling his own weapon from its weathered scabbard. 'No!' the voice repeated, quieter this time but no less dangerous for it.

'Stover,' Sweet growled as the sword point bit into the flesh of his neck. Damn it was sharp. Stover snapped his head up and looked at the newcomers with wild eyes. Sweet took the time to do the same—or those he could see anyway.

There were four of them—including the one at Sweet's back—all wearing long cloaks bearing strange markings along the hems. Their weapons were slightly curved and their faces were shrouded in shadow. Heavy hoods covered their heads, but the swirls and jags of dark tattoos could be seen within.

They were Wyns.

Sweet swallowed, feeling the cold press of the sword blade in the side of his neck. It was sharp enough to shave with—the irony of which was not lost on Sweet—and whoever was holding it wasn't shaking at all. A confident warrior, then. But he was still alive, which was more than could be said for most folk who encountered Wyns out in the wild. Were these four with Thond? If so, where was the big bastard himself? The voice from over his shoulder had been deep, and it had only spoken the same word twice, but if Sweet were a betting man he'd have gambled that it belonged to a woman all the same. More importantly than that, they were all still alive. If Thond and his men had caught them unawares, Sweet reckoned they'd be dead already. All except the prince, maybe.

'If you're here to rob us,' Sweet said, speaking slowly and keeping very still. 'Then we've not much to take, I'm afraid.'

The steel against his neck pressed harder still and he winced as he felt it cut into the skin. Another wound to add to my growing collection, he thought sourly. The woman behind him, for it was clearly a woman now, said something in a tongue he didn't understand. The words were guttural and the cadence seemed jumpy and disjointed. Sweet found it hard to even read the tone of what was being said—he couldn't tell if she was furious or elated or indifferent.

Surprisingly, their own Wyn—a sword held against his throat by a hooded warrior that could've been his twin—spoke in response. The same sharp, rasping sounds came from his mouth and his expression remained unchanged throughout. He finished and lapsed into quiet. It was the highest number of words Sweet had ever heard him say in one go, even if he didn't understand a single one of them.

'The hell are they saying?' Stover stammered, his hand twitching to pull his sword free of its sheath completely. The warrior with the blade held to Violent Fey's neck shouted something in the foreign tongue and this time Sweet had no problem reading the tone of it. The warrior pressed his weapon closer to Vi's throat to emphasise the threat.

'Stover you moron,' Sweet hissed at the other man. 'Don't. Fucking. Move.' He glanced over at their own Wyn, who seemed as calm as standing water. 'What're they saying?' he asked the tribesman.

The Wyn glanced up over Sweet's shoulder at the woman behind him, then looked back at Sweet.

'They say we invade,' he said, speaking the common tongue again. 'They camp not far.'

'Did you tell them we're *not* invading?' Sweet asked, raising an eyebrow.

The Wyn nodded.

'We take king north,' he flicked his glance over to where Prince Orsen was kneeling with a sword propped under his chin. A thin trickle of blood was running down his neck and Sweet knew the edge of the blade was just as keen as the one at his own throat. 'We not invade,' the Wyn finished.

Before Sweet could respond the woman behind him barked something in her own language again. Once more, Sweet struggled to hear if she was angry with the denial offered by their own Wyn, or if she was ordering their release. He guessed it wasn't the latter, as the swords stayed pressed against their necks. After she had finished talking, the Wyn—their Wyn—nodded and replied in the same tongue, then looked back down at Sweet.

'They say we bring warriors,' he reported. 'Warriors to kill them and take their land.'

'And you told them we didn't?' said Sweet, somewhat more urgently now.

'Yes,' the Wyn nodded again, 'we take king north,' he repeated.

Sweet resisted the urge to roll his eyes. The absurdity of the situation nearly caused him to laugh aloud but he quelled it quickly. If he was being honest, the sticky warmth from the cut at his neck helped with that process, too.

'What do they want?' Sweet asked, looking directly at the Wyn. 'Ask them what they want.'

The Wyn looked up at the woman behind Sweet and spoke, the words flowing quickly and rhythmically. It was strange seeing the Wyn speak so animatedly and Sweet found himself feeling suddenly foolish. He had always viewed the Wyn as something of a novelty. He was a skilled tracker and a deadly warrior—certainly a valued asset to the crew—but he had never really considered the man's true nature. The thought brought more than a little shame down on Sweet. The feeling didn't last long though—there were bigger things to worry about, after all. The sword-wielding woman behind him was one of them, and she answered the Wyn in kind. Sweet looked to the Wyn for a translation again.

'We not fight them,' the Wyn said, choosing his words carefully. 'We fight *for* them.'

'What?' Sweet asked, confused.

'More warriors come,' the Wyn gestured down the steep hillside. 'We not fight them,' he gestured to the four warriors surrounding their camp. 'we fight for them.'

Understanding settled over Sweet like a shroud and he wondered if there might've been an agreeable way out of this after all. Well, he considered, more agreeable than having your throats slit by a group of angry Wyn warriors.

'She wants us to help fight the men tracking us?' Sweet looked to their own Wyn for confirmation. The tribesman nodded.

'Well,' he sighed, looking across to where Stover was standing. That dumb look of confusion plastered across his face and one hand still on the hilt of his half-drawn sword. 'Looks like you got your miracle.'

*

The Wyn leader led the group higher up the slopes, eventually stopping at a narrow pass between two faces of rock. A loud crashing sound could be heard echoing from within the passage. She gestured for the group to move inside, her waving arms insinuating the need for urgency.

'I guess Thond and his men are closer than we thought,' Sweet muttered to Violent Fey as they shuffled into the crevice.

'Aye,' Vi nodded, keeping her eyes on the lean form of the Wyn leader. 'You sure about this?'

Sweet raised an eyebrow.

'Been askin' that a lot recently, Vi,' he cracked a smile at her, then softened. 'Of course I'm not bloody sure,' he admitted, 'but we were gonna stand and fight them anyway, might as well fight with four more blades to call on.'

'Not just any blades, neither,' Vi murmured, watching as the Wyn leader strode deftly up a series of impossibly angled rocks. The tribsewoman stopped at the tip of one and spun on her heel to face the way they'd come, her eyes squinting as she stared into the distance. It was a feat of almost inhuman balance, but she performed it as nonchalantly as others might take a breath.

'Agreed,' Sweet nodded. 'They'd make deadly enemies, which means they can be deadly friends, too.'

'You think we can kill the magicker's hound?'

'I do now,' Sweet admitted. Violent Fey looked at him with a quizzical eye and he shrugged, cracking another grim smile. 'Stover was right, we'd have needed a damned miracle if we tried to face them ourselves.'

'We can fight,' Vi countered, a small flash of anger crossing her face.

'Aye, we can,' Sweet nodded, then he glanced up to where the Wyn leader was poised on the rocks above them. When he spoke again he lowered his voice, almost reverently. 'But this lot can kill.'

The Wyn leader transferred her gaze away from the horizon and moved it down to where the group was walking. Sweet looked away, eager not to offend their newfound allies but mostly eager not to get his throat slashed open.

The other three Wyn warriors were stalking off ahead, already inside the rocky passage. There were two men and another woman—little more than a girl, really—all dressed in the same robes and carrying the same kind of blade as worn by the Wyn in Sweet's crew. All were grim-faced and silent, though by now Sweet reckoned that might just be a Wyn thing, after all.

Sweet glanced across to their own Wyn and saw that the man seemed to walk with his hooded head held a little higher than usual, his back a little straighter. Maybe he was imagining it, but the Wyn seemed to be walking with more purpose, now.

Sweet shook the thought clear of his head as they approached the opening in the rock. It was narrow—only wide enough for them to walk three abreast and even then that was a squeeze—and the rocky walls closed in on each other the higher up they rose. The crashing noise was a cacophony now and the constant barrage to Sweet's eardrums made him wince a little. It was like having a hornets nest between your ears.

The path wound through the rocks for a few minutes before eventually widening out again. The rock wall to their left climbed ever higher until at last it ended in a jagged edge. The rock wall to their right tapered downwards and split away from the path altogether. In the open space there, Sweet saw a drop of some twenty feet that revealed the source of the bedlam.

A rushing river, frothing white and occasionally revealing the sharp side of a dark grey stone beneath the surface, raged below. The fast-flowing water crashed into the sides of the rock and the air was thick with a wet mist thrown up by its relentless energy. Sweet could feel the moisture settling in his beard even as he peered over the edge. As he looked, a heavy log was carried into sight, hurried along by the torrent below as though it were little more than a twig. The log disappeared under a frothing rim before emerging again some ten paces further downstream, it clipped a jutting boulder and was spun madly, before hitting another with a rending crack. The log was splintered into pieces and they were swallowed by the hungry waters.

Sweet's grim assessment continued as he looked to the far side of the raging river, but there was only more rock. Another towering face of stone, darker towards the bottom where the spit of the river could reach it. The rock looked slick and the speed of the current meant that getting a handhold would be impossible. Even if you somehow did, he reasoned, the force of the current would tear you away from it—or tear your arm away from your body—before you had a chance to try hauling yourself out of the water. He turned his head, looking first upstream and then down, but saw nothing except for more of the raging river and more walls of rock. If you were unfortunate enough to find yourself in the torrent, it would only be a question of what would kill you first—would you drown or be dashed upon the jagged rocks before you had the chance?

Falling off this ledge and into the raging depths would be a death sentence.

A firm hand clamped down on his shoulder and Sweet jumped, damn near tumbling off the rocky outcrop and into the river below. He spun around to see the Wyn—their Wyn—staring at him. The man's face was as blank and unreadable as ever.

'Bloody hell man,' Sweet managed, whistling a breath of relief between his teeth, his heart racing. 'You could've sent me straight in.'

The Wyn flicked his glance down to the raging torrent, then back up at Sweet, his expression unmoved.

'She speak to you,' the tribesman said. Sweet stared at him a moment longer, then nodded and began walking across to where the Wyn leader was standing, grateful to be away from the deadly precipice..

The woman was tall and—like her companions—lean and with an athleticism only gained from time spent learning to cope with the wilderness. She'd pulled back her hood to reveal a shaven head, decorated with tattoos similar to the ones that adorned the neck and face of the Wyn in Sweet's crew. As they approached, that very same tribesman— who Sweet had known for years and had never registered so much as a gesture of greeting from—dipped his neck and touched a flat palm to his forehead. Some sort of gesture of acquiescence, Sweet reckoned, though he was too stunned by the sight of it to think of anything else.

The woman spoke, the words meaning nothing to Sweet, and the Wyn straightened once more. She spoke some more and the man turned to face Sweet.

'She is Ashan Feroq,' the Wyn said.

Sweet nodded and turned to face the tribeswoman, he held out a hand.

'Sweet,' he said, then scratched at his chin with his other hand before shrugging and adding, 'Bitter Sweet, I suppose.'

The tall woman called Ashan Feroq looked down at the offered hand, then back up at Sweet's face. Then she turned her head and spoke to the Wyn again, her voice filled with what sounded like urgency. Eventually, she fell silent and the Wyn translated again.

'Invaders come soon,' the Wyn reported, 'we will fight them in the passage, lead them back here. Ashan Feroq and her tribe will join, then.'

'Her tribe?' Sweet raised an eyebrow and flicked his eyes to the other three Wyns clustered not far away. 'Just four of them?'

The Wyn began speaking in his own tongue and Sweet realised he was translating the question for the woman. He held out a hurried hand and shook his head, cutting the Wyn short.

'Never mind,' Sweet told him, 'the plan is good, but she and her... tribe, will be better fighters than us, surely they would be better suited to fighting in the narrow passage?'

The Wyn translated as Ashan Feroq stared directly at Sweet. Her eyes darkened as the tribesman finished speaking and she replied curtly.

'No,' the Wyn translated. Though Sweet reckon he could've figured that one out himself from the steel in the woman's narrowed eyes. 'Ashan Feroq not send her warriors to die for us. She spare us. We hold passage, then lead invaders to her. We sacrifice.'

Sweet considered a retort. Then he considered negotiation. Then he realised—looking into the flinty eyes of the Wyn warrior woman, that either option would be fruitless anyway. He sighed loudly and nodded.

'Fine,' he agreed, 'how long until they get here?'

The Wyn translated and Ashan Feroq gave a single word in response. For the second time in as many moments, Sweet didn't reckon he needed a translation. The Wyn duly provided one anyway.

'Soon,' he said.

Sweet nodded and hitched his trews. He offered the warrior woman a brief smile and a nod of his head, then turned away from her and approached where Violent Fey, Stover and Daraday were standing, waiting expectantly under a cloud of river spray.

'Well?' Vi asked, raising her voice so as to be heard over the din of the torrent raging behind her.

Sweet gave a grim smile.

'Here's the plan,' he said.

The clouds had parted and the sun was shining brightly overhead. Sweet squinted against it. The gentle press of heat was making him uncomfortable. Every square of skin that it warmed—his forearms, his neck, his face—served as a reminder for the bits of his body that weren't even protected by the cloth of his garments. It made him feel exposed.

The noise from behind him was more than a little irritating now, too. The crashing echoes of the river on the other side of the narrow rock passage were constant. At times it sounded like no two moments were the same, then the noise seemed to coalesce into some sort of pattern, but then Sweet's ear would lose that pattern again and it would descend back into chaos. It was frustrating to the extreme.

But thoughts of the heat and the noise fled from Sweet's mind as soon as the shapes of the men climbed into view. There were six of them in total, all walking with their heads held high and making no attempts to conceal their approach. Five of the group were clad in long dark robes, tied across the chest and shoulder to reveal light, baked leather armour beneath. The sixth was leading them, and he was wearing thick, metal plate armour that reflected the sunlight in dazzling splashes as he moved.

'Bloody hell, has he been carrying that the whole way here?' Violent Fey's whisper came from over Sweet's left shoulder as she caught sight of the armoured warrior. Sweet swallowed, biting down fear as he watched the men walk towards them, moving slowly and calmly.

'He's a big lad,' Sweet muttered, 'I'm sure he can manage it a little while longer.'

'That's the magicker's bodyguard?' Prince Orsen asked from over Sweet's right shoulder. There was the slightest stammer to the younger man's voice, but he held his nerve well.

'Aye,' Sweet nodded, 'that's him.'

'You've some powerful enemies,' Orsen murmured.

Sweet turned to him and raised an eyebrow.

'Technically,' he told the prince, 'he's *your* enemy.'

Orsen smiled at that, but Sweet's own grin faded as he turned back to face the advancing warriors.

The armoured Wyn continued his climb, wearing his armour like it was a coat of feathers. Sweet saw the two hand-axes strapped to the man's broad back, the blades glinting wickedly in the sunshine as they peaked eagerly from over his wide shoulders. Sweet swallowed again.

'You sure about this?' Violent Fey asked. Sweet snapped his head round and saw the corner of her mouth had curled up slightly. She'd made a joke. There really was a first time for everything. His consternation turned immediately to dark humour and he felt himself relax.

'We all know the plan,' he told them gruffly, 'so let's see it done.'

They knew the plan alright. It was a simple one. Less to go wrong that way, Sweet reckoned. Sweet, Orsen and Violent Fey would engage Thond and his men just outside the rocky passage. They would quickly fall back and draw them inside. Just a few steps into the narrow cleft, Stover and Daraday would be waiting—the latter would be armed with his bow, though Sweet didn't much fancy the lad's chances of differentiating between one of them and one of Thond's group. Above them, screened by a short ledge, waited the Wyn. When the fighting moved into the passage he could drop down and ambush the attackers—it was Sweet's hope that he might be able to take down Thond himself, though the presence of all that plate armour had him doubting now. Killing the bear seemed like childsplay compared to this.

After a brief bit of fighting, they'd all then turn and flee back into the open space beyond. Ashan Feroq and her three Wyn warriors would be waiting there and—all being well—they'd overwhelm however many of their enemies were still standing. Sweet reckoned that, with a bit of luck, they'd be able to kill two of the attackers before they even got to that point. That would mean ten on four, in their favour, by the time all the dice had been thrown.

Good odds, Sweet reasoned.

His assessment of those odds wavered with every step Thond and his men took towards them. They moved with a swagger that stopped just short of arrogance. There was no pomp or ceremony, just a total belief in their physical power. A consummate understanding of their martial prowess. It wasn't something for them to boast about. Boasting about being the better warriors was beneath them. It was for blaggards. Real warriors didn't waste time or energy with tough talk, they just fought until their opponents couldn't.

It was simple, really. They were deadly and they knew it.

Sweet swallowed again.

The group stopped some twenty paces away. Even with the distance between them, Thond was still terrifyingly massive. He was wearing his full-faced helm again, so Sweet couldn't get a read on the man's face. But the faces of his companions were cold, their expressions dark. Sweet could tell that they were men who didn't bother with the bluster of threats. They didn't need harsh words and ruthless assurances. It wouldn't be part of their parlance. They just dealt in violence and death.

Thond shifted his weight and raised one enormous, plated arm. He extended his finger and pointed just over Sweet's shoulder, directly at Orsen. Sweet felt the fugitive prince shift uncomfortably under the weight of the gesture. The meaning was obvious; *give us the prince.*

'You boys are a long way from home,' Sweet called, glad to hear that his voice wasn't quavering. It was something of a surprise, because Sweet felt damn close to shitting himself with fear. The palms of his hands felt corpse-clammy and his mouth felt bone-dry. His head felt strangely light and his legs strangely heavy. He looked around at the rocks and arid plants. 'Strange place for a stroll, can we help you with anything?'

The men said nothing. They didn't bristle, or sneer, or curse. They just stood in silence, the breeze tugging gently at their dark robes. It made them feel all the more dangerous, somehow. Thond's armoured hand remained pointed at Orsen.

Sweet took a breath and tried again.

'You can see we've got our bounty,' he called. 'Bringing him back to your master now, in fact.' Sweet hitched his trews and tried to look nonchalant. 'We're just ah...taking a scenic route back to Levitan, is all.'

Thond's arm dropped back to his side, but still none of the gathered warriors spoke.

'After all,' Sweet continued, his voice lowering to more of a murmur, 'there's all sorts of dangerous folk about.'

The armoured giant slowly bent his arms behind his back and lifted the two huge axes clear of their ties. He pulled them back around in front of him, the edges of the heavy blades glinting in the sunlight. It seemed as though the big warrior was done talking.

'Fuck,' Sweet whispered.

Thond's men drew their own weapons and they began their advance.

Sweet licked his lips, though it only seemed to make them drier, and glanced to his left. Violent Fey held a borrowed shortsword in one hand and pulled a long-bladed dagger from her belt with the other, she reversed it with a flick of her wrist and bared her teeth at the advancing men. Sweet flicked his gaze right and saw Orsen had already drawn the blade of Damsen steel, it flashed brightly in the sunlight. Sweet swallowed and drew his own sword, the ringing as it was pulled from its sheath sounded weedy and hollow. He held the weapon up and waited for Thond and his crew to draw closer.

When they were just a few paces away the enemy suddenly rushed forwards, as though some unspoken command had passed between them.

There were no battle cries, no shouts or grunts of exertion. The absence of those things somehow made the whole experience even more horrifying. It was just a cold, silent wave of meat and steel that surged towards where Sweet was standing.

For a heartbeat he froze, unable to move for the shock of the sudden attack. If it had lasted any longer then he would've died instantly, but luckily the heartbeat passed and then Sweet took a big step back. More of a clumsy lunge back, really, but he dodged the swinging blade of Thond's left-hand axe all the same. Beside him, Vi and the prince had done the same, backing away from the sheer ferocity of their opponents' opening rush. There was a clash of steel as Orsen turned away one man's blade, only to cry out in surprise as a second attacker nearly ran him through with his own weapon. To Sweet's left, Vi snarled furiously as she ducked a sweeping slash that would've opened her throat, she parried away a second blade and hissed at her opponents through gritted teeth.

Sweet saw a glint of something coming his way and scrambled backwards for the second time in as many moments. Thond's second axe came hurtling through the air, right through the space Sweet had previously been occupying. Sweet reckoned the force of the blow would've opened him up from shoulder to groin, such was the strength of the big, armoured Wyn. The attack left an opening though and Sweet stabbed back with his own sword, but Thond was sickeningly fast and spun on one heel, bringing up one of his axes to deflect the blow. Sweet had to cling onto his sword to stop it from flying out of his grip. The force of Thond's parry sent vibrations running up his arm all the way to his teeth. Then Sweet was backing away again, desperately trying to avoid the deadly arcs of Thond's swinging axes.

Vi and Orsen were faring little better. The plan to back away into the rocky passage was accelerating quickly now, for all three of them knew that if they didn't do it soon then they would be butchered. Orsen cried out again as a sword blade pierced his defences, opening up a long cut across one cheek, he countered with a riposte aimed at disembowelling his attacker but another enemy tapped his sword aside with ease.

'Back!' Sweet called, narrowly avoiding another swing of Thond's mighty axes. The shout was little more than a desperate plea, but the others heard it right enough. They began moving back towards the passageway through the rocks. Thond and his men continued their advance, pressing home their advantage with a cold fury. Sweet spun away from one of the huge axes again, only to nearly impale himself on another man's outstretched sword. He brought his own weapon down to bear on it but the wielder was too fast and flicked it back as he pulled away, the length of the blade ran down Sweet's side and he grunted as a cut was opened across his ribs. The hilt of his own sword connected with the blade and he managed to push it away just as the attacker stabbed forwards again. Violent Fey saw her moment and lashed out with her long-bladed dagger—the one she spent so much time sharpening around their nightly campfires. The blade plunged through the man's eye socket and he made a piercing, gurgling sound before crumpling to the ground. The dagger was lodged deep in his skull and Vi had to let go of it in order to defend herself from yet another ferocious assault.

'Back!' Sweet called again, the pain in his side fuelling the strength of the sound now. Together they edged their way into the shadow of the rocky passageway. Sweet risked a glance over his shoulder to judge where the first curve through the rocks was. The risk nearly ended him, as Thond suddenly charged. A silent mass of metal that just appeared in front of Sweet's face. He ducked on instinct, avoiding a slashing cut from both of the man's axes that would've decapitated him. Sweet stabbed out again but it was pointless, his sword only scraped meekly along the bigger man's armour. Thond pulled his swing back and his metal-plated forearms slammed into Sweet's chest with a devastating force. Sweet was hurled backwards and hit the rockwall with a thud that knocked the wind out of him.

Sweet groaned, certain that his ribcage had been smashed to shards. Then he felt a sharp pain in his eyes as grit was kicked into his face, he glanced up to see Violent Fey had nearly back right onto him, her booted heel kicking up dust and pebbles as she dodged the attentions of two of Thond's men.

Sweet tried to rise but it was as though his muscles wouldn't obey his mind. He sat, slumped and groggy and saw that the attacking pair had opened up Vi's defences. Just as one of them was about to spear his sword through her unprotected midriff an arrow suddenly materialised in his neck. The man grunted and dropped his sword, his eyes going wide with surprise. Dark blood began to bubble around the wound and the man dropped to one knee, his hands fumbling at the shaft. Vi regained her composure and parried a strike from the remaining attacker, defending desperately.

Sweet heard Stover give a great shout, cursing and hollering as he emerged from his hiding place. The frenzy of the bounty hunter's sudden appearance seemed to give Thond's men a moment to reassess. The man closest to him repelled Stover's initial attack and then backed away.

There was the slightest lull in the fighting and Sweet felt a hand grab him under his armpit. The fingers of that hand dug into his flesh like iron bars, causing the gashes he'd received from the fight with the bear to flare in pain. Sweet grunted and saw it was Daraday who was lifting him to his feet.

Sweet nodded to the youngster, then swung his attention back to Thond and his men. The attacker that Daraday had shot was still on his knees, though his fumbling hands seemed to be lolling more now and Sweet reckoned he wouldn't be getting back up. Adding him to the man Violent Fey had killed just outside of the passage, that left just Thond and three of his crew remaining—at the expense of none of their own.

Sweet didn't have time to admire their luck as the enormous armoured Wyn suddenly lurched towards them again. His men followed and the fighting began anew. Steel clashed against steel, the noise echoing high up through the rocks all around them, sounding like the melody of a madman to accompany the din of the crashing river. The noise was interspersed with the occasional grunt from Sweet's side of proceedings. Daraday had nocked another arrow to his bow and was frantically searching for a target, but he was positioned behind Violent Fey and the others so he couldn't risk loosing an arrow without hitting one of his own. Step by step, the group was forced back through the passage. A combination of Thond's ferocity and the skill of his warriors meant that Sweet and his crew were fighting for their lives. Rarely did they offer an attack of their own, and each time they attempted to counter they left openings that nearly got them killed. Orsen tried another riposte, only to see it rolled easily. The tip of his attacker's blade pierced his shoulder, but he backed away swiftly with a grunt and slashed the weapon aside before it could be driven deeper. Stover dove aside from a slashing cut, pressing himself against the craggy rock wall to avoid the blade. The attacker's sword clanged off the stone, the blade stopping just inches from Stover's nose. Violent Fey was bleeding heavily from a cut on one arm and Sweet could see dark droplets marking their retreat through the passageway.

They were tiring, too. Sweet's own breath was catching in his chest as though someone was sitting on him, and the close proximity of the stone passage meant that he could hear similar exertions from those around him, too. Thond and his men still made almost noise at all. Their breathing seemed controlled and they continued to slash and cut with precision, rather than fury. Thond himself was still swinging his terrible axes at Sweet, who could do little more than back away each time the deadly weapons hurtled towards him. Thankfully the man's size and the close quarters of their surroundings meant that he couldn't arc the weapons at the same time, but even so he moved them with delicate conservation. The ferocity of the attacks had lessened, but they were no less deadly for it. The curved edges of the weapons flashed within inches of Sweet's face more than once as he desperately tried to fend the armoured giant off.

As he was retreating, Sweet's heel caught on a cleft in the floor. He spiralled backwards and landed on his arse with a jarring thud that sent pain running up the length of his spine. His teeth clamped together and he bit his tongue hard, the metallic taste of warm blood flooding his mouth. Sweet slammed his hands down to stop from falling flat on his back. Thond's right hand-axe came cannoning through the air and chopped into Sweet's left hand. The pain from his arse was instantly replaced by a sudden burning sensation in his knuckles and Sweet saw that the axe had bitten through flesh and bone, even cutting bloody chips away from the stone below. Thond hefted the axe clear and brought it crashing down again. Sweet had just enough of his senses left to roll madly away, cradling his wounded hand and half-crawling away with his other. He had just enough time to glance down and see that the first two fingers of his left hand had been sheared away completely. The third finger had a deep cut into the side of it that was oozing blood. Both the gash and the bloody stumps pulsed with a growing agony. Sweet swore and rolled again, seeing his severed fingers lying in a splash of crimson on the floor just ten paces away. Thond stood over them, the edge of one axe blade slick with blood.

My blood, Sweet realised.

Sweet groaned and struggled to his feet, vaguely aware that he had dropped his sword somewhere. The fighting around him was still furious and every member of his crew was still battling for their lives. If it went on much longer those battles would soon be lost.

A shadow flickered from above and Sweet saw the Wyn drop down from his hiding place. He fell silently, like a hawk descending on its prey. Just as he had done when he'd killed the bear, Sweet thought. Only this time his target was plated in metal and carried two huge axes instead of bared teeth and talons.

And this time his target spotted him first.

Thond quickly adjusted his footing, but didn't have time to bring either of his monstrous weapons to bear. Instead he raised one forearm and the Wyn crashed into it with a sound that echoed through the rocky passage. Both men were pushed to the ground and Sweet saw the Wyn quickly roll clear, his sword in hand. The tattooed tribesman scrambled over to Sweet and started dragging him back through the passage.

Thond clambered to his feet, clearly a little dazed from the impact but recovering quickly. The armoured giant began staggering after them and Sweet realised that the others had started fleeing, too. Vi was attempting a fighting retreat against a swordsman who moved so quickly Sweet could barely see his blade. The prince was doing the same as Stover and Daraday led the way back through the rocky passage. The pain throbbing from Sweet's ruined hand was excruciating now and he gritted his teeth as the Wyn pulled him along.

'Fuck,' he whispered, his mutilated fingers dripping blood as they ran.

*

The six of them burst out of the rocky passage in a heaving, sweating heap. Sweet stumbled again as the full roar of the raging river washed over him, only for the Wyn to tighten his grip and haul him upright once more. The tribesman was immensely strong and for the second time Sweet felt the stitches on the gash in his arm pull. After being dragged another few paces he felt some of them rip completely and the top of his shoulder began to add to the cacophony of glowing hot pain that seemed to be emanating from every part of his body.

They staggered out into the open space, squinting hard against the sudden brightness of the sunlight. Ashan Feroq and the three other Wyns were waiting in a half-circle around the entrance of the rocky passage. The bounty hunters limped beyond them and then turned to face the enemy.

Thond still led the way. He loomed out of the shadows like a demon of legend, his plate armour and the blades of his axes flashing dangerously as he stepped into the sunlight. His three remaining warriors followed, their swords still drawn. Sweet saw blood dripping from two of them and wondered what other wounds they'd inflicted on his crew inside the passage.

He should've felt elation. Thond and his men were now outnumbered ten to four, just as he'd hoped—but Sweet knew those numbers would count for little. The skirmish inside the passageway showed the gulf in skill between his crew and Thond's warriors. Besides, Sweet and the others were injured and exhausted now, too. If they fought them in an open space like this they would be cut down in moments. No, the hard truth was that they would now be more of a hindrance than a help.

And truth was a weapon.

Sweet felt that truth, cold and sharp, slide home as he realised their chances of survival now rested on the fighting prowess of Ashan Feroq and her tiny tribe. They were stealthy enough, that much was for sure, but how would they fare in open combat?

Thond paused for a moment. His face was still covered by his helm, but Sweet could feel him scanning these new opponents. Sizing them up like a butcher examining the meat in front of him. Ashan Feroq stood motionless, her sword still scabbarded at her hip. The thunder of the crashing river filled every moment as the two groups observed one another in watchful silence.

Then Thond surged forwards again. For someone so huge, he moved so quickly that Sweet found it a miracle that he was still alive at all. One of the man's enormous axes slashed toward Ashan Feroq, but the Wyn warrior sidestepped at the last. Her sword rang out through the din as she swept it from its scabbard and aimed a return stab towards Thond's exposed armpit. The giant clamped his arm down and spun away from the attack, his second axe spinning towards Ashan's head. The Wyn warrior woman ducked and backed away.

Thond's men rushed forwards at the same time as their leader. They were met by Ashan's warriors and the clash of steel sang out amidst the noise of the river, the sounds echoing horribly against the stone walls around them. Sweet could only gawp in amazement at the swordplay on display. The warriors on both sides moved with a graceful ferocity, their movements swift and filled with power, but not overzealous in their execution. Every attack, every parry, carried exactly the amount of energy and strength that it needed to in order to be effective. The faces of the tribesmen on both sides were set. Their focus total.

Sweet felt the grip on his arm loosen as the Wyn—their Wyn—strode forwards to join the fray. Sweet was too exhausted, his body wracked with too much pain and his mind overwhelmed by the deadly skills on show to protest. He watched as the Wyn leapt to the defence of the younger female warrior from Ashan's group. She was struggling to contain the attacks of the attacker who faced her and the Wyn parried a downward cut aimed at her head. The tattooed tribesman then spun away from a lunge, slamming his shoulder into the attacker's body and pushing him back. Stunned, Thond's warrior was now on the back foot as the Wyn pressed home his advantage, cutting and slashing with terrifying speed. The Wyn dodged a riposte, but instead of backing away he stepped in to meet his attacker once again. Sweet saw the warrior's eyes go wide with fear—perhaps he realised he was about to die—as the Wyn kicked out at his planted knee. Sweet didn't hear the crunch over the noise of the river behind him, but he saw the warrior's face contort with pain as the limb bent awkwardly under the impact of the kick, causing him to drop his sword. The man's painful expression redoubled as the Wyn's own blade bit into his chest. Sweet saw the tip of the blade extend up and out of the man's back in a bloody spray.

The Wyn turned, wrenching his blade free and letting the body crumple to the floor. He gave a curt nod to the female warrior in Ashan's group and then sought out his next opponent. Across the way, Sweet saw that the two men in Ashan's group were acquitting themselves well against Thond's remaining warriors. He could see the doubts that were starting to form in the minds of their opponents. Their attacks seemed less sure, as though they didn't want to commit themselves too much and leave themselves open to returning blows. Their confidence—the same confidence that had been on such resplendent display as they'd first strutted up the hillside—was beginning to ebb away.

The armoured giant must've sensed it too, despite his concerted efforts to kill Ashan Feroq herself. He suddenly spun away from the Wyn leader and flung one of his hand axes at the closest of her warriors. Sweet barely saw the weapon as it turned and turned through the air. The intended target obviously didn't see it either, as the heavy blade slammed into the side of his skull. The force of the blow toppled the man sideways and he fell in a heap, dark blood leaking around the axe still embedded in his head.

Ashan Feroq gave a howl—the closest thing to a war cry Sweet had heard from anyone outside of his own crew—and launched a frenzied attack against Thond. The armoured giant parried her first attacks using the plates on his arm, then brought his remaining axe up to return the blows in kind. The lithe Wyn leader dodged the heavy blade, moving like flowing water to avoid its deadly touch, then continued her assault. Sweet, his mutilated hand throbbing now, watched transfixed as the two warriors hacked and slashed at each other. Their skill was incredible to behold. Ashan Feroq was lightning fast, the tip of her blade seeking the meagre gaps in Thond's plate armour, but the giant was equal to it, closing off her openings and swinging his one remaining axe with devastating force.

Ashan Feroq danced aside from another sweeping cut and lanced out with her blade. For a moment Sweet thought she had him. The tip of her outstretched sword seemed destined to slide in the parting between plates under Thond's armpit, the blade would surely spear his lungs. But the giant was wise to the move and spun on his heel, stepping in to meet his attacker. Sweet saw Ashan's eyes go wide before the full force of Thond's plated forearm smashed into her face with a crunch that was audible even over the din of the river. The lean Wyn leader was catapulted backwards, staggering several half steps before crashing to the ground. Her sword was spun from her grip, twinkling in the sunlight as it sailed through the air.

Thond moved in for the kill. His enormous shoulders were heaving now and Sweet was glad to see that even he was tiring—at least it proved he was human. He approached where Ashan lay dazed, blood streaming from her ruined nose as she struggled to straighten her vision and prop herself up on her elbows.

A shadow stepped across her, a curved sword raised in tattooed hands.

The Wyn.

Sweet saw Thond pause for a moment, as if gauging this new opponent. Then he charged, covering the ground between them with terrifying speed. The Wyn was ready for it, and slashed across Thond's shoulder as he sidestepped the attack. The blade didn't cut into him, but it hit his armour with enough force to dislodge one of the metal plates, leaving it hanging from a broken leather strap. Sweet thought she heard an angry growl from within that full-faced helmet, but there was no way to tell over the roar of the river. Thond and the Wyn circled one another. The wind had changed and spray now clouded the scene, glittering dangerously in the bright golden sunlight above.

Thond attacked again, and again the Wyn dodged the sweeping axe blade. His sword licked out, seeking an opening. The armoured giant didn't pause to catch his breath this time, instead he rounded on the Wyn and unleashed a devastating series of sweeps and cuts with his murderous axe. At first the Wyn ducked and weaved away from the blades with the same ease of movement Sweet had come to recognise in him, but as the assault was sustained he started making mistakes. His footing wasn't quite right and it put him off balance. The price of the error was very nearly decapitation at the hands of Thond's axe. Then his riposte was wild, with the armoured giant neatly parrying it and reversing a swing that nearly opened the Wyn's throat. At the last, the Wyn didn't jump far enough back and Sweet saw the blade of Thond's axe cut into the top of his sword arm. A spray of blood leapt into the air and mixed with the mist from the river below. The Wyn lost his grip on his sword and it clattered to the stones at his feet. He had no time to retrieve it, though, as Thond moved in again, forcing him back. Closer and closer towards the precipice overlooking the torrent. The Wyn scuttled and danced away, before running out of ground to flee into. He turned and faced Thond, the heel of his left boot hanging over the edge of the drop into the raging waters below.

The armoured giant paused again, his shoulders rising and falling with his exertions now. He stooped down and picked up the Wyn's sword with his free hand—it looked like a tooth-pick in his plated grip. Sweet could almost sense the giant's triumphant smile from inside his helmet. The big warrior hefted the sword, testing its weight, then slowly advanced on the Wyn. Sweet wanted to cry out, but his throat was hoarse and no words came out. He wanted to rush over and help—unarmed and badly injured as he was—but his legs wouldn't move. Time seemed to slow as Thond stalked towards the tattooed tribesman. From his position, Sweet could see the Wyn's face—still plain and pragmatic, despite the obvious peril he was in. The tribesman's flint-like eyes met his own and it seemed like they softened for a moment, as though the Wyn was saying something. Sweet had known him for long enough to read what that look meant, though at first it didn't register properly.

He was saying goodbye.

Thond stepped closer, his captured sword raised. As he lunged, the Wyn suddenly stepped in to meet the strike. The blade pierced his chest and exited in a bloody spray out of his back. The Wyn's eyes bulged as he was speared by the weapon. At the same time, he clamped both hands around Thond's elbow and braced his legs against a jutting rock. Sweet had no time to cry out. He watched as the tattooed tribesmen threw himself backwards, the force of the movement—combined with Thond's own forward momentum—carried both men over the precipice. They seemed to tumble for an age, then disappeared into the hazy mist thrown up from the water below.

Sweet scrambled over to the edge of the rock, leaving a grisly trail of blood from his missing fingers. He looked down at the river below but saw nothing save for the raging foam and the roaring current. Sweet sagged against the stone, feeling numb. Even the pain from his hand had dissipated now. The spray from the river felt cool upon his face and he rolled onto his back, staring up at the bright blue sky.

Then all went black, and Sweet passed out.

## What it's worth

✦→→•–|—•—»●《•—|•←•←•←

SWEET WOKE SLOWLY, his eyes flickering as he tried to prise them open. Dappled sunlight filtered in, painted in an array of sharp greens and hazy browns. Shapes formed in his vision and he saw that they were the leaves of a tree, the branches bending and swaying softly in a firm breeze. A bird chirped from somewhere in the tree and Sweet heard the sound of rushing water in the distance. At first he felt groggy, unsure of where he was or what had happened, but then the memories of the fight with Thond and his warriors returned. He saw again the Wyn impale himself upon his own sword, held tightly in his opponent's outstretched hand. He saw the tattooed tribesman fasten his grip to the armoured giant and catapult them both backwards into the torrent below. His head ached with the memory, a throbbing that was growing in viciousness with every passing moment. Maybe it had all been some hideous nightmare. A bad dream to end all bad dreams.

More pain erupted from his left hand and he suddenly remembered Thond's axe, biting through his fingers and chipping at the rock beneath. It was no bad dream, then. He remembered scrabbling desperately away from a second swing, his amputated fingers abandoned at the feet of the armoured giant. Sweet pulled his hand into view and saw that a bandage had been applied to it, the fabric weaving around his palm and up between his two remaining fingers, binding them together. The first two appendages of his hand were an ugly space and Sweet grimaced as he felt a burning, itching pain emanate from the base of where they had been. He flexed his hand and the pain sharpened.

'Best not do that,' came the voice of Violent Fey, Sweet turned his head—sending another jolt of agony into his temple—and faced her. There was the beginning of a dark bruise forming around one side of her face, accompanied by a jagged cut that ran across her forehead. She looked exhausted, but otherwise unscathed. She crouched down beside Sweet with a waterskin in one hand and offered it to him. Sweet took the skin in his uninjured hand and drank, the cool liquid soothing his dry throat so much so that he nearly choked on it. 'Careful,' Vi warned him, 'take it slow.'

'What happened?' Sweet spluttered, offering her the waterskin back. Vi took it and replaced the stopper, she sighed and looked away before meeting his gaze again.

'We beat them,' she shrugged at last, though she sounded far from jubilant about their victory. 'Orsen and I killed one of them, with a lot of help from our new Wyn friends. They managed to get the other without us. And...well, you saw the big one go into the river,' Vi looked away again. 'Ain't no one getting out of that mess, especially not in all that armour.'

Sweet stayed silent a moment longer. He left Vi with her thoughts. Hell, they mirrored his own clearly enough. He pictured the look in the Wyn's eyes, just before the tribesman had leapt forwards to meet the deathblow that would be struck against him. The man had meant it. Every moment of it.

He had given his life to save theirs.

Sweet considered saying something. Truth be told he didn't know what to say. He wanted to voice his feelings at the Wyn's sacrifice, to pay the man's last deed the respect it so reverently deserved. But from the look painted across Vi's face he reckoned he didn't need to. Which was a damn good thing, too, because he didn't have the faintest clue how.

'How's everyone else?' Sweet asked, grimacing as he pushed himself to a sitting position. He was sitting with his back against the trunk of a tree, growing out the side of a gorsy slope. A rough-hewn path led away to their left, winding away out of sight. Further away, Sweet could see the river snaking its way through the rockier ground. The noise from the river echoed up to his ears, even with the distance. The bright sunlight turned the spray into a hazy mist and a myriad of colours danced among it.

'Cuts and bruises, mostly,' Vi shrugged again. 'Yours is the worst,' she added, motioning to Sweet's bandaged hand, 'Orsen got stabbed just above the hip, but it didn't go too deep. Daraday took a knock to the head but he's walking it off right enough.'

Vi paused, looked away again, then looked back, as though chewing her words a little before speaking them.

'The Wyns didn't do so well,' she continued, 'you saw what the big one did to one of the men. The other was killed helping Orsen. Only Ashan and her daughter survived.'

'Daughter?' Sweet raised an eyebrow, ignoring the pain it caused this time.

'Aye, I reckon so,' Violent Fey nodded, looking back down the path again. 'Hard to tell for sure when you don't know what they're saying, but they seem that way. They certainly look alike, anyway.'

Sweet said nothing. He hadn't really paid that much close attention to the Wyns. First they had been a threat, then a potential opportunity, then a downright essential ally. He hadn't stopped to think they might've been a family. Maybe the two dead men were Ashan Feroq's sons, or her brothers? Maybe one of them was her husband, the girl's father? Maybe that was what the Wyn—their Wyn—had meant when he'd first described the warrior woman's "tribe".

Maybe he'd meant *family*.

'How long have I been out?' Sweet asked, forcing the thoughts from his mind as he suddenly felt nauseous.

'Not more'n a few hours,' Vi shrugged again. 'We made a litter out of branches and a cloak. Pretty much dragged you up here, the river crossing's just down past those trees. The others are up ahead. It gets a little rocky and we couldn't carry you all the way up there.'

Sweet nodded, then remembered that Thond and his hunters weren't the only danger. Before he could ask, Vi held out an open hand.

'Daraday is scouting to the north,' she told him, anticipating the question. 'Reckon we're good, for now at least.'

'Aye, for now' Sweet grunted. He started climbing gingerly to his feet. He reached out to use the trunk of the tree as support and felt pain lance up his ruined hand. He grimaced.

'Easy now,' Vi warned him, 'you're pretty beat up. Take it slow.'

'I've had worse,' Sweet lied, forcing a grim smile. 'Besides, can't be sitting here in the shade all day now, can I?' Vi said nothing and Sweet managed to steady himself enough to look around for his gear.

'Your pack is up at the camp,' Vi said, watching him closely, 'your sword, too.'

Sweet gave another grim smile, then gestured with his ruined hand.

'Lead the way,' he said.

*

Sweet was exhausted by the time they reached the little cove of rocks in which the rest of the crew had hunkered down. It was a short walk from the tree he had been resting under, but the going was steep and rocky. It was no surprise they'd decided to leave him to rest a little further down the slope. The footing was loose, with stones shifting under Sweet's boots, and he nearly fell twice. The second time Vi had to snap out a steadying hand. He was breathing hard and could feel a sticky film of sweat covering his brow as he approached the camp.

Orsen saw him first. The raven-haired prince sat a little straighter and offered a smile that quickly turned to a grimace as he disturbed one of the many wounds he'd picked up in the fight with Thond's warriors, and from the bear before that. Stover was sitting a little further back and gave a curt nod, his near-permanent scowl still etched across his hatchet features. The tall Wyn leader, Ashan Feroq, sat opposite Orsen, one arm draped over the shoulder of the other robed woman. They both turned as Sweet approached and it was then that he saw the obvious similarities in their faces. They both had the same eyes, the same small nose—though Ashan's was bruised and swollen from where Thond had broken it—and the same high, angular cheekbones. They could've been the same person but for the years between them. Mother and daughter. How could he have missed it before?

Had other things on my mind, Sweet considered, dropping down close to Orsen with a grunt.

'You look like shit,' the prince observed. Sweet only nodded, too tired to even offer a weathered smile in response.

'We should eat,' Violent Fey strode into the camp and immediately began busying herself amongst their gear. 'Then get as much sleep as we can. We'll be alright here for the night, but need to get moving tomorrow.' She glared up at the clear sky, as if challenging it. 'Winter's not far off.'

Ashan Feroq said something in her own tongue, then rose to her feet. Her daughter did the same. The two Wyn warriors looked at each of the group in turn, their expressions weary, then Ashan spoke again, her words coming fast and alien. Sweet held up an apologetic hand once she'd finished.

'We're sorry,' he said, 'but we don't understand you.'

Ashan screwed her face up in frustration, wincing as it pinched at the bruising on her face, then muttered something in her own language. Finally she gestured, first to herself, then to her daughter. Then she pointed out beyond the camp, to the west. Sweet followed the movement with his eyes, then met her gaze. Understanding settled over him.

'You're leaving,' he said, motioning with his good hand and using his fingers to indicate a pair of walking legs. 'You're heading west?'

The Wyn leader brightened and repeated the gesture, nodding as she did so. She said something Sweet didn't understand. Then her tone became more solemn, her expression softened and she met Sweet's gaze with a melancholy understanding. Sweet didn't need to speak her language to understand what that look meant.

*I'm sorry for your loss.*

Sweet nodded in kind, hoping that the feeling was reciprocated in his own expression.

'We owe you both a great deal,' he said, suddenly aware that everyone in the camp was looking at him. He swallowed. 'You and your people saved our lives. You paid a heavy price. For what it's worth,' he tipped his head again, 'we're thankful for that.'

The Wyn leader nodded and motioned to her daughter. The younger woman gave a short bow to each of them—touching an open palm to her forehead as Sweet had seen their own Wyn do to Ashan before the fight with Thond—then the two women gathered their belongings and began to make their way out of the camp.

'They're leaving?' Stover stirred, dark bags hanging under fearful eyes. 'We could do with some fighters in the crew.'

'Aye,' Sweet sighed, watching the two Wyn warriors leave, 'but I don't think that's our choice.'

'We should ask them, at least,' Stover muttered, his tone somewhere close to a whine.

Sweet sighed again, closing his eyes and doing his best to ignore the thousand aches and pains that were plaguing his tired body.

'You're welcome to ask them, Stover,' he breathed.

*

The temperature had been warm for most of the day, but it quickly fell as the sun drifted below the horizon, a blazing disc of orange that soon turned into a swathe of pale pinks and deep purples. Violent Fey got a fire going as the sun set over the rocky landscape and the group—such as it was, now—huddled around it for warmth. Daraday returned not long after, reporting no signs of movement to the north of them and no indication that they were being pursued by anyone else to the south, too. He furrowed his brow when he realised they were two members lighter than before he had left to keep watch, but ultimately said nothing. He seemed to understand the reasons for the absence of the Wyns without needing an explanation from anyone. After all, Sweet thought, the boy is sharp.

It was a good thing he didn't need it explained to him, because the crew was exhausted. Daraday gave Sweet the slightest of nods to acknowledge his good health—such as it was—and dropped down beside Violent Fey. He immediately pulled out a dagger to clean and sharpen. Vi had already laid down under her blanket, though Sweet doubted that she would be sleeping. And if she is—he thought—it wouldn't take much to rouse her, no doubt with a blade already in hand. Further round the campfire, Stover was also covered by his blanket, his shoulders heaving up and down with steady, guttering snores. It would take more effort to wake him up, Sweet mused, that was for sure.

Sweet himself was tired beyond all reason. The litany of bumps and pains seemed to have dulled into one singular pulsing sensation that emanated throughout his body. It was like wearing a cloak of bone-weary, ever stiffening aches. It was uncomfortable for sure, but bearable all the same. Every now and again though, sudden fire would light from the missing fingers of his left hand and he would glance down at the bandages wrapped around it. At first he would be confused, trying to make sense of the new silhouette at the end of his arm, then the pain would flare again and remind him he would forever be short of a few appendages.

'How's the hand?' Orsen asked from his left. Sweet glanced up and saw the prince looking at him. He shrugged.

'Hurts like a bastard,' he admitted, 'but I'll get by.' Sweet thought for a moment, then added, 'and I always was bad with a bow, anyway.'

Orsen gave a weary smile. The weariness of it was only highlighted by the deep shadows cast on his face by the flickering campfire. His smile was quickly replaced with a sharp grimace and he stiffened a little.

'You look like shit,' Sweet told him, drawing a fresh smile from the prince.

'I *feel* like shit,' he replied, holding a hand to the side of his belly.

'They stick you bad?' Sweet asked, motioning to the cloth wrapped around Orsen's midriff.

'Got lucky,' Orsen grinned, 'he slipped just as he lunged. He got flesh but not much else.' He paused, his smile fading. 'I think we were due a bit of luck.'

'Aye,' Sweet muttered, seeing again two shapes—locked in a deadly embrace—plummet off a rocky outcrop and into the raging waters below. The longer he stared into the campfire the more it felt like he could see them there, flickering amongst the flames.

'He was one hell of a fighter,' Orsen continued speaking, breaking Sweet's growing melancholy. The prince breathed deeply and whistled it out through pursed lips. 'I've never seen anyone move so fast. All my life

I thought Carthin was the best swordsman in the world…but your man was beyond comparison.'

'That he was,' Sweet nodded, not entirely sure whether he was agreeing with the prince's assessment of the Wyn's skill with a blade, or simply his worth as a man. A wave of sadness washed over Sweet then, like a dark flood that drenched all of his thoughts. He sighed and looked over at the prince. 'You know we never even knew his name?'

Orsen raised an eyebrow, then looked down.

'I was going to ask if anyone knew it,' the prince admitted, 'but it never felt…right.'

'We never even asked him,' Sweet continued, 'we ran recruitment in a town somewhere north of Thradonia, I forget where. He just…joined our crew and we called him "the Wyn" – it was kinda funny at first, then it just stuck. And he…' Sweet trailed off, curbing his rising frustration by taking another deep breath. 'And he *died* for us. All of us. Without us even knowing his fucking name.'

Sweet grimaced. He felt a plague of regrets gripping at his chest, chief amongst them was the shame at his apathy towards a man who had sacrificed everything for them. Guilt sliced away bits of him with more force than any battleaxe ever could. He felt like bellowing his anger into the darkness, but instead he only sat and stared blankly into the dancing flames of the campfire, letting the misery and pitiful self-loathing wash over him.

Bitterness had dripped from every word he'd spoken. Bitterness that tasted like ash in his mouth. Bitterness that he knew he had brought upon himself. He was Bitter Sweet, after all. That was the truth. And truth was a fucking weapon.

'I don't think it mattered to him,' Orsen's voice broke Sweet's descent into his own dark thoughts. Sweet glanced up, grateful to see that the prince wasn't looking at him. Instead the younger man was staring into the fire, though really he was looking through it. Looking at nothing. His face was set, his expression peaceful. 'You said yourself, he joined your crew. I think *that* was what mattered to him.'

'Enough to give his own life for ours,' Sweet muttered.

'It was his life to give,' Orsen shrugged. 'If he decided to lay it down in exchange for yours,' the prince sighed, 'then that was his choice. Only he gets to decide what his life is worth.'

Sweet considered that for a moment. He still felt swamped by regret. His guilt still clouded his mind and his anger was still burning hot somewhere beneath it all. But there was something in what Orsen was saying.

And something was enough.

'Now,' Orsen continued, offering a conciliatory smile, 'I really do feel like shit, so I'm gonna get some sleep.' The prince paused, before quietly adding, 'you should, too.'

'Aye,' Sweet lied, knowing he'd be incapable of sleep. 'In a while,' he said.

The prince rolled over, bundling himself in a blanket and using his pack as a pillow. He settled down facing the fire and lay still. His breathing deepened within moments and Sweet knew that the younger man was asleep.

Sweet stared back into the campfire, his mind a hurricane of raging thought. Complicated thoughts. Thoughts that were more painful than any severed fingers ever would be. Regrets and questions. Bitterness and guilt and shame. All things that Sweet had tried damned hard to avoid for most of his life. He knew rest would never come whilst his head was filled with such an alien maelstrom, but he closed his eyes against the flickering firelight all the same. His mind dwelling on what the young prince had said.

And drifted off to sleep.

## All that glitters

→⟩ + ⟩•⟩• ┼»●◄┼ •⟨•⟨ + ⟨

S WEET WOKE TO an orchestra of pain. It seemed that every joint and
muscle in his body was throbbing and moaning in turn. Some of them
didn't even bother to get in line, instead lancing him with angry reminders
that they needed soothing more urgently than the others. A few even got
impatient and flared like a kicked fire, sending sharp daggers through the
back of Sweet's tired eyes. He blearily rolled over, acutely aware of an
unpleasant tingling from his missing fingers. Sweet hoped the wound
wouldn't get infected. He felt a shudder of fear as he remembered seeing
injuries similar to his go bad. The unfortunate men and women with bad
wounds would scream of a burning fire emanating from the injury. Their
blood became poisoned and further amputations often became necessary.
Even then, not all of them lived.

That bleak thought, along with the multiple servings of pain had
woken Sweet fully now and he tried to push the images of infected
wounds and agonising deaths from his sleep-addled brain.

It was morning. The sky above heaved with a brooding grey horde of
clouds and there was a metallic smell to the air that promised rain wasn't
far away. It seemed that the previous day's glorious sunshine had been an
interlude, rather than a prelude to some good fortune from the weather.
Sweet groaned and forced himself onto his back, staring up at the roiling
mass of slate-grey sky high above him. A chill wind was blowing steadily
and he felt a small sense of comfort, swaddled as he was under his thin
blanket. Still, now that he was awake the cacophony of aches and pains—
coupled with the promise of grim weather and the thought of an agony-
induced death—was chipping away at that comfort. He sighed, then
committed to moving once more.

With another heaving groan, Sweet rolled onto one elbow, stifling
a wince as pain erupted from it. He pushed himself up to a kneeling
position and closed his eyes, took a deep breath and waited for the worst
aches in his body to subside. When he was sure they were as quiet as they

would go, Sweet opened his eyes again and let out his breath. Violent Fey and Daraday were still sleeping where they had lay the night before, each wrapped tightly in the meagre comforts of their blankets. Sweet looked the other way, expecting to see Orsen still coddled in a similar position.

Only there was no Orsen.

Sweet stayed where he was for a moment, his brain struggling to process the space where the prince had been. Maybe he went for a piss, Sweet reasoned, though when he scanned the periphery of the camp he couldn't see any sign of him. Didn't need to wander that far to take a piss, Sweet thought.

Maybe he went for a walk? Sweet nearly scoffed aloud. They were all so exhausted that a leisurely stroll was the last thing on anyone's mind. Besides, what the hell was there to see other than bare rock and scree?

Sweet felt the first stab of rising alarm, an urgent sensation that gripped him deep in his guts and wormed its way up to his thoughts. It was instinctive, and Sweet relied on his instincts. He cast his eyes over the rest of the camp.

And realised that Stover was missing, too.

'Fuck,' Sweet whispered. Then he was scrambling across to where Violent Fey and Daraday were sleeping, the latter was even snoring quietly. 'Wake up!' he tried to bark, but his throat was dry and it came out as a rasp. It didn't matter, Violent Fey rolled clear of her blankets almost instantly, her eyes wide and a dagger in hand, glinting dully in the grim morning light.

'What is it?' she demanded, her bleary eyes clearing quickly as they flickered around their little campsite for signs of danger.

'Orsen's gone,' Sweet told her, his missing fingers somehow itching uncontrollably. He ignored it. 'Stover, too.'

Vi's expression darkened. She threw her blanket away and rose smoothly to her feet. Daraday wasn't far behind her, though the youngster looked a great deal more hazy than she did.

'Which way?' she growled, her knuckles tightening white around the hilt of the dagger. Sweet looked around, realising too late that he was searching for the Wyn for advice on tracking. He put aside the sudden stab of guilt and made his best guess.

'Back the way we came?' he offered, 'I don't reckon he would've pressed on, too many unknowns.'

'Why'd they go?' Daraday asked, his own alarm evident from his expression.

'Don't reckon Stover gave Orsen much of a choice,' Sweet replied, turning it over in his mind. 'Probably waited for him to get up to take a piss, followed him and took him hostage at knifepoint.'

'Why didn't Orsen shout for help?'

'Stover threatened him,' Sweet shrugged, weariness settling over him now. 'The mad bastard would've killed him if he made a sound.'

'But why?' Daraday pressed, confusion etched across his face.

Violent Fey stepped forward, shouldering her pack and drawing another dagger from her belt. Her face was darker than the clouds above, her voice colder than the wind that blew through the camp.

'Let's find out,' she growled.

\*

The three of them left their gear and scrambled down the slope back towards the noise of the river crashing through the rocky valley below. Violent Fey led the way, her eyes set and teeth gritted in a near-permanent snarl. She picked her way over the rough terrain like a predator, relentless and focussed. Daraday followed close behind, his own expression a mask of dark concentration now that he had shaken the last of his sleep away. Sweet struggled on behind them both, feeling every iota of the weight of his years, the trials of the journey north and the pain of his injuries. His breath came in heaving gulps as he battled to keep up with the other two, all the while his thoughts raced like leaves in a stormwind.

Fucking Stover! His mind screamed through a lance of pain from his mutilated hand. The silly bastard thinks he can lead Orsen all the way back south with a sword at his back! And then what? All the way back to Levitan? For what? Does he really think Sylvanus won't just kill him and take the prince? How fucking stupid did you have to be to even consider that as a viable option!

But, Sweet supposed, if there was one thing Stover didn't lack, it was stupidity.

Anger started to rise in Sweet then. Anger at Stover. Anger at the loss of the Wyn. At the loss of Bryntas. Even Jenrick, who had drowned in a festering canal. Anger at the magicker, Sylvanus and his arrogant Vol masters. Anger at the whole damn enterprise. Mostly though, Sweet found that he was angry with himself. Angry for taking on this wretched task when every fibre of his being had told him not to. Angry at his own stubbornness for finding reasonable ways forward when every last instinct had screamed at him to turn back and walk away.

That anger fuelled his resolve. It quieted his pain and surged through his exhausted body like a wildfire. He gritted his teeth and pushed on, taking long, purposeful strides until he was level with Violent Fey. He saw the same feelings of concentrated rage etched onto her features. She glanced over at him. They didn't say a word to each other. But—as with so many times before—Sweet reckoned they didn't need to.

That look said it all.

*

They crossed the river at a shallow ford. At this point in its arc, the raging torrent had slowed to little more than a fast-flowing stream. At the ford itself the water only came up to Sweet's knees at its deepest point. As he trudged across after Violent Fey he found himself wondering if the Wyn's body had washed past this point. Or had it snagged somewhere further upstream? Certainly the giant, Thond, wouldn't have made it this far downriver. With all that armour, added to his enormous bulk, it was more likely he'd been dragged under and caught somewhere against the riverbed. Caged in metal as the rushing water surged in to smother him. Sweet had to concede it was a nasty way to go, even if the big bastard probably deserved it.

Daraday splashed through the river beside him, an arrow notched to his hunting bow. They didn't know exactly what time Stover had stolen out of the camp with Orsen as his prisoner, it could've been as soon as the rest of them drifted into sleep or it could've been moments before Sweet had awoken. That meant the pair of them could be miles into the wilderness, or just around the next bend in the track. The boy wanted to be ready.

After the ford, the land rose sharply again. Crumbling dirt pathways gave way to more rocky ground. Gorse and bushes screened the sides of their way and they soon found themselves following the course of the river upstream. The path narrowed and soon they were walking with a rockface on one side and the crashing torrent below on the other. The ground was slick with spray and they moved carefully as well as quickly.

Before long the path widened again. They rounded a bend and Sweet saw that they were back in the same open, rocky expanse where they had fought Thond and his band of hunters. The sky was still dark, despite the lateness of the morning, and the whole place had taken on a more sombre tone now. The bodies of Thond's men were nowhere to be seen, maybe Vi and the others had rolled them into the river, maybe wild animals had taken them, but dark patches on the rock remained where they'd fallen.

Sweet saw the lip of rock that the Wyn had catapulted himself and Thond into the river below, condemning them both to watery graves. And in the middle of the rocky circle—making for the narrow passage where some of Sweet's fingers had been liberated from his left hand—were two hunched figures. One of the men carried a drawn sword and was shuffling a step or two behind the other.

The rage that had been welling inside of Sweet became uncontrollable then. He took a deep breath and bellowed as loud as his weathered lungs would allow, forcing the noise to carry over the din of the crashing river.

'Stover!'

The two men froze and turned. The noise from the river was enormous, but Sweet's shout had cut through it like a hot knife through butter. Sweet saw Orsen's face brighten, at the same time as Stover's mouth fell open in surprise. His expression went from its usual fixed derision to one of fear. His eyes went wide and he scurried closer to where Orsen was standing, positioning the prince between them as Sweet, Violent Fey and Daraday marched across the stone towards them.

'Stover you traitorous fuck!' Sweet barked, stopping some ten paces away from them both as he suddenly became acutely aware of the steel in the other man's hand.

'No closer, Sweet!' Stover spat, levelling his sword against Orsen's back and moving half a pace to his left to show them what he was doing. 'Or I'll stick him like the royal swine he is.'

'And then what, Stover?' Violent Fey hissed, a dagger still gripped in each of her hands, the knuckles bone white. 'You kill him and we kill you.'

'I could've killed you all!' Stover shouted, his voice nearly a shriek. 'Could've slit your throats while you slept! But I didn't! I *let* you live!'

'You couldn't risk waking one of us more like!' Violent Fey retorted, her lip curling in anger. 'Fucking coward!'

'Rather be a coward than a dead man!' Stover bellowed back, locking eyes with Sweet. He bared his teeth and tipped his head back. 'You'd have killed us all with this mad fucking plan o' yours! First Bryntas! Then the Wyn! We nearly got killed by a damn bear. Any one of us could've bought it back in that whorehouse in Scarvin.' He coughed a laugh, but there was no humour in the sound. 'Hell, Jenrick didn't even make it out of Levitan! It was only a matter of time. And for what? This bastard?'

'Enough, Stover,' Vi growled.

'Half a million in gold!' Stover tightened his grip on Orsen, his eyes bulging with a heady mix of fear, anger and excitement. 'With that big armoured bastard out of the way it's a clear ride back now!'

'He's our only way out of this mess!' Sweet shouted back. 'That magicker'll kill you and take the prince before you get within fifty miles of Levitan! He would've done the same to all of us!'

'I'll take my chances,' Stover sneered, tightening his grip on the sword pointed at Orsen's spine.

'No you won't,' Sweet told him. 'Vi's right, you've got no options left, Stover. Drop your weapons and walk away now. You get to live. But we won't let you take him, and if you kill him then we'll kill you, I promise you that.'

'A promise from you ain't worth shit!' Stover spat. 'Lies is all we ever get from you, *Bitter* Sweet.'

'Well this one is worth your life, Stover,' Sweet told the other man, his voice cold. He meant every word. Meant them more than anything he'd ever said. This was a cold truth, a hard truth. And truth was a weapon. 'We *won't* let you take him. And if you kill him, we *will* kill you.'

There was a moment of quiet—save for the thrashing of the river behind them—as Stover looked at each of them in turn. His expression alternated between fear, resentment and anger. He was cornered, and he knew it. His whole body shook with the dawning realisation of his predicament.

'Fuck you!' Stover burst at last, his voice quavering. He was somewhere between apoplectic rage and bursting into tears. 'Fuck you for bringing us out here! And fuck you for making us enemies of the fucking Vols!'

'He didn't do shit!' Violent Fey hissed again, slowly moving around the side of where Stover and Orsen were standing. She cocked her head dangerously. 'Or don't you remember that it was *you* who made us take this fucking bounty! *You* got us into this mess!'

'*I* got us into the deal of a lifetime!' Stover was shrieking now. He pointed a trembling finger at Sweet. 'It was *him* what turned it into a fucking nightmare! Lost his senses! Got caught up in a fucking fairytale and this bastard's pretty words!' Stover gave Orsen a sharp shove with the point of his sword, drawing a wince of pain from the prince's face. 'And pretty words is all they is! Sweet-talking, rancid bullshit! Promises of honour and redemption and more pay than the purse that the Vols put on his head! As if some runaway prince has more coin than the *fucking Vols!* It's all bullshit and you know it! And you got taken in by it like a bunch o' rubes! You got spun around by this bastard's fancy, shiny words! Well words don't put money in your pocket!' Stover's face was glowing red now, the veins on his neck bulging like tightened cords. 'And all that glitters ain't fuckin' gold!'

Something—a blur of movement—crashed into the side of Stover, knocking him sideways with a grunt. Orsen was caught by the blow and toppled forwards, landing awkwardly as the air was forced from his lungs. Sweet watched as Stover and the shape wrestled briefly on the ground, the unsheathed sword swinging wildly and clanging against the stone underfoot. It was then that he realised that the shape was Daraday. The younger man must've circled wide as Stover ranted and raved at them—blinded by his own vitriol—and now the lad had rushed in and was grappling with the grizzled bounty hunter.

The pair rolled to a sitting position, with Stover sat—groggy and with a bleeding split on his forehead—between Daraday's splayed legs. They were sat the way lovers might cuddle together, enjoying the sunshine of a summertime picnic, only their faces were both contorted into murderous rage. Sweet something flash, bright and sharp, in Daraday's hand. The youngster swung his arm up, curled it around Stover's chest and pinned him tight. The bright thing in his hand was a dagger, no doubt honed to wicked sharpness. Daraday—a cold snarl set across his face—drew it up to Stover's exposed neck and pulled it harshly across the stubbled skin.

Stover's throat split open like a ripe fruit. Crimson spilled out over Daraday's hands and splashed down onto Stover's chest. His eyes went bolt wide, like a mad horse caught in a fire. His free hand fumbled at the gaping wound in his neck as it yawned even wider. Sweet felt a moment of revulsion as he saw the grimy tip of one of Stover's fingers actually slip into his own slit throat as he tried desperately to stop his lifeblood from draining away. Stover gurgled something and more blood bubbled out from his mouth, popping and foaming with spit. A stark line of it, dark as ice at night, ran down the side of his chin to join the flood below. Stover's leg kicked and bucked twice, then his wide eyes rolled backwards and he went limp. They stayed there for a moment, Daraday straddling Stover from behind, his right arm slick with blood, before the younger man pushed himself backwards. He gave an angry kick at Stover and the dying bounty hunter toppled to one side. Blood immediately began to pool around him in a dark spread.

Sweet was breathless. The combination of his rage and exhaustion made him barely able to register what had happened. He saw that Violent Fey had rushed to Orsen's side, checking the prince for wounds. Orsen seemed to reassure her that he was fine and Vi quickly turned her attention to Daraday. The youngster was still standing over Stover's body, his bloodied arm—the dagger still gripped between white knuckles—dripping scarlet to the ground. He was glaring down at Stover's corpse with a hard look on his face.

Bloody hell the boy has got steel, Sweet thought. The notion made him feel strangely empty somehow. And there was unease, too. Sweet had seen the look on Daraday's face before, just never on the lad himself. Sweet had seen it plenty of times in his many seasons as a bounty hunter. He recognised it instantly—even instinctively—as the face of a man to be given the widest possible berth. A man to be avoided. A man not to be tested. A man most certainly not to be fucked with.

It was the face of a killer.

'Dara,' Vi was speaking, her usually steely voice now calm and soft. Almost like she was reasoning with the youngster, as though the dagger in his hand was levelled at her rather than pointing towards the dead body on the ground. Her approach sounded so alien to Sweet that it took him a moment to realise that she was exercising caution. She had seen the look on Daraday's face too, and clearly didn't fancy being on the receiving end of it. Hell, something in her voice sounded like it had strayed beyond cautious. Sweet reckoned she was worried.

Scared, even.

'I'm fine,' Daraday said, his voice flat as he continued to stare down at Stover's body. The grimy bounty hunter had fallen onto his side and flopped slowly onto his back, his slit throat had stopped pumping blood and instead now merely leaked it. Stover's dead eyes stared up at the slate sky. Daraday turned away from the grisly display and met Violent Fey's worried gaze. 'I'm fine,' he repeated, more assuredly this time.

Something in Vi's posture relaxed a little and Sweet suddenly realised he had been holding his breath for what seemed like forever. He let it out, as slowly and steadily as he could manage, scared that releasing it all at once would somehow tip things back towards sudden violence. Vi stepped towards Daraday and did something Sweet had never seen her do before. Not to anyone. She embraced the youngster, wrapping her whip-lean arms around him and holding him tight like a mother would her child. No, not like that, Sweet thought—more like a big sister hugging a younger brother after something terrible had happened. Sweet was wholly unused to seeing any kind of emotion from Vi, and being party to it now somehow seemed wrong. He felt uncomfortable and looked away as she clung to the boy.

After what seemed like an age, Vi stepped back from Daraday. Sweet saw that some of Stover's blood had transferred from Daraday to her own clothes and he tried not to stare at it.

'There was no other choice,' Daraday spoke first, almost startling Sweet. His voice carried like steel, cutting through the racket of the crashing water that continued unbothered behind them all.

Sweet looked up at him, seeing the resolve in the younger man's eyes. No, not resolve. Damn, was there a hint of defiance there? Was Daraday sizing up Sweet's take on what had just happened? Daring him to speak against it? Hell, did Sweet even want to? Just moments ago he had been threatening Stover with just the same outcome.

Well, not quite the same, Sweet reasoned. I offered Stover a way out. All he had to do was walk away. Daraday had given him no such chance. He had tackled him unawares, fought with him, then opened his throat without so much as a word of warning.

'We couldn't let him go free,' Daraday spoke again, as though reading Sweet's thoughts. The boy's tone was firm. Final, even. 'Not after all this,' he waved his bloodied arm around the scene. Sweet followed the sweep, keeping his expression as unmoving as he could manage. Eventually his eyes landed back on Daraday. Finally, slowly, he nodded his agreement.

'Aye,' Sweet said, meeting Daraday's eye and seeing the younger man relax a little. His grip on the bloody dagger seemed to loosen a touch, and Sweet found himself wondering what might've happened if he'd voiced any sort of disagreement over the notion that Stover had to die. 'Aye you're right,' Sweet nodded again, more strongly this time. He stepped forwards and looked down at Stover's lifeless body. His vacant eyes stared up at the sky above and his jaw had fallen slack to one side. Even in death he looked confused. Sweet couldn't tell if he felt pity or relief or something else entirely. He looked down at the corpse, knowing that—of all his many, many fuck-ups—Stover's final one had been his biggest, too. The more he considered it, the less grievance he truly felt at the man's death. One less whirlwind of shit in the world was no big loss, he reckoned. He looked up, his face grim, and saw that Orsen was moving towards him.

'You good?' Sweet asked gruffly.

The prince nodded, holding his side and breathing hard.

'The old wounds, rather than anything new from him,' Orsen explained, motioning down to Stover's corpse. He took another deep breath. 'So what do we do now?'

Sweet didn't say anything for a long while, then he looked up at the grey sky.

'Still got some daylight left,' he sighed. 'Let's get back to the camp and get some more rest. I bloody well need it.'

Orsen grinned his agreement, but without much enthusiasm. His smile faded as his eyes lighted on Stover's body once more.

'What about him?' he asked.

Sweet glanced down again, his expression cold.

'He made his choices,' he said. 'Leave him.'

*

The pains in Sweet's aching body had dulled from a cacophony to a chorus by the time he slumped back down in front of the campfire. He sat, slumped and hurting, idly twirling a small stick between his fingers—or what was left of his fingers, anyway.

Violent Fey and Daraday had rebuilt a fire in the ashes of the one from the night before and it flickered and wavered in the rolling breeze. It was late afternoon now and the sunset was already beginning to shimmer behind a bank of clouds. The temperature had dropped and Sweet was vaguely grateful for the presence of the fire to warm him.

Across from him, Violent Fey sat staring into the flames. Her expression was stony and unreadable, but Sweet reckoned he could detect something downbeat in the way her shoulders were set. Something deflated about the hardness in her eyes. She was drawing a whetstone across the length of one of her daggers, but even the scraping screech sounded lessened somehow. Like it was more an act of monotony than a considered effort to actually sharpen the weapon.

Daraday left the camp shortly after the fire had been started, dully announcing he would scout to the north again, looking for any signs of Malvadas' crew—or for any further hints of the Vol soldiers that the Wyn had spotted. The lad's arm was still damp from where he'd washed the blood away in the river ford on their way back across. Well, he'd washed away as much as he could, anyway.

Orsen watched the youngster leave. A few minutes of silence passed—save for the occasional crackle from the campfire—and then the prince turned to Sweet.

'You're worried about him,' he said, his voice soft.

Sweet didn't turn to face him. Instead he sighed and threw the stick he'd been playing with into the fire.

'You reckon?'

'I know,' said Orsen, more firmly this time. 'Carthin taught me lots of things, he was good at lots of things, but reading people was the one he was best at.'

'A worldly man, your Carthin,' Sweet observed, still staring into the fire.

'He was,' Orsen agreed, 'and he'd say that you're worried about Daraday.'

'He'd be right,' Sweet replied, his voice soft and low.

'Why?' Orsen asked, shifting his position and wincing a little as his stitches pulled. 'He's got courage. He can clearly take care of himself.' Orsen thought for a moment, before adding. 'He's certainly not a man I'd want to cross.'

Sweet sighed again, exhaling through pursed lips so that it came out as a long, low whistle. Orsen's eyebrows slowly rose as he read the expression.

'That's your concern,' the prince observed, 'that he's not a man you'd want to cross.'

'He was barely a man at all when he joined our crew,' Sweet sighed, scooping up another errant stick to toy with. 'Just a boy with dreams of catching bad folks and bringing them to justice.' Sweet coughed out a dead laugh, remembering the days of his own youth. 'He'd not been with us long when we happened upon a bounty—some mad killer who'd taken his business through a place called Woodbyrne—and one of our crew got stuck by him. A lad named Aribor, not much older'n Dara was himself.' Sweet remembered the cloying heat inside the woods. He remembered the sweat on Ari's brow, on his own brow. He sighed again. 'The boy had grown close to him, so losing Aribor hit him like a hammerblow.'

'Can't imagine that happening now,' whispered Orsen, his gaze following the direction that Daraday had left the camp. 'He's a hard bastard.'

'Aye,' Sweet sighed again. He found himself thinking about when Daraday had first joined them, wide-eyed and skittish. The boy he had been was long gone now, replaced by this stone-cold killer. 'Ridin' with us'll do that to a lad. That's the truth o' things.'

'And that's what you're worried about?' Orsen pressed. 'That you made him a hard bastard?'

Sweet shifted uncomfortably. The move sent a flare of pain running up his side and he swore quietly before settling again. He considered the question.

'It's not that we—that *I*—made him a hard bastard,' Sweet thought for a moment. 'Hell, you *need* to be a hard bastard in this business, or it'll eat you alive and shit you out for fun. But there's shades to it, I reckon.'

He shivered, picturing gold teeth in a wolf's smile. 'You're never more'n a few steps from turning into someone like Malvadas.' He coughed out a chuckle. 'Or Stover, for that matter.'

Orsen left it for a moment, but when he spoke again his tone was soft.

'Are you worried about having a monster in your midst then?' he asked, raising an eyebrow. 'Or that you might've created the monster?'

Sweet turned to face the prince, scrunching his face up and observing the man more closely. He thought for a moment that he might be being mocked, but Orsen looked sincere. He had the face of a man waiting patiently for a response. The questions themselves had been unexpected and Sweet suddenly felt a flicker of anger. Resentment, almost.

'Why're you so desperate to unseat the Vols?' Sweet countered, fiercely changing the subject. The question landed like an arrow and Orsen seemed surprised by it. Sweet continued anyway—in for a copper, in for the purse and all that. 'I mean, they invaded your lands, but you escaped them. You could go anywhere and live any life you want. Instead your first thought is to reach Thradonia and start planning how to get your kingdom back. Is being a *king* really so damn important?'

Orsen thought for a moment. Sweet had been cornered by the prince's line of questioning and had responded with something he'd hoped would hurt in return. He'd hoped to raise some anger in the other man. Anger he could deal with right now. But the prince seemed merely pensive. Saddened, almost.

'I don't know,' Orsen admitted at last, his shoulders dropping. 'Perhaps I don't care all that much. Perhaps it was just something to hold onto. A purpose to keep me going. Carthin always said anger could give you strength,' he sighed loudly, 'maybe I just used it to keep going.'

Sweet felt guilty looking at Orsen's face so he turned his gaze back to the fire. The guilt lingered until he threw the new stick he was playing with into the flames, angry with himself now.

'I didn't mean nothin' by that,' he told the prince. He forced another dry laugh. 'It's just been a real shitty few weeks.'

'Not looking much brighter for the weeks ahead either, is it?' Orsen gave a wry smile. Sweet nodded grimly.

'No it ain't,' he said. Sweet thought for a moment, then sighed. 'And I don't reckon you want the Vols out of Pratia just because you're angry.'

'No?'

Sweet shook his head.

'I reckon you're doing it because you care,' he said, still looking into the flames. 'I reckon you don't want some bloodthirsty gang o' murderous

Vols running your country into the ground. That's why you want them gone.' Sweet took a deep breath, then let it out slowly. 'We saw the cairn you left at Scarvin. Don't reckon an angry man would've taken the time to do that for the dead.'

Orsen looked even more surprised than before.

'You found it?'

'The Wyn did,' Sweet nodded, then he reached inside his cloak with his good hand and dug around a little. Eventually he pulled clear the ring he had lifted from the cairn beyond the battlefield, the jewel sparkled in the light of the campfire. Orsen's eyes widened further still.

'I'm guessing that one weren't Carthin's idea?' Sweet continued, turning to face the prince with a raised eyebrow of his own. He offered the ring out to Orsen. The prince's initial surprise gave way to another wry smile and he took the ring, sliding it back into his finger and looking down at it, shocked.

'No,' he admitted. 'Carthin said it was a waste of time. I did it anyway.'

'Aye,' Sweet nodded and chuckled drily, 'I reckon your man Carthin and I would've agreed on that one.'

'Probably,' Orsen laughed, this time with real feeling. The sound felt strange inside the camp, but Sweet reckoned it was welcome nonetheless. When it subsided, the prince looked across at Sweet again. 'So what about you?'

'What about me?'

'If I do what I do because I care,' Orsen smiled, 'why do you do what you do?' He raised an eyebrow and mimicked Sweet's own words. 'Do you like bringing bad folks to justice?'

Sweet sighed and thought about it.

Why did he do what he did? He didn't give two shits about justice, or whatever folks called it. Maybe one day he had done—right at the start of things—but not anymore. A life of violence and grime and lies had quickly crushed those notions out of him. Even if it was about restoring some sort of balance, he wasn't bothered. Two wrongs didn't make a right, but Sweet reckoned you couldn't right some wrongs no matter what you did anyway. Sometimes wrong was just wrong. He didn't even care about the coin, though he reckoned he'd always convinced himself that was what he was after. He remembered the sinking feeling when he'd considered that the magicker's offer might be legitimate. The idea of never wanting for money again had made him feel empty and terrified. Maybe after he'd stopped giving a shit about thoughts of justice and nobility he'd needed something to fill the void. Something to give him purpose. Something to keep going. Thoughts of gold had simply been the neat lie that he'd told himself. So when that had been put out in the light, exposed as the falsehood it was, what was left? Sweet reckoned he knew the answer.

For the first time in his life, Sweet was uncomfortable with the truth of it. He reckoned there was one, but it was so stark that the pointlessness of it might just finish him off, here on this damn hillside in the arse end of the north, while a fugitive prince looked on, bemused.

The simple truth of it was that he didn't know why he did what he did.

And truth was a weapon.

Sweet sighed again.

'Not sure why I do it,' he admitted, with a shrug. When he saw Orsen starting to level a challenge he continued more forcefully. 'Not sure any of it's got much meaning. It probably should have—a purpose or some such, that is. But the hard truth is it doesn't. Not really.' He sighed again. 'It's just the work what needs doing.'

'And what about all this?' the prince questioned, gesturing around them.

'What about all what?'

'Turning your back on the contract,' Orsen pressed. 'Siding with me—the very bounty you were charged with bringing in? How is that *just the work that needs doing?*'

'You offered us more money,' Sweet reminded him.

'Come on now,' Orsen looked a little sheepish, 'we both know I'm going to struggle to see that promise through—although I'll do everything I damn well can to make sure that I do,' he added. 'So why'd you really do it?'

Sweet shifted a little and thought about the question. He scratched at his chin.

'Some work doesn't need doing,' he answered at last, then cracked a small smile, 'and I've got a golden rule about who I refuse to work for, too.'

The prince said nothing, and Sweet found the growing silence uncomfortable, so he filled it himself.

'Besides,' Sweet sighed again, 'maybe this one can mean something. Maybe we get you to Thradonia and you rise up against the Vols and take your kingdom back. Maybe you stop their empire from swallowing everything and everyone in the whole damn world.' Sweet smiled wryly. 'Maybe you stop the greatest tyranny of the age!'

Orsen scrunched his face up at that and Sweet chuckled. He had been joking, of course, trying to turn the conversation away from such reflective topics. Topics that never failed to make him anything but profoundly uncomfortable. But that uncomfortable feeling remained all the same and Sweet knew that all the jokes in the world wouldn't cover it up. Not today. He sighed again and whispered, almost to himself.

'Maybe this one can mean something.'

## Shadow of the mountains

+|+ → • • ⇒✗●✗⇐ • • ← |+

S WEET WOKE IN the pale light of the upcoming dawn. He still ached, but the multitude of pains felt lessened somehow. Not good by any stretch, just less bad. He felt less exhausted, too. It was still an effort to rouse himself completely—throwing a few sticks onto the smouldering remnants of the fire as he did so—but it was manageable.

The others seemed buoyed a little somehow, too. Violent Fey was more herself again, all fluid confidence and hard edges. Orsen seemed to have slept off the worst of his own agonies, as the young so often did. Even Daraday seemed less tense. The boy had returned to the camp just as the darkness of the night was fully settling in, having reported no movement so far as he could see. It seemed that, for now at least, Malvadas and his crew were happy to lay a trap for them on the way ahead, rather than continue the hunt. The thought of the gold-toothed sonofabitch waiting somewhere up ahead filled Sweet with a mixture of creeping dread and dull rage. Though it seemed like an age ago, he still remembered burying Bryntas in a shallow grave by the side of the road. Bryntas, who had been murdered in cold blood. Malvadas had done that—or at least he had ordered it done, and that made him responsible in Sweet's eyes.

The thought of running into him and his band of cutthroats was a grim one at best. Despite this though, Sweet felt weirdly optimistic. More optimistic about things than he had done since they'd rode into Levitan, in fact.

His good mood lasted only a few hours.

They had packed up their camp and continued climbing north, cutting along a ridge that had patches of ice and standing water along its way. By the time noon swung around—or what Sweet reckoned was noon anyway, as the sky was filled with greywhite cloud—the temperature had dropped considerably. They had wrapped themselves in whatever extra winter cloaks and clothing they could muster, but it made little difference.

The wind began to bite harder and sharper than it had done before, cutting through the smallest of gaps between clothing and stinging the bare skin of faces and hands.

Not long after that, it began to snow.

The first tiny flakes drifted down, lazy and arrogant, as though announcing their presence was barely worth the effort. Sweet followed one as it dropped right onto the tip of his nose, leaving it tingling even in the bitter winter wind. It was chased by a second, then a third and fourth. Before long the air was fuzzy with specks of drifting white, accentuated by the occasional flurry as a gust rippled across the high ridges on which they walked. Within the hour, patches of snow began to appear on the ground underfoot, ever growing and merging with one another, threatening to carpet the land under a stark blanket of white.

The wind picked up again as the afternoon wore on and Sweet called a halt to their arduous trek, pulling the group into the relative comfort of an overhanging boulder. They huddled around, red cheeked and puffing breath, and ate a meagre meal of whatever they could scrounge from their packs. Their food was running low, though Sweet's spirits were lifted when he found that Stover had been lying about what provisions had remained in his pack. The bounty hunter had concealed just how much his own personal stash had amounted to, so there was plenty to share amongst the four of them now. It was no surprise, really. Stover had always been a deceitful liar. Unfortunately the bastard had not been lying about his lack of taffa, and Sweet would've sacrificed even more fingers for just a single drag on one of those papersmokes.

'How much further?' Orsen asked, trying to keep the shiver from his voice.

Sweet scrunched his nose up, the strange sensation of his missing fingers making the gaps on his knuckles itch.

'Not too far now, I reckon,' he said, fighting the urge to scratch at them. 'The weather might be hiding it well, but we're not far from the shadow of the mountains. The pass is just to the northwest.'

'Will it be snowed in?' Violent Fey asked. The question was posed with no concern or panic. She sounded calculated and ambivalent again, just wanting the facts so she could deal with them. Sweet found the return to her usual demeanour more than a little comforting.

'Only one way to find out,' Sweet shrugged. He glanced up at the bunching clouds overhead. 'Don't reckon this is heavy enough just yet, but it might be worse further north and the longer we leave it,' he shrugged again, 'the more likely it is.'

'Well then,' Orsen attempted a smile, 'what're we waiting for?'

\*

The four of them hiked on until the light began to fail. Mercifully the whipping winds carried the clouds further east, leaving a dusty pink sky in their wake. Far to their west, the sun was rapidly dropping below the faint line of the horizon, burning like a forge fire as it shimmered over the dark brown smudges of land.

Ahead of them, the mountains that marked the northernmost border of Pratia loomed out of the twilight like an impossibly high, ominous wall of stone. The peaks were topped and scratched with huge swathes of snow, but Sweet knew that didn't necessarily mean anything for the state of the pass itself. The peaks were so high that the snow barely ever left—and if it did then it made a swift return to wreak havoc on anyone foolish enough to attempt to climb over the mountains.

That didn't stop folks from trying, of course. Some even made it, scrambling down the far side of the mountains into Thradonia or—if they attempted the crossing further west, into Vol territory. Most who did it once didn't bother with a return journey, having clearly received a deeper appreciation for the deadly challenge that the mountains posed—and probably a healthier perception of how much lady luck had smiled upon them the first time they crossed, Sweet reckoned.

But for every one person who managed the feat, there were half a dozen who turned back, frostbitten, blistered and beaten—and a dozen more who didn't come back down on either side at all. And now here we are, Sweet thought. Not trying to go over them, sure, but still trying our luck getting through a pass that might not even be there anymore. Not only that, but we've got the small matter of being hunted by a bunch of violent, dangerous bastards all the while.

The thought made Sweet shiver as he stared up at the shadowy sentinels, or maybe it was just because he was horrendously cold. The last blast of snow-driven wind had left ice crusted into the hairs of his beard and they pulled at his skin as he tried to warm his face with his hands.

The land dipped a little—cutting away the worst of the wind's hateful gale—and Sweet called a halt to the day's walk.

'This is about as good as it's likely to get,' he told the group. 'Leastways before we're stumbling about in the dark, anyway.'

They didn't need telling twice. The precipices and drops that had accompanied their journey now were staggeringly high. If you were to fall then you'd have time to consider what awaited you when you met the jagged rocks and unforgiving stone below. None of them fancied navigating through the terrain in the dark.

They pitched their roughly-packed tents as best they could and practically fell into them. There was little point in trying to start a fire as they didn't have enough fuel to keep it going. Besides, the four of them were dead on their feet anyway. Vi shared her tent with Daraday and Orsen climbed in with Sweet. The pair of them collapsed back-to-back, still clothed in their gear from the day's march. They pulled their blankets over themselves and shifted until they found something that vaguely resembled comfort.

Exhaustion did the rest for Sweet and he was asleep in moments.

*

The following morning Sweet was drawn from sleep with a groggy sigh. His body was all aches again and he wondered how he ever could've felt that they were improving. Of course, the growing cold didn't help. Neither did the thin layer of white powder that fell from their tent as Sweet clambered out of it. It had snowed again during the night and the shallow valley they had chosen to hunker down in was neatly covered by it. The covering wasn't too deep, Sweet reasoned, but the fact it was there at all was cause enough to worry.

If the pass was blocked when they reached it, they'd have no choice but to turn back or starve to death in the shadow of the mountains. That would mean heading south again, and Sweet didn't reckon that he fancied seeing those sights for a second time. Even if the pass were clear when they arrived, it would take nearly a full day to get through it, maybe even two—considering that they were all close to collapse already. If the weather turned when they were still inside they would likely become trapped. Stuck between walls of stone and blocked by mounting walls of snow and ice, where they would most certainly freeze to death. Not the preferred outcome, Sweet considered.

Gotta get there first, anyhow, he thought, trying to distract himself from the notion of an icy death. That means getting around Malvadas and his crew, and all their watchful eyes and sharp weapons. The distraction didn't provide the comfort he was looking for, and Violent Fey must've had similar struggles, because she came alongside Sweet not long after they'd packed up their camp and set off again.

'Where'd you reckon Mal will set up?' she asked, her husky voice ducking under the worst of the wind. Sweet shrugged as he walked.

'I know where I would,' he said, turning to meet her gaze. The steely look in her eye told him she'd probably had the same thought. It was the only logical thought for any bounty hunter worth their salt, really.

'Where's that then?' Orsen asked, coming up on Sweet's other side. The lad was clearly still in some pain from his ordeals—youth or not—but he was battling on gamely enough.

'Easy thing about hunting someone when you know where they're headed,' Sweet sighed. 'If you get ahead of them you can just wait for them there.'

'The mountain pass?'

'That's where I'd set my trap,' Sweet muttered.

'It used to be a mining camp,' Vi answered the prince, 'there'll be shelter—even if it needs patching up a bit—plus plenty of cover for them to hide in. They can wait, well-fed and warm, for us to come to them, hungry and tired and needing to get through.'

Orsen didn't blanche, but he looked downtrodden at the news. Sweet didn't blame him, he felt the same way.

'That's where I'd set my trap,' Sweet repeated.

*

The weather eased off as they continued trudging north. They had plenty of drinking water; they refilled their waterskins with snow and packed them between their clothes, letting whatever heat remained in their bodies turn it into meltwater—but food was a different matter. What remained of their provisions had been evenly split between them now, but even with Stover's stash divided up Sweet reckoned they'd need to scavenge something right on the other side of the mountain if they were going to keep going. No point getting into Thradonia only to starve to death in the borderlands there, he reasoned.

Gotta get there first though, that helpful voice chimed in again. Sweet was beginning to think it wasn't much help at all. Seemed to him that voice was great at announcing problems but much less vocal when it came to offering solutions.

Each step they took north became more monotonous than the last. The trek had become a dreary trudge. Aching legs became too numb to ache. At one point Sweet startled himself, snorting and flailing his arms as he was roused from this routine by a harsh gust of wind. He didn't know if he'd somehow fallen asleep whilst walking, but the very notion that it could happen was scary enough to help him keep a firmer grip on his wits. He didn't fancy taking a wrong step and tumbling down one of the many steep drops that now scarred their way forwards.

They made camp as the sun was setting once more. This time they found enough shelter—and enough wood from some measly looking trees—for a fire. The smoke drifted lazily overhead but Sweet didn't give it much mind. It might've mattered if they were being tracked, but Malvadas had a significant advantage in knowing exactly where they were heading. It didn't much matter if they signalled their position every step of the way. Sweet reckoned they might as well arrive at the pass with a bit of warmth in their bones.

He thought sheer exhaustion would take him swiftly again, but Sweet struggled for sleep that night. His thoughts were plagued with doubts and voices from his past. He saw the faces of his crew. Stover, the Wyn, Bryntas, Jenrick. first alive and then slack and dead. They floated and drifted across his mind like phantoms. At first he just saw their faces, floating apparitions in the darkness. Then he saw their hands, sliding out of the shadows. All of them were reaching for him and he tried to squirm away from them.

No, not reaching for him. Their hands were all upturned, as though presenting their palms to him one by one. Palms that were drenched with blood. They pressed in towards him, each of them moaning softly as they floated ever closer. It took him a moment, but Sweet realised they were calling out his name.

'Sweet….Sweet...Sweet!'

*

'Sweet!' Vi's whipcrack voice jerked Sweet awake and he thrashed wildly. She caught his injured hand in a vice-like grip and held him firm. 'Sweet, it's me.'

Sweet blinked. The memories of the ghosts of his crew still swarming his senses. Memories of bloodied hands and mournful moans.

No, he thought. Not memories, nightmares is all. Nightmares because I'm nearly all-in, and my mind is deciding it wants to go before my body does. Well, he thought, forcing anger through his exhausted limbs and stiffening his resolve, tough shit. I'm not done yet.

'I'm alright,' he said, blearily using Vi's grip to help him up and out of the tent. The day was lightening already and he scrunched his face up at the gathering clouds. 'How long have I slept?'

'Sun's been up an hour,' said Vi.

'You should've woken me up,' Sweet muttered, not sure if he meant it or not. 'We need every hour we can get, ahead of the snow.'

Vi shrugged.

'You needed the rest,' she said, simply. 'I only woke you up now because you were thrashing and hollering. You sure you're alright?'

'Aye,' Sweet nodded, shaking the images of bloody hands from his mind. 'Aye I'm fine. Shitty dreams is all.'

'No roaring fireplaces and spiced wine then?' Vi asked, a crooked smile in place.

'Not so much,' Sweet replied, still hearing his name echoing mournfully somewhere in the back of his mind. 'Where're the others?'

'They ranged up ahead. I told them to stop if it got to noon and we hadn't caught up. They didn't leave long ago.'

'Well then,' Sweet grumbled, the sweat from his nightmares already turning into an uncomfortable chill against his skin. 'Let's get this tent packed and catch up with them.'

\*

They didn't have to hike for long, eventually coming across both Daraday and Orsen slumped lazily across a rock formation that half-resembled a bench carved by a giant. Both men looked strangely content, like they were enjoying whatever meagre sunshine found its way through the ceiling of clouds that seemed to be growing darker with every passing moment.

'What's got you two so chipper?' Sweet grunted, breathing hard from the last little climb, it had been a steep bastard.

'See for yourself,' Orsen reported, barely able to contain a smile. He turned and scrambled up the back of the stone shelf. Sweet was bone-weary, but he had enough strength to follow the raven-haired prince up the series of rocky ledges. As they neared the top, he saw Orsen keeping himself low and mimicked the behaviour, more out of instinct than any conscious thought. Sweet peered carefully over the lip of stone.

Ahead of them, nestled in a tight bowl of a valley and covered with a generous layer of crisp white snow, were a series of ramshackle buildings and lean-tos. Most were still standing, but the roofs of some of the larger ones had buckled inwards. One even boasted a collapsed wall, the remnants of the building jutting out from the snow like a cracked tooth.

To the west of the camp was a stand of tall, thin trees—the branches laden with snow and bending deeply. A semi-covered stack of logs, roughly hewn but neatly arranged, was hidden away to one side. A vague outline of a path could be seen between the structures, winding this way and that as it led up the steep slope until it disappeared into an opening—buttressed by square-hewn logs—at the foot of the mountain. Sweet saw some kind of wagon, abandoned and weathered, waiting silently besides this opening with the traces rotting in the breeze.

The mining camp.

Sweet felt, rather than saw, Orsen's victorious smile widen beside him. Moments later, he saw the reason why.

At the far corner of the camp, another rough outline of a path snaked further into the shadow of the mountains. It was barely visible, and already a big snow drift was forming to one side of the opening, but it was there all the same.

The pass through the mountains.

And it was open.

## Lights in the dark

S WEET STARED AT the winding passage for several moments. He kept his eyes open, scared that blinking might somehow magick the pass away. Like it was some kind of illusion, and startling it would somehow cause it to disappear.

Only it wasn't an illusion, and it wasn't disappearing.

At least, not right now. Snow had begun to fall again, but it was light, the flakes barely visible as they frittered down from the sky. It would take a harsher word from the winter weather to close down the passage through the mountains. But if recent days were anything to go by, this was a whispered promise of louder things to come.

The drift that had begun forming across the pass entrance was already piled high, but Sweet reckoned that had been from a single blizzard. The rest of the pass—as much as he could see anyway—still looked traversable. It would be a long, hard trudge through knee-deep snow—nearly all of it uphill—but it was still there and it was still open.

Sweet tried to quell the rising excitement he felt in his chest. He knew all too well that feeling was often chased by a swift and heavy dose of disappointment. He scanned the area around the pass for potential sources of that disappointment. It was true that the mouth of the mountain pass looked clear, but further in there could be anything. A rockfall might've blocked the way decades ago, or an unseasonably early avalanche might've barred the passage with a wall of snow and ice.

Then there was the camp itself. The buildings looked derelict and—although he couldn't see the telltale flicker of firelight in any of the windows or doorways—that didn't mean they were empty. Malvadas was a sly bastard, and Sweet knew that this would be the best place for him to lay a trap. With that being the case, he'd likely tell his men to keep a low profile and avoid advertising their presence.

Sweet glanced up at the rock formations surrounding the camp, looking for a way around it to the pass—but there was nothing. The camp was hemmed in by walls of sheer stone, slick with ice and capped with snow. The only way to the mountain pass was through the mining camp.

Malvadas had sacrificed half of his men in the ravine—damn that felt like a lifetime ago—to capture the prince, but that would still leave him with six or seven cold-blooded killers at his disposal. That wasn't a huge force to work with, but they still outnumbered Sweet, Vi, Orsen and Daraday—and all four of them were nearly spent. If they ended up in a scrap, Sweet didn't fancy their chances all that much.

That meant avoiding detection was key. They would have to sneak through the mining camp and hope that Malvadas' men were either dozing or not watching the shadows closely enough. Perhaps we could wait for another blizzard, Sweet thought, then dismissed the idea just as quickly. Although it would provide ample cover, they also ran the risk of getting completely lost in the snowstorm—or the blizzard lasting long enough and blowing hard enough to close the passage north.

Sweet swore under his breath and observed the mining camp once more. Most of the log-built buildings were single-storeyed, but a taller one was set against the rock wall just beside the mine entrance. Some sort of gallery, set above a rickety-looking lift-and-pulley system, stretched out to the left of it. If Sweet were in Malvadas' shoes, he would definitely put a pair of eyes up in that tower. The spotter would have a good view of the whole camp and could raise the alarm if they saw so much as a flicker of movement between the buildings below.

The other buildings were spread around fairly haphazardly. A few of the smaller ones seemed to have been erected close to a larger, rectangular building in the centre of the camp. Sweet reckoned that would be the mess hall, where the miners would've gone to eat and enjoy whatever passed for recreation in this godforsaken part of the world. Sweet frowned, thinking about where he would position his people if the roles were reversed. After a time he decided it was pointless. Any of the buildings would give good cover and a decent view of the open lanes and wide alleys between them.

Then there was the pass itself. Sweet reckoned if he was hunting someone who needed to get to that gap in the mountain, he would set a pair of eyes on it at all times—maybe even two pairs of eyes, just to make sure. Malvadas was sure to have done the same. Luckily there were few buildings set close to the pass, so Sweet scoured the sides of the mountains themselves, looking for signs of a concealed cave or a roughly put-together lean-to. Anywhere that might serve as a little nest for hunters tasked with watching the pass. After several minutes of fruitless observation, Sweet gave up with a frustrated sigh. His eyes weren't as good as they used to be, and even then they'd never been great. We need the Wyn, Sweet thought. The notion brought on another wave of stinging guilt and Sweet quashed it. No time for mourning dead men, he told himself sternly, or we'll be seeing them soon enough, for sure.

What about the horses? Sweet suddenly thought. Malvadas and his crew had been riding north when the Wyn had last seen them, so where were their horses? Sweet squinted across the camp once more but couldn't see anything. That meant nothing, of course, the mountains to either side of the mine snaked in and out to create great walls of rock either side of it. Malvadas' hunters could've left their mounts out of sight and then walked the rest of the way into the camp. Again, that's what Sweet would've done. It did mean you'd have to leave someone to watch over them. Or at the very least send someone to check on them every once in a while—to keep them warm, watered and fed—which meant someone would have to leave their post. That gives us an opportunity, Sweet thought. If we can watch the camp until someone leaves to check on the horses, we'll know where one of their watch posts is. That might help us figure out where the others are, Sweet considered.

It was as good a plan as any, and Sweet was just about to relay it to the others when another thought occurred to him.

Where are the Vols?

Just after they'd disturbed the bear, the Wyn had spotted two groups heading north. The first had been Malavadas and his crew—and Sweet had no doubt that they were down in that mining camp now, waiting patiently for their prey to stumble into their trap—he could almost feel it. But the second group had been larger. Large enough to send up a small cloud of dust on the distant horizon. Sweet guessed it had been Renauld, the Vol lieutenant from Levitan. He and his men had been led on a wild goose chase in the west and then charged north when they realised their mistake. When the Wyn had first spotted them, they'd been closest to the mountains. That meant they should be here by now.

So where were they?

Sweet didn't know Renauld like he knew Malvadas, but the Vol lieutenant had seemed cunning and able. Unlike Malvadas though, Renauld would've had little or no need for secrecy here. No need to skulk about in the shadows. He would've brought enough soldiers to man the camp, light fires *and* watch the pass. They would be patrolling the camp with torches and dogs—if they'd brought any with them. They'd be well armed and well trained, too. Vol soldiers were not lightly trifled with.

So where the fuck were they?

'All looks pretty quiet,' Violent Fey appeared beside him. He startled a little, despite the fact she'd been sneaking up on him like that for years. Must be tired, he thought. Hell, he *was* tired. Vi cocked her head a little and frowned down at the seemingly deserted camp below, then she added, 'didn't expect that.'.

'Aye,' Sweet whispered, 'figured they'd have pretty much blockaded it by now.'

'Maybe the Vols and Mal got into a disagreement?' Vi offered, 'fought each other?'

Sweet shook his head.

'If they ran into each other Mal would've backed down,' he said, rubbing at his neck with his good hand, 'he's reckless, but not stupid enough to think he can take a troop of Vol soldiers with just a handful of men. They would've left the pass and come looking for us in the wild.'

'Maybe we passed them by?'

'Could be,' Sweet said, though he thought it unlikely. 'But then where are the Vols? If they took the camp, why didn't they keep it?'

Violent Fey stayed silent. Her expression was even, but Sweet could tell she was turning the question over in her mind. There was a slight tension in the corner of her eyes that told him she was even troubled by it. Hell, Sweet was troubled by it. He could deal with absolutes. You see an obstacle, you figure out how to overcome it. You spot a problem, you find a solution. It didn't make shit easy, but it at least made it doable.

Mysteries like this—on the other hand—were tricky bastards.

Sweet watched the camp a few moments longer, then sighed. He crawled carefully back away from the rim of stone and gingerly climbed down a few more feet. Orsen and Vi followed, with Daraday climbing up the incline to meet them all. The three of them looked to Sweet expectantly.

'We'll take watches,' he told them, acutely aware that the stumps of his missing fingers were itching madly again. 'Keep an eye out for any movement down there. We'll do that for the rest of the daylight,' he glanced skyward, guessing they had a handful of hours before the sun would start fading behind the horizon. Sweet sighed again. 'We'll start moving when it's good and dark.'

'Tough going,' said Vi, 'getting down there in the dark.'

'We've had tougher,' Sweet tried a grim smile. It didn't feel right on his face so he pulled it down just as swiftly. 'Once it's dark we'll make our way down to the camp and see if we can sneak through it.'

'This feels like a trap,' Orsen said. He looked uncomfortable with the plan, but accepting of the fact that their options were limited, to say the least.

'Aye, I reckon it is.' Sweet nodded his agreement, then he pointed up to the sky. 'But we can't wait up here forever. And the longer we leave it the more chance the snow starts coming in proper. Not only that, but we're running out of food. Better we take our chances getting through than starving to death waiting for some good luck.'

Orsen nodded and offered no objections. Sweet looked to the others, but both Vi and Daraday were stony-faced.

'Good,' he told them. 'Get rid of anything in your pack that rattles, tie off anything in your gear that jangles. Wrap anything shiny, keep it as hidden as you can.' He sighed again, before adding, 'but keep your weapons close, just in case.'

\*

The hours passed slowly. Sweet didn't mind, he had gotten good at waiting—decades spent hunting men and women across several kingdoms had provided ample practice—and, if he was being perfectly honest, it felt good to just stay still for a moment. Even in this cold and miserable place.

Sweet reckoned he knew why the mining camp had been abandoned, and it was probably only in part due to the mountain's bounty of precious metals drying up. It was cold and grey in this part of the world. Savage and unrelenting. There was an awesome beauty to it—no doubt—but it made Sweet feel incredibly small and insignificant. It felt bleak and hopeless. Not somewhere men were meant to be for too long at a time.

After an hour, Daraday climbed up the rocky shelf and took over. Sweet carefully navigated his way back down to where Orsen and Vi were huddled in blankets. They hadn't dared start a fire this close to the mining camp and so wrapping themselves in layers of whatever they could manage was about the only way to stay warm. Sweet coddled himself inside his own threadbare coverings and dozed for a while, listening to the steady howl of the wind and waiting for the sky to darken.

Violent Fey and Orsen took their shifts watching the deserted camp. None of them saw any signs of life in the stand of buildings below. Vi reckoned she spotted a white fox slinking about in the treeline to the west of the camp, but other than that the place was as still as a tomb.

Sweet took the last watch before the light began to rapidly fade away.

The shadows cast by the buildings below lengthened, then they were swallowed by the oncoming night itself. The sky was still smothered by cloud so after a bit more time even the outlines of the buildings vanished from view. Occasionally when the wind blew right, the clouds cleared a little and a glimmer of moonlight made its way through, illuminating the mining camp a dull, silvery blue.

After a few more minutes of trying desperately to squint through the darkness, Sweet eventually relented and returned to the others. It took much longer in the darkness as he had to carefully feel his way with his feet, which were damn near numb from the cold. He was puffing hard by the time he made it down. The others looked up at him, he could just about make out their faces in the gloom.

'Can't see a damn thing down there,' he whispered to them. 'Get some rest. We'll leave it an hour, then get moving.'

*

Sweet could hear his own heart beating—loud as a parade drum—and he was sure that at any moment a door to one of the cabins would spring open and armed men would come rushing out. Either Malvadas' grimy bounty hunters or Vol soldiers in their well-tended armour. Maybe even both, he thought, knowing how fickle luck could be. He cursed every crunching footfall on the ground covering of snow, then cursed again for every breath that puffed out as a cloud of mist in front of his face— certain that the little plumes of fog would be what an eagled-eyed spotter would catch a glimpse of in the darkness.

At least his missing fingers had stopped itching, though he reckoned that was mainly because the cold had made the rest of him so numb that it was hard to feel anything save for a prickly tingling all over.

Still, Sweet thought, ducking between two more dilapidated buildings, I'll take it. Better to feel the cold than be dead to it. He remembered hearing tales of folks who got lost in the wild during the winter months. When they were found—if they were found—some of them were found completely naked. The explanation offered was that, as the cold had set in, they became disoriented and mistook the prickling discomfort for overheating. In a panic, they would've shed layers of clothing in order to combat the feeling—only for it to increase their exposure to the biting cold and kill them all the more quickly. Frost mad, Sweet had been told it was called. It made him a mite grateful for feeling the icy touch of every shiver, at least he wasn't suffering from that just yet.

The dark-haired figure of the prince arrived beside him, tucking himself tight and low against the wall of the building that provided them with cover. He looked alert and ready, and Sweet again found himself impressed by the young man's spirit. Fleeing through the wildlands under constant threat of capture or death was no mean feat, but the young royal seemed to have a deep well of courage and resolve, and was drawing from it regularly.

After him came Vi, and then Daraday. Both of them held one hand close to their hips, no doubt just inches away from the hilt of a concealed dagger. They moved lithely, their tiptoeing steps barely making an impression on the carefully laid carpet of snow.

With the four of them assembled, Sweet slowly leaned round the side of the building and watched for signs of movement. When he was sure there was none—or as sure as he could be, anyway—he retracted his head and nodded to the others before ducking out of cover and scurrying across the way to the next building.

They'd done this twice already, and it had barely taken more than a few minutes, but to Sweet it felt like a lifetime. Every time he broke from cover he expected a shout to go up or torches to flare into life. Every time he poked his head round the corner of a building he expected an arrow to come hurtling through the air at him. But there was nothing. The night was still and silent, save for their shuffling movements and quietly crunching footsteps as they stalked through the darkness of the camp.

They arrived at the next building and Sweet peered round it again. The distance between their cover and the dim outline of the next cabin up ahead—barely visible in the meagre light of the stars—was the greatest yet. Sweet swallowed, watching carefully for guards in the darkness. He was about to turn back to the others and nod for them to go again when he heard something. A slow creak, like a board shifting under weight. The noise was close, too.

Sweet turned back to face the others and saw from their expressions that they had heard it too. Violent Fey had even craned her neck so that she was looking at the cabin they were huddled beside. The creak sounded again and Sweet realised why it had sounded so close.

It was coming from inside the cabin!

Sweet instinctively shifted an inch away from the log-built wall, as though the cabin itself was the thing hunting them. He caught Vi's eye and realised that neither of them knew what to do. What did the sound mean? Was someone inside the building? Should they try to sneak in and subdue them or carry on dashing between cover? What if there was more than one person inside? What if it was nothing? It could be an animal, or just the wood of the cabin itself flexing in the cold?

Sweet took a deep breath and steadied himself. He blinked slowly then motioned for the others to follow him, all the while listening carefully for that telltale sound again.

Sweet rounded the corner of the building and began slowly creeping towards the shadowy outline of the next cabin along. With every careful footstep he felt more and more exposed, sure that at any moment they would be discovered, or that he'd feel the cold, hard touch of steel on his flesh.

They'd made it about halfway across when the creaking groan sounded again, longer and louder this time. It was followed by another, then a shuffling kind of thud. Sweet stiffened, then began hurrying towards the perceived safety of the next cabin, he could hear the soft, quickening footsteps of the others behind him and knew that they were following.

They arrived at the building and Sweet immediately turned, squinting back into the darkness to see if he could see signs of pursuit. There was only shadow and snow and nothing in between. The only tracks he could see were their own, leading back the way they came until the snow bled into the darkness of the night.

Then a light flared. Bright and piercing in the darkness. But it wasn't torchlight. It didn't even look like fire, not really. It was bright and blue and strangely luminescent. It flared in the distance and then coalesced, swirling and hovering some five feet off the ground. The light cast shadows all around it and Sweet saw the shape of the cabin they'd just been hiding behind.

Then he saw the outline of a figure. Someone holding the strange, gently pulsing light aloft and staring out into the darkness.

'Inside!' Violent Fey whispered, her voice hushed but sharp.

As if snapped from a trance, Sweet tore his eyes away from the glowing light and the ghostly figure. He followed as Vi led the way along the wall of the building until they reached the doorway. She grabbed for the handle, at the same time as she rested one hand on the leather of the uppermost hinge. Daraday crouched beside her knees and cupped his own hands around the lower hinge. Vi turned the door handle and eased it open, the groaning creaks of the weathered hinges were lessened by the pressure they each applied.

It was completely black inside, yawning at them like an open grave.

They hurried in and Vi carefully swept the door shut behind them.

*

'What was that?' Orsen whispered, reflecting Sweet's own thoughts—only his thoughts had been more urgent, and more sweary.

'Magick,' Daraday's voice sounded in the dark.

'What?' Orsen's hissed response.

'Magick,' Daraday whispered again.

Sweet's mind raced and his heart was beating more wildly than ever. The near-total darkness of the cabin interior wasn't helping matters either, though he noticed some light was spilling in away to his left. Violent Fey must have seen it too, because she moved towards the source, her shadowy figure detaching itself from the gloom.

It was a small window, set high into the wall. Vi slowed as she neared it and then edged her face around the portal, peering out into the darkness of the night.

'What can you see?' Sweet whispered, taking careful steps towards her and cursing every board that groaned under his weight.

'He's still there,' Vi reported, 'hasn't moved yet.'

Sweet neared the window and ducked underneath its frame, positioning himself on the opposite side to Violent Fey. Slowly, carefully, he moved his head into place so that he could see out into the darkness beyond.

Sure enough, the shadowy figure hadn't moved. The glowing ball of blue light was still raised high, swirling and roiling. It took Sweet a moment to realise the figure was holding it aloft in the palm of one hand. Daraday was right. It was magick.

The figure wasn't completely unmoving, though. The pulsing ball of magick light picked out enough of them to show that their head was turning, this way and that.

'They're looking for us,' Violent Fey whispered, echoing Sweet's thoughts.

'Aye,' he agreed, 'and it won't be long before they see the tracks, we best get moving.'

It was then that the smell hit Sweet's nose. It was pungent and acrid, burning his nostrils as soon as it swept across them, but it was somehow sickly sweet, too. He grimaced and turned away from the window, squinting in the darkness and trying to spot the source of the odour. He recognised the smell all too well and his eyes soon landed on the ghostly outline of what he was looking for.

Away at one end of the cabin, stacked in the shadow of the far wall, was a pile of corpses. A sticky patch of drying blood stretching out beneath them.

As Sweet's eyes adjusted to the gloom once more, he saw that there were dozens of them. Piled in a neat stack, almost like firewood, save for the odd arm or leg that had slipped out and hung loose and pale in the darkness.

'Shit,' Orsen breathed.

'"Shit" is about right,' Sweet replied, his heart quickening. He surveyed the pile of bodies further and saw that they were all young men. Most of them had been stripped naked, but he saw the tattered remnants of a uniform hanging from the chest and neck of one of them. He was about to voice his thoughts when Daraday got there first.

'They're Vols,' the youngster whispered, taking half a step towards the pile of bodies.

'Dead Vols,' Vi breathed.

'What're dead Vols doing here?' Orsen asked.

'I'll bet *he* can answer that,' Sweet whispered, nodding towards the window and the shadowy figure beyond.

A groan in the darkness behind them made them all spin on their heels. This time the groan wasn't from a creaking floorboard. Sweet's mind raced and he had to fight to keep from wrenching his sword clear of its scabbard.

That groan had come from a man.

They waited in tense silence until the groan came again, it sounded tired and strained. Sweet freed up a dagger with his good hand and stalked across the room, his heart beating so loudly he could hear it pulsing through his head. As he moved through the shadows he passed the door through which they had entered the cabin. Just beyond that was another door, plain and unassuming. Sweet reached out for the handle just as the groan came again, he reckoned whoever was making the noise was just on the other side.

Sweet licked his lips and flexed his fingers around the dagger, he felt Orsen and Daraday just behind him, as tense as coiled springs. Sweet slowly turned the handle and then pulled the door open with a sharp yank. Thankfully the hinges were in better condition than the one leading outside and the door opened with the merest swoosh of disturbed air. Sweet half-threw it aside and stepped into the darkness beyond, the knife raised.

He stopped and drew a sharp intake of breath.

The room beyond was small, but it had its own window and the ethereal light from the moon spilled inside, painting everything inside a ghostly silver colour

Not that there was much inside, save for the prisoner.

The man was on his knees, naked and wretched with his chin resting limply on his chest. His arms were drawn up high above him, shackled to the wall behind him with heavy iron manacles. Sweet saw the telltale chain from a second set that must've been binding the man's legs. He was deathly thin, and his skin was so pale that in the moonlight it looked nearly translucent. The man shuddered—a thin mist of breath puffing out from his downturned face—and groaned again.

'Shit,' Orsen whispered a second time.

The prisoner shuddered, causing his chains to rattle against the wall behind him. He slowly raised his head towards the noise and Sweet gasped again as he recognised him.

The man was Renauld.

His face was drawn and sallow, with heavy bags hanging under his eyes and the rough beginnings of an unkempt beard sagging from his sallow cheeks, but it was the Vol Lieutenant all the same.

'What the fuck…' Sweet managed.

'H...help me,' the man whispered, his voice scratchy and hoarse.

'What the hell happened here?' Sweet breathed, swallowing his fear as he met the man's desperate gaze. It took the Vol lieutenant a moment to register the question, then he blinked and shuddered again.

'The...the magickers,' Renauld managed, then his eyes grew even more desperate. 'P...please help me.'

Sweet knew that the man was beyond help. It was a wonder he was alive at all, naked and chained in icy temperatures that were plummeting further with every passing heartbeat. Being inside the cabin would've helped, of course, but there was little warmth in here and he wouldn't last much longer. He knelt down in front of the bound Vol soldier, the dagger still resting in his uninjured hand.

'What happened?' Sweet asked again, a little harder this time.

'T...the magickers came,' Renauld managed, 'they said they were here to help us. They led us north.'

'The bodies,' Sweet motioned over his shoulder, 'your men?'

Renauld nodded, his eyes glassing over with tears.

'They...they killed them,' Renauld nodded, 'said it was for bl...blood magick. Made them stronger.'

'Sylvanus,' Sweet whispered, almost to himself. He swore, then looked back at Renauld. When he spoke again his voice was nearly a growl. 'Is Sylvanus here?'

Renauld shivered again, damn near uncontrollably this time. The movement caused his chains to rattle. The noise was uncomfortably loud and Sweet stiffened a little. After the man had gotten a semblance of control over his trembling, he shook his head. No.

'How many?' Sweet demanded.

'F...five of them,' Renauld croaked. 'They...they said they were here to help!'

'Sweet!' Vi's urgent hiss came from the other room. 'He's on the move!'

Sweet cursed again. The magicker must've spotted their tracks in the snow.

Renauld must've guessed the same thing because his eyes grew wide with terror and he began to babble.

'P...please,' he mumbled, struggling against his chains, 'please help me! Help me!'

The man's voice grew louder and more desperate as he talked and Sweet shifted uneasily at the noise.

'Quiet!' he hissed at the man.

But Renauld persisted, babbling and moaning as he begged for help.

'T...take me with you!' he cried, his chains slapping against the wall behind him with a dull clanking sound, 'I can help! P...please don't leave me with them! Please I can—'

Renauld stuttered and trailed off as Sweet's dagger plunged through his ragged chest, piercing his heart. His face didn't even have time to register surprise and his final breath came as a rattling rasp. Sweet reckoned he might've even seen a glint of relief in the Vol's haunted gaze, before the man's head slumped forwards once more. This time for good.

'Sweet!' Violent Fey hissed again.

'What's going on?' Orsen asked as Sweet pushed himself to a standing position, wiping warm blood away from his knife hand.

'Looks like Sylvanus sent his own team after you,' Sweet told him, wiping Renauld's blood from his hand on his coat. 'Magickers, five of them. They killed the Vols as some sort of sacrifice.'

'But Sylvanus *is* a Vol,' Daraday's voice.

'Aye, but don't reckon he's all that loyal to his own.' Sweet nodded towards the pile of bodies in the other room. 'His magickers used those poor bastards like fuel. He must want you pretty badly,' he looked at the shadowy shape of Orsen.

'He killed his own men?'

'Must be how they get their power,' Sweet shrugged, he didn't know enough about magick to fully understand it. Truth be told, right then he didn't much care either. His mind raced as he considered their chances. There was only one magicker out there right now, so they outnumbered him four-to-one—could they take him? Sweet frowned at the thought. Renauld had a whole troop of soldiers and they'd been subdued and summarily massacred in some kind of twisted blood ritual. Sweet didn't fancy their chances.

'Shit,' he whispered, scrambling to think of a plan. He saw the urgency etched onto Violent Fey's face in the other room and knew that the magicker was closing in on the cabin.

There was a sudden creaking noise and more light spilled into the building. Sweet, Daraday and Orsen all wheeled round to see the doorway leading outside swing open in a wide arc, the hinges screaming as it went.

A figure—a man—stepped inside, snow-covered boots clomping against the boards underfoot. He wasn't overly tall, but he put both hands on his hips as though he commanded the room. Sweet's eyes were still adjusting but he saw something glint in the darkness of the man's face.

Gold teeth.

'Well, well, well,' Malvadas chuckled loudly, 'what have we got here?'

'Shit,' Sweet whispered again.

# A better plan

⊣• ⟶ •) •• ✗•●•✗ •• (• •⊦

For a moment all was still.

Breath misted from between Malvadas' shining teeth. His face was fixed into a grin that would've soured milk and his eyes glittered dangerously in the dim light. Sweet saw other figures behind him— two members of his crew no doubt—silhouetted inside the doorway. Moonlight glinted off of the exposed steel in their hands. Orsen and Daraday had frozen in place beside Sweet, and—off to their right— Violent Fey was still crouched by the window, her eyes wide as they lighted on the newcomers.

'Sweet!' Malvadas' grin grew wider and threw up his hands in feigned friendship. His smile faltered as he added, 'you don't look happy to see me.'

'Mal, listen—' Sweet started, his eyes darting to Vi to see if he could get a read on how close the magicker was. But she was fixated on this new development and the angle was all wrong for him to see through the window himself.

'My my my,' Malvadas clucked, interrupting Sweet and taking a deliberate, menacing step into the cabin. He transferred his gaze to the body of Renauld, still slumped in his chains and with blood leaking freely from the hole Sweet had put in his chest. Malvadas cocked his head at the sight and frowned a little. 'Didn't take you for a torturer, Sweet.' The bounty hunter sighed loudly. 'Still, looks like you've been a busy boy.'

The men behind Malvadas took a step inside, following his lead. One was whip-lean, his narrow eyes scowling at Sweet, Orsen and Daraday. The other was an enormous brute, wide-shouldered and stony-faced. Both held swords in fight-ready grips.

'Mal, listen to me—' Sweet tried again.

'Talking's all done, I'm afraid,' Malvadas made an apologetic gesture with his outstretched hands. 'We'll be taking our bounty, now,' he pointed at Orsen. 'Can't be letting the rest of you live, though.' He cocked his head again, all false apology. 'Nothing personal,' he chuckled, 'just wouldn't want you tryin'a steal him back again is all.'

'Mal, just listen!' Sweet barked, his attention darting to Vi once more. She was looking out through the window once more and Sweet saw her eyes grow wide. She flinched away from the opening and Sweet's next words were cut off by a sizzling crack and an enormous bang.

The whip-lean bounty hunter standing beside Malvadas jerked awkwardly, as though struck by a sudden fit. His neck arched back and his mouth gaped open in what Sweet took to be a mixture of surprise and pain. In the same instant, blue light—bright and alive—coalesced in the back of the man's throat. Sweet even saw some of it light behind the man's eyeballs, making the little spider web of veins there glow a sickening purple colour.

Then the man's head burst into blue flame.

The bounty hunter jerked again, spinning sideways and landing spasmodically, his ruined neck ablaze with the magick fire. Malvadas and the brute both spun on their heels, just in time for a second bolt of magick to come careening towards them. This one caught the big man square in the face. With his back now turned to them, Sweet couldn't see exactly what happened to the bounty hunter, but the collateral force of the impact hurled Malvadas further into the cabin—he hit the wall with a grunt and crashed to the floor.

The sword fell from the open grip of the big bounty hunter with a clang and the man crumpled at the knees. Sweet had shielded his eyes from the savage glare of the magick and now saw that the big man was also headless, just like his comrade. A few hungry licks of blue flame clawed upwards from his open neck, already blackened and charred, before his body toppled forwards..

The entire thing happened in no more than a few seconds, but it was more than enough for Sweet to know what they needed to do next, that was for damn sure.

'Run!' he bellowed.

*

All at once the cabin was alive with the sounds of scrabbling boots, slick with meltwater, scraping and thumping against wooden boards as Sweet, Orsen and Daraday all lurched to their feet. From the other room, Violent Fey gestured madly with one arm.

'This way!' she yelled, turning and not waiting to see if they would follow.

Sweet scrambled across the narrow hallway—his left boot slipping on something that might've been snow or might've been blood—and led Orsen and Daraday into the other room. He saw the silhouetted figure of Vi clambering over the stack of corpses that lined the far wall and for one moment he thought she'd gone mad. Then he saw the window beyond the bodies, facing out to the other side of the cabin, half hidden in the shadow of the dead men. He followed after her, taking care to keep as low as he could, expecting another bolt of the terrifying blue magick to come screaming into the cabin at any moment.

Sweet scrambled over the pile of bodies, too scared to be disgusted by the feel of them. The corpses were cold and firm, but limbs rolled and the weight shifted as he clambered over them; it was like climbing a pile of logs. At one point Sweet's foot slipped into a neat gap between two bodies, his leg disappearing all the way down to the knee, bringing him almost nose-to-nose with the glassy-eyed stare of one of the dead men. Sweet cursed and heaved himself further up the pile. Vi had made it to the window and unceremoniously threw the shutters wide. She poked her head out briefly before grabbing the sill and pulling her legs up like an acrobat. She slid through the gap, feet first, and disappeared from sight.

Sweet grunted and followed. Behind him, he could feel Orsen and Daraday climbing the pile of corpses, too. Their movements shifted the bodies further still and Sweet sent an aimless prayer that the whole stack of dead men wouldn't come crashing down. After what seemed like an age, Sweet made it to the window and half-jumped at it, his right shoulder tipped out through the opening and he fell through it with all the grace of a sack of vegetables. He landed hard on the same shoulder and groaned as pain jarred up his side. The covering of snow did little to soften the impact of the frozen ground beneath and Sweet cursed as it awoke all the other aches and pains he had been trying so hard to quash. Sweet had the good sense to roll away just as Daraday's boots landed in the space that he'd previously occupied. Orsen followed shortly after.

Sweet was about to speak when there was another blue flash from inside the cabin, the light spilling out from the window in a streak that illuminated on the snow at their feet. There was a huge crashing sound and Sweet saw flames burst into life from somewhere within. This was followed by more movement, and then a shadow appeared in the window, before dropping down to the ground just as Sweet had done. The shadow moaned and rolled onto one side.

Malvadas.

Sweet ignored the groaning figure of the gold-toothed bounty hunter and turned to Violent Fey. Her eyes were no longer wide with fear and she'd drawn a dagger, the blade glistening in the pale moonlight.

'They'll be watching the pass,' Sweet whispered to her, 'we need to get out of the camp and hide, figure out what to do next.'

'Sweet?' Malvadas groaned again. He shook his head and pushed himself to his feet, 'what the fuck is going on?'

'Quickly,' Sweet motioned to the others, ignoring Malvadas' question and keeping his voice low. 'This way.'

Sweet crouched low and headed back along the length of the cabin. He peered around its corner to check for signs of danger, but he could barely see twenty paces into the darkness and had to settle for assuming there was none. Keeping his shoulders hunched, Sweet lurched away from the cabin and headed across the mining camp, expecting at any moment to be catapulted from his feet by a bolt of flaming magick.

Fucking Sylvanus, he thought as he raced across the snow, his boots crunching loudly as he ran. He heard similar footsteps behind him and knew that Vi, Orsen and Daraday were following close behind. Probably Malvadas too, if the man had any sense. Fucking Sylvanus and his fucking magick, Sweet cursed again. The Vol magicker must've sent his own team after the prince. What was it he had said to them, back in Levitan?

*I'm far too cautious to put all of my eggs into your basket. I even have my own men looking for the prince.*

Sweet had assumed he'd meant Thond. And he'd been half-right. The armoured Wyn and his trackers had been hunting them just as they had hunted the prince himself. Stupid, really, to assume that Sylvanus wouldn't have a second team in pursuit. An insurance policy, of sorts. Hell, if Sweet had half the resources that Sylvanus had then it's exactly what he would've done. Sent a team of men to cut off all hope of escape, just in case.

Not just men, either, Sweet thought.

Fucking magickers.

Renauld had said there were five of them. Five magickers that had overpowered the man's entire Vol unit and then used them in some kind of ritual—blood magick, he had said— to elicit more strength for their black craft. At least one of whom had killed two men using some sort of blue fire he could conjure with his bare hands—all in the space of a few heartbeats.

Sweet cursed again as another cabin suddenly loomed out of the darkness. He had to swerve awkwardly to avoid crashing straight into the wall and he skidded on the icy ground. A quick glance over his shoulder told him that the others were following. Malvadas had limped after them, too, his greasy hair flying wildly in all directions. The bounty hunter looked dazed and terrified, but at least he'd stopped asking questions Sweet had no answers for—or at least, no appetite to answer right now.

Sweet's mind raced as he strained his eyes for signs of pursuit. Some way in the distance the cabin they had taken refuge in was starting to catch fire—the flames a more regular orange and yellow now, though that was of little comfort.

Magickers. Sweet had never fought magickers before. There were so few in the world that he'd only ever met a handful, and most of those were like Sylvanus—men in positions of power who didn't need to concern themselves with men like Sweet. Not until now, anyway.

Sweet had no understanding of the craft of magick, and even less about the power they might wield. Could they see in the dark? Maybe. Could they read a man's thoughts before he acted on them? Possibly. Could they kill a man with just one thought of their own? Probably.

'Sweet?' Vi's hissed whisper came from the darkness to his left..

'This way,' Sweet nodded, taking off again. He didn't really know where he was leading them all, he was just trying to put as much distance between them and the burning cabin as possible. He tried to picture the layout of the camp in his mind's eye, and then place where they had been when the magicker had discovered them. It was all guesswork, of course, but Sweet reckoned heading away from the burning cabin full of corpses was as good a call as any.

Five magickers, Sweet tried to gather his thoughts again as they hurried—hunched and fearful—through the abandoned mining camp. Five magickers with unknown powers. They were here for the prince, and they obviously knew that he would be making for the pass through the mountains. At least one of them would be stationed there, then. One other was behind them somewhere, back at the cabin they had just fled. That left three others unaccounted for. Sweet could be leading his crew straight to them. He shook the worry from his mind and carried on scrambling through the snow-covered lanes between buildings. It didn't much matter where the other magickers *might* be, there was *definitely* one behind them, and he'd burst a man's head open like a ripe tomato—that was reason enough to head in this direction.

They stopped by the corner of another ruined cabin. The roof of this one had collapsed inwards and snow had covered much of the interior.

Shadows consumed the rest. Sweet had paused, partly to get his bearings but also because his lungs were burning now. Every breath of ice-cold air he sucked into them hurt like hell. The others joined him, keeping their backs to the ruined building. There was a brief scurry as the wiry form of Malvadas scrambled closer to where Sweet was hiding.

'Sweet,' the bounty hunter huffed, his gold teeth glinting in the moonlight. 'What the hell is going on?'

'Magickers,' Sweet answered, his eyes darting around in the darkness, seeking out signs of pursuit. 'That Vol bastard back in Levitan sent five of his own to head us off at the pass.' A thought suddenly occurred to Sweet and he raised an eyebrow at Malvadas. 'Where's the rest of your crew?'

'They're at the opening of the pass,' Malvadas answered, 'me, Falk and Rebin saw you go into that cabin and—'

'Your men are dead,' Sweet cut him off. 'The magickers'll be watching the pass. You want to stay alive, you fight with us.'

'Sweet!' Violent Fey raised her voice. Sweet heard a note of protest in there and waved his mutilated hand frantically in the darkness.

'We can argue about it later!' he hissed, 'for now let's just get the hell out of this damn camp.'

Without waiting for a response, Sweet took off again. He rounded the corner and ran along the length of the ruined cabin, still hunched over in a bid to make himself a smaller target. As he passed the cavernous opening caused by the collapsed roof he saw movement in the shadows.

Movement followed by a flicker of blue light.

'Down!' Sweet cried, hurling himself forwards into the snow.

There was a fizzing crack, followed by the sound of something whooshing overhead. Sweet felt a wave of heat pass over him, pressing at his skin and tingling at the hairs on the back of his neck, then it was gone. He rolled onto his side and saw a figure standing in the middle of the ruined cabin. The magicker was hooded and cloaked. His arms were bent at strange angles and his pale hands were contorted, extended out towards Sweet and the others. A quick glance backwards told him that most of the others had heeded his warning. Malvadas and Orsen were both facedown in the snow just behind him. Behind them, Violent Fey and Daraday were still standing, stunned but unhurt by the bolt of magick that had flown from the shadows of the cabin.

The magicker turned at the hip, focussing his attention onto where Vi and Daraday were rooted to the spot. Sweet saw the magicker's elbows tense, and small flickers of blue light began to coalesce around his fingers. Sweet was about to cry out again—to try and warn the others—but then the magicker suddenly jolted. The blue light faded as quickly as it had appeared and the magicker dropped to one knee and half-turned. Sweet saw a shape protruding from his shadowed face. Something short and sharp-angled. It was the hilt of a dagger. The magicker crumpled further and toppled over inside the ruined building.

Sweet looked back to see Violent Fey straighten. She had thrown overarm—the dagger slamming into the magicker's eye socket—and now pulled her extended hand back in. She turned to Sweet and let out a long breath.

'Time to go,' she whispered.

Sweet nodded and pushed himself roughly to his feet, ignoring the stinging bite of the winter cold in his finger stumps. He took one last look at the magicker's body, just to be sure. The hooded figure lay unmoving, half-covered by the shadows of the broken cabin walls. Satisfied they wouldn't be getting up again, Sweet continued scurrying along the side of the building.

His mind was racing and his heart was beating wildly. He'd been moments, perhaps just inches, from a sudden and fiery death. So many things could've gone differently that his mind reeled with the thought of them. He might not have seen the magicker rear up in time. The magicker's aim might've been better. Vi's aim might've been worse. All in all, he was lucky to still have a head to worry about such things.

Just keep going, he told himself, willing more energy into his aching limbs and scanning the darkness for further signs of danger. If there had been five magickers, he thought, now there're four. And at least we know that—powers or not—they can't stop a well-thrown blade.

Just keep going.

*

They made it to the edge of the camp without further incident, though everytime Sweet broke from whatever meagre cover they could find he still expected to be spun from his feet by a magicker's bolt. The constant sense of fear was beginning to drain him now, and he felt more exhausted than ever as they reached the walls of the last building on the outskirts.

They'd struck east through the mining camp after their encounter with the magickers, heading away from the direction of the pass. Instead they were now closer to the looming entrance of the mine itself, even in the darkness of the night Sweet could see its cavernous opening etched into the star-bathed slopes of the mountain.

'Sweet!' Violent Fey's voice again, whispering harshly in the darkness. 'What's the plan?'

Sweet considered the question. Truth be told there hadn't been much of a plan, just to get the hell away from the camp. The magickers had turned it into their killing field and it would only be a matter of time before they happened upon them. And next time they might not get so lucky with Vi's knives.

'The mine,' he breathed at last, 'we can hide in the mine.'

'No,' it was Orsen who responded, his voice authoritative but not confrontational. 'No, we'd be stumbling around in the dark and they'd find us eventually.'

Sweet pondered the reply, then realised the boy was right. Who knew what condition the mine was in. They could fumble around and pitch themselves down an open shaft, or cause a cave-in and get themselves trapped or worse. They couldn't light torches, for that would draw the magickers right to them, and even then the magickers needn't even follow them inside. They could simply stand guard at the mine entrance until their prey had to emerge from the darkness. Sweet cursed inwardly at his own foolishness.

'You're right,' he nodded grimly, then brightened, 'got a better plan?'

He saw Orsen crack a small smile in the darkness, the first he'd seen from the lad since they'd entered this accursed little camp.

'A false trail,' he said.

*

Orsen's plan was blindingly simple, but no less good for it. Not for the first time, Sweet found himself admiring the boy's calmness under pressure. He'd a cool head on him, even when Sweet's own was starting to unravel.

They broke cover from the cabin and made for the mine entrance, shuffling through the snow as it began to deepen the further they made their way up the mountain foothills. They arrived without encountering any problems, skirting a rotting wagon that had been left beside two empty carts. The entrance to the mine yawned ahead of them and the group made their way into the shadows. Sweet shivered as they entered this new darkness. It was a different kind of fear to the one he'd encountered in the camp. Out there, the danger had been in the open darkness of not knowing who or what was just a few feet away. In here though, the same darkness felt cloying. The rock walls and ceiling above quickly closed in on them and he became acutely aware of the fact that an entire mountain was currently positioned directly above his head.

Once they'd gone in deep enough—when the snow gave way to bare rock, slick with meltwater but impossible for them to leave tracks in—they backtracked on Orsen's instruction. They carefully picked their way back through their own tracks, stepping backwards in a bid to tread inside their own footprints again. When they'd gone far enough, Orsen whispered for a halt and then turned to face the rock wall beside him. Sweet saw the boy reach out and pull himself up onto the rock face, then he slowly began to shuffle his way along it, back the way they had come. Vi, Daraday and Malvadas followed suit. Sweet himself wondered briefly if he had any strength left in his body to manage the feat, but the thought of being blown apart by blue flames seemed to give him a bit more life and he clambered onto the rock wall beside them. The missing fingers of his left hand made the manoeuvre awkward and sent fiery tendrils of pain lancing down his arm, but he gritted his teeth and followed his companions.

As they shuffled back along the wall of rock, it slowly curved away from the entrance to the mine. Sweet glanced back across and saw their tracks in the snow, scuffed and piled as they'd waded up the slope and into the mine. As he saw the tracks he found his admiration for Orsen growing further still.

This might just bloody work, he thought.

Not only that, he considered, but if it did it might even provide them with an opportunity for escape. With just four magickers remaining—and assuming they took the bait and surmised that their quarry had holed up in the mine—they might leave the mountain pass unguarded. Orsen's plan might see them slip the noose and scramble through the mountains undetected.

The thought brought fresh energy flowing through his aching body and Sweet scrambled along the rockface after the others. Once they were safely clear of the mine entrance, Orsen climbed down from the rocks and began carefully skirting them along the base instead. The others followed. Sweet was glad to be free of the climb, as his remaining fingertips were somehow both numb and painful at the same time. They kept close to the rocks, to avoid leaving obvious tracks, but slowly circled away from the mine altogether.

The ground began to rise again and after a time, Orsen led them all behind a stand of boulders that had slipped free of the mountain. Sweet hunkered down beside the others and looked back down the way they had come. He realised for the first time that the sky was beginning to lighten a little. The deep dark of the night was giving way to the paler blue of a dawn twilight and he could see further now. Some two hundred paces down the slope was where they had disembarked from the rockface. Another hundred or so paces beyond that he could see a rough line in the snow, leading towards the mine entrance. Those was the tracks they had left for the magickers to follow. The false trail. Then there were the small shapes of the wagon and the carts, no bigger than Sweet's thumbnail from this distance. Off to his right, Sweet could see the outlines of the buildings in the camp beginning to emerge from the darkness now. The flaming cabin had burned out, but Sweet could see curls of smoke drifting from its ruin. There was no other movement in the mining camp.

'There!' Violent Fey's harsh whisper cut through the air again. Sweet could see her more clearly now and followed her pointing finger. Just at the edge of the mining camp, three shapes had emerged. All were hooded and cloaked and walked close together. They were bent forwards, as though examining something on the ground.

'They're following our tracks,' Orsen whispered. Sweet heard a note of victory in the boy's voice, but grimly quelled his own feelings of elation. Not until the bastards disappeared into the mine itself would he celebrate, and even then he was unlikely to jump for joy. Then there was the other problem. There were only three magickers down there. Where was the fourth?

Sweet watched, peeking over the edge of the rocks, as the magickers slowly made their way out of the camp, following the same path he and the others had taken less than an hour before. At one point one of them raised a hand and created a blue luminescence around it. Sweet instinctively ducked back down behind the boulders, before realising the magicker was probably just lighting their way. Checking to see if the tracks were still there.

It began to snow again, and Sweet cursed under his breath. Not only would snow eventually close the mountain pass, but it might also now obscure their carefully-laid false trail. Thankfully the snowfall was still light and Sweet reckoned the magickers would still be able to follow them right enough.

*If* they followed them, he thought.

Sweet could practically feel the hopes and prayers of his companions as they watched the magickers approach the entrance to the mine. Even Malvadas was crouched, watching wide-eyed as he willed their pursuers into the darkness of the mine. Beside the bounty hunter, Daraday had slung the bow from his shoulder and held an arrow in his grip alongside the riser. Better safe than sorry, Sweet thought.

The three figures neared the rotting wagon. The one still holding the pulse of glowing magick stopped to examine the dilapidated vehicle for a moment. He glanced up in the direction of the rocks and for one mad moment Sweet thought that he had spotted them. After what seemed like an age, the magicker turned and followed his companions further along the path. Sweet exhaled—long and slow—unaware that he'd even been holding his breath. The three magickers were still stooped over, carefully following the tracks that led into the mine.

But where the hell was the fourth?

Sweet cursed again. He reckoned they'd been savvy enough to at least leave one of their number in reserve. No doubt still guarding the pass itself. They were careful bastards, that much was for sure.

Sweet looked along the line of his companions, seeing Orsen with his hand flexing close to his sword, Vi's daggers sheathed all across her body and Daraday with his bow in hand. Hell, even Malvadas had a long-bladed knife and a stumpy little hatchet. Between the five of us, Sweet thought, I reckon we might stand a chance against one opponent. Especially if we can take them by surprise.

Below them, the three magickers walked further into the mountainside until they disappeared from view, obscured by the wall of rock that curved away from the mine entrance. Sweet and the others waited for a few long moments, but none of the magickers reemerged.

'It worked,' Orsen breathed, a victorious grin stretched across his face, making him look even younger than he was. Sweet nodded, but couldn't muster the strength to return the gesture.

'Aye,' he whispered, 'it might keep 'em busy long enough for us to slip back to the pass,' he looked at each of them in turn, the dawn twilight growing brighter with every passing moment. 'But there's still one of 'em out there,' he told them, 'so be on your guard.'

The group nodded, determined and ready. Sweet carefully picked his way back from the stand of rocks and started heading west, away from the mine. They'd made it no more than twenty paces when Sweet heard Violent Fey's voice, hushed but sharp and full of alarm.

'Sweet!' she hissed.

Sweet turned his head. Three hundred paces behind them, he saw a figure—hooded and cloaked—standing beside the shape of the old wagon. The figure stood facing up the snow-covered slope, staring directly at them. The magicker raised an arm and there was a short flash of light. The echo of a cracking noise followed shortly after.

A signal.

Then the magicker began stalking up the slope towards them.

'Fuck,' Sweet cursed.

Behind the lone magicker, other shapes came scrambling out from the entrance to the mine, all hurrying to join their companion. They were heading straight for them.

'Fuck,' Sweet cursed again.

# *Blood and snow*

T HEY SCRAMBLED FURTHER up the slope, kicking chunks of snow behind them in their wake. Sweet could feel every breath burning in his lungs as they desperately tried to put distance between themselves and their pursuers. Glancing back over his shoulder, he saw that their efforts might well be in vain.

The cloaked magickers advanced at a steady pace, relentlessly striding up the snow-covered hillside. There were four of them, moving in a line with some three paces between them. Sweet reckoned two must've been moving close together as he'd watched them leave the mining camp. In the poor light he'd mistaken them for a single magicker and assumed they were just a trio. Then they must've left one behind by the wagon whilst the others followed the tracks into the mine. A sentry, posted in case the tracks leading into the darkness were a ruse—which of course they had been. Idiot, he cursed himself, would we have done any different in their position?

Didn't matter much now, Sweet reasoned, turning back to their course and struggling up the slope after Orsen, Vi and the others. He wondered how long it would be before a bolt of that hellish blue fire would come screaming up the hill towards them.

'Spread out a little!' Sweet cried, the exertion taking the wind out of him, 'don't bunch together!'

They heeded his call and both Orsen and Daraday shifted their direction a little to widen the gap between themselves. Sweet risked another glance and cursed again as he realised the magickers were closer still. Not by much, mind—but step by step they were eating away at the distance. They stalked ever closer with steely purpose, not rushing, just moving steadily towards their quarry.

Sweet considered their options as he toiled after his companions, every aching muscle and swollen joint shrieking in protest. They could turn, stand and fight—but what would be the point? The magickers were clearly deadly opponents, even at a distance. They wouldn't get within twenty paces of them before being incinerated just like Malvadas' men back in the cabin. Did that mean struggling on then? Leading the magickers further up the mountain? To what end? Eventually they would tire and have to stop. Besides, the magickers would probably catch up to them long before that point. Were they not just prolonging the inevitable?

What else was there then? Negotiate? Sweet would've coughed out a laugh if he wasn't fighting for breath, scrambling up the snow-covered path with his life in the balance. He didn't reckon Sylvanus' magickers would be open to sitting down and talking things through, especially since they'd probably discovered their comrade with a throwing knife still embedded in his eye. Not only that, but what did Sweet have to negotiate with anyway? The prince was the prize, but Sweet got the feeling—given how the magickers had handled things so far—a dead prince was just as good as a live one, despite what was on the contract Sylvanus had given to Sweet and his crew. Even if they did surrender the prince to the magickers alive, Sweet thought it was unlikely they would repay the gesture by allowing them to leave unharmed.

Not only that, but Sweet reckoned turning on Orsen now would just about cement his place in whatever passed for a hell in the next life, for sure. The boy had shown incredible courage and resolve in the short time they had known him. Not exactly things you could live off, but Sweet reckoned they were worthy of something all the same, even if that something was sticking with him—and probably dying beside him—to the end.

Bloody hell, Sweet thought, maybe Stover was right after all. Maybe I have lost my senses.

'Down!' Daraday bellowed, his eyes going wide as he caught sight of something over Sweet's shoulder. Sweet didn't need telling twice and hurled himself into the snow. There was a flash of light, then a great whumping noise, followed by a vibration that Sweet felt in the hillside underneath him. A smatter of snow and ice and splinters of stone rained down around him. He looked up and saw a gently smouldering crater away to his left. Snowflakes falling from the sky landed inside the crater and instantly puffed into steam. One of the magickers had loosed a bolt—and it had damn near taken Sweet right between his shoulder blades.

Ahead of Sweet, Daraday nocked an arrow to his bow and drew back the string. He aimed, took a deep breath and then fired. Sweet followed the arc of the arrow through the dim light of the predawn sun. He lost it for a moment in the semi-darkness before catching sight of it again close to one of the magickers. They were near enough now for Sweet to see that the magicker was a man with a thick red beard, just visible beneath the shadows of his hood. Daraday's shot was a good one, but the cloaked figure stopped mid-stride and waved a hand at the missile. More of that bastard blue luminescence appeared and the arrow was brushed off course to plunge harmlessly into the snow. The magicker continued up the slope after his comrades, seemingly unfazed by the attempt on his life.

'Keep going!' Sweet bellowed, more for his own benefit than that of the others. Judging by the looks on their faces, they didn't need much encouragement.

The group continued staggering up the slope. At one point the magickers below them released another bolt, but it fell short and impacted on the hillside below them with another whump. The climb was getting steeper now, arcing around to one side, and Sweet realised they were following a natural path up the side of the mountain itself. To their left, the drop became increasingly sheer and increasingly high. To their right, rows of rocky outcroppings lined the way, creating fissures and gulleys all leading up towards the peak hidden somewhere in the clouds. The snow was falling heavier up here, too. Long gusts of wind blew across the unprotected flanks of the mountain, carrying flurries of white powder across their path and whipping it into their faces with the sting of a thousand tiny needles. Ahead of them, a rockslide had created a natural fork in their way. Boulders as big as wagons and man-size stones were stacked in a ridge that piled away to their right.

'Vi!' Sweet bellowed, seeking out Violent Fey in the whirling snowscape. When he saw her turn, he gestured wildly to the fork. 'Take Orsen and Dara left!' he told her, 'Mal and I will hook right.'

'Like hell we will!' Malvadas protested breathlessly, stopping in his climb. 'I'm not splitting up to lead those bastards—'

There was a roar, followed by a deafening crack as another bolt of blue magick cannoned into the slope just behind Malvadas. The gold-toothed bounty hunter was thrown to the ground and came up spluttering snow.

'Go!' Sweet barked, grabbing Malvadas by the shoulder of his cloak and hauling him to his feet. He half-dragged the other bounty hunter towards the right side of the fork and watched as Vi and the others split off to the left. Sweet risked a glance behind and saw that the magickers were pairing off to do the same. The red-bearded one grabbed the man beside him and made after Sweet and Malvadas. The other two angled themselves towards Vi and her group.

'This ain't my fight,' Malvadas hissed, wrenching himself clear of Sweet's grip. 'I ain't part of this shit.'

'Yeah?' Sweet grimaced, then motioned back down the slope. 'You can go down there and tell 'em that then, eh Mal?'

Without waiting for a response, Sweet clambered over the slippery lee of a big rock and began pushing on through the narrow gulley behind it. Moments later he heard Malvadas scrambling through behind him.

*

They worked their way through the rocks, occasionally scrambling up steep inclines that barred the way forwards. Sweet didn't dare look back. His thighs were burning with exhaustion, his lower back was as stiff as a board and he felt like he couldn't catch a single breath long enough for it to make a jot of difference to his empty lungs. Each inhale brought a sharp pain to his chest and he wondered if their pursuers were feeling the same. Probably not, he reasoned. What had Renauld said? They'd gained their power from killing the Vol soldiers? Blood magick? Who knew what kind of physical advantages that gave them? These bastards could probably climb this mountain all day if they wanted to, Sweet thought bitterly.

Behind him, Malvadas cried out as the blade of his hatchet caught on the rock. Sweet saw it had dug into the man's hip and reached back with one hand to offer help. Sweet expected Malvadas to eye the gesture with his usual mixture of suspicion and scorn, but he did neither. Malvadas grabbed him by the wrist and Sweet hauled the gold-toothed bounty hunter up over the stones. They were both breathing hard and Malvadas leaned back against the nearest boulder.

'Don't...reckon...there's much more...in me,' he gasped.

Sweet could only nod his agreement. Though he didn't want to admit it, he was done in. It would only be a matter of time before the magickers caught up to them. They were finished.

The thought was strangely comforting, somehow. No more running in terror, no more looking back over his shoulder. No more bastard climbing. Even the biting cold felt oddly relaxing, now. Was this what it was like to be hunted? He thought. Was this what all of those bounties—all those men and women—over the years had thought, as he and his crew had hunted them? Sweet managed a wry chuckle at the strangeness of those thoughts. Malvadas' head dropped down from the sky and he raised an eyebrow at Sweet.

'Somethin' funny?' he asked, between breaths.

Sweet nodded.

'Been a hunter most'o my life,' he said, 'never thought I'd go like this,' he motioned to the mountainside. 'Hunted, y'know?'

Malvadas only nodded and swallowed hard. He glanced back down the way they'd come. No sign of the magickers yet.

'Reckon they'll listen if I try to talk?' Malvadas asked at last. Sweet only gave a grim smile. Malvadas caught his eye and shrugged. 'Didn't think so.'

Sweet took a deep breath. This one felt less painful and he revelled in it for a moment. Then he glanced away to one side and saw a shallow opening burrowed into the mountainside. It wasn't deep enough to hide them, not for long anyway, but a plan formed in his mind all the same.

'Mal,' he motioned to the recess, 'get back in there, I've got an idea.'

The bounty hunter obeyed—weary and half-heartedly, but he obeyed all the same. Sweet risked a quick peek down the path they had come but still couldn't see either of the cloaked magickers. He could hear them now though, their scrambling footfalls scratching and scrabbling as they climbed after their quarry. Sweet grabbed at a length of his cloak and ripped at it, pulling a raggedy piece of the fabric clear. He placed it on the rocks behind him, stuffing it into a gap between the stones so that the wind wouldn't wrench it away. Then he joined Malvadas inside the shallow cave. Sweet slowly drew his sword.

'That's your plan?' Malvadas raised an eyebrow again, he unlooped the hatchet from his belt, wincing at the shallow wound in his hip. Sweet only shrugged.

'Might be enough to distract them,' he reasoned, 'just long enough for us to get close. You ready?'

'Aye,' Malvadas nodded, hefting the hatchet. 'But—for the record, Sweet—this is a shit plan.'

*

The red-bearded magicker was the first one over the rocks. Sweet and Malvadas heard him long before they saw him. Magick powers or not, he was breathing hard as he hauled himself over the boulders and onto the little rocky platform. Up close, Sweet saw that he was heavily built, with broad shoulders and a powerful chest underneath that thick robe. The magicker's eyes were fixed on the path ahead and Sweet saw them light on the scrap of cloth flapping in the wind. The man's comrade scrambled up the stones just a few heartbeats later. Another man, barely more than a boy, actually. This magicker was clean-shaven with rose-coloured blotches on his cheeks and dark curls of hair that hooked over his ears. His hood had been pulled back by the weather and he looked decidedly pissed off at having to chase people up a mountainside.

Without a sound, Sweet sprung from his hiding place, Malvadas beside him. They offered no war cries or bellows of defiance. Sweet knew that those kinds of things were mostly for stories anyway. In close quarters like this, fights with blades tended to be short, brutal and bloody.

The curly-haired magicker saw them first. He had barely caught his breath from the short climb up the rocky lee when Sweet was upon him. The look on his face quickly turned from pissed off to one of complete surprise. That surprise then turned into pain as Sweet's sword point plunged into his belly. The boy gurgled as the blade tore through him before he could cry out properly.

The red-bearded magicker was quicker to react. Sweet heard a sudden rushing noise, as though the air around him was being sucked away, then pinched his eyes shut as a sudden flash of blue erupted in front of him. Heat threatened to engulf him and for a moment Sweet thought he had been hit. He cracked open one eye to see that the magick bolt had caught the curly-haired magicker in the back. The youngster—now very dead—slumped over, his cloak ablaze with blue flame, pulling Sweet's sword down with him.

The impact of the blast had wrong-footed Malvadas, giving the red-bearded magicker enough time to react to their ambush. Sweet saw the magicker pivot expertly on one foot. At the same time he drew both hands together and then pulled them apart, gritting his teeth all the while. Sweet was mesmerised as he saw a ghostly blue sword emerge in the space between the man's palms. It shimmered and glowed ethereally, but looked no less deadly for it.

In one smooth motion, the red-bearded magicker dodged aside from Malvadas' overhand swing and cannoned his shoulder into the bounty hunter. Malvadas was thrown backwards and hit the rocks, stunned. The magicker followed in and levelled his glowing blade at Malvadas. The weapon stabbed through Malvadas' stomach, just as Sweet's had done to the magicker's young comrade. Malvadas gave a grunt, followed by a second, louder cry of pain as the magicker pulled his blade clear. The gold-toothed bounty hunter gave a pained sigh and then slumped down to the ground.

The red-bearded magicker rounded on Sweet, the glowing blade crackling faintly in his hand, it's point now slick with dark blood. Sweet, unarmed, met the man's gaze.

Sweet felt two things then. The first was fear. True, unbridled fear as he knew for certain that he was staring into the unflinching eyes of the man who would be his killer. Unparalleled fear as he knew for certain that his death was at hand. Sure, he'd been in dangerous situations for most of his life, but this—he knew—would be the last.

The second was an eerie sense of relief. The feeling that soon, very soon, all of the running and the fighting and the cheating and the lying would be over. Soon he would be free. Quite madly, that feeling was stronger than the fear, too. Sweet was ready, that was the truth of it.

And truth was a weapon.

The magicker took a menacing step towards Sweet and tensed as he raised the glowing blade. Sweet watched the man advance on him, his mind coursing with these two emotions—such strange bedfellows and yet, somehow perfectly suited to one another. He watched as his death approached, as his freedom neared.

Then the magicker jerked. His fingers flew open and the magick sword dissipated into nothingness.

Sweet saw something had replaced the man's left eye. Something that gleamed dully in the pale light of the upcoming dawn. The magicker dropped to his knees and his head flopped forwards. Sweet saw an arrow shaft embedded into the back of his skull. Behind the slumped form of the magicker, he saw the outline of a figure set against the brightening sky.

Daraday straightened up. The strange sensation of terror and relief flooded away from Sweet in that instant and he suddenly felt all of his pains and burdens weigh down on him once again. The ache in his muscles and the stinging in his missing fingers returned with a vengeance. The exhaustion, his empty lungs and burning legs all started screaming in unison.

Grunting, Sweet bent low and yanked his sword free from the body of the curly-haired magicker. Off to one side, Malvadas groaned and clutched at the wound in his belly with both hands.

'Back to the others!' Sweet ordered Daraday. The lad lingered for a moment, then nodded and disappeared from sight.

Sweet watched him go then knelt beside the stricken bounty hunter. Blood had bubbled up in his mouth, giving his gold teeth a sickening glean.

'Never thought I'd go...saving your arse, Bitter Sweet,' Malvadas coughed.

'Been a strange few months,' Sweet agreed, inspecting the wound and knowing that the man was dying. 'I've normally got a golden rule, y'know? About who I work with.'

'Aye,' Malvadas nodded, 'everyone knows it.' He coughed a barking chuckle, spraying more blood into the snow. 'Who you don't work with, right?'

'That's the one,' said Sweet. 'Good thing it got broken for this little jaunt, eh? Else you wouldn't have been here to take that hit for me.'

Malvadas coughed out another laugh. Sweet's face hardened then.

'Can't say I'm sorry to see you go though,' he told Malvadas, meeting the dying man's gaze. He meant it, too. A man dying weren't no reason to forgive all his past actions. Especially not one with a history as dark as the one that Malvadas had. Sweet stared hard at the dying bounty hunter. 'For Bryn, you know?'

Malvadas said nothing, but Sweet reckoned he saw a moment of confusion flicker across the man's face, as though he hadn't understood what Sweet had said. Or maybe he was just noticing the mortal wound inflicted on him for the first time—some men wouldn't believe they were dying right up until they went. Malvadas shuddered and grimaced down at the terrible wound.

'You didn't have to kill Bryntas,' Sweet told him, his face set, 'he deserved better'n that.'

Malvadas juddered again, and Sweet reckoned the bounty hunter hadn't heard him this time. He spluttered for breath and then went still with a long, drawn out sigh. Blood leaked out between the man's fingers as his hands relaxed their grip on the wound in his stomach.

'Hell,' Sweet straightened up, 'we all deserve better'n this.

# What winning looks like

SWEET CLAMBERED OUT of the rocks, leaving the bodies of Malvadas and the two magickers for the snow to claim. It was falling heavier now and the wind seemed to be whirling ever stronger, knocking great tufts of it up into his face. Sweet put an arm out to defend against it and looked for tracks. After a few moments of searching he saw a scuffed trail leading further up the mountain. Daraday's trail. It would lead him to the others for sure—if they were still alive.

Three magickers were dead. That left only two now, and—so far as Sweet knew—they had sustained no losses themselves, save for Malvadas, who was no great loss to anyone. Add to that the worsening weather and poor visibility and Sweet was beginning to favour their odds. After all, they couldn't fire their damned magick at what they couldn't see.

Sweet struggled up the slope, slipping several times as the footing beneath him became more and more treacherous. A small break in the swirling snow storm gave him a glimpse of just how high they'd climbed. On reflection, he wished he hadn't been privy to it. The drop was staggering and the longer Sweet stared at it, the more the mountain itself seemed to sway precariously in the whipping wind. The cold was biting into every inch of exposed flesh, too. Sweet's ears sang with pain and he could feel ice forming on the patchy beard that covered the lower half of his face, pulling at the skin like a million tiny needles.

Sweet was beyond exhausted now, and every trudging upward step felt like climbing a mountain itself. He wearily stamped his left leg down and threw his arms up in alarm when it kept right on going, plunging through the snow and falling away into nothingness. He lurched sideways and knew then that he was tumbling off the side of the path. The drop he had glimpsed just moments ago meant that a bed of unforgiving rocks awaited him after what would be an agonisingly long fall through the air. Long enough to consider what awaited him at the bottom.

Strong fingers wrapped around his wrist, digging in deep and righting him once again. A second hand clutched at his weather-beaten coat and hauled him away from the drop. Sweet nearly fell into his rescuer and the two of them stumbled sideways into the deepening snow. He turned his head and saw that it was Violent Fey, her face set into her usual expression of grim determination. He wanted to thank her, but he was too exhausted to muster any sounds, and so settled for a nod instead. She returned the gesture and pushed herself to her feet, pulling him up after her. Vi motioned at something in the maelstrom of snow—the wind was howling too loudly to be heard but Sweet got the gist. She wanted him to follow her. He trudged after her, more aware of his footing after his brief dalliance with a savage, brutal death.

Vi led him away from the worst of the whipping wind, and Sweet soon realised she'd found shelter. Soon the snow was no longer whirling around his face and he was able to drop his arm to see again. The sun still wasn't quite up yet—and the storm was making it damned difficult—but there was enough light for him to be able to make out the beginnings of a low-ceilinged cave that stretched into darkness.

A shape loomed out of the shadows and Sweet flinched, instinctively throwing his hands in the air. It was Orsen, sword in hand and ready to plunge straight into Sweet's chest.

'Not the warmest welcome I ever had,' Sweet breathed, lowering his arms again.

'But not the worst either, I imagine,' the prince smiled at him.

Another shape emerged and Sweet recognised Daraday, a fresh arrow nocked in his bow and a dagger gripped tightly in his bow hand. He relaxed a little as he saw Sweet.

'The gang's all here,' Sweet murmured, offering a dry chuckle. 'The magickers?'

'Lost them in the storm,' said Vi. 'I went looking to see what I could see, found you.'

'Caught me,' Sweet corrected, 'just before I could take a tumble off the cliff. Maybe the magickers didn't get so lucky?'

Vi shrugged.

'They did or they didn't,' she said.

'Daraday tells us the other two are dead,' Orsen put in. Sweet nodded. 'Malvadas, too.'

'Good riddance,' Vi spat.

'That leaves only two left then, right?' Orsen asked, skirting Violent Fey's outburst. 'That's good.'

'Aye,' Sweet agreed, scratching at his chin and regretting it instantly. The clumps of ice there pulled hairs from his face and he winced. 'Still two more'n I would like, though.'

'So what should we do?' Orsen asked.

'We can wait them out in here,' said Vi, her fingers dancing over the hilts of her daggers. 'If they stumble across the cave, we kill them.'

'Aye, that's one option,' Sweet agreed, 'but if this storm doesn't blow over soon,' he paused for a moment. 'It could close the pass.'

This suggestion was greeted like a rotten stink. Sweet saw each of his companions absorb the information before coming to the same, bleak conclusion that he had already found himself.

'We have to leave,' Orsen said at last.

'Heading down in this weather will be worse than coming up,' Vi pointed out. 'It's a long way to fall.'

'Aye,' Sweet nodded, remembering the sight of those jagged rocks far below, 'but it also means there's less chance o' those bastards finding us. If we slip by them, we can get to the pass whilst they're still fumblin' around up here lookin' for us.'

'Or we could run right into them,' said Vi.

'Or that,' Sweet nodded grimly, then added, 'if that happens, we kill 'em.'

'Right then,' Orsen said, sheathing his sword. 'What're we waiting for?'

*

Sweet didn't relish the thought of heading back out into the swirling winds or the frozen landscape. The brief respite he'd received in the little cavemouth had been downright heavenly. He was still cold, tired to his bones and beaten to bloody hell and back, but at least his ears had stopped stinging. A part of him—a big part of him—wanted to ignore his own advice and just wait out the storm inside the cave. They had a little food left, and the entrance should be more than defensible against just two attackers, particularly if they took them unawares—but he knew they were running a terrible risk every minute they spent up here. If the pass through the mountains became snowed-in, they'd be forced to turn back entirely—and with the condition the group was in, Sweet didn't reckon they'd survive long in the wilderness.

So, with a heavy heart and a body that was nearing its limit of physical punishment, Sweet ducked under the rocky ledge shielding the cave from the worst of the wind and forced himself back out into the snowstorm.

And crashed straight into someone.

Sweet was so shocked that he barely had time to register what had happened. The person he slammed into was equally stunned. They were about a foot shorter than he was and of a much slighter build. As Sweet crashed into them, knocking them back a step, he saw a glimmer of a face—a woman's face—and recognised a look of surprise that quickly changed into one of anger.

A blue light began to form.

She was one of the magickers.

Sweet had no time—and barely any strength left—to reach for his sword. Instead he lurched towards the magicker and swept his arms around her, gripping her in a bear hug as tight as he could muster. She cried out and he pinned her tighter, throwing his weight sideways at the same time. He didn't know much about magick, but he'd seen enough in the last few hours to reckon that freeing the woman's hands would be a pretty big mistake. She was quick, though, and readjusted her footing well. Sweet's attempt to drag her down failed and she pulled her head back sharply. Sweet recognised what she was doing just a moment too late.

Pain exploded between his eyes and he felt his nose crack and flood with warmth. His vision swam as he recoiled from the savage headbutt, but he kept his grip tight. The woman snarled at him and hissed something in a language he didn't understand. He was vaguely aware of a second figure in the snow, hooded and cloaked. He heard the others call out and a scuffle began.

The magicker in his grip tossed her head back a second time and Sweet tried to turn his own head to avoid the blow. He only half-succeeded, this time her headbutt glanced off his cheek. It was no less painful for it and he felt a bit of the strength in his arms leech away.

The magicker must've felt it too, because she snarled again—this time as though sensing victory. She wrenched her head back a third time, preparing to butt him again. Sweet did the only thing his addled brains could come up with.

He headbutted her first.

The pain was unlike anything he'd ever experienced before. His temples throbbed so much that he thought his head would fall in on itself. Strange lights bubbled and burst in his eyes. Then he lost his vision—everything flickering black and brown—but only for a few moments. He was down on one knee but couldn't remember falling. The snow seeped cold and wet through his trews. Ahead of him, the female magicker was still on her feet, just three or four paces away. She was holding her head and her legs looked shaky—or maybe that was just Sweet's vision blurring madly.

The magicker pulled one hand away from her head and held it down by her side, fingers splayed in a contorted pattern. Her fingertips began to dance madly.. Sweet saw a strange glow begin to emanate from the palm. In its light, he saw her glaring at him, blood streaming down her face from her smashed nose—it glowed black in the eerie magick light.

Sweet knew he had to get up. Knew he had to get to her.

Get to her or die. Die kneeling in the snow atop a nameless mountain.

Summoning every last vestige of strength he had, Sweet bellowed—though the sound came out as more of a hoarse croak—and charged at her. The blue glow formed into the shape of a knife, the blade roughly half a foot in length.

Sweet reached her—his hands grabbing for her throat—and a lance of fire stabbed into his side. He didn't need to look down to know that he'd been run through with the magick dagger, he could feel its burning presence inside his flesh. Hurts just the same as steel, Sweet thought. Hurts more, if anything. Letting the pain fuel his anger, Sweet bellowed again—there was more strength to the sound this time—and bore himself down on the magicker. His weight carried them over and she landed on her back with a grunt, Sweet atop her with his hands—mutilated finger stumps screaming with pain—wrapped around her neck.

The magicker struggled in the snow, but the hand she had used to stab him with the dagger was pinned between them and she could only get one arm up to scratch at his grip. Sweet gritted his teeth and squeezed as tightly as he could, ignoring the woman's protesting swipes. She thrashed and wriggled but Sweet held on, his face pitted in a determined snarl. After a time, her struggles began to lessen, her flapping protests growing weaker. Then they abated altogether.

Sweet managed to hold his grip a moment longer, just to be sure, before his strength failed him and he collapsed atop her. The pain in his side had weirdly lessened now, though he could feel something warm leaking from his abdomen and down over the top of his thigh. Sweet groaned and rolled off the dead magicker.

The storm wind calmed for a moment and the scene cleared a little. Off to his right, Sweet saw other shapes in the snow. His vision swam in and out of focus until he saw a cloaked figure lying still on the ground. The hilt of a dagger sticking out of his chest. Above the body stood

Violent Fey. She was breathing heavily and sported a fresh cut above one eye. Further back from the scene, Sweet saw Daraday crouched beside another still figure lying just inside the mouth of the shallow cave.

Orsen.

Sweet groaned and suddenly Violent Fey was by his side, her face pinched with concern. Sweet didn't reckon he'd seen her concerned more'n three times in his life—all of them on this cursed job—and he gave a dry chuckle.

'What the hell's so funny?' Vi asked him, checking something around his waist.

'Never seen you look so damn serious,' he told her, coughing out another laugh. 'And you *always* look serious.'

Vi didn't return the smile, and that confirmed what Sweet already knew. He'd seen that look before. Hell, he'd *given* that look before. He knew the simple truth. That he was more than just hurt. The grin faded from his face and he glanced over Vi's knee towards where Orsen lay.

'The prince—' he started.

'He's alright,' Vi pushed him down with one hand, her touch was gentle but firm. 'He got thrown against the rocks, hit his head is all. He's groggy, but reckon he'll be ok.'

Sweet read the undertone in her voice as she spoke.

'Not so much me though, eh?' he tried another chuckle, but this time the pain in his side returned anew and he winced harder still.

'I've seen worse,' Vi lied. She'd always been a bad liar, and Sweet would know. Daggers and knives were her weapons, truth and lies had always been his.

'Bullshit,' he croaked again, 'I'm leaking like a damned sieve.'

'What do you want us to do?' Violent Fey asked. When she spoke her voice was soft, and Sweet had to quell another snorting laugh. He'd never heard her speak like that before. Sweet grimaced.

'Get me out of this fucking snow,' he told her.

Vi yelled for Daraday and the youngster appeared at Sweet's other side. Together they carefully manoeuvred him towards the cave, half-carrying, half-dragging him out of the elements and into the relative sanctuary of the rocky overhang. They positioned him next to Orsen, resting his back against the cave wall. Sweet looked across at the other man. An angry lump was forming on the prince's forehead, dark bruising already starting to blossom around it. He was unconscious, but his breathing looked steady enough.

'He's gonna have one hell of a headache,' Sweet chuckled, wincing as the pain in his side flared again. The flow of blood seemed to be slowing now—or maybe I just can't feel it so much anymore, he thought. It was hard to tell where the numbness from the cold begins and the numbness from bleeding to death starts.

'He'll live,' said Vi, staring down at Sweet with a sorrowful look on her face. That was almost too much for Sweet and he forced another choking laugh.

'Come on now, Vi,' he tried a grin, 'we won didn't we?'

'Is this what winning looks like?' Vi snorted.

'Got all the bastards, didn't we?' Sweet grimaced through his grin as a fresh burst of pain flared from the stab wound in his midriff. Then his expression hardened. 'Now you just need to get Orsen down the mountain before the snow sets in. Get him through that pass.'

'It's calming down a bit now,' Vi told him. Sweet looked behind her and saw that she was right. The snow was falling more lightly again, and the wind was only listing it a little. There were even glimmers of the sunrise in the distance. Delicate pinks and a touch of gold that coloured the clouds on the horizon. 'We can wait awhile, I reckon,' she added. Sweet met her gaze. He saw that her eyes were brimming with tears. This time he didn't force a laugh. Or crack a joke. He only nodded slowly in return.

'We *have* been waiting a while,' Daraday's voice cut through the exchange like a jagged note. Sweet winced again at the sinister tone, confused by it. What the hell was the lad talking about?

Daraday loomed over Violent Fey's left shoulder, his eyes as hard as flint. Sweet saw a long-bladed dagger in his hand. Before he could understand what was happening, Sweet saw Daraday's arm curl up in front of Violent Fey's neck.

And he wrenched the dagger across her throat.

## The weapon of truth

E VERYTHING SEEMED TO happen at once then, and Sweet understood precisely none of it.

In fact, his first thought was that he'd already died from his wound, and he was simply watching one final nightmare play out before he slipped into everlasting darkness. Then his body reminded him he was still alive—just—by sending waves of pain rippling out from the stab wound in his stomach. They were triggered by him jolting upright, so shocked at what he'd just seen that it demanded a physical, visceral reaction. Sweet's eyes grew so wide the edges of his face hurt. His heart was beating so wildly that he was sure his heart would give out before the mortal wound in his belly could claim him.

Vi's face turned from sorrow—her glassy eyes fixed on Sweet's own—to a look of the utmost surprise. The blade in Daraday's hand sliced across her throat in a wide red line and dark blood began to immediately flow from the deep cut. Vi's legs buckled and she toppled to her knees, that look of confusion still carved into her features like a silent scream. She tried to say something but only a gurgling noise came. Then her eyes rolled back into her skull and she pitched forwards, face down just a few inches from Sweet's outstretched legs. Blood began to pool around her, staining the stone black and the snow pink. It seeped across the floor of the cave towards where Sweet was slumped against the wall, transfixed with horror.

'Dara, what the—' he tried

'We've been waiting *years,*' Daraday hissed, the knife down by his side dripping with blood.

Vi's knife, Sweet thought. Vi's blood.

He killed her.

'Dara, what the fu—' Sweet tried a second time.

'Better you hear it from someone else,' Daraday interrupted him again, as though explaining something to an unruly child. 'He wanted to talk to you again...before we finish it.'

Sweet's mind reeled. The shock of what had just transpired was passing now, but it was no less confusing and he could only stare wide-eyed at Violent Fey's unmoving body.

Dead, his mind told her. Her *dead* body.

Violent Fey, who had stood beside him all these long years. Who had helped get them out of all sorts of trouble time and time again. Who had saved his arse on more than one occasion and never so much as looked for a word of thanks for it. Violent Fey with all her sharpness and all her beauty and all her cleverness and all her madness rolled into one. Power and danger and loyalty all swirled together like an unstoppable maelstrom. The person Sweet trusted most in the world, and that was the truth of it. Hell, the person he liked most in the world. The person he loved most.

His only friend.

Dead at his feet.

A fresh wave of shock hit Sweet and he could only stammer.

'D-d-dara what the fuck—'

'Hello, Bitter Sweet,' a voice sounded from away to Sweet's left. A slow, drawn-out drawl that dripped with triumph.

It was a voice he hadn't heard in a long time. So long in fact that he wasn't sure he was really hearing it at all. Maybe the blood loss had truly addled his brain. Maybe he was dead already and this was just one last ghost come to taunt him. It was certainly the voice of a ghost, anyway. It had changed a little—time would do that to most things—but he recognised the speaker all the same. He turned his head slowly, his mind still disbelieving what his eyes and ears were telling him was true.

A cloaked figure stepped inside the cave.

'Aribor?' Sweet breathed.

*

It *was* Aribor.

His face was weathered, the skin pinched tight around his eyes, and his cheeks were a little more gaunt than Sweet remembered. He had a beard now—and slightly longer hair—but it *was* Aribor. The same Aribor that had joined Sweet's crew all those years ago. The same Aribor who had helped them track the killer just outside of Woodbyrne. The same Aribor who had taken a blade at the hands of that killer. The same Aribor that Daraday had wanted to go back for. Had wanted to help. Had been *desperate* to help.

But Sweet had talked him out of it.

A wave of realisation washed over Sweet then and he felt sick. Aribor must've seen it, too—swallowing Sweet like cold, dark floodwater—as he smiled down at him. Only there was no mirth in that smile. No warmth. No happiness or affection. Behind that smile there was only hatred.

'You remember me then?' Aribor asked, malice glittering in his eyes. Sweet didn't speak.

He couldn't speak. Even if he could, what the hell would he say?

'Not used to seeing ghosts, eh?' Aribor smiled that sickly sweet smile wider still. 'But I assure you that I'm truly here, in the flesh.' He patted his chest as if to prove his point, then his smile faltered a little and his voice grew cold, 'ghosts are for dead men.'

'And he ain't dead,' Daraday added, his voice grim, the knife he'd killed Vi with was still in his hand. Still dripping her blood to the cave floor in slow, sticky droplets. 'Strange really, considering you told us that you *took care of him.* '

'Ah yes,' Aribor chuckled, but there was no humour in the sound. 'Another of Bitter Sweet's infamous, oh so sweet-tasting lies.' He met Sweet's gaze and the hate there was so palpable Sweet could practically feel the heat emanating from it. 'Pure. Fucking. Poison.'

'Ari—'

'There's no point, Sweet,' Aribor cut across him, waving a hand with a show of finality. 'No point in even *trying* to talk your way out of this one. We pieced this shit together a *long* time ago and I reckon you're just starting to do the same now, eh?'

Sweet could only nod. He felt numb. Even the pain in his stomach had faded. He felt loose, floaty somehow—like he was dreaming and sort of knew it. Only it wasn't a dream, and he knew *that* for sure.

His mind returned to that forest. That cloying, sticky forest towards the end of summer. A world away from the snow-covered mountain top where they were now. He remembered that the heat had prickled at his neck. The sweat had run between his shoulder blades and made the hairs on his back itch something fierce. He remembered Daraday's puppy-dog eyes and his pining requests to go back and tend to his wounded friend. To help him. To save him.

'You told them I was dead,' Aribor cut through Sweet's memories, his voice dripping with venom now. 'You told them all that *you took care of me.* Told them you put me out of my misery, eh?'

Sweet remembered the fight with the bounty they'd been tracking.

He remembered the murderer with the mad eyes dropping down from the tree. He remembered Aribor getting stuck with the knife. He remembered the others all seeing the wound. He remembered them all walking away. He remembered being alone with Aribor.

*I'll take care of him.* That was what he'd told Daraday.

It was a lie, of course—the only care he'd intended to deliver was the final kind. Releasing the wounded Aribor from a world of pain and sending him into whatever counted for an afterlife. That's what Sweet had meant when he'd said he'd *take care of him.* That's what he'd said.

Only...he hadn't done that, either.

The truth was that Sweet had been lying to himself as much as he'd been lying to the others. He had been sick of it all, even as far back as that. Sick of everything. He'd been sick and tired of all the violence. The danger. The killing. Fuck, the killing most of all. Yes, he'd told the others he'd *taken care* of Aribor. He'd let them believe that he'd done the deed and put the wounded youngster out of his misery. Hell, he'd even pulled a hunting knife from his belt, fully intending on cutting the man's throat to help ease his passing. Maybe slice the artery in the top of his leg—at least that way Ari wouldn't have to choke on his own blood.

Instead Sweet had done nothing.

He had knelt by the wounded boy, knife in hand, staring down at him. Sick of it all.

Aribor had been drifting in and out of consciousness by that point, and Sweet had reckoned he was good as gone anyway. Why help him along? After all, there was enough blood on Sweet's hands already without getting them even bloodier. And what was one more lie on top of a whole heap of them? A whole lifetime of them? After all, it wouldn't be a lie for all that long anyway. Before long the lie would become the truth. The boy wouldn't last.

Only somehow, he had.

And now he was here.

That was the truth. And truth was a weapon.

'A deer hunter found me,' Aribor hissed, jerking Sweet away from his hazy memories and back to the cave on the mountainside. 'Only he didn't reckon I was as gone as you did,' Aribor jabbed an accusatory finger at Sweet. 'He took me in, patched me up. Didn't give me much of a chance,' Aribor shrugged angrily, 'but he gave me *something.*'

'You survived,' Sweet mumbled, he was feeling a bit faint now. Lightheaded. Was that because he'd lost so much blood? Or because of the insanity that was unfolding before him? Both, probably.

'I survived,' Aribor nodded, 'and I never forgot what you told them all.'

'I'll take care of him,' Sweet whispered, almost to himself.

Aribor nodded again, shaking with anger now.

'Only you didn't,' Aribor continued. 'So I reckoned it should be *me* who *took care* of all of you.' He slapped at his chest as he spoke, a line of hate-riddled spittle dropping from his lips and into his beard. His anger was fierce. Raw.

Sweet looked up then, a fresh wave of confusion washing over him. Aribor smiled at him again, that sense of sick triumph returning to his twisted features.

'Daraday was the first,' Aribor said, motioning to the raven-haired youngster. The lad was still standing solemnly over Vi's body, his face as unreadable as hers had ever been. 'I caught up with him about a year after Woodbyrne. Put a dagger to his throat, fully intending to open him up and watch him die in front of me.' Aribor paused, looking reflective for a moment. 'Only I didn't,' he said, speaking quietly now, his eyes glazing over at the memory. 'Because he recognised me, and then he wasn't frightened no more. He was *happy* to see me, knife at his throat an' everything. Can you understand that, *Bitter Sweet?*' Aribor spat Sweet's name as though it was poison on his lips.

Sweet nodded. He could understand it. He was starting to, anyway.

Daraday and Aribor had been fast friends, back in the day. The lad had taken Aribor's death—false as it now turned out to be—hard. He had mourned for Ari for a long time, whereas the rest of them had put him from their minds before the week was out. Besides, back then the boy had still been soft as puppy shit, it was no surprise his friend's return from the dead had inspired such a reaction in him, even if he was there with murderous intentions.

Not soft now though, Sweet thought, glancing down at Vi's lifeless body, then back up at her killer. Now he's hard as stone—and we made him that way. I made him that way, Sweet thought. As he looked, he began to feel the first stirrings of anger. They flickered in him like the embers of a dying fire under a firm breath.

'So I decided not to kill him,' Aribor continued, clearly enjoying himself now. Small wonder, really. Years of resentment, built-up and festering, were finally being allowed their moment in the light. Of course he wanted to make a damn show of it. 'I decided to *recruit* him instead. He would be my man on the inside. He'd help me *take care of you.*'

'All this time,' Sweet breathed, keeping the emotion from his face.

'All this time,' Daraday agreed, his expression sombre.

'We got Jenrick first,' Aribor began to pace around the cave, an arrogant swagger in his step. Sweet's eyebrow shot up in alarm. 'Oh yes,' Aribor chuckled, 'that wasn't an accident. That was Daraday. He waited until Bryntas left, then sat down to drink with the fool for hours—or rather, he *watched* as the fool drank himself into a stupor—then they took a walk by the canal…'

'One quick tap to the head and I pitched him in,' Daraday finished, his voice cold. 'Idiot probably would've done it himself anyway.'

'But we like to be *sure,*' Aribor added with a hiss, narrowing his eyes at Sweet. 'We're not as careless as you, Sweet.'

A realisation dawned on Sweet then, and he felt the anger flicker more brightly still. He embraced it. It gave him strength. Fuelled his dying body.

'Bryntas,' he breathed, gritting his teeth hard.

Aribor tossed his head back and laughed again, the sound rich and dripping with sick delight.

'That one was Daraday, too,' he said. 'He left you under the pretence of going hunting, gave me the bow though—I was always the better shot. The big man recognised him. He thought he'd come to join him in scouting the road ahead.' Aribor smiled slyly. 'Didn't even see the blade coming.'

'*You* killed Bryn?' Sweet narrowed his eyes at Daraday. He remembered the confusion on Malvadas' face when he'd accused him of the big man's murder. Sweet thought it was Malvadas' own imminent death that had puzzled him, but it hadn't been. Malvadas truly didn't understand what Sweet had been accusing him of. He hadn't even known Bryntas was dead. He hadn't had anything to do with it. Because…

'I did,' Daraday nodded, his face still set. 'And then the Wyn took care of himself. Damn glad of that, too—he wouldn't have been an easy man to kill.'

Sweet said nothing, but he felt the anger boiling up to a rage inside his chest now. He glared balefully at the raven-haired youngster.

'Stover,' Daraday continued, a ghost of a smile touching his face. 'Stover practically killed himself too, trying to steal away your bounty like that. I thought you'd stick him for me, but then you told him he could leave if he gave up the prince.' Daraday shrugged. 'So I had to step in.'

'And then there was Violent Fey,' Aribor continued to pace the little cave, milking every moment of his twisted little victory. Sweet though he saw a pang of sadness touch Daraday's face at the mention of Vi's name, but in a flash it was gone. The boy's loyalty to this rotten bastard was obviously stronger than his adopted kinship with her. Figures, Sweet thought. The boy had—after all—just cut her throat. But then why the flash of sadness?

'Like the Wyn,' Aribor was still talking, tapping at his bottom lip as he spoke. 'She was always gonna be a tricky one to manage. But we just had to be patient. Stay alive and be patient.' Aribor laughed suddenly. 'Although I've got to say, Sweet—you made that first bit mighty difficult with this mad little quest o' yours.'

'You tracked us this whole time?'

'That I did,' Aribor nodded. 'Followed you right out of Levitan, through Scarvin, up through the wildlands and right to the mining camp down below. I thought the magickers would get you, I really did. But my my, you are a truly *resilient* bunch.'

'Still stood back until we took them all down though,' Sweet coughed, pain wracking his body. He gave a dry chuckle of his own. 'Hiding in the shadows like a fucking coward.'

'Needs must,' Aribor shrugged, still smiling and shaking off the insult like he was swatting away an irritating fly. 'And there's no point trying to rile me up Sweet, I've no anger left in me. That all passed a long time ago. It burned hot for a time, but it's gone now.' The smile faded, and despite his words to the contrary, Aribor's eyes glittered with hate. 'All that's left is *bitterness,* now.'

'And Daraday?' Sweet nodded up at the youngster. 'What was your plan for him, if the magickers got to us first? Let him die at their hands, too? No loose ends?'

A flicker of doubt flashed across Aribor's face. Sweet saw Daraday tense a little as he asked the question. The knife was still in his hand, though Vi's blood had stopped dripping from the blade now. Sweet saw Aribor glance at it with more than a little nervousness in his own eyes.

'Or did you play us all at our own game?' Sweet continued, sensing there might be a gap in the lines. A weakness to exploit. A lie to uncover. 'Did you spin him a little tale about getting him out if things went bad?' Sweet fought down a wracking cough. 'A little story about saving him at the last moment?'

'Quiet,' Aribor warned him.

'You did, didn't you?' Sweet forced a laugh, but found that he meant it anyway. He ignored the stab of pain it brought from his midriff and laughed with more feeling. 'You told him once we were all dead, that would be it? Vengeance complete, you'd both walk off this mountain, alive and well! Didn't you?'

'Quiet,' Aribor hissed again. One hand moved slowly into the folds of his coat.

'Ari?' Daraday turned to face his companion. Gone was the flinty look in his eye. Gone was the hardness in his voice. Gone was all the ruthlessness and the toughness he'd grown into over the years. Gone was the man that Sweet had moulded. The hardest bastard in the room. The cold-blooded killer that Sweet had created. Daraday was suddenly that frightened little boy again, riding along the trail on the outskirts of Woodbyrne under the late summer sun, asking questions that no one wanted to hear and that Sweet would never answer with the truth.

Aribor spun quickly. Sweet saw a blade in his hand. Quick as lightning, he plunged it deep into Daraday's belly. The boy grunted and doubled over. Aribor wrenched the blade clear and stabbed him a second time. Then a third. Each blow landed with a wet thumping sound, followed by a squelching slice as the blade was pulled clear. Daraday let out a harsh, breathy grunt with every strike. When it was over, the youngster collapsed with a shudder and a groan. He writhed for a moment, then fell still beside the body of Violent Fey. Sweet didn't have time to cry out. He barely had time to move at all.

Aribor stared down at the corpse for a moment. At first Sweet thought he looked regretful, but then he realised that it wasn't truly regret. It was the look you gave a task that had become an unfortunate necessity. A job that needed doing.

Apparently content with his inspection of Daraday's lifeless body, Aribor returned his attention to where Sweet lay slumped against the wall. His eyes were bright with anger now. Anger and a deep, dark madness. Sweet had seen that look a few times before. It was the look in the eyes of the kind of bounties he normally steered clear of.

The look of a true madman.

'Of course,' Aribor hissed at him, that madness bubbling over. 'I would've preferred to have done that *after* I'd taken care of you.' The man took a moment to compose himself, taking a steadying breath. 'But,' he continued, with an exaggerated sigh, 'I suppose there is something poetic about doing it this way. You're the last of the crew now, Sweet. Then it'll just be me.'

Beside Sweet, Orsen gave a low moan and shifted a little, drawing his leg up towards his body.

'What about the prince?' Sweet asked, the pain in his belly redoubling now and causing him to wince. 'You'll leave him be? He weren't there in

Woodbyrne. He ain't got nothing to do with any of this.'

'He never did,' Aribor agreed. 'All this time you were worried about everyone who wanted to get their hands on him. The Vols, Sylvanus, Malvadas' crew, that big Wyn bastard, the bloody magickers.' Aribor smiled again. 'All the while, you should've been more worried about who was after *you.*'

'So you'll let him be?' Sweet asked, his breath was hard to come by now and his vision was swimming dangerously. The cave was lurching like the deck of a ship.

'No,' Aribor shook his head, almost sadly. 'You see, Sweet, unlike you. I don't leave loose ends. When I say something, I fucking mean it. I take care of things properly. And now,' he sighed, 'it's time to *take care of you.*'

Aribor advanced on him, the knife in hand.

## Something with meaning

**B**ESIDE SWEET, THE prince groaned again as he stirred slowly back towards consciousness.

Aribor took several grim steps towards where Sweet was slumped against the wall of the cave. Sweet could hardly move, let alone defend himself. The lifeblood was still leaking away from the mortal wound in his belly and he could barely raise his right arm now. The knife in Aribor's hand was gripped tightly, still slick with Daraday's blood.

This was it. This was how he would die. Helpless and exhausted, at the hands of a vengeful madman. The realisation gave a little heat to Sweet's anger and he clenched his teeth so tightly that he heard them grind together.

As he closed the distance, Aribor hunched forwards to deliver the killing blow.

Closer.

Closer.

At the last, Sweet suddenly lurched towards him, using the final bits of strength afforded him by his anger. His anger at everything. His anger at the lies, at the betrayal. At the killing. But most of all, at the sheer senselessness of it all. He hadn't had it left in him to kill Aribor all those years ago. He'd baulked at sending one more soul into the darkness. Baulked at having one more thing to bother him as he tried to sleep at night. One more dark, grisly deed atop a mountain of them. And because of that, his crew—his family—were all dead, with him soon to follow them into the darkness.

Sweet used that rage and lunged forwards, one arm snaking out.

But not for Aribor.

Instead, Sweet plunged his hand into Orsen's boot, his fingers clenching tightly around the hilt of Vi's dagger. The one she had gifted Orsen after he had helped fight off the bear. The one he had concealed there ever since. Sweet pulled it clear and thrust it up towards Aribor just as the other man descended on him.

More fire exploded, this time in Sweet's chest, as Aribor's dagger plunged deep. But the man yelped as Sweet's own blade slammed into his side. Sweet gripped it tightly, grimacing through gritted teeth as he glared up at Aribor.

The other man straightened, the motion dragging Sweet half to his feet. He used what remained of his rage-fuelled strength to push himself all the way up, until they stood eye to eye. Sweet bore into the other man's gaze with that burning anger. Aribor's pained expression turned to one of fear as he saw the depth of that fire and he struggled to be free of their strange embrace.

Sweet twisted the knife and Aribor cried out again. The other man pulled the dagger from Sweet's chest and stabbed at him again. Twice more Sweet felt the fiery pain lance into his body as his former crew-member stabbed him with the knife. He felt his newfound strength fading quickly, but summoned enough to pull the dagger clear of Aribor's side and slam it in again, a little higher this time. The other man howled in pain and Sweet pushed off the cave wall with his back foot. His weight drove them both out into the snow, blood pouring from their wounds and staining the white ground a deep red, tinged with edges of infection pink.

Aribor stabbed Sweet again, though he barely felt it this time. He barely felt anything anymore. The snow had stopped falling and the sunrise was brighter now, almost blinding as the sun began to peak over the distant horizon. Still Sweet pushed at the other man, gripping him tight despite all his struggles and protests. He angled them away from the cave. Together they powered through the knee-deep snow drifts, picking up speed.

Until there was nothing.

Just a feeling of weightlessness. Unbridled and freeing.

Sweet saw Aribor's face change again. This time it malformed from one of pain and anger into one of abject horror as he realised what was happening. As he realised what Sweet had done.

Too late though, Sweet thought, bitter and vindicated even as he knew his action would kill him, too. His strength failed him and he let go of the knife buried in Aribor's side. The other man tumbled backwards, falling out into nothingness as he fell from the mountainside. Sweet found himself following, that weightlessness replaced by a lurching force that started dragging him towards an inevitable end on the jagged rocks far below.

A hand gripped his own. Searing pain fired up his arm from his ruined fingers and he spun his head.

It was Orsen.

The prince had grabbed his hand and was hauling him back.

Back to the snowy ledge. Back onto the mountain. Back to safety.

From far away, he heard a man scream. Aribor. The sound grew quieter as it faded into the distance, then it was cut short by a sickening thud. Echoes of the noise sounded through the mountains like ghosts.

Then there was silence.

Well, nearly silence. All was quiet save for the ragged, heavy breathing of the prince, slumped beside Sweet in the snow.

*

'What...happened?' Orsen breathed, holding one hand to his head. 'In the cave! The others! What the hell happened?'

Sweet sighed, the sound low and rattling.

'Long story,' he responded weakly, his head lolling.

It was then that Orsen noticed the other man's wounds. Sweet was bleeding from at least five different punctures to his torso. Already the snow between his legs was darkening with it. It was a damned miracle he was still alive, let alone alive and talking.

'Sweet!' Orsen took the grizzled bounty hunter's shoulders and steadied him. 'Sweet can you hear me?'

'Clear as day,' Sweet tried a weak smile, but a lance of pain stopped it short. He looked confused, as though he wasn't even sure which wound had caused it.

'You need to rest,' Orsen told him, his eyes darting over all of the injuries and knowing that simply getting some rest wouldn't be enough. Not by a long way.

'In a little while,' Sweet whispered, 'I'll get some rest...in a little while.'

Orsen looked into the other man's eyes and saw something there. It looked like relief. No, not relief. Not quite. It looked more like a clarity of some kind. A distant tranquillity. Like he'd finally let go of something that had been weighing him down for a long time.

Like he'd made peace with something.

'Still lots of work to be done,' Sweet said, still smiling. His misting eyes were fixed on the far horizon. Orsen had to lean in close to hear him, so quiet were his words. 'Gotta take back your kingdom now, eh?'

Golden light suddenly bathed them both as the sun rose above the eastern horizon. The sky blazed with it and the clouds were tinged with a dusty pink. The warmth from the sun touched both of their faces and Sweet closed his eyes, still smiling.

'Lots of work to be done,' Sweet repeated, barely a murmur. He opened his eyes and looked at Orsen, his glassy stare clearing momentarily. 'Only one of us left to do it now, though.'

Orsen nodded solemnly.

'I'll make sure of it,' he told the other man, trying to smile back at him but falling short. 'I'd never have made it this far without you. Without any of you,' Orsen whispered, 'thank you.'

Sweet coughed and winced at the movement, then looked up at Orsen, his face solemn.

'Gonna be hard…to spend all your gold, now,' he said.

Orsen laughed, the sound choking in his throat.

'What do you want me to do with it?' the prince asked. 'The gold?'

Sweet only shrugged, then grimaced.

'Spend it on getting the damned Vols out of your kingdom,' he coughed again.

'Aye,' Orsen nodded, holding Sweet's good hand in his own. 'Aye I'll do that.'

Sweet nodded back, blood still pulsing from his many wounds, but more slowly now. He closed his eyes again and tipped his head back in the golden light of the dawn sun. He whispered something as he nodded, but Orsen didn't hear him at first. He leaned in even closer to hear it the second time around.

'Aye,' Sweet whispered, 'aye...make it all mean something,' the grizzled old bounty hunter told him, with a long, final sigh.

Orsen sat a while in the morning light, cradling the body of Bitter Sweet.

# EPILOGUE

## Work to do

TARDARIAN HAD BEEN a soldier for most of his life. At just thirty-three years old he'd fought in five different campaigns already. One had been a short war with the tribes to the north of Thradonia, but the other four had been against the Vols. Or at least, three had been against them via proxy forces—such had been the way of their empire-building in those early days. The fourth though, he'd fought the Vols themselves.

They had been true to their reputation. Tough and disciplined bastards. Good soldiers. They'd fought like devils, relentless and merciless. They were known to not take prisoners—and if they did then it was only to extract information by means of hideous torture. Tardarian had barely escaped the last conflict with his life. Most of his unit had been less lucky. That had been three years ago, and ever since then Tardarian's hatred of the Vols had only grown stronger as news had come of their conquests elsewhere in the world. They'd been spreading like a cancer for decades, unchecked and left to devour all in their path. Thradonia might've repelled them, but other nations had been less equipped to deal with the ever-growing threat at their borders.

And now Pratia had fallen. Less than a year had passed since news had reached the kingdom that the capital city of Levitan had been sacked. The Pratian armies had been routed at a battlefield north of the city and the kingdom had toppled. The king had been killed and the rest of the royal family were also presumed dead, though some rumours persisted that the crown prince had survived the siege. If that were true, Tardarian thought, then he wouldn't have made it far. The Vols were meticulous campaigners when it came to war and they wouldn't have left a loose end like that just flapping in the wind.

They'd been close allies with the Pratians, at one time, Tardarian recalled. But the Pratian king had been an arrogant whoreson, and had rebuffed closer ties in light of the threat from Volsgard. He saw the offer of Thradonian aid as simply trading one tyrannical master for another.

Where they had offered friendship and closer allegiance, he had seen servitude and subordinance. He had rejected the Thradonian offer—and with little civility, too.

And then his kingdom had fallen to the Vols.

That left Thradonia with one less ally, in a pool of them that was shrinking with every passing season. Before long they would be the only ones left standing against the ravenous beast that was the Empire of Volsgard.

Worse still. Pratia had been a buffer between the Empire and Thradonia. The fall of Pratia left a corridor open to the heart of Thradonia itself. That thought made Tardarian sick with worry. Vol regiments could now march unaccosted through Pratian lands, directly to the western border they now shared with his homeland. Already there were reports of Vol troops massing, relocating from various parts of their sprawling empire into what used to be Pratian territories. They had various old rebellions to put down to the east, and new insurgencies were always springing up in their conquered vassal states, but it would mean a delay at most. It wouldn't stop the inevitable, Tardarian knew.

A new war was coming with Volsgard, that much was for sure.

And yet here he was, hundreds of miles away in the rugged lands of the north. Sent to answer some cryptic dispatch from the arse-end of the kingdom whilst his brave brothers and sisters readied themselves for the fight to keep the blood-thirsty invaders out of their lands.

Tardarian figured he must've done something wrong to warrant such a low assignment. Maybe he'd offended an officer somehow, or said the wrong word to someone somewhere and it had drifted along to the wrong pair of ears. Or maybe the gods themselves were displeased with him. Truth be told, Tardarian wasn't much of a believer, but he made a mental note to be more pious if it would help get him back to a place where he could defend his kingdom. Anywhere instead of here.

The troop of soldiers he led didn't seem to share his concerns. Most actually seemed relieved to be away from what would no doubt soon become the frontlines of battle. Tardarian knew why, too. He was no man's fool, after all. He knew that the battlefields were little more than charnel houses where men went in and bloodied, mutilated corpses were spat out. He wasn't a fresh-faced cadet anymore, and all hope of winning glorious praise on the battlefield were gone from him now.

But dammit, he wanted to *fight* for his kingdom.

None of his unit would admit to being pleased at such an assignment, of course. Several would even defend this pig-eared task as being an important one anyway, their patriotism stretched to its very limits in order to define it as somehow heroic. Tardarian tried to convince himself with their arguments—that *every* action, no matter how small, would contribute to the war effort—but it was no good. His mood was sour as they rode up to the little town.

In truth it was barely a town. More a ramshackle collection of mismatched buildings perched around the crest of a low hill. To the south, the long mountain range that marked the border with what had been Pratia stood like a row of ominous sentinels, the peaks still snow-covered from the winter that had barely just passed. Further east, they curved off to the north, marking another border with Volsgard—though it was impossible to get an army through that one.

Tardarian reined in his horse and took off his helm. He tucked it under one arm and observed the little village. The spring-melt had yet to get going in earnest and there were still patches of snow here and there. And where there wasn't snow, there was mostly mud. Townspeople went about their day, moving to and fro as they set about their chores. Farmers toiled in their fields surrounding the settlement, or led oxen pulling ploughs, preparing them for the next season. A group of washerwomen carried baskets of clothes down the slope towards the stream at its base, chatting amiably amongst themselves as they went. Tardarian frowned at the village as his second-in-command, the sandy-haired Dolma, walked his horse alongside him.

'This is it?' Tardarian asked him, his frown deepening.

'Must be,' Dolma replied, checking his map, 'there ain't another place for fifty miles.'

Tardarian sighed and replaced his helmet. He sighed as he tied the straps under his chin.

'Very well,' he said, 'let's get this over with.'

Tardarian heeled his mount forwards and led his troop towards the settlement. The villagers saw them coming and most stopped what they were doing. Tardarian wondered how often these folk saw armoured horsemen, but the presence of their Thradonian uniforms seemed to settle any unease and most just watched them out of curiosity, rather than in fear. After speaking to several of them, Tardarian was directed to the building at the centre of the village, closest to the peak of the hill.

It was a little larger than the other buildings, but no less ramshackle for it. Patchy, clay-baked walls and a sod roof that needed re-sowing on one side. It would've been regarded as a hovel back in more civilised parts of the kingdom. Tardarian rode through the settlement and dismounted outside the squat building. Handing the reins of his horse to Dolma, he pushed open the door without knocking and entered.

Inside were three people, two men and a woman, talking quietly amongst themselves. They fell quiet as Tardarian entered. The first man was dressed like a peasant, though he wore some kind of wooden necklace that no doubt identified him as an official of some sort. Tardarian wasn't sure of the custom in this part of the kingdom, but the woman—also a peasant, judging by her simple cotton dress—wore a similar necklace. The head man and head woman of the village, maybe? Most definitely, Tardarian decided.

The third man was altogether different. Raven-haired, he stood straighter than the others, taller and more composed. Despite his bearing, he looked even more physically dishevelled than the others. He was gaunt of face and looked weathered beyond reckoning. There were several cuts to his face, only half-healed, and he looked to be favouring one hip over the other as he stood. He was dressed in the cloak of a traveller, but Tardarian had been a soldier long enough to also recognise items of Pratian uniform when he saw them. A soldier, maybe? What the hell was a Pratian soldier doing all the way out here?

The man also wore a sword strapped at his waist. Even just seeing the hilt, Tardarian reckoned the weapon was not a standard-issue blade. A Pratian officer, perhaps? The weapon looked expensive though, even for an officer. Tardardian couldn't quite be sure but he thought it might be Damsen steel—but that would be impossible to afford for even the most well-connected of soldiers. He observed the man a moment longer, then cleared his throat.

'I am Captain Tardarian Danilis. I was told there was an urgent message,' he reported, 'something of great importance to the kingdom'

'To *both* kingdoms,' the raven-haired man corrected, extending out his hand and showing Tardarian a ring on his finger. Tardarian's eyes widened as he recognised the object, then his eyes flicked to the man's face and he realised whose description he fitted, damn near perfectly.

'Crown Prince Orsen,' Tardarian breathed. 'You escaped?'

'A story for another day,' the Pratian prince nodded, his face steely with resolve. 'I need to speak with your king,' he straightened. 'We have work to do.'

.

Milton Keynes UK
Ingram Content Group UK Ltd.
UKHW010635141123
432548UK00004B/244

9 781739 279202